CUT HAND
By
Mark Wildyr

STARbooks PRESS

Herndon, VA

Published in the United States by STARbooks Press PO Box 711612 Herndon VA 20171 Printed in the United States

Many thanks to graphic artist John Nail for the cover design. Mr. Nail may be reached at: tojonail@bellsouth.net.

Herndon, VA

CONTENTS

PROLOGUE

Autumn 1831 along the Allegheny River

But for improvident fate, angry, boiling clouds would have unleashed nature's cold fury upon this Yankee river valley the day he buried his ma and pa. Perversely, a rose-hued dawn washed the tall forests and granite bluffs in a warm autumn glow.

Prosperous Tory farmers, his forebears had rallied to Benedict Arnold's American Legion during the Great Rebellion, participating in raids on Ft. Griswold and New London. Their lands confiscated, their very lives at risk, the family joined the migration of a hundred thousand Loyalists to Canada and the Mother Country upon the Crown's surrender to the victorious Continental rebels.

At the turn of the century, his pa brought the little family south from Toronto to unsuccessfully petition for the restoration of their prosperity, but old hatreds die lingering deaths, and Tories were subjected anew to high prejudices with the burning of the President's House in the War of 1812. The Marquis de Lafayette's return to these shores in August 1824, and the old revolutionary's warm reception by James Monroe, the last American President to fight in the Rebellion, put the barm on the brew, sentencing the family to hard labor merely to meet the cain on farmland that once had been their own.

Life doubly rocked the slender young man with hair the color of sandy soil and hazel irises shot with brown and green and gold when the tragic deaths of his parents in a farmhouse fire followed hard on the heels of a doomed affair with the daughter of a family of Patriots, who had no use for Tories – real or reformed. The discovery of a hundred carefully horded gold English Pounds in the ashes of the family cabin confirmed his determination to abandon this hateful land and retrace the footsteps of his boyhood idol, Jedediah Strong Smith, the legendary trapper and explorer of the Far West.

CHAPTER 1

Spring 1832 at the edge of the Little Island Mountains, the Dakota country

From our place of concealment, we silently watched the tribesman ease cautiously out of the draw and press up a steep slope littered with broken boulders and sparse-leafed mountain scrub, exposing himself to two warriors on sturdy Indian ponies methodically working the rims of the coulee below. One threw up a long gun and shattered a stone near the fleeing man's shoulder. A third brave, nearer his quarry, loosed a wild yell and wheeled his pony, raising a tomahawk as the pinto churned awkwardly across the sharply pitched ground. His prey evaded the hatchet and snagged its wicked head, bringing down both man and mount.

The two adversaries tumbled in a dog-fall over the cruel, stony ground. Only one, the fugitive, staggered to his feet, swiped a bloody knife on his slain foe's leggings, and broke for the scrambling pinto. A second shot roared; the pony screamed in pain and flopped to the ground, sliding in the loose scree.

The runner dropped behind the downed beast and clawed a weapon from beneath the heavy body. Easing the barrel over the horse's side, he pulled the trigger. Nothing happened. Abandoning the useless musket atop the dead horse, the brave slithered on his belly to the sanctuary of a narrow fold of rock and began a slow climb up the escarpment. The other two Indians, most likely believing their prey now armed, dismounted and carefully approached the fallen pony.

Hidden by a thin, serrated outcrop of granite crowning the ridge, we witnessed the deadly drama unfold below us. The lone Indian, clad only in breechcloth and moccasins, slipped through the thin cover of the slope, gaining significant advantage over his cautious pursuers in this ghastly game of hide-and-seek with human lives in the forfeit. I hold strongly to the view red Indians are human even though this brings me into conflict with much of society. I have the same opinion of black slaves. Neither conviction is often voiced aloud.

Beyond the promontory we occupied, the high plains stretched below puffy thunderheads to the northern horizon broken only by a distant, barren mamelle. These broad, short-grass champains cut a swath through the country four hundred miles wide from Canada to Tejas, interrupted by occasional ranges such as the Little Islands at our backs and the Great Shining Mountains rising well to the west.

Splitlip Rumquiller surveyed things with an expert eye on my far right. Wild Red Greavy lay in the middle, taking in events through mere slits, and I anchored the left, shivering with excitement and a modicum of fright.

The runaway, making clever use of scant cover, was now close enough to distinguish his features. He was tall, appearing to be over six English feet and well formed. The Indian, who was probably no more than my own twenty and one years, glanced up suddenly. I froze. To move was to invite discovery. In that brief moment, I was struck by how likely he was. Comeliness was not something I equated with the natives I had encountered back east.

The horsemen, remounted now, crisscrossed below him, secure in the knowledge that he had no long-range weapon. The youth would have breached the ridge in a clump of mountain mahogany twenty paces to our right had not one rider suddenly urged his spotted pony straight up the slope, forcing his target into the shelter of a small draw leading to where we lay hidden.

The second brave reined his mustang left to box in their prey; then both deliberately worried their way up the slope no more than two hundred yards behind the man on foot. Within seconds, slight noises came from directly below us; strong, red-brown hands grasped the upright granite, and the brave vaulted over the crest with his eyes scanning the slope behind him.

In an instant, Split was on him, tumbling the Indian on his back in the dust. Red vaulted atop the savage, leaving me to grab a flailing right arm. It was all I could do to hold on; the fugitive tossed wildly before my weight gained the advantage. Split grunted a few guttural words, and the Indian settled down. Red, caught in the blood lust of the moment, raised a knife high above his head. Without thinking, I thrust myself between them.

"What th –" Red was barely able to slow his killing stroke. I seized his wrist in both hands. Even so, the blade drew blood from my left breast.

The man beneath me stirred not a muscle, although I trembled with belated fear. Sweat popped out on my forehead.

"Don't kill him!" I implored. Men killed one another, sometimes for no reason, but I did not cotton to being a party to it.

"Billy, ya damned fool!" Red raged quietly. "Thet siwash'd lift yer crown he git half a chance. Now git outa my way."

Splitlip's quiet rumble brought us to our senses. "Ya don't stop squabblin', we'll be in fer it right quick. Them other two's gittin' mighty close. Red, keep a eye on this feller, but don't do nothin' rash." He beckoned me away from the ridge and silently signed for me to hurl a stone off to the left and below the horsemen. I gave it my best heave.

A moment later, we returned to where Red sat atop the fallen Indian with a knife tip threatening his exposed throat. A quick look showed my companion had not given in to a murderous impulse in our absence.

"They's takin' the bait," Split informed us in a whisper, "but it ain't gonna fool 'em fer long. They ain't gonna be able to bring the horses straight up, so they'll look fer another way to the top. We's hightailin' it, and we'll take this 'un with us. Ain't gonna leave 'im fer them ta find and git curious. Let's move!"

"Ya crazy old galoot!" Red grumped. Nonetheless, he stowed the Indian's knife in his boodle and came up with a set of manacles. Where they came from I didn't know and was afraid to ask. After securing the prisoner's hands behind his back, Red fixed a rope to the chain and handed me the fag end. "Ya like 'im so much, nursemaid 'im."

Mutely accepting the chore, I followed our shackled captive as he trailed Red into the pine forest on the high side of the ridge. Split tarried to erase our sign. After a few minutes, I stopped casting about for hostile Indians and studied the one in front of me. Thick black hair, worn loose, tumbled over wide shoulders and cascaded down a muscled back that tapered to a waist no bigger than mine despite his larger frame. Firm buttocks, only half covered by a leather apron, flexed with each step. Suddenly embarrassed, I realized I was studying a near-naked man the way I had admired Abigail on the rare occasion she deigned show a spit of flesh. That was a queer thought for a Christian-raised gentleman, one dismissed as excitement over my first proximity to a pure-quill Indian.

Split joined us shortly before the light failed and picked a thick copse of locust for our camp. Nights were chilly at this altitude, but it was colder in the grave, so we dared not risk a fire – not with two armed and mounted warriors in the vicinity. If the flames failed to give us away, the smoke most certainly would. More than one immigrant party had been betrayed to hostiles by such carelessness. We took a cut of a meal, jerky and hard tack, me sharing mine with the Indian.

After we ate, Split sat cross-legged in front of our prisoner and talked gibberish for a while. Splitlip Rumquiller, who took his byname from an old hatchet wound, had preeminence among us by dint of superior experience. Nearing fifty, he spoke several dialects and knew the tribes to avoid and those who would do business with the white man. He had walked this particular route north of the Santa Fe Trail twice before. The Indians called him Splitrum.

At last the battered old frontiersman turned to us. "Name's Cut Hand, 'cause a that scar." Split indicated a long-healed wound on the youth's left hand. "Tribe's sorta a cousin ta the Sioux. The argot's near the same. Unnerstands me good enough, though some words is different. Calls 'is band the People of the Yanube. Thet's a river off ta the north. Pappy's the misco, the headman. Cut Hand was off in another camp visitin' a gal. Musta been good gash, 'cause them others flat out jumped 'im on the way back home. They kilt 'is pony, but he hightailed it fer the hill country." Split hawked and spat even though he'd used up his chewing tobacco a week past. "Been tryin' ta shake 'em fer half a day."

Split turned to Red. "Sos ya'll rest easier, he's gonna stay with us till we put some distance twixt him and 'is village. Won't give us no bother less'n ya have 'nother go at 'im. When we's satisfied, he'll take 'is knife back and head home."

Red was a small, grum man of rusty hair and crazy green eyes who tended to rise at a feather. A shanty Irishman from somewhere around Boston, he reputedly had a wife and five carrot-topped fry. No one knew why he took to the willows and appeared on the Santa Fe Trail five years back, although the set of iron ruffles that now confined our prisoner's wrists might provide a clue.

"I say we jest kill 'im," Red proposed. "Ain't no use takin' chances. Then we's free ta worry 'bout them others. Shoulda give them two a lead ball twixt the eyes when we had the chance. Now they knows 'bout us, it's bound ta be harder."

"Ain't my way, ta kill 'thout no need," Split growled in a low voice.

Red gave in sourly. "Jest don't let 'im git in my way. And them irons stays where they is. Yer gonna have to watch 'im." He shot a thumb at me. "Ya don't git no sleep, thet's yer plight." He turned back to Split. "I'd feel better we git some water twixt us and 'is people. They a river anywheres close?"

"One south a us. Said to be 'nother trail to Ft. Wheeler thet a way."

Red spoke to me again. "I ain't sleepin' with 'im. Find yerself a place off in the woods and chain 'im to a tree. If them other los come, they'll take your topknot and leave mine whur it be." I took "los" to be a scurrilous name for red men.

"Ain't a bad idee," Split mused. "Them others found our sign by now. If'n ya got chores, best git on 'em. I'll find a spot fer ya ta bed down."

"Chores?" Then understanding dawned. "Oh! Come on Cut Hand," I said, getting up. The big youth rose effortlessly, listened to Split for a minute, and then strode off, dragging me along by my rope.

We walked half a league before he found a spot he considered satisfactory. I shrugged. It appeared no different from a dozen others we had passed by without pausing. The Indian ignored my eyeballing his nakedness as he stepped out of his breechclout, but he spat staccato sounds until I stood on the other side of the bush as he went about his private business. I tied my end of the rope to a sturdy branch to perform my own, fully realizing this was a useless effort as he could easily escape by merely jerking it free.

As we washed in a cold, clear freshet, I was unable to keep my eyes off him. A tight, black bush crowned his long, thick log of a cock sheathed in flesh darker than his belly. If he noticed my observation, he gave no sign. When we were finished, he was unable to tie his flap one-handed, so I did it for him. As I performed the awkward chore, my hand – necessarily, I thought – pressed against his thigh. My reaction took me by such surprise that I fumbled. My staff hardened so abruptly, had I not already passed water, it would have been impossible to piss. My fingers lost their grip, dropping the leather apron to the ground. Quickly, I bent to retrieve it and found my eyes on a level with his manhood. Purposeful or not, I lost my balance and grasped his thigh to regain my equilibrium. My thumb invaded his freshly washed cock hair. I scrambled to my feet and aggressively went about fastening his drawstring without daring to meet his eyes.

That task finally done, I cast about for the way back to camp. Cut Hand gave a subdued snort and immediately set off in the wrong direction – leading us straight back to the others.

Split had scouted a spot fifty yards down the hill well protected by a grove of hemlock and scrub. I laid out my bedroll while the old man and Cut Hand grunted at one another. Before he left, Split put the prisoner on a blanket with his back to a small, sturdy tree and ran the chain around the bole.

After slaking my thirst from a canteen, I tipped the container to Cut Hand's lips. He finished drinking and nodded his thanks. I thoughtlessly wiped a dribble of water from his chest. As I touched him above the left nipple, I was lightning-struck. My finger caressed his dark aureole independent of my will. My nerve ends jangled; the hair on my arms bristled.

Jerking back, I sat cross-legged in the gathering darkness faintly broken by moonlight filtering through the forest canopy. "I didn't mean to do that. I don't know why I did. Never met a real Indian before! That's stupid!" I gabbled. He comprehended none of my protestations. To get off a treacherous subject, I put a finger to my own chest, "I'm Billy." I touched him on the sternum, burning my digit. "You're Cut Hand; I'm Billy!" I droned.

Sucked into a mysterious vortex, I flattened my palm against his breast, feeling the thud of a strong heartbeat and experiencing the power of his chest muscles. I swallowed hard and moved my fingers along his ribs and across his belly. Light-headed, giddy, and lacking the strength to resist, I dropped my hand to his groin. Deliberately, my fingers closed around his rod, an act so heinous my muscles froze. Suddenly, he cocked his head.

"You fellers all right in there?" came Split's raspy voice.

"Y ... yes." I snatched my hand away.

Split entered our little clearing. "Jest wanna make sure I kin git here in a hurry if needs be. They likely won't come till first light, but that ain't somethin' ya kin count on."

"You think they'll come?"

"Never kin tell 'bout Injuns."

Cut Hand spoke in a low voice. My ears flamed in the belief my shameful actions were revealed.

"He says they'll come," Split explained. "They's Pipe Stem warriors, long-time enemies. They knows who 'is pappy be. Be big

8

medicine ta count coup on the headman's son. And he kilt one a 'em, don't fergit. Asks ya ta chain him kinda loose, give 'im room ta move. Do whut yer easy with," he added, taking his departure.

As I nodded my thanks for not betraying me, Cut Hand lay back on the blanket with his arms confined above his head. I loosened my clothing and settled on the bed roll. My other coverlet went over the top of us. Boldly, I edged up so the whole of my backside rested against his thigh. Fighting a mysterious list for this strangely erotic plainsman and denying a lewd urge to mold myself to his long frame, I lay listening to the night sounds long after he slept. Too confused for keener introspection, I considered the events that had brought me to this strange land.

My name is William Joseph Strobaw, and I have earned no sobriquet except for Billy. Despite my pa's firm conviction I aspired beyond my station, I managed graduation from a small but excellent college back east. I coveted Harvard, but we could ill afford the three hundred dollars it cost. Moorehouse College was hardship aplenty at half the price.

My parents' death in a fire and a failed love affair with Abigail, whose Patriot family would hold no truck with the descendent of traitorous Tories, combined to determine me upon foreign adventure. Financing my poorly planned scheme with my dead parents' life savings, I abandoned the familiar world of intolerance, slavery, and black uprisings for the opportunity of the frontier, a promising place of new beginnings where a man's reputation was what he painted upon himself by his own actions. Another considerable influence on my rash decision was my hero, Jedediah Strong Smith, rumored to have been killed recently by the fierce Comanche along the Santa Fe Trail.

So it was that I made my way over the long winter to Independence, Missouri, where I met Splitlip and Wild Red in an ordinary two months back and learned they were headed to the Dakota country to trap and trade. During a round of drinks, it was somehow propounded that I accompany them to Fort Wheeler rather than undertake the eight-hundred-mile Santa Fe Trail along which my hero died. My rash admission to twenty dollars for the poke was likely the reason for the invitation. In truth, I had other such pieces secreted in my wallet.

The adventure almost came unraveled before it was firmly knit. Wild Red went on a drunken tear with a sleazy doxy and appeared the following morning still under the influence of strong drink and reeking of sated lust. I managed to overlook his jadish deportment, but when Splitlip went over the edge, ranting like the Marquis de Sade over fascinating and horrifying creatures no one else could fathom, I began to reconsider. Red, once he recovered his own senses, assured me Splitlip Rumquiller was a solid fellow except when he got his hands on a button. It took some inquiry to discern the button in question was hallucinogenic peyote trundled up from the Spanish Territory of *Nuevo Mejico* by some enterprising trader.

As the old frontiersman appeared entirely sane and sound the next day, and since I did not wish to be cozened out of my twenty dollars, I pursued the enterprise, although I confess to some disquiet because we walked. I am certain my gold piece was sufficient to provide adequate mounts for the trek.

# # # # #

Red was no less hostile the next day, nor did Cut Hand rest any easier around him. Nonetheless, we made good time with Split or Red occasionally dropping back to check our rear. Discovering the warriors were on our trail, Split sent us wading down a mountain brook while he turned north, muddying the water and leaving careless prints. Red took us out over a broad stretch of flat rock after a league in the frigid water. Split rejoined us at nightfall.

Cut Hand and I camped seventy yards from the others that night. My willpower was insufficient to prevent me from touching him as he lay shackled to a tree. I stroked his heavy chest and flat belly, feeling his accelerated heartbeat. Anger? Excitement? Like his breast, his stomach was hairless. Loosening his garment, I timidly caressed his bare flesh. His skin was taut, smooth. I moved to the black hair above his cock and entangled my fingers.

Inflamed beyond restraint, I put my tongue to him. He smelled fresh and masculine. Grasping his yard in my hand, I stroked it, vainly seeking to bring some life into that fascinating cock. Disbelieving what

I was doing, I took it into my mouth, sucking at him until he grew and slowly filled my oral cavity.

Fighting a sudden urge to choke and gag, I placed a hand around him and found I had swallowed no more than a third of his shaft. I spit him out and tugged back his foreskin, I tongued his big stones, astounded by the pleasant sensation this occasioned in my own groin. Then I worked over him awkwardly, inexpertly, intent on bringing this handsome creature to climax. At length, the stomach muscles tightened beneath my hand, and I shared the excitement of his orgasm. His taste should have been revolting, but the unexpected sweetness of his seed made me struggle to take all of his copious flow. I swallowed greedily, licking what few drops I had lost from his flat, hard belly. Except for panting slightly, he remained still and silent as his big yard slowly softened.

Afterward, ashamed yet wildly exhilarated, I contemplated the youth I had debauched. The enormity of my actions struck me; I had corrupted a man. A shiver played down my spine. I was a monstrous hydra, no better than the pathetic creature we called Faggot John back home. Even as I shuddered to recollect the disgust we accorded that abomination, I callously laid aside my apprehension. The morrow might bring regrets, retribution, even damnation, but my only concern at the moment was my own need.

Lying across his strong legs, I tore free of my britches to expose my own hard, hot pole. Frantically, I gripped myself and beat a steady rhythm until giving myself release, the excitement of the act immeasurably heightened by the fathomless black eyes that watched my every move by the weak moonlight. Shaken by powerful conflicting emotions, I rose, cleaned us both, and restored our clothing. Then I took my life in my hands and removed the iron bracelet from his right wrist to snap it around the bole of the sapling, giving him the length of the chain to maneuver and the full use of one hand, should our stalkers appear. Thereafter, I covered us with a blanket and slept.

I woke with dawn tinting the sky above the trees, although no light yet penetrated the glade. Cut Hand's lips brushed my cheek as he uttered something unintelligible. Seizing my hand, he turned it to the north. I understood. Then he pointed it across his body, letting me know one came from that direction. As he did so, his chain rattled. Grasping my ten-pound Common rifle, I rolled silently out of the blankets to the far side of the small clearing where I gained my feet and froze.

Nothing happened except the coming sun built its golden light slowly. Then my peripheral vision detected movement. The brave had almost reached the tree where Cut Hand lay shackled before I was certain. I threw up the gun and fired, dropping the warrior as he pounced. He lay still.

Suddenly, a second figure vaulted from the trees with a screech, bringing his hatchet down on Cut Hand. But my prisoner rolled into his attacker's legs, sending him tumbling into me. I lost the grip on my rifle along with the ability to use it as a club. The buck came up fast, but I clung to him, grappling for control of that deadly tomahawk. Silently, we struggled, thrashing around in the grass, crashing against trees. I saw stars. My eyesight blurred, but I stubbornly fought for the weapon. Suddenly, he released my right hand to force my left free of the axe. Snatching my knife from its sheath, I rammed it into his side. He continued struggling, and I feared the warrior had shrugged my thrust aside, but gradually, he lost strength until he slumped over and sagged against my legs. Badly shaken, I looked up to find three figures staring at me through the new dawn. Cut Hand strained against his chain while Red and Split held weapons at the ready.

"Ya done good, boy." Split nodded approval. "We best go scare 'em up."

"Scare up who?" I gasped, holding my blood-imbrued shirt away from me. Suddenly revolted, I snatched it off and stood shivering in the cold morning breeze.

"Horses, boy," Red answered. "Them two had horses."

I had almost finished soaking the blood and its stink from my blouse when Split and Red returned with the ponies, a sturdy mustang and an Indian calico, which whites tend to disdain, although Split assured me they were good horseflesh. We distributed the loot among us. The Pipe Stem braves had Indian trade rifles and forged tomahawks. One had carried a spiked axe; the other, a Missouri war hatchet.

Unaccountably uneasy, I bade my companions keep an eye on our prisoner while I wandered off as if on personal business. Once out of sight, I grasped a tree limb and stood with head bowed. In the clear light of the dawning day, the beastliness of what I had done descended upon me. I had forced a man to submit to my depraved desires. He was shackled, pursued by enemies bent on slaying him. I was his gaoler; he was under my authority. Yet I abused him in an unspeakably disgusting manner. Dropping to my knees, the Christian part of me begged my God's forgiveness. Somehow Cut Hand must be made to understand my repentance.

About as transparent as my Aunt Felicity's bobbin lace, I was no sooner back than Split cast an eye on me. "Ya feeling bad 'bout whut happent?" he demanded. Startled and confused and ashamed, I stared like a pole-axed ox. "Adrat, boy!" he swore. "Them two bucks was tryin' ta kill ya."

Relief made my knees go watery. Amazed my prayer had held no confession of guilt for the taking of two human lives, I ran my hand over my face.

Red grinned at me. "Them the first?"

"And the last, I pray."

"Son," Split said, his tone sad, "if them's the last, then yer a dead man. Sure as we's standin' here watchin' God's sun rise in the east, yer gonna have ta kill agin afore this trek's done. And Cut Hand here says ta thank ya."

We resumed our journey riding two to a pony with my perversion still hidden from the world. Cut Hand's arms remained shackled, so I rode in front to control the pinto.

That evening we camped where the trail forked. Our planned route ran to the northwest; the southern trace led to the river and a rumored second trail to Fort Wheeler. I promptly forgot my covenant with the Lord and proposed a split camp, laying it at the door of Red's hostility.

The redhead laughed. "Fine by me. I ain't anxious ta sleep with 'im. But ya ever stop ta thank thangs is different now?"

"What do you mean?" I demanded in alarm.

"Whut he means ta say," Split interjected, "is that there ain't two redskins on Cut Hand's bum. He needed ya last sundown; he don't now."

I glanced at the big youth attempting to chew a piece of jerky while his hands were pinioned behind him. There was also nothing to keep him from exacting his revenge. "We'll sleep up in that grove where the stream bends." I indicated the place with a nod of the head. Cut Hand's eyes flickered to the spot.

The others had hobbled the horses, so they could forage and were making ready for the blankets when we returned from our chores. Cut Hand engaged Split in a short discussion, and once again my ears reddened as I imagined being exposed as a pariah.

"He says ta tell ya he'll behave hisself," Split translated. "I figger he's beholden fer them two bucks. But he wants ta know when we gonna let 'im go."

"Not yet!" Red interjected. "I want that river 'tween us, Split."

"Ya gotta unnerstand, Red, he coulda left any time he wanted after Billy took care a them two fellers."

In our own grove, Cut Hand waited patiently as I spread our blankets and snapped his manacles around a tree. I recited prayers for half an hour, begging for strength before reaching for him. Such was the sway of this primeval Adonis that the moral shield of my Christian upbringing crumbled, exposing the raging beast of carnal lust. Aware he was free to raise an alarm, I was still powerless to protect either of us from my passion.

"Damnation, Cut Hand, you've put some kind of spell over me. What is it you call it? Medicine? You took away my self-control. I'm helpless around you. If I didn't know better, I'd say it was love –"

Astounded by my conclusion, I bit my tongue!

Abandoning talk, I placed my hand across that broad chest. He did not flinch or call out. I touched his cheek, astonished at the purity of the skin. His face was virtually free of a beard. A smattering of soft hair in his deep, mysterious armpits was all until his thick, black nether bush. Pulling at the hairs gently with my teeth, I slipped down to nuzzle his full, round sac. His great organ failed to stir. As before, I bent to my task, sucking at him until he grew hard and working with my greedy mouth until Cut Hand exploded once again, spasming and filling me with an abundance of his seed. Without pause, I threw myself atop him and ground against his hard belly until the storm broke, and I sprayed his naked flesh with milky cum.

Awed and excited, I sought confirmation this was something other than involuntary muscular contractions. I pressed my lips against his. He failed to respond. I peered at him so closely our noses touched. I kissed his eyes, moved back to his lips, and had my answer. He felt nothing. Disappointed, I muttered apologies and begged forgiveness though whether from a disapproving God or this reluctant lover, I could not say.

Sleepless, I put aside questions of morality and searched for the perversion that drew me to this man. I had known many comely youths, but the idea of lewd intimacies with them stirred me to illness. With a profound shock, I realized the truth; my heart was lost to an enterprise as hopeless as the pursuit of Abigail Carnes!

My childhood provided no clue to my folly. A loving mother and a perpetually exhausted father had raised me on prunes and proverbs. Curiosity about the fairer gender never obsessed me. I was eighteen before I had a leap with a girl, which turned into no more than a pleasant flourish that ruined a budding friendship when I showed no further interest.

I recalled no undue curiosity about my own kind beyond a shy comparing of yards, as youngsters are wont to do. When I was twelve, an older boy from a farm down the road and I went skinny dipping in the local crick. I remember him initiating talk – dirty talk – about a girl we both knew. When I refused to participate in such unseemly gossip, he groped my naked flesh. I protested, but was not unduly offended until he tried to stick his roger up my bum. I ran away, but in the safety of the woods I noticed my thing had stopped being a penis and become a cock – it was stiff as a rod.

That was the sum of my animalistic experiences, save for occasional self-gratification. Now, I had twice acted the deviant with this comely savage.

CHAPTER 2

I woke at daybreak when Cut Hand moved. He stood with his back to me at the extreme length of his chain to urinate, and like a proper sodomite I grew excited. Turning away, I restored myself to order.

We walked through the forest to where our companions were breaking fast to discover they proposed a run south to survey the river, leaving Cut Hand and me behind with the gear. Upon their return, we would decide upon a route.

Split added to Red's growing dyspepsia by delaying their departure to give me a score of words in dialect, so Cut Hand and I could communicate basic needs. I was both pleased and petrified at being left alone with him. If the chickens were coming home to roost, now would be the time.

Split and Red were no sooner gone than Cut Hand grabbed my pack, leaving the extra gear for me, and strode several hundred yards off the trail to a rill of clear spring water. As he dropped my boodle in a small clearing well-screened by trees, he bent his knees and stepped backward through the chain of his manacles. His hands now in front of him, he spun me around and imprisoned me against the trunk of an ash to search my clothing for the key to the iron cuffs.

Freed of his chains, Cut Hand retrieved a knife and rifle from the spare gear before beckoning me to follow. At the creek, he motioned me still and spent a quarter of an hourglass scouting the area. Finally satisfied, he stripped and waded into a pool of waist-deep water. When he plucked a soapweed and set about washing his skimpy garment in the suds, I ran for my soiled clothing and blankets, all of which cried for a good cleaning.

Cut Hand washed our blankets; I worked on my clothes. He examined my shift, my set of short underclothing, with amused curiosity. Once everything was draped over bushes to dry, he scrubbed himself until his skin squeaked. I followed suit, praying my fair flesh would not react adversely to the plant.

When we gathered our damp garments and started for the grove, Cut Hand blinded our trail. Once inside the small copse, we spread our things to dry and sat naked on the grass facing one another. Suddenly anxious about our situation, I began to babble, pointing to my chest and repeating my name. When he more or less mastered "Billy," I started in on his, deciding to shorten it.

"You'll be Cut," I said, touching his exciting breast.

I fell silent and studied him frankly. Hair like rain-drenched Pennsylvania coal drying in the sun framed a heart-face with a wide, smooth forehead. His skin was nut brown with an underlying reddish hue. Close examination revealed why his gaze was so disconcerting. The eyes were restless black orbs liberally flecked with tiny golden splints that gave them an inner light. I have never seen eyes like that before or since – until years later.

His nose on anyone else would have been weighty, but its Roman curve perfectly balanced a generous mouth and strong chin that stopped just short of stubborn. Powerful, corded arms swelled with each movement. His chest made me think of fornication.

He endured my examination silently for long minutes, and then he suddenly rose. Uncertain of his intentions, I waited until he pressed my head against his groin. Then I joyfully surrendered to my shameless need for him. Opening my lips, I licked at him. Clasping my head in his hands, he moved me over his belly and testicles and thighs before taking me back to his flaccid penis. I sucked him into my mouth, coaxing the glans from its silken sheath. He reacted, filling me with his solid flesh. I surrendered to my lust and drank the ambrosia of his seed. When it was over, I desperately yearned to understand what he was thinking.

Although my own need was nakedly evident, I was loath to make a move. He was in control now, and it was not clear he would welcome my flesh. He sat back comfortably against the tree and permitted his eyes to close. Disappointed, I lay quietly with my leg against his. I woke to his gentle touch. His big hands explored my body, as mine had his. His finger tickled my arms where tanned flesh met white skin. He pinched a tit, stirring unexplainable currents within my breast. He ran the flat of his hand over my chest and belly, toying with the thin line of brown-blond hair snaking down to my navel. He totally ignored my needful tool, hefting my stones as if weighing them. I understood what he intended when he lifted my knees and leaned his hot, hard erection into me.

18

"No!" I cried, pushing him away. He grasped my shoulders with those powerful hands and pulled himself back to me. His searching, throbbing organ teased my proud flesh. Suddenly realizing I countenanced what he wanted, the fight went out of me. Watching his incredible eyes stare into my own, I fearfully permitted him his way. The first penetration was like a flaming brand. His long, straight pipe with its large viper's head drew cries of pain. As I opened to him a slight mustiness rose in the air.

Undeterred, he pressed against me as his massive column steadily invaded my bowels. Finally, he rested, allowing me to adjust to his foreign presence. As the pain died, I experienced a great pressure within me. His hips pressed firmly against my bum; he penetrated me with those eyes as certainly as he pierced me with his roger. Satisfied with what he saw in my face, he began to move. The pain evaporated except when he stabbed more deeply than before. In its place came an incredible awareness of hot, hard flesh exercising my insides.

Cut thrummed me masterfully, in no hurry to draw the experience to a conclusion. Calmly and deliberately, he thrust first hard and then gentle; and each had a thing to recommend it. My universe shrank to the small bower sheltering my lover and me. Sweat gathered on his brow and dropped onto my lips; I savored its briny tang. Exploring his flaring ribcage, I wondered why no other man's physique claimed my attention as did his. The thick bush tickling my flesh, the stones spanking my bum were as erotic as the massive column plowing my channel. I was consumed by pagan lust, savage love, naked physical dominance. And it was magnificent! I hoped it would never end.

That was, of course, beyond human endurance – even Cut Hand's. At length, the pace of his movements increased. His jabs grew deeper and more frantic. His eyelids slowly closed, lowering long, curled lashes to his cheeks. After what seemed an incredible length of time, his shuddering orgasm spewed seed into my depths in strong, hot waves. He ceased his movements with his torso resting against my knees as he fought for breath. Finally, the handsome Indian raised himself to his knees, his heavy chest heaving from his exertions.

As he started to withdraw, I locked my heels behind him. Understanding, he pressed against me again as I slowly stroked myself to ejaculation. Never had self-abasement been more wonderful. Never had I spilled so much sperm. It was magnificent. Tumultuous! When we rested, he dipped into the seed smearing my belly and sniffed it curiously before wiping his finger on my chest. I laughed, expelling him, and that was the signal for us to move. Side by side we strode back to the rushing stream where he unceremoniously threw me into the pool and bathed us both. It was a lustration, a ritual cleansing with water.

At nightfall, I luxuriated in his presence, lying against him to watch a firmament of stars without number. Completely comfortable, perfectly at ease, I marveled at the lack of disgust, at the absence of shame or mortification. I experienced no withdrawal from him as I had noted after the tumble with that girl so long ago.

We spoke little except to comment on a meteor or an especially bright planet. The words were meaningless, yet their import was as clear as the crescent moon. When we went to our blankets, I lay with my back against him. During the night, I woke to find him spooned against me. His arm across my shoulders gave me a feeling of safety so complete I failed to sleep with one eye open for the first time since arriving on the frontier.

The next morning, we stalked and shot a yearling buck as it came to water. I butchered the animal while he scouted to see if the gunfire had excited any unwelcome interest. After a meal of fresh venison, he fashioned a bow of bois d'arc and arrows from dogwood, making a quiver out of the green deer hide.

Late in the afternoon, as we stood shoulder-to-shoulder to pass water, he playfully turned his stream into mine. When things were stowed away properly, he sat nude on his blanket while I lay beside him in the same condition. He looked at me intently, but I sensed he was not contemplating sodomy. At length, he pointed to my eyes and said a word. Finally understanding, I responded, "Eyes."

"I-ze."

"No. Eyes," I enunciated the word clearly. He did better the second try. Patiently, he worked his way down my body. Nose, ears, chin, neck, chest, nipples, belly, right down to the toes. After we repeated the process three times, he touched each part of me and mouthed the words. This aroused me again and occasioned learning the English vernacular for the male penis in repose and in a state of excitement.

He motioned me to sit beside him and drew stick figures in the dirt. The first was a standing male with another on his knees, head joined to groin. Embarrassed, I provided the vulgar words for fellatio. He then drew stick figures in a position requiring a term for anal intercourse.

He repeated the words dutifully, and then put together his very first sentence in elegant King's English. "Cut ... fuck ... Bil-lee."

"Quite adequately!" I agreed, blushing deeply.

Before we were finished, he knew I had no family, and I understood he had living parents, one sister, and no spouse. He sat in deep thought a few moments before venturing conversation again, pronouncing my name and adding a strange noise that sounded like 'windy.' Frustrated, he used his fist and forefinger for the unmistakable sign of sexual intercourse. "Splitrum? Red?"

Shocked, I made it plain only he excited my interest.

The light was fading and with it, the warmth. He placed a blanket around my chilled shoulders. I awakened in the darkness as he used me for an oyster basket to deposit his semen, thrusting like a stallion mounting a mare. When he finished, I fell into a dreamless sleep, untroubled by images of a vengeful God. That came in the early morning hours as a wave of belated shame and self-loathing wracked me so violently Cut Hand pulled me against him to share his warmth. An hour of silent pleas for forgiveness eventually allowed me to drowse.

# # # # #

My companions returned on the morrow. Split laid a calming hand on Red's arm when they spied Cut Hand standing unfettered at my side.

"The Injun's free; he might as well skedaddle fer home," Red grumbled unpleasantly.

"Thet's about the way a it," Split agreed. He spoke to Cut, who nodded but made no move to leave as Split explained to me they had determined to build a boat for the next part of the trip. When Cut and I returned to gather my gear and the butchered stag, he detained me with a hand on my arm.

"Bil-lee," he said in his beautiful bass. He pointed to himself and swept his hand in the direction we had come.

"Yes," I answered with a puckering of my guts. "Cut's going home."

He frowned. "Bil-lee. Cut." He pointed to the northeast again. "No, Split, Red, Billy." I waved to the south.

Shaking his head, he held his hand to the northeast. "Cut. Bil-lee."

"You want me to come with you?" I asked. "But … but that's barking at a knot. I can't! I've got to go to Fort Wheeler!"

"Bil-lee come," Cut said firmly. Frowning in frustration, he labored to create a sentence in English. "Cut talk Splitrum."

"No!" I panicked. "You can't talk to Split about this!"

"Cut talk," he said resolutely. The matter was obviously settled in his mind.

As I studied his black, gold-flecked eyes, my objections floated away like suds in rinse water. "Billy, Split come here." I surrendered to his determination and made a walking motion with my fingers. "You wait."

Satisfied, he set about gathering our things as I went to fetch Split. Once back in the glade, I couldn't figure how to start, but since Cut was not so inhibited, I blurted out something before he had the opportunity.

"Uh, Split. Cut Hand … I think he's asking me to go with him."

"Whut? Ere that so, son?" Split turned and barked something in Cut's tongue. The Indian nodded solemnly. "Be damned. Thet's whut he wants all right." Split slung out another series of staccato sounds, and when Cut answered, the old man's eyes widened. "Whut the hellfire's been goin' on? Damnation, Billy, whut'd he do, bugger ya?"

I felt the flush rise in my chest and paint my entire head a bright crimson. My ears burned. I grew near unto founding. The dizziness passed; my embarrassment did not. Dumbly, I nodded.

"Well, I'll be a sum-ma-bitch!" the mountain man cussed. "Shoulda seen it a comin.' Ever since Cut Hand joined up, ya been schemin' ta git off by yerself. Ya thank I don't ken, son? Hellfire, been times I ain't seen a woman fer months, and I git a hankerin' fer some handy fella. Been eyein' yer arse fer a while now."

He laughed as I blushed again. "This here's 'bout the best lookin' feller I ever cast eyes on, so I can see how it happent. Go tell Red we ain't leavin' till the morrer. Go on. I wanta talk ta this rascal and straighten this all out."

Red did not take the news well. He was all for packing the horses and starting out right then. "Damnation, I don't like it a 'tall! We oughta be hittin' the trail," Red shouted, halting me as I set off for the glen. "Oughta be advantagin' these good days. Won't all be like this, ya know. Weather's gonna git us one a these short days! Thet buck give ya trouble?" he asked, changing the subject.

"No," I answered, swallowing hard. I had not been anxious for Split to learn of my folly, but I certainly did not want Wild Red Greavy knowing about it. "Just got free of the chains and took me hunting. Showed me a plant they use for soap. Got my clothes and blankets clean," I rattled on.

"Whut ya so nervous 'bout?" He shifted an uneasy eye in the direction Split had gone.

"Nothing. Cut Hand's staying tonight, so we're gonna split camp again."

"How come he ain't lightin' out? Guess it's fer the best if we's lollygaggin' around here another sunrise. Warn the Injun I got my short gun right handy."

"I'll tell him not to shoot you with it," I snapped, leaving Red staring after me as I started for the bower once again. Cut and Split were seated cross-legged in the middle of the clearing taking animatedly. They ignored me until Cut got to his feet.

"Set down!" Split ordered, indicating the spot Cut had vacated. "Well, ya done got yerself innit! That big buck wants ta be yer *sannup*, yer Injun husband. Wants ya ta split the blankets with him like a squaw!"

"Like what?" I gasped.

Split sighed and took out an old ivory toothpick he carried. Worrying the thing was his substitute for chewing. Tobacco was hard to come by except for the *Kinnikinnick* he got from the Indians now and then. "Billy, these folk don't thank like we do. They's been *Berdaches* among the tribes fer a long time."

"*Berdaches*?" I asked.

"Sodomites. Double-faces. Men that likes men and lives like females."

"I ... I don't want to live like a woman," I stammered uncertainly, thinking of Cut Hand's pipe buried in my fundament playing my nerve endings like a drum.

23

"Didn't thank ya did, but ya got yerself all mixed up with this feller, and he's got purty firm idees about how thangs oughta be."

I shook my head slowly. "This is all my fault! It was me, not him. I forced myself on him when he was shackled."

"Don't take me wrong, son, but ya ain't got the ability ta force nothin' on thet young buck he don't want. He mighta let ya make the first move, but he don't allow nothin' he don't countenance." Split paused for a minute. "Billy, I knowed a few fellas gone Injun. I even knowed a couple went ta live with bucks. Seen one ten years later, and he was satisfied on 'is life. The other'n ended up a wore out old man 'fore 'is time. Didn't have no sane word to say about Injuns. So I ain't got no value fer ya on this. A Injun looks at this world a lot different from whites," he went on. "Everthang has its place and use. If thangs is in harmony, the world's okay. If they git outa balance, then they needs right'n."

"But aren't people like that out of balance?"

"They don't figger it thet a way. In some a the nations, *Berdaches* got a place a respect. Somethin' 'bout their connection ta the spirit world. Allus some folks don't like 'em, but thet's jest the way a folks, red er white. Like as not, a *berdache* don't make no waves, they's as welcome as anybody else."

"What do you mean, make waves??"

"Well, fer instance, like chasin' boys."

"Hellfire, Split, what do you think I am?"

The old man fixed me with a pale blue eye. "Son, we jest been talkin' 'bout thet. Ain't ya 'cepted it yet?" He ignored my shocked look and continued. "Soma the bucks marries *Berdaches*."

The concept staggered me. "Marry men?"

"Not 'zactly. They figger *winktes*, thet's whut the Sioux calls 'em so that's likely how Cut Hand knows 'em, ain't a man ner a woman neither."

Winkte! Was that the word Cut used back in the grove?

"They's a whole diff'rent thang, I guess ya'd say," Split continued. "I ain't got no idee how they'd take ta a white *berdache*, but they ain't likely ta look on it as bad medicine if'n ya behave yerself." The frontiersman took a deep breath. "Son, it ain't none a my business whut ya do. Yer a free white man, and if ya want ta be Cut Hand's country wife, thet's yer affair. He's a fine figger of a man, and I got a s'picion he's a rum 'un, too, but I cain't see 'im goin' 'thout no woman

24

fer long. They's a good chance he'll git ya back with 'is people and sooner er later jest cut ya loose."

"What will they think about him if he brings me home ... like that?"

"Likely ain't gonna bring 'im no harm. Thet buck'll be the man whoever he marries. But then they's the problem a who he be. Thet's the stumper. I ain't tryin' ta poke a spoke outa yer wheel, but one a these days 'is daddy's gonna die. If'n they look ta Cut Hand ta lead 'em, he's gonna have ta live in the middle a 'em with a wife and family. They puts great store by families and small fry. Headman er not, makin' babies is 'is first duty, else the band dies away. They'll come a time he'll have ta own up ta his duties. And I gotta figger he's a standout, the kinda man who faces 'em right square. He marries and gets little 'uns, the seed he wastes on you ain't gonna bother nobody."

We talked a mite longer without settling anything until Split suggested we ask Cut Hand to come help build the boat while I considered his proposal.

"Does Red have to know?" I asked.

"Sooner er later he'll figger it out, but I ain't gonna tell 'im."

Cut joined us in the grove, his face solemn – formal even. This was serious business to him. He spoke gravely.

Split turned to me. "He wants ta say somethin' ta ya, and wants me ta deliver the straight goods."

The next few minutes turned bizarre as the tall, handsome Indian spoke earnestly in one tongue, and the short, dumpy man translated Cut Hand's declaration of devotion and kinship into his own version of the King's English. Then using Splitlip Rumquiller as my tongue, I expressed pleasure at Cut Hand's words, but said I had to think hard about changing my life so drastically.

Cut Hand responded in his deep voice, echoed by Split's lighter tones. "He says 'is heart is yers ta hold till ya wants ta give it back. Even if 'is duty do git in the way a thangs, and he ken it will someday, ya'll still have 'is heart."

Split drew a deep breath. Sweat broke out on his upper lip as he strained to come up with the right words. "Lord, I sure need some tobac, er better yet a button! Anyways, he'll help ya build a little cabin at the edge a camp. Problem is, these people move 'round, so yer apt ta be buildin' one badger hole er t'other the rest a yer life. And he says whenever the day comes ya wants ta go back ta yer people, he'll accept it even if ya carries 'is heart clear across Turtle Island. Thet's their way a saying this here part a the world. He'll go with us ta the river, but he ain't gonna sleep nowheres near old Red. Course, I don't thank thet'll pose no problem fer ya." The old man worried his torn lip while he thought for a minute. "Son, I'm gonna come up here after supper and teach ya a little more a the lingo."

Before Split began his instructions later that night, he warned that Red had tumbled to the situation, adding when Red came off his snort, he wanted it made it clear to the gut-eater "he'd never laid a hand on the boy."

# # # # #

It took four-days to make the day and a half trip to the river. Things were going smoothly until Cut started getting nervous. Then Split put his nose in the air. They exchanged glances, and a few minutes later, Cut handed me the reins and slipped off our pinto to disappear into the woods. Split left the mustang to Red and hoofed it to the opposite side of the trail.

Red spoke quietly, the first words he'd directed my way since learning of my tendency. "Jest keep on slow and steady, boy. False alarm, like as not."

I had been so bedazzled riding behind Cut I failed to notice there was not a sound from the forest. When the wood is truly silent, watch your hair. As soon as we got to a spot where we could put our backs to a small bluff, we reined in and dismounted.

Split showed up first, uneasy even though he had found nothing. The better part of an hourglass elapsed before Cut slipped in on cat's paws and huddled quietly with Split.

"Cut Hand found sign," the old mountain man said in a near-whisper. "Six er eight barefoot ponies on a game trail ta the west. Figgers a raiding party's short-cutting across the Little Islands. We best wait 'em out. Me'n Cut Hand's gonna go up the trail a piece and blanket our tracks."

It was the shank of the afternoon before either Split or Cut rested easy, so we camped at the base of the bluff. My young swain regularly eased away to cut for sign, and that made me nervous. Finally, I grabbed my long gun and fell in beside him, ignoring his displeased look. We found nothing alarming, and the forest was slowly returning to normal – save in our immediate vicinity.

We put the ponies on a picket and hit the blankets early that night. Deciding against a separate camp because of agitation over the mounted party, Cut and I spread our blankets a short distance from Split and Red. During the night I rebuffed Cut, so he settled for putting his arm around me while whispering in my ear. In my imagination, he was telling me what our life would be like together. When he finally slept, I lay in the comfort of his proximity and wondered at the absence of guilt. After worrying that to rags, I came to the conclusion it had something to do with the overwhelming feelings I held for Cut Hand. Was that sufficient?

Going north would strike twice at my psyche! I would live with a strong, virile male; at the same time severing all ties to my own people. To travel among foreign peoples is one thing; to cut your tap root is another entirely. What I contemplated amounted to abandoning my gender and my culture! Could I do it? More to the point, could I prevent it from happening?

Strange, even while exercising these limbic doubts, I perceived myself safe and comfortable beside him. It impressed me as right and good, not something the Almighty should condemn. I could not imagine Gentle Jesus frowning down upon us. While I am not an ecclesiastical scholar, neither am I a free thinker, so I prayed earnestly for celestial guidance.

# # # # #

We raised the river after three more days of backtracking and laying false trails. This gave Cut and me more time to practice his tongue, but it put horrendous carnal temptation in our way, which I resisted with uncommon strength.

The night we arrived, Cut and I sat beside a fire and practiced our language skills while Splitlip and Wild Red went about their own business. Cut's argot was beginning to make sense to me now, and I found it less exacting than English. Cut was as hard a taskmaster as I, insisting on the correct pronunciation and not allowing laziness with the language. That would come later, as it always does when one grows comfortable with a tongue.

"Damnation!" Red flared suddenly. He had been on the nettle all afternoon. "Don't ya never shet yer trap? Bad 'nough the red belly's manglin' good American, but yer gruntin' 'round in thet pig tongue is gittin' me down! And 'nother thang, tell thet heathen ta shut his hole tonight. Like ta never got no sleep him moanin' like he done last night."

My ears reddened, and I had my mouth open to decry a false accusation when I realized it would accomplish nothing. "What put you in such a heat?"

"Aw shat!" he spat a vulgarity. "Ya wanta be this red heathen's luffee, I ain't gonna grutch ya, but we hadn't run onta this 'un," he threw a thumb Cut's way, "we'd be long down the trail now. We gotta find work ta git us a poke we wanta handle next spring." By "handle," he meant trade. "We oughta git goin' 'stead a settin' 'round here watchin' two growed men makin' moon eyes at one 'nother. Never seen nothin' like it. I had a gittern, I'd pick ya a tune so's ya could serenade 'im."

Sensing Cut beginning to bristle, I snapped back. "Climb down off your horse! This man is here to help build a boat to make your journey easier and faster. He doesn't deserve that from you!"

"Fawk!" Red cursed. "Jest leave me be. And don't go disturbin' my sleep, neither." With that, he turned away from the fire and tossed down his roll.

Taking us all by surprise, Cut moved the bedding he had claimed from one of the dead warriors over beside Red.

The carrot-top sat up. "How come he done that? Tell 'im ta git outa here!"

"You tell him," I replied, moving to the other side of the man. Now he had a heathen on his left and a deviant on his right.

Splitlip Rumquiller let out a laugh like a donkey's bray. "Tarnation, Red," he gulped between chortles and hiccups. "Ya sweet-talked yerself inta two bed partners!"

Red gave him a murderous glance and flopped back down.

Wild Red wasn't on such a high rope the next morning. After a breakfast of fraise with lap, or rabbit, in the pancakes instead of bacon, we set to work on the boat. As Split preferred a dugout to a birch bark, we felled a cottonwood something over four English feet in diameter. Without adz or proper axe, using only fire and forged hatchets taken from the slain Pipe Stem warriors, the four of us slowly crafted a twenty-foot canoe. The sides were a more or less uniform width of two finger knuckles; the bottom, a full finger length thick. Two solid strips of wood left in place served as bulwarks to strengthen the craft and hold cargo more securely.

It was a sight watching the Irishman and the Indian work together. Occasionally, the redhead would pause to look at the youth laboring alongside and shake his head. He simply could not believe a man like that could lust after a boy. Occasionally, I caught Red seeking the sodomite in me, and from his puzzled look, he didn't find it. Good! Even if I say it myself, there is nothing of the priss about me.

The afternoon the boat was finished. Cut washed himself in the river and strode over to put the question to me.

"I'll answer you on the morrow," I hedged. He frowned. "Morning," I said.

Spinning on his heel, he went fishing and provided our evening meal.

The conversation around the fire was less jadish that night. Split spoke slowly, taking care to draw Cut Hand into the conversation. Even Red exchanged a few words by way of unspoken apology for his previous outburst, the cause of which still escaped me.

"Damnation," Split lamented as he slapped at a nighttime gallinipper. "Whut I wouldn't give fer a twist! Even soma thet Indian weed. Course, a button er two'd be a sight better."

"Me, I'd settle fer a cag a Spanish wine. Er maybe a low bunter," Red grinned. "With big dugs and no expectation I'd take it easy on 'er."

"How about a honey-soaked gammon?" I pictured the fat ham so vividly my mouth watered.

"Whut 'bout you, Cut Hand. Whut'd ya like ta have?" Red made an effort to be civil.

Cut looked the redhead in the eye and uttered a single word. "Bil-lee!"

I don't know if I was more embarrassed or more prideful.

Split killed off the evening regaling us with tales of the tub, cock and bull stories of his travels. I was surprised to learn he was at the fourth Fur Trapper's Rendezvous on the Great Salt Lake in 1828 and claimed to have been on close terms with Jedediah Smith.

# # # # #

Over the past few days I had wrestled more aggressively against the idea I was offensive to the Lord God, that I was reprobate, abandoned in sin. Despite my Christian upbringing, the power of my need for Cut Hand ate away the base and exposed the noble in my emotions. And there were noble elements: loyalty, companionship, steadfastness, friendship, love. Perhaps love made our coupling acceptable.

I toyed with the idea Cut should come with us to Fort Wheeler, but soon purged that worm from my mind; nowhere in my world would a union such as ours be tolerated.

When I touched his shoulder in the middle of the night, Cut sat up immediately, alert to some unknown danger. I found his hand and clasped it in mine. "Splitrum. Red," I whispered in his ear, raising both our hands and motioning toward the river. "Cut. Billy." I waved to the north.

His smile broke the night. "Cut ... Bil-lee good life. Good!"

"Yes," I agreed, suddenly assailed by a myriad of fresh doubts.

CHAPTER 3

The next morning, Red and Cut tested the dugout on the river's iron-gray water while Split instructed me in dialect. Although I spoke the tongue childishly, Cut and I knew enough to permit fluency to eventually flourish.

Dividing up the boodle fairly gave Split and Red the extra rifle while Cut and I took possession of the axes and horses. We took more of the cate, the store-bought food, since they would likely encounter white civilization long before I did. My new companion and I took leave of my friends at high sun on a day I calculated to be a Saturday in April, Year of Our Lord 1832.

Cut claimed the mustang, which he named Arrow Wind because he was as swift as an arrow's flight. We called the pinto Long Wind; he was slower but clear-footed, and could run the other horse into the ground. When we first acquired the mounts, I had twice boarded the pony from the left and found myself sprawled on the ground. Long Wind was Indian-broke and accustomed to riders mounting from the right or off side. The saddles were mean things, merely surcingles fastened around the ponies' barrels with some sort of stirrup leathers and scraps of buffalo robes as cushions.

The open forest cast an airy green blanket over broad glades little troubled by thickets of underwood, quite unlike the brushy woods of my youth. Occasional fire scars heralding past conflagrations provided clues to the likely reason. The vicinage teemed with shy wildlife: white-tailed deer and squirrels and the barking wolf, the coyote, who slunk away at our approach.

A distance down the trail, I dismounted. Cut appeared at my side, worry burning in those strange eyes. He was, I realized, concerned that I had changed my mind.

I tried out his tongue. "Not easy to leave friends. Maybe never see again."

"We will see Splitrum again," he replied with certainty, correctly perceiving where my affinity lay. We walked in unaccustomed silence a few steps. "Did you do wrong to come with me?" he finally asked what preyed on his mind.

31

"Never!" I answered in dialect before going back to English. "That is the only thing I am certain of. Whatever the future holds, I want to face it with you."

He nodded emphatically. "Good. You see. Be good." His English words exhausted for the moment, he switched. "It is good we can talk to one another."

I gave a rueful laugh. "I speak your tongue like a child."

"But every sleep you get older. By the time we get home, you will talk like a man. I'm five winters old in American," he added proudly. "Soon I'll get to the age when hair grows down there."

Cut's people measured years by winters, months by moons, and days by sleeps. A broken sleep was a partial day.

"What Splitrum say for Cut, Cut now say to Billy. Billy take Cut heart!"

I had finally gotten him to pronounce my name correctly. Next I had to work on pronouns or he would wear out our appellations.

Absent his shackles and shed of the restraint of strange men, Cut Hand became his true self, one fully as likeable as I had anticipated. He turned the teaser – trying to convince me arboreal limbs rubbing in the wind were tiny tree squeaks, mythical birds of the imagination. He tested to see if I showed a dread of owls and the two-noted poorwills, night creatures he claimed were souls of departed warriors.

"What did you think when you came over that ridge and found yourself in the middle of us?" I asked in English as we walked the ponies.

"Run from grizzlies; find wolves," he answered in his tongue.

"And that first night when I was trying to talk to you?"

"Sounded like a loon going Billy-Cut Hand, Billy-Cut Hand!" he joked in argot.

"And ... and when I touched your chest?"

"I thought about kicking you in the stones," he answered in his tongue. "But you saved me from Red's knife, so I let you feel around. Besides I didn't know when the Pipe Stem would show up."

"When we ... laid on the blankets?" I pressed.

He tried out his English again. "Billy do wrong thing; Billy die."

A shiver ran down my spine. He meant, of course, if I had tried to roger his bum.

"Were you sorry afterward?"

"Why? Cut no do nothing. But feel funny when Billy shoot on belly." He turned serious and went back to his own tongue. "I looked on you as a handsome man, but when you put your lips to me, I was confused. He's a *winkte*, but he does not act like one ... except when he plays with my pipe." He pronounced the word "Win-tay." "But if he is not Win-tay, then this is wrong," he finished.

His answer gave me my first inkling there was something more to this Win-tay business than simply being his word for a sodomite. I broached the subject obliquely. "What does Win-tay mean?"

"It is what we call the special people who can see with the eyes of both a man and a woman. *Win* is a short way of saying *winyan* or woman. *Kte* means about to happen. So it is an about-to-happen woman, a not-woman."

That night he asked a question in English as I settled in his arms on the blanket. "Why Billy say no to Cut at river? Two times!" He held up dual digits.

"Because of Red and Splitrum."

Surprised, he responded in dialect. "What would that matter? As long as we were private about it, why would they care?"

His amazement revealed the depth of the cultural gulf between us. "White men," I started hesitantly using English, "don't believe men lying with men is a natural state. They believe it is wrong. That God condemns it."

He turned to me, frowning uncertainly. "Two men lying together is against natural law, but a man lying with a Win-tay is not wrong."

Recognizing this as a pivotal moment in our relationship, I replied carefully. "I am a Win-tay, Cut Hand, but only yours."

He apparently perceived the danger as well because he dropped the subject. It was some time before I felt confident enough to speak again.

"Tell me the truth, what is it going to be like when we get to your village?" Some of my uncertainty leaked out with that question.

"I always speak the truth. If you are proud of who you are; if you be yourself, everything will be good."

"Be myself," I snorted. "I don't know who Billy Strobaw is any more."

"Stro ... baw?"

"Strobaw. That's my family name. What we call a last name. All my immediate family was called Strobaw."

He stored that for future use and tried his English again. "Billy Stro ... baw good and strong and brave ... and pretty to look at."

Ignoring the "pretty" comment, I moved on to what concerned me. "Can Win-tays be brave and strong? I'm scared I'm going to make things go bad for you."

"Why Billy worry? Cut like Billy. People like Billy like Cut does."

"I hope not!" I snorted. He saw the humor and laughed deep in his throat, raising my excitement level. "Your laugh makes my pipe hard."

"It has been seven sleeps since it did anything but pass water, unless you helped yourself to some pudding," he said in his tongue. "It will be good, Billy. You will see. Now I'm going to laugh some more and see if Pale Hunter stands up." Pale Hunter danced a jig in my pants.

That night when his pipe, which I dubbed Dark Warrior, delivered its semen, he masturbated me so thoroughly that I shivered as if ague-stricken. Never had a decision seemed more right! I resolved to enter this new world with curiosity and hope rather than anxiety and despair.

When I fell asleep to the subtle night sounds of the mountain forest, the Lord Jehovah raged at me and pissed in my face in disgust. I woke to thunder and a drizzling rain and had difficulty shaking that blasphemous image even after Cut Hand pulled me to his powerful body.

"It is only *Wakinyan* cleansing the earth," he murmured quietly, drawing a blanket over us.

Wakinyan, whoever that was, thoroughly soaked us and put a chill on my flesh. The next day, however, the forest flourished from her ministrations. Mourning doves, which Cut called medicine birds, sang to one another from sodden tree limbs, and small game, invigorated by the night's rain, flitted among damp boles. As the sun sent shards of warmth through the canopy and chased away my puckered flesh, I noticed how frequently we stopped to talk and scout the area. That led me to wonder how the Pipe Stem ambushed him. Likely he was besotted by some woman and staggered right into their arms. A pang of jealousy seized my innards.

To stir me from my snit, I asked about the small, leather pouch he wore around his neck. He explained it was a medicine bundle containing a piece of his umbilical cord and small rounded stones called *tunkasi*, which protected him against negative energy – bad medicine.

We dawdled away most of the phase of a moon gaining fluency in one another's languages. I shuddered to think I had been bound for the Santa Fe Trail where I would have missed him. But, even the joy of Cut's presence could not purge the occasional guilt I experienced in private over my libertine practices.

"Don't you understand, Cut?" I snapped once when he challenged my mood. "I love you, but my God says that is wrong. Men don't lie with men!"

"This God of yours must be the same Great Mystery who made me. My creator gave me a hunger in the loins, so I can make children, but he never said there was only one way to enjoy the act. Why would he make it pleasurable if it was not to be used?"

"Even you said it was wrong for two men to lie together."

"Yes. And it is wrong for two women to lie together, and two Win-tays to lie together. That is against nature."

"But I am a man," I cried in anguish. "I have a yard and stones like you! We are two men lying together, Cut!"

He went so quiet that I grew deathly afraid. "If that is true, I will leave you here and hang my head in shame. But a pipe and stones do not make a man, Billy. You are not a man because you were born with a penis. You are not a man because you are brave and strong and killed two warriors." He tapped his heart. "Your spirit determines what you are, not your genitals."

"That can't be right!" I protested. "God makes you a man or a woman. There isn't anything else!"

Then I learned one of the great differences between the Red and the White worlds. To the European, life begins, progresses, and ends along a linear. A man is a man and behaves as such or suffers for it; a woman travels an even narrower pathway. They are opposite sexes.

The Indian perceives life as a Sacred Circle. There is no "only-man" or "only-woman," no opposite genders, merely complementary ones. Cut drew a hoop in the earth. Humans, according to his notion, might fit anywhere within the circle. A man was a man according to his spirit; a woman was a woman because of hers. A man became a man by accepting a man's responsibilities. His sexual appetite had less to do with his orientation than his choice of responsibilities.

If a boy child selected a bow as his toy, he was allowed to grow into what he would become, a man. If the boy chose a woman's tool, he was allowed to grow into what he would become, a Win-tay, a not-woman, a double-face, a human being with male genitals who accepts the responsibilities of a woman.

One male may appear more manly than another, or less so, but his spirit determined his lifestyle. So men or two-spirits or women fit at various places on that great circle according to choices made before the Soul Journey ever commenced. The point was that humans belonged wherever they felt natural, and one man's "natural" was not necessarily another's. It was a powerful philosophy allowing a person to live where he fit, rather than fit where he lived – a staggering concept that brought me some ease of mind.

That night, Cut bestowed a new name on me. "You will be called Teacher by my people."

"Why Teacher?" I asked.

"How many people would be speaking my tongue so well in so short a time? We haven't said very much in American for several sleeps."

"English," I corrected him automatically.

"See ... like a teacher. You will be a good teacher to my people. Teachers are important to my *tiospaye*, my band. Those called by the Double-Faced Woman are often teachers. She enters the dreams and instructs those who will be Win-tays." He pursued the significance of his new name for me. "They say all the tribes will have to face the white man someday. But with you as our teacher, we will learn his way without being infected by it. We will take what is useful and ignore what is not."

As we shared information and grew to truly know one another, I was able to see beyond my blind infatuation with the physical and appreciate the man. I genuinely liked, admired, and respected the object of my devotion. Nor did the trail lead just one way. I grew confident Cut felt much the same about me.

One day near the northern edge of the Little Islands, he asked me a casual question. "Did you couple with women?"

I noted the past tense. "One. I was never much interested in sex."

"I like to do it," he said in perfect English as he reached for me. His lips, his mouth, his tongue drew the bones from my body, leaving me weak and dizzy. Then they bestowed some of his great strength, so I was suffused with power and contentment. He delivered his seed before pulling mine from me and rubbing it on his chest like a potent ointment.

I sensed danger in his next words. "Does it bother you that I fill you with my seed, but take none of yours into me?"

"No. We each have our place. I know mine; I know yours."

Not completely masking his relief, he responded. "Perhaps someday."

Still on uncertain ground over this Win-tay concept, I shrugged. "If you wish. If not, I will be happy to be the flower to your bee."

He gave a low chuckle. "Said like one of the People. You are learning my tongue very well."

"Just so long as one of them isn't acting the flower to your bee!"

Cut Hand laughed again and pulled me to him, gently kissing my eyelids. "Ri' eye, lef' eye," he intoned, mimicking our anatomy lesson, as he mounted me.

Much later, he dragged me to my feet and tossed me into the stream. The cold water turned my skin blue, which he thought was hilarious.

# # # # #

Our carefree life came to an abrupt end the next day. We were afoot to give the ponies a rest when Cut suddenly stopped me with a hand against my chest and bent to study the print of an unshod hoof in a sandy spot among the rocks. He carefully backtracked until he found where the rider had left a more sizeable party.

"A scout," he said in a low voice. "Main party close." He was cautious; I was downright terrified.

Cut led Arrow back over the trail, seeking the origin of the tracks of a large number of horses. After checking my rifle load, I followed along behind. At length, Cut halted and raised his hand. He needn't have bothered; Long took his cues from Arrow.

Motioning for me to remain still, Cut slid off his pony, handed me his reins, and cautiously made his way to a thick grove of trees to the right of the trail. I dismounted to gentle the ponies with a hand to their muzzles.

Cut returned and led me to a scene I will never forget no matter my longevity. There were two wagons. One was overturned with its right front wheel smashed against a boulder. The scalped, carrion-ravaged body of a white man lay nearby. The second Conestoga stood in perfect condition with a bloodied man slumped across the seat. Each corpse was literally covered by bullet holes and arrow shafts. Judging from the items spilled from the overturned wagon, the dead men were traders.

After laying them out and protecting what remained of the bodies with a covering of stones, I rummaged around in their goods. All food, tobacco, weapons, and whiskey were missing, but other gems lay abandoned. There was a veritable library of books on carpentry, medicine, physics, Washington Irving, Fennimore Cooper, Shakespeare, and Poe. A well-stocked Pandora's Box of medicines held bitters, which some call quinine, ground amber for epilepsy and hypertension, balm and barley water; a whole passel of familiar and strange curatives. Cut wouldn't let me bring the saws and levels and other priceless stores.

I hounded him into helping drag the undamaged Conestoga well off the trail and loading it with items from the wrecked wagon, after which we eliminated any sign leading to our hidden trove. Nervous over spending too long in one spot while hostiles were in the area, Cut demanded we leave. I gave in gracefully because I fully intended to return and retrieve that wagon. Its contents would make my future life infinitely more secure. As there was nothing to identify the men, there was no moral quandary over appropriating their belongings since it was no less sinful to abandon such riches to the elements.

We tracked the war party for the rest of the afternoon with only a St. Anthony's Meal, in other words no meal at all. Once, Cut freed himself from his breechclout and pissed off the side of his moving pony. When I tried it, all I managed was to paint my leg. Thankfully, he was ahead of me, or he would have laughed in spite of the danger. Even so, when we finally halted in the dead of night, I heard him sniffing. To his credit, he didn't ask after the source of the odor. We neither bathed nor made love that night. The forest did not feel right to him, so we lay silently in one another's arms with the ponies tied at our shoulders. Sometime during the dark hours, I heard distant voices that held the sound of drunkenness.

"Are they Pipe Stem?" I whispered.

"No. Pipe Stem would have headed straight for their camp. They are most likely renegades. We'll find out tomorrow."

"Why?" I hissed. "Let them go their way, and we'll go ours."

He paused before answering. "This is not the white man's world, Billy. Here, you need to know what is going on, or someone may rise up and scalp you."

I accepted his reply, although some part of me wondered if the danger of the thing was not the attraction. With that thought came another. Could the same be said for his bringing me home with him?

We broke the party's trail early the next morning. Their horse apples were stale, dropped the day before, but freshened as we grew closer. Catching the sound of renegades ahead, we dismounted and hid the ponies before cautiously making our way up a sharp rise some distance ahead of us. The stony ridge fell sharply away to reveal a small natural lea where four Indian ponies, eight heavier horses, obviously trace animals, and two riding mounts that could have been military grazed contentedly. Four warriors stood jabbering, each louder than the other. By the abundance of broken earthenware jugs littering the area, they were likely roostered.

Cut was signing that the party totaled six men with two out scouting when a horseman raced up, chattering and pointing back over his shoulder. He had cut our trail. Two of the others left with the scout; two remained behind.

"The horses!" Cut whispered, frantically scrambling down the ridge. Suddenly, he crouched down out of sight behind a stunted cedar. Not twenty-five paces ahead of us, the missing scout led his pony by the reins as he padded along in our tracks. Laying aside his rifle, Cut shrugged out of his bow and quiver.

The raider's head went up a fraction of a second before Cut leapt from cover. The man fought to raise his rifle, but Cut was too close. His knife sliced into the scout's belly and jerked upwards. The

39

stricken warrior froze, his scream died, and his paralyzed finger failed to squeeze the trigger.

Suddenly, a savage apparition rode down on Cut, hatchet raised, face twisted into a mask of rage. I stepped from the trees and swung the stock of my long gun. It crunched against bone. The man rolled in the dirt. Instantly, I was atop him to put my skinning knife between his ribs.

Recovering quickly, Cut caught the reins of the pony as it passed and collected the other dead scout's mount, which had shied away to munch placidly on bunch grass. As we gathered up the slain men's weapons, Cut and I concluded the rider had been sent to collect his companion.

Mounted on the captured ponies, we raced back to the small vale where the raiders held the horses, gambling that anyone remaining would assume it was his own men returning. The guard actually had his hand raised in greeting when Cut sent two feathered shafts toward him. The man dropped without a sound.

We paused long enough to make certain the raider was dead and collect his rifle, a breach-loading carbine. I now had three weapons; Cut, two. The tracks of the remainder of the party led straight to our trail. We dismounted and tied our ponies. Two of the men crouched in the trees not far from where Arrow and Long were hidden. The third warrior was somewhere ahead investigating our mounts. Cut signed he was going to circle around to the far side of the trail where the missing man was probably hidden.

An hourglass passed, and my two were beginning to exchange glances, doubtless wondering why we had not yet appeared. I took a bead on the more distant warrior, afraid one of them might make some sort of move. One did. He checked his rear and found the bore of my Common centered on his chest. He let out a cry before I shot him.

I grabbed a second rifle as the other man whirled and fired. The ball gouged a furrow out of the meaty part of my right arm. He dropped his weapon and charged, loosing a horrendous scream that almost paralyzed me. Finally reacting, I adjusted for his movement and fired the second rifle. His body twitched, but he rolled out of sight behind a tree and came at me from a different direction. I drilled him with the third gun before he covered half the distance. Horrified, I saw the last remaining brave rise out of the brush. Cut was on him before he could raise his weapon.

My companion stepped out of the trees across the trail and quickly assessed the situation. Lifting his rifles, he gave a piercing cry of triumph. Damned if I didn't join right in. I let out a whoop and tore open my britches or I would have pissed my pants. Cut gave a roaring laugh before freeing his great cock and loosing his own excited stream. Then, we examined each other's wounds.

My arm bled freely, but I considered that favorable, as it would drain any contaminants from the lead. Cut had a gash on his hand, probably from his own knife when he took out the brave who almost got me. We hugged joyfully for a moment, found a small spring where we washed and bound our wounds, and then went to collect our spoils. Cut absolutely refused to bury any of the dead, so we abandoned them to the same carrion creatures who had feasted on their victims.

By the standards of the country, we were wealthy when we finally set out on the trail, anxious to put some distance between the recent battleground and ourselves. A dozen and a half breech-loaders and six Indian trade rifles as well as considerable ammunition comprised only a portion of the booty. The exciting thing to me was the discovery of more books: tomes on chemistry and wheelwrighting and all sorts of useful subjects – and the Holy Bible. Neither Cut nor I understood why the raiders had taken them. A few pages had been torn out, so perhaps they served as sanitary papers or fire starters.

There were also trade items such as bolts of cloth, needles, thread, beads, dyes and many other useful commodities – truly a treasure. The last thing we discovered stumped me. It was a whole canvas bag stuffed with coins, many of them gold, and a sheaf of bills of various issue. I'd have to sort it all out later. Of course, to Cut the real wealth was the eighteen horses we now owned.

That night we camped above the cedar break that gave out onto the high plains easting of where we originally met. As I finished a supper out of our stores, I realized some military units were not armed with rifles of the quality we now possessed. Why did the Indians have so much gold and paper currency, things they were not known to value? And why did the white men drag heavy wagons up mountain trails when relatively unbroken plains stretched in every direction like an endless roadway?

The more I thought on the matter, the clearer it became this had been a rendezvous to buy guns where greed on one side or the other

41

resulted in tragedy. Honest gentlemen or nefarious cheats, it made no matter. Either way the traders were dead.

In the midst of my cogitation, Cut covered me with a wild abandon born of the day's blood lust, making me wonder if killing always brought an urge to pizzle and a need for passion as I matched him stroke for stroke. I came with a loud groan; he with a great roar.

CHAPTER 4

The next day we hazed our horse herd down out of the wooded Little Islands onto the awesome plains under a bright blue sky broken by puffy, white clouds. It was a different world. A fresh breeze ruffled new grass in a rhythm of nature's making. A swath of torn sod revealed a broad buffalo run, a trace the great beasts had used for centuries. Cut explained deep sandy depressions as wallows where the shaggy creatures covered themselves in dust to defend against insects and other pests. We came across a bleached bison shoulder blade bearing man-made markings in red and black, an Indian signboard.

Two hours after the sun's zenith, Cut pulled Arrow to a halt as four horsemen materialized out of a thin line of trees marking a stream a hundred yards ahead of us. Warily, I cradled my rifle. Cut held up a restraining hand and let out a wild yell. Immediately, the others replied and kicked their horses forward, swarming around us joyfully. Two appeared about Cut's age; the other two were younger.

"Bear Paw, you thought you were rid of me!" Cut laughed. "Buffalo Shoulder, have you learned to shoot straight yet?"

"Cut Hand!" a broad man, heavy but not fat, drew up in front of Arrow. "Are you this white dog's prisoner or is he yours?"

"This white dog has killed five of the enemy since I've been with him. Three of those times, he saved my life."

"Hah!" the bigger youth laughed. "Cut Hand has a white man to guard his backside now."

"The man with the big shoulders has an even bigger mouth," I snapped, letting pique precede good sense.

A fired granado loosed among them would have caused less consternation than a white man speaking their own tongue. Cut's quick frown told me I had made a bobble.

"Bear Paw," he addressed the young man. "This is Teacher. His name is Billy Strobaw, but he is called Teacher. He is my friend. Do you understand? Billy, this is Bear Paw, so named because his big feet make a track like bear paw. We have hunted and fished and stolen horses together ever since we could walk. Don't ever play the hand game with him or he will win all your ponies."

43

The big youth kicked his mount to my side and gave me a long, insolent look. His locks, which tended to curl slightly, were restrained by a beaded hairbine across his brow. Splatterdash leggings covered his lower limbs. His torso was brown and bare and heavily muscled. He struck me as a sport – a brash, showy man. We probably would not be friends, but Cut had purged the sting from our exchange.

Arrow moved to another man's side. "Buffalo Shoulder and I played in the dirt before we could walk. This is the only man who can keep more shafts in the air at one time than I can when we play the arrow game. I think we covered our first girl together."

The young man grinned loosely, and I wondered if he was somewhat fishy, although he did not reek of strong drink. Yet his words firmed up my observation. "Got drunk the first time together, too."

My heart dropped like a stone as reality – as welcome as a blizzard in autumn – set in. My beloved had a history with these people. How would I weather that? I swallowed hard and put on a good face as he continued.

"These two pups are Little Eagle and Otter."

Little Eagle was thirteen or fourteen, the other boy about three years younger. Ages were difficult because these people appeared young in countenance and developed in physique.

From that moment, I looked upon Cut's people as handsome and well put together; made from the same leather, so to speak, as my beloved. Of course, in time I found a number of them had crooked noses or squinty eyes or the usual imperfections, but on the whole they were attractive people. These members certainly fit that image. They were all fairly tall and ranged from almost chocolate to nutmeg in skin tone.

As soon as introductions were completed, the others plied questions, liberally laced with teasing remarks. Cut put them aside, promising to reveal all after he greeted his family properly. The youngest, Otter, galloped away to spread the news of Cut Hand's return. Little Eagle rode at my side and asked countless questions about my clothing, my rifles, the bandage on my arm – and the dried stain on my trousers. The others scattered to herd the horses.

The stream beyond the trees proved to be the Yanube, a broad, shallow, cottonwood-lined waterway, more a creek to my mind than a river, although I was to learn of its immense carrying capacity during spring runoff. Once we forded the rapidly moving water, we turned north, moving across the undulating terrain on a parallel to the river for less than a league before we raised a snarl of new riders shouting in raucous welcome. The horsemen, mostly young and exuberant, wheeled about us on their sturdy ponies, trying not to allow their curiosity to cross the bounds of rudeness. Two more seemly figures rode among the tribesmen.

One was Cut Hand's father, Yellow Puma, a swamping, impressive figure astride a white mount. Solemnly, the chieftain clasped his son's forearm and spoke in a low tone that did not reach my ears. It was amazing how much the colt resembled the stallion. I was looking at Cut twenty years from now.

The other man, older than Yellow Puma, was something of a dry-bones, skinny as an orphaned calf except for a small, rounded paunch. His hard, suspicious eyes studied me obliquely; he was well practiced in the native art of seeing everything without directly engaging another's eyes. I pegged him as a Jesuit, a designing, cunning man. This must be Spotted Hawk, the shaman Cut had warned must be won over to our side. I eased Long's nose to the ear of the man's pony.

"Greetings, Spotted Hawk."

Of course, Otter had told of the white man who spoke like the People, but this one would likely have shown no surprise even had he not been forewarned. It would be difficult to get on his high side.

"I am Billy Strobaw, a friend of Cut Hand's come to seek the shelter of your lodges."

The medicine man took my measure in one glance. "A man who comes in peace is never turned away," he intoned. When called upon to speak at council, that low, rumbling voice would serve him well. "You are welcome to rest from your journey," he continued, not once allowing the curiosity hiding behind his eyes to show.

"Billy," Cut spoke at my side. "This is my father, Yellow Puma. Father, this is the man called Teacher." As coached, I performed the clasped forearm greeting. The muscles of that arm were as firm as those of his son.

"You are welcome, Teacher. Cut Hand says he has a great story to tell. We will hear your side of it to make certain he does not blow smoke in our eyes."

The village, which boasted about thirty skin lodges, gave Cut Hand a tumultuous reception. Joy at seeing their kinsman safe overcame the natural reserve I learned they generally accorded

45

strangers. All were similarly clad. The men boasted girdles of buckskin, sturdy moccasins, which I called shoepacs, and little else except for occasional shell disk ornaments or gorgets, which looked to be French. A few wore bone breastplates. The women dressed modestly in soft shifts of buffalo hide or some sort of herba, a grass cloth. Their habit occasioned a more liberal use of dyed porcupine quills and beadwork. Hair on both male and female was uniformly long and thick, and customarily worn in braids falling to either side of the face.

Mongrel dogs yipped with unrestrained pleasure; fat, dark children shouted or laughed or cried according to their nature. As we threaded our way between clustered tipis, I noticed armed sentinels on horseback at the distant edges of the village. The procession halted before an unadorned lodge no larger and no smaller than all the others. The women of the band gathered in a large clearing before the tipi around a handsome matron attended by a beautiful young woman some years my junior. This was Bright Dove, Cut Hand's mother, and his sister, Butterfly, exactly as he had described them.

Cut Hand greeted his mother with an awkward embrace. Butterfly received an affectionate bear hug. Not so restrained as the older woman, she peppered him with questions and recriminations for worrying them so.

After I was introduced, Cut showed me to the bachelors' tipi where I stowed my personal gear. Left to my own devices, I changed clothes, discovering my white skin to be the object of some curiosity among the three young men in the lodge. Uncertain whether to hize or haze, that is sequester myself or wander aimlessly, I settled on something useful.

Before I was halfway finished washing my soiled clothing at the river, Butterfly took them away and shooed me back to camp. Allowing her to handle my under clothing was acutely embarrassing to me; apparently it was of no concern to her.

The evening meal in Yellow Puma's tipi, which I was invited to share, was buffalo pluck, a mixture of heart and liver, with French beans, corn, squash, rape, and what I would call jonakin, a sort of cornbread. Conversation did not once touch on our recent adventures, but centered on me. Because of Cut's proclamation that I was "The Teacher," I described my time at Moorehouse, although images of a calculus classroom were not especially impressive at the moment. The women of the household supped on the south side of the lodge, and their silence indicated the men's conversation was of more interest than their own.

When we moved outside, the entire village had congregated on the *Hocoka*, the important open space before the headman's lodge where the Four Directions meet. Spotted Hawk took a seat beside me on the buffalo robe spread for the occasion. The members of the council arranged themselves in a circle. One, a man of middling years with a dark, wolfish look about him, was the biggest Indian I had ever seen. He was not obese, but carried a bulk that complemented his great height.

Yellow Puma, who sat to my left, made a production out of lighting a calumet, offering the pipe to the sky, earth, and four cardinal directions. I am not a consumer of tobacco, and kept a straight face with difficulty as I drew the acrid smoke into my lungs. When the pipe had made the circle of the council, the misco turned to Cut.

"We rejoice at your safe return, Cut Hand. We found your pony and the dead Pipe Stem, but your trail went cold in the mountains. Now you have returned with a guest and riches and a story."

Cut Hand rose and gave a sign to Little Eagle and Otter while I discretely tried to cough smoke from my innards. Spotted Hawk took note of my actions. The boys lugged several large bundles over and laid them at Cut's feet.

"My father," he began in the manner of a born storyteller. "Three Pipe Stem warriors ambushed me as I was returning home. The cowards shot my pony from under me."

I swallowed a smile when no one asked how they accomplished that feat, but doubtless the teasing would come when he was alone with his peers. I suspected the big Indian I noticed earlier had picked up on the omission.

"I headed for the mountain country, moving as stealthily as a serpent," Cut went on. "For half the span of the sun, I worried my way through a draw, over a hillock, through the buffalo grass, taking what cover I could."

Oh yes, he was going to make an epic of it. I felt eyes on me and knew Spotted Hawk watched me closely. Had he ever seen a white man before? When I turned my attention back to Cut, his physical beauty distracted me for a moment, a dangerous thing with the old shaman's eyes on me.

Cut told of slipping over the crown of a ridge to find himself in the clutches of three savage white men. Savage white men? I suppose a fair-minded citizen could reach that conclusion if he didn't know us. Some of the People nodded in recognition of Splitrum's name. Cut identified me as the third of the savages, and told of his deliverance from Red's deadly knife.

Splitlip lived up to his reputation in the epic by cunningly outwitting the remaining Pipe Stem bent on murdering Cut Hand. The old man's wood lore grew near unto magic as he slurred the trail of four people from the sharp eyes of the enemy. Somehow the subject of manacles never came up, but Cut rendered me full credit on the morning the two warriors attacked. Nobody asked why he left both of them to me.

Cut Hand came into his own when we left the river, boon companions now, bound for his village. The battle with the renegades was exciting enough to be told without embellishment, and this time we were heroes together. The fact the six raiders had been liberally sampling the traders' liquor stores escaped the telling. He finished with his invitation for me to come live with the Yanube to learn their ways and earn their friendship.

Yellow Puma bade me welcome and thanked me for saving his son's life three times over. I reminded him Cut Hand had saved me once, which was as good as thrice, because to lose one's life is a singular event. There were quiet chuckles around the fire and subdued titters from the women at the back of the crowd.

The Yanube misco expressed disappointment the mighty Splitrum had not accompanied us and invited me to speak. Even though Cut and I had rehearsed this to the extent of him putting words into my mouth, I was leery of the effort. I stood and faced the waiting throng.

"Thank you, Yellow Puma. I hope my poor words do not fail me. You can be proud of your son. With my own eyes, I saw Cut Hand avoid three mounted warriors with long guns bent on slaying him. I watched as he killed one in hand-to-hand combat. I witnessed his bravery in confronting three white men, one of whom wanted to put a blade in his heart. Despite this, he helped us construct a canoe, so my companions could safely travel to Ft. Wheeler.

"Cut Hand and I have fought together and killed together. To kill a man is not an easy thing because to my teacher's mind it is better to learn from a man than to slay him. Yet sometimes it is necessary.

Cut Hand told me of his people and made me long to sit at their campfire. But we do not come empty handed."

On cue, Cut opened one of the packs, drawing out a fine breech-loading rifle, which we presented to Yellow Puma. Another went to Spotted Hawk. Keeping only a few of the breechloaders, we asked Yellow Puma to distribute the remainder of the rifles to the People in accordance with their need. The gigantic Indian helped himself to one of the better weapons without waiting for Yellow Puma's largesse.

We also gifted the band with our horse herd less three of the ponies and enough trace animals to pull the wagon I intended to retrieve. The trade goods went to the women, setting off a scramble for pots and knives and trinkets. When things settled down, I continued.

"I ask to live among the People of the Yanube to learn their ways and draw wisdom from their lore. I will share my own knowledge with you. I do not come as a trader or a trapper or a factor of the white government."

I drew a shaky breath before proceeding. "I am aware the appearance of white men among you is not welcome, but it is a fact of life that they will come. I began my Soul Journey far to the east – beyond the great River of the Missouri and even beyond the Big Muddy, the Father of Waters, where the white people number as the blades of grass. Like their red brethren, they do not all speak the same language or dress the same way, but they all do one thing and do it well. They plant their roots and send their increase to the west to put down their own tentacles.

"Already they have taken the tribal lands of the Six Nations, beaten down the Cherokee, pushed the Choctaw and the Chickasaw to the west. I was a babe when they defeated the great Tecumseh of the Shawnee and took his lands. I was but little older when General Jackson, who is now chief of all the Americans, overcame the Creek Nation.

"Far to the south, the Seminole are under attack. The Congress – the great council of the Americans – has decreed that all of the red men east of the Big Muddy will be moved to the west. Even as we speak, Black Hawk, chief of the Sauk, is battling the Illinois militia. And already other white men travel through your country to explore the far west. Before I was born, white men named Lewis and Clark passed near here to travel the Yellowstone and Columbia River country until they reached the great lake to the west where a man can walk no farther.

"Others have been to the Great Shining Mountains and down into Spanish Santa Fe seeking land and furs and the yellow metal that comes from the earth. Someday they will come here, as well. But I have come first to offer a bargain. I do not covet your land. I came west seeking to learn, and in return I will teach. I know my people. I know they can be unspeakably savage, and unbelievably kind, not much different in that respect from many others. Someday you or your children will have to face great numbers of them. What I can teach you of our ways will help prepare for that time.

"Cut Hand told me of a savannah not far from here bordered by tree-covered hillocks. The land is flat, yet sheltered. There is good water from a brook. I would build a home at the edge of that clearing and plant seeds. While I am not a trapper, I would snare peltry for my own requirements. While I am not a handler, I would trade fairly any possessions I do not need for those I do. I will earn my keep without becoming a burden to your people."

"And I will help him build his home," Cut declared, "and share that life with him – until my duty calls me back," he hedged.

Spotted Hawk spoke into the sudden silence. "Teacher, there is no yellow metal along the Yanube."

"Good," I said emphatically. "Then my people will be slower in coming. I will be privileged to learn from you as you are, not as you will be. And as you come to know me, then you will have a better understanding of my people."

The tall, gangly brave I had noticed spoke suddenly. His voice seemed to rumble around in his massive chest before making it past his lips. "It would be better if you simply go away," he announced.

Cut started to interrupt, but I held out a hand. "There is no variance between us on that. Yes, the Yanube would be better off if I went away and spoke nothing of the beauty of the land – provided none of my people ever followed in my footsteps. Better if my people never come here. But they will come. When they do, the world will never be the same again. If I can make you understand my people, perhaps the meeting will be easier."

There was silence around the fire for a moment before Yellow Puma nodded and filled the void. "Your words are good. They did not fail you. And I believe your heart is good, as well. You have saved my son, and while this is sufficient for his mother and me, I have a responsibility to all of the People. You will rest in the tipi of our bachelors until a decision is made. You are welcome in my lodge whenever you wish. Bright Dove and Butterfly will see to your needs."

"Thank you. I could not ask for more."

Cut spoke up. "Tonight I will sleep with my family. Tomorrow I will join my friend in the bachelor's tipi."

It was obvious a great worry was lifted from Cut as we walked back to the bachelor's lodge. "You did well. Thank you for not speaking of the buffalo."

I had wanted to say that wherever the whites appear, they kill off the native game. As these people lived so completely on the buffalo, I had intended to warn them of this until he convinced me that would likely cause them to consider my words as silly prattle.

"I should have, Cut. They deserve to be warned. These things I have spoken are all true."

His voice mirrored his disbelief. "Not even the white man can destroy the buffalo. They have always been here. They will always be here."

I moved to more personal matters. "When you told them you would share my home did they fathom our relationship?"

"No. That is a matter to broach with my father when I decide how to do it."

"You don't know how?" I asked, my voice rising. Somehow this was not working out the way I envisioned.

"Billy, do not press this thing too fast. It will take time." He paused before continuing. "We must be careful with Spotted Hawk. Some Win-tays are considered sacred because they are powerful people. Tonight, you spoke as a man of power. You hinted at the future. Spotted Hawk must not become jealous of your power. He cannot see you as a threat."

"Who was the big man who questioned me?"

"That was Lodge Pole. He's an outlander, a Lakota who came to the *tiospaye* when he married one of our women. He also has some weight with the council." His tone left me to wonder if there was more to the story of this giant.

\# \# \# \# \#

During the days that followed, we hunted with others of the band, and as I am a fair marksman, I brought in my share of wild game. Many of the Yanube were friendly, but others kept their distance. Little Eagle and Otter hung around to satisfy their adolescent curiosity about a stranger. Bear Paw aligned himself with those who kept their distance. I amended my initial harsh judgment; he would have made a stout friend.

The lack of intimate contact caused Cut to cast long looks at the young women, sending one more chill of fear down my near-frozen back – icy from fretting rather than the clime. The weather was magnificent: warm days followed by cool nights and more rain than I associated with plains country. Cut assured me the Thunder-Being, *Wakinyan*, was busier than usual.

One day, Cut and I hauled my boodle to the spot he had selected for my cabin. No decision had been made by the council, but he understood I needed reassurance, and this was his way of providing it – plus we gained a little privacy. Little Eagle or Otter or someone else usually dogged our footsteps.

Trees are scarce on the plains except around rivers and creeks and mountains. The two worlds merged in this little piece of heaven on earth. Three pine-covered hummocks anchored a small forest straggling off to the northeast on the trail of a fair-sized brook. That stream, which in later years bore the name Strobaw's Crick on military maps, was eternal, running with pure, spring-fed water four seasons of the year.

The meadow, hemmed on three sides by the hills, opened to the south with a view of the Yanube about a third of a league distant. A game trail or Indian path rode the edge of a tree line between the river and the mead. It was an ideal home site, flat with a slight drainage toward the distant river. One deep, ugly draw crept from the northern hill into the flatland marking where the creek had flowed before changing course.

Cut, bearing a burning brand, entered a large grotto by means of a hole screened by bushes on the near face of the north hill. My love, clad only in his loincloth, was goose-fleshed from the chill, as the temperature in the cave was regulated by a frigid spring arising at one end to seep from the cave and join the creek within fifty paces of where I intended to build the house. The water was pure; perfect for domestic needs. This would be our cool room for hanging meats and preserving all manner of root vegetables. There was a tiny entrance on the far side of the hill, opening out onto the forest.

Emerging from the cavern by this smaller adit, Cut grasped my hand and led me like a swain to a thick grove of trees. Without words, he laid me atop my abandoned clothing and relieved his Cupid's cramp by covering me with an eagerness that matched our first couplings. I discovered anew the strength and power of Dark Warrior, the fullness of Cut Hand's stones, the endurance of his thighs. He came quickly, and then rested while he stroked Pale Hunter gently. When I was about ready to ejaculate, he released my rod and rogered me long and hard. Judging him ready, I seized my own pipe and brought myself to climax as he exploded into my fundament. Had I but possessed a woman's vagina, he would surely have lined me with child. We lay joined like dogs after our exertions, enjoying an intimacy we shared with no other human on earth.

Our need sated, I examined a few of the items recovered from the trader's wagons before moving my goods into the hollow hill for safekeeping. The medicine bag held a truly impressive variety of remedies and restoratives.

The money canvas contained a veritable fortune in crowns and doubloons and pieces-of-eight and Spanish dollars and Portuguese half joes and a host of others that would require time and consideration to calculate. Most were gold, fewer were silver, and very little was copper, the reverse of the usual case. The bag also held paper money, some issued before the reevaluation of 1780. There was new tenor and old tenor, 1781 Maryland red, and currency I did not even recognize. Then, of course, I had the remaining gold pieces of my heritage. There was sufficient to wallow in velvet for eternity.

While fascinating and stimulating to the imagination, these were, of course, the least valuable items. It was the tools and the barrels of nails and other treasures I hungered to recover from the wagon.

Back in the meadow, I plotted my pan, the foundation to the house. It grew from a simple cabin into a structure to accommodate my store of goods, a double house with one side mirroring the other. The east porthern would be our living quarters; the west would have a large keeping room where Cut's friends could swap stories. Tired of my prattling, Cut dragged me to the horses. As we made our way back to the village, I released some of my spleen.

"Damnation, Cut, they've had time to plot the future of Turtle Island!"

He ignored my outburst and stunned me with his next words. "Some are questioning whether you are truly a Win-tay."

"So you finally broached the subject with your father, and they are finding excuses to keep us apart. Who's causing the problem, Spotted Hawk?"

Cut fidgeted uneasily. "No. Lodge Pole."

"What about people living anywhere on the Sacred Circle? What about an individual's nature determining whether he's a man or not? His responsibilities –"

Gently, Cut Hand laid a hand on my arm. "The responsibilities you choose are those of a man. You hunt. You fish. My father's women clean your clothes and cook for you. You do not sew –"

"Give me a place to live, and I'll cook and clean, by God!"

"Good. Because you must move out of the bachelor's quarters and make a lodge like one of the People."

"Hellfire and damnation, Cut! How am I supposed to do that?"

# # # # #

To say my first home among the Yanube was an oddity is a vast understating of the fact. I cut and trimmed lodge poles while Butterfly and her friends prepared enough buffalo skins to make a cover. I spent a night in the open at the edge of the village nursing peeled knuckles and barked shins surrounded by skinned poles and half-sewn hides. Otter was the only male willing to help with "women's work," sewing as fine a stitch with his bone needle as I did with my metal.

Cut Hand showed up after dark and endured my goosiness stoically. He eased my depression by holding me close as we lay beneath the stars. Exhausted, I fell asleep without arousing Pale Hunter, who preceded me in slumber.

The following afternoon, I raised my tipi only to have it flop back to earth in a jumble of poles and ripped skirts. Otter again came to the rescue. He showed me how to bind four poles near the top and spread them to provide support. Then we added other poles to steady the framework. He was as proud as I when the cursed thing managed to stand. By the time it was properly draped with repaired coverings, another day had turned into night. It only took two days to do what any Indian wife accomplished in mere hours. Cut Hand handed out lavish complements, ignoring the fact my lodge opened to the west when all others faced east, the First Direction. Then I learned about such things as backrests to serve as lounging chairs and parfleches to hold our goods.

It was all worth it when Cut Hand covered me in the privacy of our own lodge. He chose that night for his first act of reciprocation, lowering his head and struggling with Pale Hunter until I shuddered through an unbelievable orgasm. After that, we worked over Dark Warrior until he was scoured!

The next morning, Cut dropped the other moccasin, and the nearest neighbors sought refuge in another part of the village. "Billy, I want you to wear women's garb. A dress, a shawl. Something!"

"What!" My face went livid. "Never!"

Eventually, we arrived at a compromise. I took to wearing bright red galluses, which some call suspenders, or a crimson belt, or brilliant garters tied to my trousers below the knees, all dyed with colors mixed by village women. Later, I managed to acquire some crimson ferret, narrow tape that scriveners use to tie up documents, to festoon my arms. I sported something flamboyant every day. There came a time when these red men with their wry sense of humor labeled me, a white man, the Red Win-tay.

Next, I wove one of the willow frames that serve the People as chairs. Unfortunately, my first attempt fell apart and dumped Cut Hand into the dirt. He had the good sense to withhold complaint.

The following morn brought a double blow! My handsome lover started the day off wrong as we broke fast.

"Can I be what?" I roared.

"You don't need to act like a woman, just be a softer man," he reasoned.

"Hah!" I sputtered. "I am not a womanly man, and I won't be a womanly man. I built your bloody wigwam and dressed up like a bawdy house madam, and if that's not good enough, then so be it! I'll be myself, as you instructed me in the mountains! They'll accept you if you're just yourself, Billy! And I always tell the truth! Those were your words, Cut Hand, Scion of the People of the Yanube!" I added as a deliberate stricture.

"I did not lie!" he protested. "I just … miscalculated."

"Say it, Cut Hand! How did you miscalculate?"

"Men already have children before they marry Win-tays," he said hastily.

"If you think I'm going to wait until you marry and have two or three fry, you can perform an unnatural act upon yourself!" I raged.

He drew himself up proudly. "I will resolve this."

"Is there anything else I should know?"

He shook his head firmly.

I do not believe Cut lied to me, but there was definitely something else I needed to know. A handsome man of middle years showed up and announced that he would lie with me until his wife was over her menses. He left deeply offended, not by my refusal, but from my torrent of English vulgarities.

My next visitor was a child in his teens. When I sent him packing, he swore I sounded like every shrew of an Indian woman he'd ever heard. He didn't get half of what Cut Hand received when my love showed up for the evening meal!

When he had his fill of my ranting, he reassured me as only Cut can. Most of my anger, he understood, came from fear and uncertainty over the future.

"Why haven't we heard, Cut? What if they don't agree to let me stay?"

"Then we will go somewhere else."

"You will leave your people for me?"

"As surely as you left yours for me." He rose and held out his hand to pull me to my feet. "We will go hunting tomorrow."

"Are Win-tays permitted to hunt with the men?"

He ignored my sarcasm – as I had hunted with them often – and replied jauntily. "That's one of the advantages of having such a wife. She can do your hunting for you. I can grow as lazy as a new pup with a full tummy."

"Yes, but if you ever call me 'she' again I'll take my skinning knife to you."

CHAPTER 5

The days stretched and drew out my anxiety. In a small community such as the Yanube village, privacy does not exist; yet it became clear I was being observed especially closely. Natural, Cut Hand claimed. A stranger among the band naturally fueled curiosity.

One day, an attractive matron scratched on my tipi, which I had scornfully dubbed the Wacky Wigwam, and asked after some medicine in aid of her cramps. I had withdrawn to seek out something from my medicine bag when I halted in my steps. I had come within an eye's blink of providing her laudanum before Cut's warning about Spotted Hawk leapt to mind. Reluctantly, I denied having anything to help her.

Later, a young man joined me as I washed at the men's bathing place in the river. Introducing himself as Badger, he demonstrated an uncommon curiosity about the white man's religion. Suspecting necknackery, I guarded my tongue carefully.

"I learned of the Great Spirit from Cut Hand," I replied, "and have come to believe he is the same as my God, Jehovah, who created all things. From what I can see, we share the same Great Mystery, although there is a difference in our creation stories. My faith teaches that the Great Spirit sent his Son, whom we call Jesus, to live among us as a man."

Badger pursed his lips, but I could see he was not rejecting my words, so I continued.

"This Jesus is accepted as our savior. He came to earth to live and suffer among us to show us the proper way of living."

"Hah," was Badger's reaction to this news. That was a word liberally used to express – just about anything.

"Jesus was persecuted and slain by others because he was too perfect to live among imperfect men."

This time his "hah" expressed disbelief. "The Creator allowed mere men to slay his son?"

"Has the Great Spirit never done anything to surprise you?"

He frowned and turned thoughtful over that one. "It is true that mortals are jealous of perfection."

Cut later told me Badger was Spotted Hawk's nephew.

57

I crossed paths with Lodge Pole one day, giving me my first good look at the man who displayed the same grotesque form, bony features, and lumbering gait of a freak I saw in a sideshow during my Moorehouse days. The circus billed the man as Sampson the Invincible. But I perceived he had been afflicted with something called gigantism; a weakness, not a strength.

Lodge Pole continued on his way without speaking, but he examined me obliquely, that is without staring directly at me, with a fierceness that was disconcerting. This was one – as my father used to say – to watch his waters; that is, a person who bears close scrutiny.

Later, when we were alone, I pressed Cut for more information on this strange man. He eyed me for a moment before answering.

"He has no quarrel with you," he assured me, "but if he can use you to cause me trouble, he will do so."

"Another little detail you neglected to mention," I said. "Why does he wish you ill?"

"He's ambitious. He covets my father's place."

My heart gave a timid leap. "Is the leadership not something you inherit?"

He shook his head slowly. "No, the People will choose their next leader. But most will look to me."

"This is the answer!" I allowed my joy to surface. "If he wants it, let him have it. It solves our problem. The leadership can pass, leaving us free to live our own lives." My beloved's sour grimace pierced my bubble of hope.

"There is a reason he does not live among his own people," Cut said slowly. "He led a raiding party into an ambush, and some claim he deserted them to save his own hide. Others, mostly friends of his, I understand, said it wasn't his fault. He was injured in some manner and unable to come to the aid of those he led. Whatever the truth, his own *tiospaye* made it uncomfortable for him, so he joined his wife's band. I do not trust him, Billy. Yet, he has his followers, and if I do not seek the mantle, he might prevail."

"And that would be a catastrophe?" I knew in the bottom recesses of my heart his assessment of the giant merely confirmed my own.

"I fear it would be the end of the *tiospaye*." he responded.

I thought for a moment. "It could be the threat will take care of itself. I judge him to be … what, thirty-five snows?"

"Or more." Cut watched me intently.

"Chances are good your father will outlive him."

His mouth dropped open in surprise. "And how do you know this? Among your other talents, you can see into a man's future?"

"Hah," I replied. "Would it were so. I would look into my own. No, it is his condition that foretells his future. He is afflicted with an abnormality. That is why he is so huge. Likely in his younger days he looked relatively normal, but now his bones are becoming enlarged. He walks with a jerky gait. People who suffer this malady do not normally live long. I think there is something about this in one of the traders' medical books. We will look it up."

We left it at that, each mulling over what he had learned.

# # # # #

Bear Paw, Little Eagle, and two others joined Cut and me on one of our hunts. We were only moderately successful, as the normally curious antelope were unaccountably wary. Little Eagle claimed the sight of a white man frightened them. As we returned to the village, the buzzing of a buttoned viper spooked Bear Paw's pony. The animal reared, and unbalanced by a pronghorn carcass slung across its crupper, went down hard, breaking Bear Paw's right leg and sending one of the antelope prongs deep into his back.

Cut sent Little Eagle racing for Spotted Hawk, but all agreed we dare not wait for the medicine man. Cut sat behind the injured hunter and held him for me while I examined the wound in his back. No large blood vessels were punctured and his breathing seemed normal, so I allowed the wound to bleed out poisons while we tended the leg. I stood in front of Bear Paw and tried to muster a grin.

"You are not going to like me very much. This is going to hurt."

"Don't like you much now," he tried to keep a light tone. "Do what you have to." For such a big man, he looked terribly vulnerable.

"Fair enough. Hold him still," I told the others.

Bear Paw did not utter a sound as I set the leg and bound it between two strips of wood from a nearby shrub. Then, I cleaned the stab wound in his back with antiseptic from my ever-present travel kit and cauterized the injury with a heated knife blade. After this painful process, I smeared on ointment of the black poplar to succor the burn.

59

Lastly, I bandaged Bear Paw with strips torn from my shirt, and put his arm in a sling made from the remainder of it. Spotted Hawk arrived as I finished.

I worried over the old shaman's reaction all the way to the camp. This might be precisely what Spotted Hawk needed to reject my petition. He struck me as a closed and suspicious man, although he saw to the needs of his people adequately from what I could judge.

The first thing I did on reaching the Wacky Wigwam was to dig out a spare shirt and cover my naked torso. Two messages reached me at almost the same time. I answered the summons from Spotted Hawk before I went to see Bear Paw.

The shaman invited me inside when I scratched on his tent. Entering nervously, I sat to the right of the doorway, as was expected of a polite guest. He occupied the *catcu*, the seat of honor. As a courtesy, I endured a ritual pipe in silence, which did little to calm my anxious stomach.

"Tell me what you did before you closed his wound," he said when our smoke was exhausted.

He sat in stony silence during the telling of my treatment, showing some curiosity about the black poplar ointment. Then he rendered his judgment. "You did well."

Relief made me giddy but not incautious. "Thank you, but we must wait and see if the sickness sets in."

"If it does, it was not because of what you did." He paused a moment. "I think you will be allowed to live among us."

I wondered if I had misjudged the old man. "Spotted Hawk, thank you for your aid. I know the decision could not have been made without your support."

"Hah," he said, and the interview was over.

Bear Paw was ensconced on a backrest in front of his tipi. His young wife disappeared inside as soon as I showed up. He waved me to a spot on the other end of the blanket, and I endured a second smoke I did not want.

"Thank you for helping me," the young man said, stoically enduring the pain in his leg. His dark skin had gone even darker, and he demonstrated signs of lethargy. "Tell me the truth. If it had been Cut Hand would it have hurt as much?"

I laughed. "Yes, in truth, it would."

"You did not make it harder because I have not come over to your side?"

"I do not cause pain on purpose, my friend."

"I want you to know I am on your side now. Remember that if there is another time."

As we both chuckled over his wit, his wife came out of the tipi and handed me a beautiful, incredibly soft and supple buckskin shirt.

"Since I am wearing yours," Bear Paw indicated the bandage circling his broad chest, "Half Moon thought you should have another in its place."

Permission to stay was granted around a council fire that same evening. The *tiospaye* held a dance in celebration, a wild and exhilarating affair. Dances have a spiritual meaning for these people – as do most things. The big, booming drums and the piping flutes and raucous rattles stirred the blood unaccountably. For the first time, I heard the men's songs of love and war and bravery. The women's screech-owl trill was somehow more savage and primordial than all else.

Men, resplendent in a variety of feathers – eagle, hawk, turkey, pheasant – danced together while women in dresses adorned with beads and shells and colorfully dyed porcupine quills danced apart. Occasionally, there was a social dance where everyone participated. They even prevailed upon me to shuffle along on these latter.

Once, an eagle feather came loose from a headdress and fell to the ground. Immediately, everything came to a halt. Four mature men, or round bellies, approached the fallen plume from the four cardinal directions to retrieve it. Lodge Pole reverently bore the sacred feather to Spotted Hawk. After the old shaman performed a brief ceremony to restore the quill's potent medicine, the dance resumed and continued until the early hours. Even my bed in the Wacky Wigwam looked good when I finally got there.

The next day, Cut and I gathered six of the roach-maned trace horses and set out to recover the traders' wagon. I had hoped to have him to myself for a few days, but that was not to be. Buffalo Shoulder and Little Eagle insisted on seeing the Place-of-the-Wagon-Raiders-Battle, as they termed the site.

They proved good and gregarious companions, although I could have done without the jugs lashed to Buffalo Shoulder's mount. He drew from one steadily, but was unfailingly generous in offering it to the rest of us. I had a single swig of the bumblebee brew, but its sting was too much for me. Cut partook sparingly; Little Eagle, liberally. I chewed on my tongue to refrain from sharing the common sense that children should not indulge in spirits. The boy could not be more than fourteen. But this was their world, not mine.

Nature and carrion animals had not been kind to the rotting carcasses of the slain raiders. Fortunately, the tribesmen have an aversion to cadavers, so the curiosity exhibited by Buffalo Shoulder and Little Eagle was quickly exhausted. None too soon for me, we moved on to the Place-of-the-Broken-Wagon-Ambush.

The hidden Conestoga was serviceable with only minor repairs. I exasperated my companions by taking time to dismantle and salvage most of the second, damaged vessel. I was glad I brought six of the big horses because the scoop wagon was heavily loaded. Once I figured out which was the hand horse, I lashed the spans in place with salvaged harness, and we set off.

Darkness fell before the wagon broke out onto the plains, so we marooned in the foothills. Cut and I slept in the Conestoga, but the others merely toppled over in place once their jug was empty. I reached for Cut as soon as everyone was settled, deftly spilling his big yard from his loincloth.

"I want to suck you, Dark Warrior," I addressed his cock solemnly. Dark Warrior understood and raised his hooded head. I freed him of the foreskin and washed the bulb of his head lavishly. Then I set to work in earnest. Cut was not entirely successful in muffling his exclamation of release.

Happy, I lay back on my blanket and sighed. He had my trousers open and Pale Hunter exposed before I realized what he was doing. His hand set me afire. I came quickly and thoroughly. Instead of lying back down, Cut left the wagon to look for signs of danger. He was back within an hour, rolling himself into our blankets and settling his big form beside mine.

\# \# \# \# \#

My back was virtually broken before everything was unloaded back at the meadow with the hollow hill. The place was now called Teacher's Mead by most. These people named everything. I wanted to sleep in the wagon again, but Cut refused. It was not long before I understood why. Had he made love as violently in the wagon as he did beneath it, we would have rolled down to the Yanube and floated downstream. He took me again in the middle of the night, this time from behind. I rather liked that, except I could not watch his beautiful face while he flanked me. His mouth was at my ear; however, and I savored the rush of loving words as he pounded into me. When he came, everything was right with the world.

I created a marquee, a shelter similar to a military officer's large field tent, from the wagons' canvas covers to serve as our quarters while we constructed our permanent dwelling. Then I gleefully tore down the Wacky Wigwam and moved the rest of our belongings to the Mead. Thereafter, Cut declared us married before the council. Although not pleased by the idea, Yellow Puma chose not to make things uncomfortable for us.

From time to time, the young men of the *tiospaye* dropped by to lend a hand constructing our permanent home or to sit and smoke while they harassed others for doing woman's work. In their vale, the women made and owned the lodges. Yet, this was no simple tipi and clearly required a man's strength. Before it was finished, most of the village had aided our endeavor in some measure.

The exterior was native rock, cemented with a tabby of clay and small stones surpassing the hardness of plaster. The gavel, or gable, faced south, so the door opened out onto the meadow. The women scraped hides incredibly thin as paper lights to admit brightness through the window casements, so we would not live in a dungeon. When time allowed, I would construct stout drawn windows with gun slots for defense.

The two keeping rooms, the big parlors, were fire rooms with large fireplaces backed onto one another and vented by a double stack. Each was fitted with lug poles and reckon hooks to hang pots and other vessels for cooking. A windowless interior room at the rear of the western porthern served to store weapons and other precious goods. The east side was one big room for sleeping and general living with a sizeable pantry for dry goods, and a bathing room at the rear. With the ready availability of good water, I intended to use gravity to bring it directly into the house.

With the approach of the summer solstice, a great excitement gripped the *tiospaye* as invitation sticks passed from village to village for something called the Sun Dance. Indians from all the tribes in the area converged at a chosen spot north of us for a holy ceremonial to demonstrate the continuity of life and interdependence of all nature. A Men's Cycle Ceremony, it was dedicated to *tatanka*, the buffalo, who willingly sacrificed himself so the People may live. A Win-tay from another tribe opened the ceremony by blessing the Sun Pole of the Sun Dance Lodge. Men danced four days without rest or food to induce visions. Some endured self-mutilation to contribute blood to the Sacred Circle of Death and Rebirth. All this was described to me, as I was not allowed to attend. Cut remained at the Mead, missing the ceremony for the first time in his life.

While Cut worked on the drawn windows, I excavated the ugly gash in the earth running from the north hill down to a jetty beneath the house, roofing the tunnel and covering it with stones and dirt to create a secret passageway to the cavern. Both outside entrances to the cave were barred with strong doors and secured with stock locks.

The day scouts reported *tatanka* was coming, the Yanube village was deserted within an hour. This time Cut joined his people, as the buffalo provided the band's food for the coming winter. I remained behind to build my necessary on the windward side. Cut thought my plan laughable; he could not imagine performing toilet duties in such a close and smelly place.

Concealed pipes made from reeds and pitch pine tar carried water into the house; carved hardwood spigots controlled its flow. A small fireplace in the bathing room heated water for a shower made of an elevated basin held together by tar and gravity. Upon his return, an exhausted and filthy Cut gratefully made use of the device and then fell into his blankets to sleep the night away.

Not long thereafter, Spotted Hawk decided upon an auspicious day to begin the band's journey down the near side of the Yanube two full days and a broken sleep to join related bands in the winter camp. As the *tiospaye* was capable of moving about thirty miles a day, Cut would be separated from his loved ones by twenty-five leagues for the entire winter. Would he be happy? His sour visage made no promise in that direction when the move began.

I was well on the way to completing a sturdy front door by the time Cut returned from accompanying the band a distance. Recognizing his disquiet, I allowed our labor to provide its own balm. The door was soon hung against the coming weather, fitted not only with a sturdy stock lock, but also backed by two solid beams to guard against battering. Teacher's Mead was now virtually a fort.

Although northers soon rattled the gables, we tried to get out every day to avoid cabin fever. Like any two people cooped up together, we sometimes became miffy. Fortunately, we recognized the danger signs before minor spats became blazing anger. One or the other would go to the west side of the building and busy himself with a solitary task until his grum estate qualified. It was particularly hard on Cut, who would have had duties aplenty to distract him had he been where his heart said he belonged – with his people. Neither of us strayed far from the house alone. Sometimes the snow drifted four or five feet deep, but rackets, which Cut called snowshoes, expanded our environ a few leagues except when it was storming.

I braved the cold to construct a wooden linter, a commodious lean-to on the outside of the house to provide some meager shelter for our animals. By next winter they would be snug in their own barn, I vowed. During the short, cold days, we worked on furnishings to make us more comfortable, including a bed, a big-framed affair with extra cords strung to support the vigor of Cut's nighttime exertions. Both the mattress and the under-mattress were rude until I could lay hands on the proper materials. Cut used the bed as an accommodation to me, but he appreciated the spring of the thing when he flanked me.

Our first time in the bed, his tongue invaded my mouth and reached for my throat. His exciting, naked body lay against me from head to toe. Dark Warrior pushed between my legs. Cut went slowly, reinvestigating all my secret places. Probing with his mouth and hands and pipe, he set me afire. When he finally presented himself, his thrusts were strong; the orgasm, shattering.

Then he pulled me atop him and allowed Pale Hunter between his legs to ride against his sac. Imprisoned between his strong thighs, I came. Shot through with exquisite convulsions, my body ultimately reclaimed itself from wherever it had gone, and I could finally speak of my deep, undying love.

The long nights were spent teaching Cut to play chess and checkers on rudely carved sets. I studied the Holy Bible, seeking insight into my deviancy. The Old Testament railed against lying with your own kind, as well as denouncing Onan's sin and adultery. It also prescribed eating rituals and other behavior widely ignored by much of the Western World. Why then did these not carry the same stigma? Nowhere did the Lord Jesus decry my kind. I remained confused, but also cautiously reassured.

Once, when I wrote something in one of the traders' ledger books, Cut demanded to learn to read and write. A piece of flat planking covered with sand served as writing paper, and our fingers became pencils, just as in my earliest schools. Once he mastered some new lettering, he would ply it to scrap paper to see what it looked like for real. He did well except for paying proper attention to his tittles, those dots over 'i's and 'j's. As he learned quickly and easily, I was struck anew by the realization this was truly a man of many parts.

# # # # #

That first winter with Cut was one of the happiest times of my life, and I am convinced he came to feel the same despite the strain of separation from the *tiospaye*. The cold clung hard to the land that year. Late in the season, the nearby clamor of howling wolves pulled us out of the safety of the house. The animals had proved a problem at times, harrying our horses as food grew scarce.

Mounted on rackets and armed with two rifles and a hatchet each, we followed the baying wolves over the west hummock to the edges of the thin forest where a pack harassed four moose driven down from Canada by the long winter. Wolves are medicine animals, and Cut was as reluctant to destroy one of them as he would have been to shoot a kinsman; they were brother warriors. Yet, though skeletal, the moose would yield considerable fresh tallow for the People. Four shots brought them down, but it required six more and some flailing with the hatchets to ransom our bonanza from the wolf pack. It took three days to butcher the meat and hang it in the cavern.

Worried by the prolonged winter, we increased the feed to our horses a *senight* – a full week – before Cut sensed a change in the weather. By the time the first break came, the team horses were in shape to drag the Conestoga over a half-frozen, half-thawed trail. Even though the spring runoff had not yet fully begun, the river was high, and walks normally easy to ford, roiled with angry, white water. Cut said that when warm weather arrived, even the trail we now traveled would be inundated. It took four full sleeps to make the two and a half day trek.

The village, swollen by other bands to some hundred lodges, was in decent shape. While winter game had not been plentiful, the population was in no danger of starving thanks to stores of jerky and pemmican. The supply of green meat provided by the Canadian moose was welcome and immediately shared among other *tiospaye*s. The People were not known for what they had, but for what they gave away.

When another storm threatened a few days later, Cut and I headed back home to find wolves had pulled down one of our smaller animals. A barn was definitely the first order of business when the weather turned.

We knew spring was really upon us when a group of Yanube raised three tipis at the south edge of the meadow almost in the tree line. As soon as they were set up, Cut and I took gifts of food and discovered Bear Paw and his family, as well as Little Eagle and Otter, were among our guests. We got little work done that day and talked far into the night. When the last Indian had gone back across the clearing, Cut and I lay in our bed, not the least sleepy.

"Do they treat you differently?" I asked, studying his strong, handsome face by the firelight.

"No," he answered easily, stroking the back of my head slowly, "but some of the girls are jealous of you, and right now I am going to give them something to be jealous of." He lifted my head and touched his broad, generous mouth to my eyes, my forehead, my lips. Tonight, it was loving, but he achieved an orgasm no less forceful, no less exciting.

Afterward, he studied my face as if seeing it for the first time. "I love you, Billy Strobaw. I love you with the *nagi* that makes me Cut Hand. I cannot imagine my life without you."

No sooner had he spoken the words than I frowned.

"We will find a way," he said. He understood what puckered my brow.

CHAPTER 6

Looking back, it is amazing that first year worked out so well. How I chose to live my life often defied the vogue of a male wife, but as Cut Hand and others often observed, I was a strange Win-tay. I was masculine, refusing to soften to people's expectations. I hunted, fished, and played stickball with the men. Of course, I also performed the housekeeping chores and kept us in presentable clothing. Becoming swept up in the idea of fancy dress, I added to my red suspenders and belt and leg ties with a crimson hatband and dyed buckskin shirts, truly earning the sobriquet of Red Win-tay.

Perhaps it was because I was white they allowed me to blur the line between man and "not-woman." Or maybe it was my total lack of interest in women, except to develop friendships and gain knowledge from them. The most valuable thing I learned about my adopted people was that they were human.

Buffalo Shoulder was constantly in his cups, half a dram short of an outright sot. Bear Paw, while a good, decent man, tended toward sloth. No, that's too harsh a judgment. He merely did the minimum required to get by. Little Eagle? Suffice it to say he was an adolescent with all the ills that condition conveys: a bit of a bite and always seeking advantage over others. Cut was the best of the lot but drawn toward taking personal risks. Otter was a pure delight, mayhap too young and unformed to have developed his own eccentricities. If pressed for a fault, I would say he was too eager to please. Overall, I deemed them as fine a group of people as I have encountered. I did not find Fennimore Cooper's *Noble Savage*, but I met many noble men and women.

Thanks to the buffalo, the Indians of the area were prosperous. Even so, the life span of a tribesman was often short; therefore many men married more than one wife to assure a succession of children to replace the loss of his own life. A slain warrior's wives often went to his brothers for protection and succor. None of the People were abandoned to hunger or the elements upon the loss of a provider.

This relative wealth allowed the bands to remain small and widely dispersed except when gathered in a large winter camp. *Akicita,* or warrior clans, what whites called Soldier Societies, often spanned bands and even nations. Dog Soldiers existed among both the Sioux and the Cheyenne. Cut Hand belonged to the Porcupine Society, which acted as policemen for the villages, keeping order and providing protection when the people were on the move. Even now Cut was often away from home scouting the *tiospaye*'s territory.

The wisdom of constructing a double house, done solely by instinct, was proved countless times. When Cut and I were at home, there were usually young men puddering about. Little Eagle and Otter oft times slept in the west fronting room. Only at night were we truly alone in the private east porthern of our home.

One day, I walked around the corner of the house to find Cut's friends teasing him about me. Unobserved, I backed away in embarrassment.

"Cut Hand doesn't have to worry about a toothed vagina," Bear Paw ventured.

"How about it, Cut Hand?" Little Eagle's young voice asked. "Does his backside have teeth?"

"No, but his mouth does," Bear Paw rejoined.

"How does it feel to stick it in a man?" Buffalo Shoulder asked. As usual, he was halfway into his cups.

"If you want to know, you'll have to find out for yourself!" came Cut's easy retort. "Bear Paw, drop down on your knees. Or maybe Little Eagle should bend over and bare his buttocks."

In a flash of understanding, I realized this was a good and natural thing. They were always teasing one another, and none of the banter was mean-spirited. Reassured, I stomped around the corner and said the first thing that came to mind.

"Why don't you do that, Little Eagle? That butt looks good to me. Cut Hand, you'd better watch out or he'll take me away from you!"

Little Eagle manfully laughed with the others. "You're the one who better look out, Teacher. More likely, I'll bury my big prong between your white buns!"

"Better try mine," Buffalo Paw chuckled. "You will think his little thing is a grub worm."

"Hah!" Buffalo Shoulder snorted. "Everybody knows a bear's bone is short. Now if you really want to see what a man –"

"Too late," I interrupted. "The best man here has already plowed a furrow the size of which none of you can match!"

They chortled and poked at Cut Hand playfully. Thereafter, none bothered to guard his tongue around me.

The outhouse – what we called a barn back home – was built of stone with a wooden roof topped by thick sod to moderate temperature extremes and discourage fire. It had a loft that allowed for storage of winter fodder. Warm weather required a different approach. Collecting enough fallen timber for a horse walk, we built a Pennsylvania worm fence, one of those zigzag structures of stacked rails, around a large area to the west of us.

In a moment of inspiration, I traded for four pups that promised to grow into large, aggressive animals. We devoted long hours to training each dog to guard a certain territory. At nightfall, we had four efficient sentinels, one in each cardinal direction. Whether we were at home or away, no stranger could approach nearer than a hundred yards without dealing with a big, mean dog. They were self-hunters, so we fed them only to supplement their diet and bind them to us.

That spring, we were called away for two days to celebrate Butterfly's marriage to a young man who recently joined the band. He was a likely buck, and Butterfly was eager for his hand. Yellow Puma was pleased with the bride price, which virtually beggared the young couple. Cut and I each gave a gift of horses, one a young colt my mare had recently dropped. Broad Fist, named after the big hands at the end of his strong arms, seemed a good man.

Cut drank to excess on their wedding night, the first time I had seen him in that condition. Fortunately, he was not the low, glowering drunk I encountered so often in ordinaries, but grew playful, hazing and harassing the newlyweds mercilessly until the wee hours. If the couple consummated their union, it must have been near unto dawn because as Cut wore out, Bear Paw took over.

When he finally staggered into the bachelor's tent sometime in the middle of the night, Cut fell on me, totally unmindful of anyone else in the place, all of whom vacated immediately. While his performance was drink-impaired, he still managed to get the job done quite adequately before sleeping the sleep of the innocent, his nose hard against my neck. I loved him even more than before.

# # # # #

As spring blossomed, the sap rose not only among the flora, but also among the young bloods of the *tiospaye*. The drums and rattles came out and they danced themselves into a frenzy. When the drums fell silent, talk turned to the formation of raiding parties to harass their enemies. Of course, my hot-blooded mate organized a Porcupine foray against the Pipe Stem. Fearing his penchant for pursuing personal danger, I demanded to go along. Rather than forbid it, he begged me to help protect the *tiospaye* in case of attack in his absence. We closed up the house, left the dogs on guard, and departed for the village, taking our stock with us for safety's sake.

The dance the night before he was to leave seemed especially savage. War dances and scalp dances stirred the blood of everyone there, including this white man. Cut and the others I had come to love and respect reverted to a wilder, fiercer time as the fever rose in them. I watched in fascinated fear!

Cut, Bear Paw, Buffalo Shoulder, and four others left with the rising of *Wi,* the sun. Little Eagle and Otter accompanied them to tend the mounts and serve as messengers. A *senight* later, the group returned with twenty-six horses taken from the Pipe Stem main herd. Cut had counted coup on one warrior and killed another.

Such successful raids were bound to generate reprisals. Despite my reluctance, I was talked into returning to the Mead while Cut remained at the village in his capacity as a Porcupine. He argued, with reason, one of us should be at the meadow because a deserted homestead is a great temptation to passing parties bent on mischief. Although merely youngsters, Little Eagle and Otter were designated to accompany me as messengers. In truth, they were probably safer with me in case of raids.

Arriving at the Mead, we wasted no time getting inside the house although nothing seemed amiss. During the night, a bout of excited barking warned us of strangers in the area, but nothing happened. Early the next morning as *Anp*, the cold red light that leaves no shadow, led in *Anpetu*, the daylight, the dogs commenced again. As I stepped to the porch and called the animals back, three armed warriors stood in full view on the path across the meadow. I watched until they turned and went into the forest. An hour later, a lead ball shattered against a stone three feet to my left when I stuck my head out the door.

As I ducked back inside, Little Eagle poked a weapon through the paper light of the nearest window. His shot cut leaves from the tree where the assailant had been standing. Our dogs took cover without being told. Moments later, Otter warned that two attackers had taken shelter behind the barn. Fortunately, my animals were still with the band's herd.

We traded maybe fifteen shots. Little Eagle hit one of them, but the wounded warrior limped away under his own locomotion. The dogs were quiet that night, so we managed some sleep. I sent the mongrels scouting the next morning, and when they returned in an agitated state, I came to the conclusion the enemy had merely sought to keep us penned up inside the Mead.

Worried, I left the two boys to protect the house and made my exit through the secret tunnel, gaining the forest on the far side of the north hill undetected. Laden with three long guns, I set off at a trot. Half a mile from the village, I heard a battle raging. Unexpectedly encountering a line of warriors firing into the village from a fall of rocks, I sheltered behind a tree at their rear. Most of the Pipe Stem were afoot, alerting me this was an unusual raid. These warriors took more pride in individual exploits of daring than in sustained siege. There was greater honor in one warrior facing another on horseback than firing from cover.

The attackers were in force and had obviously made a run through the village as there were two burned lodges and a third toppled and collapsed. Once their surprise was spent, the Pipe Stem had been expelled. The Yanube horses were strongly guarded in a huge corral at the far end of the village, but the raider's mounts were hidden somewhere.

Overcoming the temptation to rush, I crept from tree to tree until I found the horses strung on picket lines in a small meadow guarded by three warriors. Working in as close as possible, I picked off the most distant of the three. One of them whirled toward his fallen companion, assuming the attack came from that direction. I winged him with the second long gun, but the third brave was not fooled. He got off a ball, which whipped past my cheek. My last rifle brought him down. A fourth man surprised me but squandered his lead ball before attacking with a hatchet. My rifle stock rendered him senseless.

Cutting their restraints, I stampeded the ponies down on their masters. I then settled behind a tree and plunked away. The raiders, finding themselves besieged from two sides, scurried to find new cover. My bag was modest; I was more interested in chasing them off than in killing them. When they withdrew, I went into the village to see if I could be of help while the Porcupines set out in pursuit.

An hour later, the tired party returned. Cut dismounted and embraced me in full view of everyone. He stepped aside, allowing Bear Paw and a couple of others to do the same. I was no longer the stranger who lived among them as Cut Hand's Win-tay mate; I was accepted.

The defense of the camp was not without cost. Two young men and a seasoned round-belly were laid away in the rocks. One of the fallen was Broad Fist, Butterfly's new husband.

Something about the Pipe Stem raid bothered me, so I cornered Cut as he moved through the camp checking on what mischief had befallen his people.

"Where were the scouts?" I demanded a bit more stridently than intended. His Porcupines were responsible for security and ordinarily knew when there was a stranger within a league of the village.

His murderous look told me this was not the first time that question had been put. Nonetheless, he brooked my interference.

"It was Buffalo Shoulder," he sighed. "He and three others were scouting our boundaries.

"Let me guess; he got drunk."

"He and one of the other guards were in a gully with a jug when the Pipe Stem passed through."

"He ought to be horsewhipped!" I thought of Butterfly's young husband lying wrapped in blankets.

"There will be trouble over this," my mate acknowledged.

Although the *tiospaye* remained in a high state of alert, that effectively ended the raiding season for the year. A few additional clashes took place when individuals met accidentally, but there were no further outright raids. I know warfare is considered manly and exciting, but I frankly prefer the calm of peaceful times. Was that one of my womanly fribbles?

Cut stayed in the village with the Porcupines until it was clear the danger had passed. Occasionally, Little Eagle or Otter or both would stay with me, providing company in Cut's absence. They were so bright and likeable and curious and full of energy that I began teaching them English.

When Cut returned a few days later, he greeted me with all the enthusiasm of a bridegroom. We made love first, and then we fucked.

74

By the following morning the thing he had been holding within poured out like flux from a lanced pustule.

"There was a council meeting." He sat at our table pushing biscuits around his plate.

I halted in the process of forking a griddle cake. "And the result?"

But it required more of the telling than that. He needed to purge his mind. "Some wanted Buffalo Shoulder banished."

My blood froze. To be thrown out of the *tiospaye* was the most severe form of punishment these people meted out, except for individual acts of retribution. "That seems harsh." I felt my way gingerly.

"Yes, but three of the People died because a drink was more important than his responsibilities."

"Did they demand the same of the other guard?"

"No. He is but a youth who fell to Buffalo Shoulder's drink. His father will see to his punishment." He paused. "Lodge Pole led those who wanted Buffalo Shoulder sent away."

"And you? What did you want done?"

"We dismissed him from the Porcupines. That will hit him hard enough, I think. He's not a bad man if he stays away from liquor."

"Who spoke for him?"

Cut ducked his head and pushed his plate away. "I did. And Lodge Pole will make much of that. For the moment, Buffalo Shoulder is to be left alone. They'll shun him, but they didn't demand he leave the camp."

"He may, anyway," I ventured.

"Yes," Cut acknowledged sadly. "That is true." He looked up at me. "I hope I did right, Billy! But he's a friend."

"That is so, Cut Hand, a childhood friend. But you have a responsibility to look at things as a leader, not a friend." I hesitated as my mouth went dry. "You will be called upon to make more difficult decisions than this one. Perhaps you can begin to appreciate the burden your father bears. You can be guided by only one thing, my love, and that thing is not friendship or personal loyalty. It is deciding what is best for the *tiospaye*." When I finished speaking, my words reverberated in my ears like a prophesy.

Cut sat quietly, looking suddenly diminished. "I know," he whispered.

The newly widowed Butterfly, deeply saddened by the loss of her husband, began spending time at the Mead. To tempt her out of her grum estate, I cajoled her into learning to read and write. Otter was eager to join in, and we sort of pressured Little Eagle. Soon there would be four of Yellow Puma's people conversant in the English language.

# # # # #

The tide of American settlers moving over the plains increased. The *Uoceti Sakowin*, or Seven Council Fires – called the Sioux Nation by whites – was finding it increasingly difficult to avoid immigrants; and while their cousins, the People of the Yanube, were more remote, the Europeans came even here occasionally. The first were traders who showed some sense, standing off across the river until Yellow Puma sent them to Cut and me.

Without revealing that several gathered on our front veranda could understand every word they said, I greeted the two men who looked to be drovers recently converted to the trade. Nathan Hatcher and his partner, Bill Rickles, showed no disrespect to the dozen or so Indians who hovered around curiously. The larger of the two, Hatcher, made his greetings and allowed as how they didn't know there was a white man within fifty miles until they learned about me from the Sioux.

"These look like good people. Ya keep 'em handled?" he asked, meaning did I keep them supplied with trade goods.

"Do what I can." Indicating the two homemade chairs on the veranda, I invited them to sit and asked after news from the outside.

"Let's see. You come out here when?"

"I left the Allegheny River Valley in the fall of '31. Got to this country in April of '32, as best I can calculate."

"Ya made good time."

"River-boated most of the way to Independence."

"Well, Old Hickory got re-elected since then." Hatcher said. "And old Charley Carroll died." The name did not ring a bell until he added, "They say he was the last one still alive ta sign the Declaration." He meant, of course, the Declaration of Independence. I gave no indication that to a Tory's way of thinking this was one of the most dastardly scraps of writing ever committed to parchment.

"Black Hawk got hisself whupped," Rickles volunteered. "Illinois militia 'bout wiped 'im out in a big battle on the Bad Axe River. Them Injuns is finished."

Most of the rest of their news concerned troubles down in Tejas, that being their home country. The American settlers were bound on breaking away from Mexico and setting up an independent republic; the Mexican President, General Santa Anna, was just as determined to stop them. There were bloody times ahead. That, I surmised, was why they had gotten out.

The two men did not seem like bad sorts, but I was relieved when they traveled on after some hard-bargaining. My spare team of hog-maned wagon horses trailed behind their Conestoga as they moved off to the west while new treasures crowded our storage room, a supply of powder, lead sheets for casting shot, and a few items the Yanube women would need. Despite my claim to be no handler, the Mead was beginning to look suspiciously like a trading post. One of the items they left behind was a dressing glass I intended to hang above the rude table holding our toilet items. I had long coveted such a mirror.

A black-frocked preacher showed up next. Lacking the good sense to await an invitation, he blundered through the fast-moving Yanube, missing the walk by a hundred yards and almost foundering his mount. He thundered at the band gathered in the *Hocoka* that night, unconcerned that most of his congregation did not understand a word he said. I hid out with the women at the back of the crowd and tried to explain he was not angry, which I perceived was not fully the truth, but caught up in the excitement of a spiritual experience.

The good reverend overindulged in the local fermented drink, made an indecent proposal to one of the Yanube matrons, and was escorted across the plains the next morning preaching incoherently to his horse. I never expected to see the man again. Someone, be he red or white, would jack-roll him for his coat or his shoes or his jaded pony before the year was out.

# # # # #

The next visitors were of another stripe entirely. Cut Hand was in the village, and I was alone except for Otter when the guard dog in the south put up such a clamor I stuck my head out the door to see what was going on. Three strange warriors calmly stood just beyond where the dog seemed willing to go. One gave the sign for peace. I barked a command to the dog and held up one finger.

Obediently, one of the men handed his weapons to a companion and approached the house. I stepped inside and told Otter to stay out of sight. If there was trouble, he was to use the secret tunnel and summon Cut Hand. I walked back to the door without my rifle.

The warrior was tall and handsome and obviously someone of standing within his *tiospaye*. He moved with a regal bearing despite his obvious youth. I judged him to be my peer and suspected that I was in the presence of one of the dreaded Pipe Stem. In addition to a modest loincloth and low moccasins, he had a small blanket thrown over one shoulder. Despite my deep commitment to Cut Hand, I felt a flare of interest.

"Greetings," he intoned formally. "I am Carcajou, son of Great Bull, Headman of the Pipe Stem Draw People. You are the one called Teacher?" His dialect was similar to the Yanube's. These two bands must be related, yet they fought one another bitterly.

"I am," I responded gravely. I knew Carcajou was French for wolverine, a cunning and ferocious beast of the north woods.

"I will tell you what I want," he said abruptly, sinking cross-legged to the grass. Apparently, he felt he owed me no courtesy, as it often took hours of polite small talk before these people would come to the point of a visit. His words, however, were respectful.

"This blanket is a small thing woven by my mother. It serves no purpose except as decoration, but she asks that you accept it."

"Gladly." I sat opposite him and took the red cloth, which was finely worked and richly dyed. "You must permit me to select some trifle for her," I responded, recognizing the blanket as an Indian gift, one for which something of equal value is expected, a sort of diplomatic exchange of presents.

"Our shaman has been injured. A pot of boiling water overturned on his hip, scalding him. He is old, so his repair will be lengthy and painful."

"How can I help?" I asked.

"We wish to spare him what pain we can. Do you have some of the drink-that-kills-pain among your stores?"

"I have a small amount of laudanum, sufficient to give him ease for a little while, nothing more. Since he is your healer, do you have someone capable of assisting him?" I poked my nose where it was not invited.

He seemed to take offense. "We take care of our own."

"Forgive me, I merely wished to know if my attendance was required."

He unbent a little. "Thank you. There is another who can attend the burn. Your lau ... da ... num will be enough."

"Will you come inside while I get it for you?"

The man cast a curious eye over the building before declining. I came back with a flask of the liquid and a fine metal bowl that would accept the rigors of household travel. He rose.

"There is something else," I said, holding up a small packet. This is called populeon. It is an ointment of the black poplar that succors burns and scalds. Ask your healer to apply some to the wounds." He accepted these and handed over a derringer hidden in his loincloth. "This is too great a payment for what I have given," I protested. "Perhaps a bag of lead balls and a little powder will even the bargain."

Carcajou hesitated and then nodded. When I returned with the items, he spoke. "You do not act like a Win-tay."

Caught short, I puzzled over my answer. "Perhaps a white Win-tay is different from a red Win-tay," I finally answered.

"That must be it, though they call you the Red Win-tay. You are a person I can respect, I think. Thank you for listening to my needs."

"Thank you for coming in peace."

They were no sooner gone than Little Eagle slunk out of the trees. "You betrayed us to the Pipe Stem! If I had someone with me, I would have slain them, like you should have."

I looked down my nose at him. "I do not slay people who come in peace. Nor do I think Yellow Puma would have done so!"

"You gave them shot and powder! I saw you. They'll use it to kill our women and children."

"I gave them a small amount in payment of this handgun. Certainly not enough to slay women or ... you children," I added in a deliberate stricture"

Doubtless Little Eagle would have taken offense, but his attention was claimed by the pistol. He examined it like the fifteen-year-old he was, not the adult he had been pretending.

79

I called Otter outside and gave him instructions. "Ride to the village and tell Yellow Puma what you heard and saw."

Little Eagle almost broke and ran for his pony hidden in the trees, so he could be first with the news, but dignity reestablished itself and he remained with me, requiring I relate all that was said. With an inward smile, I told him most of it. As he matured, he was acquiring an arrogance that sometimes sat well and sometimes rendered him obnoxious – like most who reached that difficult age.

# # # # #

Our homestead was completely finished by the time the band's out-parties reported the buffalo herd that fall. Excited over my first hunt, I refused to listen when Cut bade me remain behind. Most of the warriors of the camp rode out ahead of the women who followed with knives and hatchets and travois for packing the meat. The hunters were in high spirits, each describing how he would slay more of the animals than his neighbors.

What followed numbed the senses. The Indians rode their hardy little ponies into the midst of the shuffling, snorting herd to fire point blank into the side of both bull and cow. Several of the ponderous beasts fell before the stampede started. So began the most blood pumping, exhilarating adventure of my life – pounding alongside a wooly, half-ton beast fleeing for its life while I fought to stay aboard a racing, pitching horse.

Beyond the deafening thunder of the stampeding herd, the grunts of the fleet ponies, and the yelling and cursing of the hunters, the most overwhelming impression was of smell, of powerful odors: feces, urine, intestinal gasses, blood, slobber, mucus, musty pelts, dry choking dust – and fear! Fear has its own stink, and mine is as different from Long Wind's as his is from the huge bison bull we pursued. Drawing his breath in great, lowing gasps, the buffalo veered, almost sending Long to his knees and me beneath a thousand flying hooves.

Flouncing wildly atop my racing mount, I fired blindly, unable to take proper aim. The massive beast did not even grunt. Struggling to bring up my second rifle, I loosed a ball behind the shoulder. The mammoth beast stumbled and tumbled. Long cut to the left, away from the stampeding herd, and I saw there were yet more of the beasts behind us blindly following the panicked dash of their brethren across the ancient trace. Fumbling to reload, I picked out a cow and ran her to her death.

Done with the carnage, I hauled up and watched the dreadful spectacle with rising excitement. When rifles were empty, the Indians relied on arrows. In less than an hourglass, fully five score of the beasts littered the landscape with groups of women hacking and hewing at the carcasses.

The hunters transferred to fresh mounts and turned over their buffalo horses to youngsters who would walk the beasts while they cooled off. The men once again became warriors and proceeded to scout the area for danger. The hunt had taken us a far distance from the village, and the Yanube would not be the only band engaged in such a slaughter in our vicinage.

I sat astride my gallant little pinto, allowing him to blow and took in the tableau that stretched for miles over the prairie. Then I dismounted and began walking to allow him to recover and to consider what I had observed and participated in this day.

Given that *tatanka* provided all of the instruments of the People's existence, the kill today was well measured. There was sufficient meat for food to last the winter, not to mention wooly hides for tents, blankets, and clothing. Nothing would be wasted. Bones, intestines, hooves, marrow, all would be utilized. The existence of the band was assured for another season.

Cut drew alongside on Arrow and paced me. "You did well, my love."

I looked up at him sharply. He did not often utter endearments except in the blankets. My eyes roved his excited form. Apparently a hunt such as this was as efficient an aphrodisiac as warfare. I grew aware of my own arousal.

"Cover me now!" The stimulation of the chase settled in my loins, and I tingled from every orifice.

His eyes danced. "Buffalo running is bloody work."

"I don't care! I'll clean off the blood and sweat with my tongue."

"Do you wish Butterfly and Half Moon to watch us copulate?" he asked as the two women dropped beside the carcass of a half-grown calf nearby. He laughed. "Be patient, my handsome wife. Tonight you will beg me to stop."

"That is a promise you'd best keep!"

We were late in returning to the Mead, and he dallied with his bathing, but after that, he delivered on his promise. He had to help me to the chamber pot to void my bruised bowels. I took a small measure of satisfaction the following day when he complained Dark Warrior was sore to the touch.

CHAPTER 7

Canadian northers heralded an early winter, and with the appearance of chill winds, the dress of the People changed. Buckskin leggings covered red-brown legs, soft hide shirts hid bronzed chests, and moccasins rose to the knee. Coats and robes and body blankets draped broad, muscled shoulders. My deviancy apparently now clasped me in a firm grip as I frankly preferred the summer months when the men's habit usually consisted solely of loincloths. Although tempted by none beyond my ability to resist, there was nothing to prevent me from enjoying the sight of such flagrant masculinity. I knew full well that Cut peeked down a maidenly bosom on more than one occasion.

We decided to accompany the People on their trek south to haul the heavier provisions in the Conestoga. This was my first move to winter quarters, and the epic of an entire town traveling across the plains with the precision of long practice was a novel experience. Moccasins and hooves and travois poles tore a wide track across plains littered with horse apples and dog date and the occasional human offal when some child could wait no longer. Plodding mounts, seemingly resigned to a long trail, bore the young and the ancient and sleds containing household goods. Decorated umbrellas of buffalo hide stretched over bone or wood poles sheltered men and women alike from the still potent autumn sun. The spare horses, herded by boys and young men, traveled to the west of the column to avoid the lung-clogging dust.

Even the dogs labored on behalf of the People, hauling a load, sometimes in a pack, sometimes on a miniature travois. Only the pups – human and canine – ran free, yipping and yelling and laughing and crying, nipping at fetlocks or tugging at skirts. Toddlers made some portion of the journey on short, stubby legs supported by leading strings firmly held by sisters or aunts. The smallest rode strapped into cradleboards on their mothers' backs, viewing the retreating world through huge dark eyes.

Cut Hand and his Porcupines rode wide circles around the lengthening column to scout danger, lend assistance, and hurry along stragglers. I rode drag in the Conestoga.

83

The journey was to take four sleeps, which calculated to around a hundred and twenty miles. Excitement gave way to drudgery ere the first day saw its close. To break the monotony, I invited Butterfly to share my seat and bring me up to date on her life. She had dropped out of our circle of regulars at the Mead. As neither Cut nor I understood the reason, I asked her plain out as we rolled across the prairie avoiding ha-has, those hidden gullies that unexpectedly cut the rolling countryside.

"I could not handle all the happiness." She pronounced this enigmatic answer and then firmly shut her lips.

Butterfly had no sooner abandoned me to solitary travel than a gruff voice requested permission to ride a distance. Startled, I beheld Lodge Pole at my off-wheel. Waving him aboard, I prepared to halt the team, but he accomplished the transfer from horseback to wagon seat on the move with only mild awkwardness, using strength in the stead of grace and balance. The slat beneath my bum buckled alarmingly as he settled his great weight.

I cast an eye on his mount, curious as to the beast that handled such bulk. The horse was a bosomy, puddle-footed draft animal fully eighteen hands high with short, wide hindquarters and a broad back, the antithesis of the usual plains pony, which was bred for speed and stamina.

"Greetings, Teacher. Thank you for allowing me to rest my weary bones," he boomed.

I laughed. "Hold your thanks a league or two. This contraption is more apt to rattle bones to pieces than give them rest."

"True," he acknowledged, his teeth clacking audibly. "But the agitation is to different parts of the body."

To my surprise, the big man was a pleasant companion. He gossiped easily about the *tiospaye*, giving me insights into several individuals. I gained the impression he was as well informed as Yellow Puma and Spotted Hawk. After a time, I began to relax, which was doubtless his intent.

"I was baffled by Cut Hand's defense of Buffalo Shoulder," he said out of the blue with a big eyeball watching me closely, "although I suppose it was no surprise to you."

My eyebrows shot up so forcefully they shoved the hat back on my head. "How so?"

"Were you not the one who wished him to remain?"

"Me!" I seemed stuck on monosyllables. "Why do you think that?"

"Buffalo Shoulder is a handsome man ... personable," he added, perhaps intending to soften the stricture.

"Handsome young men or clumsy old giants," I spewed before my mind wrapped itself around things and controlled my tongue, "dereliction of duty resulting in the death of anyone merits punishment." Abashed at my effrontery, I glanced at him and was repulsed by the enlarged, bony features. He no longer seemed presentable company. "Lodge Pole," I blathered on, "let's understand this thing clearly. Cut Hand does not consult me on matters of the *tiospaye*."

He pursed thick lips. "Strange. Was not your counsel to be of such value when you petitioned to remain?"

Unfortunately, I am a fair-skinned man who shows his condition. I felt my cheeks flaring. "In matters relating to the Americans, he learns from me. In matters of the People, I learn from him."

As much as I desired it, I dared not order him from the wagon. He had too much standing in the community to be treated rudely by an outsider. No matter, having taken my measure, he was prepared to leave. I halted the wagon while he negotiated a transfer in the reverse.

The days passed slowly, and I saw little of my mate even during the night, but eventually the band reached its destination without undue difficulty. I gaped in awe at the efficiency of the women as they erected their tipis. Within hours, the village looked as if it had sat in that very spot for years. Other bands arrived to add lodges to those already standing. Cut and I intended to sleep in the wagon.

I found a quiet moment as we stood aside from others at the edge of a small grove of trees to relate my encounter with Lodge Pole – almost to my regret. Incensed, Cut Hand was well on the way to confronting the giant before I convinced him that was exactly what the man wanted. Frustrated, my love hacked at a poplar with his knife as if assaulting his nemesis.

"He is a pimp! He cannot talk to a man's wife like that!"

"Yes, but he knows I'm not a traditional wife. He'll claim that fact to excuse his boldness. Damnation, Cut, many take liberties with me they wouldn't dare with a woman."

He turned to face me squarely, and I read the thoughts behind those magnificent eyes.

"It cannot be helped," I said, spreading my hands and shrugging. "I am who I am, and I behave according to my nature."

He relented. "And I would have you no other way. So what do we do about Lodge Pole?"

"Ignore him. That will injure him more than anything. But this is only his opening salvo. He may begin starting rumors."

"I'll kill him if he does!" my outraged love breathed dragon's fire.

"No. We'll figure out what to do when the time comes. Just promise me one thing. Don't let him drive a wedge between us."

"No one will ever be able to do that!" my mate cried, clutching my shoulders and drawing me to his breast. As there were others within sight, he released me quickly.

Although Cut determined to stay with the *tiospaye* a few days, I insisted on returning home. He argued but stopped short of forbidding me to go, possibly because he reasoned it might carry an afterclap, a consequence. To avoid a series of brutal gullies requiring long detours, I crossed to the south bank of the Yanube to commence my journey.

I do not know how long the warrior paced me to the west before I finally spotted him. Woolgathering about Butterfly's mysterious attitude and Lodge Pole's slur robbed me of the alertness so essential in this country. Three others rode at some distance behind the wagon. When three appeared in front of me, I hauled up on the reins. The river was to my right with no walking place or ford within eyesight. I was totally cut off. Deciding to make a run for it rather than simply surrender to fate, I slapped the reins and urged the hand horse to action.

The wagon slowly gathered speed. Gambling they would not shoot the horses, I scattered the three braves in front of me. The warriors let out whoops of joy and fired shots into the air, anticipating the sport of the chase. The fastest mount belonged to a man who immediately lost his grip on the tailgate when I deliberately swerved to the left. My leap of satisfaction was short-lived. When I topped the next rise, it looked as if the whole Sioux Nation blocked my way. I hauled back on the reins, deciding the time to outrun trouble had passed. Now it was time to talk.

The big Conestoga clattered to a stop a hundred paces from the nearest Indian. He immediately held up a hand, and those pursuing me drew to a halt. I remained seated as a solitary figure urged his horse into a walk. Had I stood, I likely would have stained my britches, and that would be both unseemly and dangerous. There is nothing these people disdain more than a coward. These were not Sioux, I decided; they were Pipe Stem. Recognizing the approaching man as Carcajou gave me no clue as to whether this encounter was promising or foreboding.

"Hau, Teacher," the Pipe Stem scion gave a solemn greeting as he drew up beside the wagon.

"Hau, Carcajou. How is your medicine man?"

"Come see for yourself," he said, beckoning a rider forward. The brave exchanged places, taking the reins of the wagon while I claimed his pony.

The entire band, which looked to be larger than the Yanube, ranged across the plains on its journey to winter quarters on the south side of the river. The column halted as we neared. I knew without being told the tall man riding beside a travois was Great Bull. As we neared, Carcajou motioned me to wait while he rode forward to speak with his father. The older man signaled me to approach.

Great Bull had seen more snows than Yellow Puma, but was every bit as impressive. Authority rode his shoulders like an aura. "So you are the great Red Win-tay," he said. These people were given to hyperbole as well as dry humor, and I was helpless to determine which this represented.

"I am William Joseph Strobaw," I intoned, proving I could pontificate, too. "I am on the way to my home at Teacher's Mead."

He turned to an old man strapped to a horse-drawn sled made of two trailing lodge poles spanned by buffalo robes. The patient looked amazingly like Spotted Hawk. "This is Small Horse, our shaman. Your medicine is helping him mend, and your kill-the-pain drink eased his way."

The small, wrinkled man gazed at me through squinted eyes. For something to contribute, I said I wished there was more of the laudanum.

"It was enough," the old shaman wheezed.

"Good," I answered inanely. Had it not been for the inherent danger, this would have seemed a hazy dream.

"Your land boat is here," Great Bull said, pointing behind me with his chin. "You are free to go on your way."

"Great Bull," I said, prompted by a sudden urge. "If I visit the village of the Pipe Stem after the winter snows are gone, will I be welcome?"

He considered the question for some time before replying. "It would be better to remain with your Yanube friends." He urged his pony forward, leaving Carcajou to oversee my repossession of the wagon and safe conduct through the remainder of his column.

Now the danger had passed, I silently acknowledged the strong sexual attraction I felt for the striking warrior who rode beside my near wheel. Immediately, I was shot through with a sensation of treachery.

I crossed to the north side of the Yanube and gained the safety of my home three days later without further incident. The dogs and the horses were glad to see me. I unhitched the team, pitched fresh hay to the animals, and fell into bed exhausted – mentally and physically.

# # # # #

Cut returned home two days after my arrival, smashing the north cavern door to enter by way of the secret tunnel. He had followed my tracks and understood I had been captured. He knew the Conestoga had returned to the Mead, but who was in the wagon? The dogs' calm demeanor led him to believe I was in the house, but was I alone? He first expressed relief at finding me safe before growing angry because I ignored his wishes and returned without him.

He relented somewhat after I explained what had happened, but continued to withhold his pardon until we replaced the smashed door to the cave with one twice as strong. He now realized the value of the secret entrance.

"You are a strange Win-tay," he said, not for the first time, as he drew me to him that night. "You disobey your husband in front of the whole family, kill more of the enemy than he has, confront the entire Pipe Stem band, and walk away without harm or loss. And still your husband loves you."

He seldom referred to himself that way. "Your Win-tay wife loves you, too, husband," I replied in kind.

"You show it in peculiar ways."

"I'll show it now in ways even a dolt can understand," I moved down to his pipe. Dark Warrior, already stirred by the excitement of my near catastrophe, needed little encouragement to rise rampant and ready. It required only a modicum of tonguing. Tonight, it was gentle and loving, perfectly fitted to both our moods.

Our personal relationship restored, we settled in for a long winter. Cut worked hard on his reading and writing and developed a clear, running hand. Once able to understand how full and complete sentences were structured, he applied this to conversational English. Soon he would be better at my language than I was at his. We also took up ciphering so that in future dealings with traders he could not easily be cheated.

Cut paid me due attention during the cold months, leaping me frequently and on occasion accepting my seed in reciprocation by way of apology after a particularly tense day. I loved him without reserve, regardless of his mood.

We had to rescue of one of the dogs shortly before the snow melt began. The wolf pack chased West – we'd named them for the territory they patrolled – onto the stoop of the house. We put three of the dogs in the barn with the stock and took South, our favorite, into the house with us. He was a big brindle that looked ferocious even when he was lying on his back slobbering over a good belly rub.

Yet, by the tail end of this winter season, Cut was more testy than the previous year, likely because the band was at a more distant remove. He was also concerned over Yellow Puma, who had suffered from a lingering ague during the move south.

At long last, the Chinooks blew a warm breath across the Mead, giving false promise of spring and making further delay an unbearable burden. When the weather eventually broke, we undertook a horseback trek to the winter grounds the first week of the thaw. Bedding down in the snow had never been my favorite pastime; however, a snow cave with Cut Hand's big form wrapped around me was a surprisingly comfortable shelter.

The camp was in decent shape; Yellow Puma was not. He still coughed and raled as badly as last autumn. I broke out the Pandora's Box of medical supplies and got some saffron down the man. Within an hourglass his persistent hack eased. I looked up old Spotted Hawk and turned over some of the medicine, suggesting it helped to alleviate the croup. When he asked after the manner of its administration, I knew Yellow Puma would be medicated until the shaman's supply ran out.

As I walked out of Spotted Hawk's tipi, gunfire broke out to the east. A young guardsman raced in from the horse herd, yelling that two white men had snatched a couple of horse tenders. Otter was one of the youngsters taken.

Leaping aboard our mounts, Cut and I raced to where the abduction had occurred. The tracks told the story. The ruffians had the boys double-mounted with them. I did not know the other lad, but Otter was around twelve or thirteen and good-sized for his age. The men must have knocked them in the head and tied them in some manner.

"Man-stealers," I muttered. "They will sell the boys as slaves."

The shock in Cut's eyes changed to rage. Without another word, we crossed the ha-ha and sped along the plainly laid trail. From the look of the tracks, their mounts were big horses, no match for the small, tough Indian ponies.

We dogged the fleeing men as they tried but failed to cross to the Yanube in three different places. The tracks were growing fresher, and Cut's natural caution reestablished itself none too soon. An angry bee buzzed between us, followed seconds later by a distant report. A heavy caliber rifle! Buffalo hunters.

Cut dismounted and worked his way along the riverbank while I took Long over a rise opposite the point where I thought it likely the shot had been fired. Dismounting, I topped the hill and saw one of the men had taken advantage of a rock fall at the edge of the water to track Cut's movements. The other desperately tried to coax his balky mount into the water with his captives tied to trailing ropes. The fool! The boys, both afoot, would be swept away and drowned if he managed to get his horse into the stream. Cut would have to fend for himself. My rifle ball punched the man from his saddle. He flailed in the rapids and disappeared downstream.

The second man whirled and loosed a shot that knocked me from my feet. Stunned of mind and numbed of body, I crawled through the snow to the ridge, straining to see what had occurred below. One of the boys, still tethered to a nervous horse, rushed the man who had shot me and was slapped to the ground. That cost the ruffian dearly. Cut's ball entered one side of his head and exited the other. This was more than the horse could stand; it bolted, dragging the boys along behind.

Still not certain of how badly I was hit, I staggered to Long and clawed my way aboard. The panicky runaway was not hard to catch; the boys' unaccustomed drag slowed him considerably. Unwilling to risk truly stampeding the pony, I took up a second rifle and spent anxious seconds trying to draw a steady aim. My eyesight faded in and out, but I managed to shoot the beast before pitching headlong into the snow.

# # # # #

I woke after dark in a tipi with Cut sitting at my right and Yellow Puma on my left. Spotted Hawk hovered over me. "What –" I asked before exhaustion robbed me of speech.

"The ball bounced off your thick skull," Cut joked feebly, and I knew I would live.

"Drink this," Spotted Hawk ordered, shoving a buffalo-horn cup filled with some vile concoction beneath my nose. I almost threw up.

"Otter?" Did that horrid croak really issue from my throat?

"He is well. They both are. Bruises and scrapes and sore heads."

That was all I heard until morning. Finding myself abandoned, I managed to crawl to my feet and stagger outside without falling flat on my face. Otter was immediately at my side to lend a steadying hand. I mussed his hair.

"Good to see you, boy," I said.

"Boy!" he snorted. "Who's a boy? I was about to jump that man and knock him from the saddle when you robbed me of my opportunity. Then you scared the horse and nearly killed us."

"Such gratitude," I snorted at him. "You're as bad as Little Eagle."

He sobered. "Thank you, Teacher. Don't tell anybody, but I was scared. Why did those men want us?"

"To sell you to someone who would chain you and work you as a slave for the rest of your lives," I sought to frighten him into greater caution.

There was a dance that night to celebrate the boys' safe delivery, but these people danced at the drop of a hat. The drums and rattles and whistles about tore my poor aching head from its wretched neck.

We returned to Teacher's Mead when I could sit a horse decently. It may have been the merest coincidence, but the moment our homestead hove into view, my head mended. Feeling fitter than I had for a week, I insisted on checking the dogs and livestock. Repelled by the mess in the barn, I sat on the front porch and worried with saws and hammers and planes until I had a good start on a tumbrel to cart manure. When he finished with whatever he had been doing, Cut joined me on the porch and watched as I whittled a wheel into the round.

"Do you know how frightened I was?" he asked at length. "When that buffalo hunter fired, and you fell to the ground, I thought I would die. I jumped up and ran straight at him. I wanted to hatchet the man to death! I wanted his scalp! Then Otter kicked at him, and I was afraid for the boy, so I shot the man-stealer. I was relieved when you got up and rode after the runaway. But when I caught up, you were flat on your face sucking wet snow into your lungs." He looked at me intently. "Don't ever frighten me that way again."

I returned his stare but held my tongue for a long moment, savoring what I saw in those strange gold-flecked black eyes. At length, I laid a hand on his corded arm. "Now I truly believe you love me. You understand the small death I die with each raid you undertake. Remember this feeling the next time you needlessly expose yourself to risk."

He chose to ignore my gentle rebuke. "If that is love, it is a terrible thing."

"Yes, but it is a wonderful terrible thing. Aren't we anxious when one of the dogs is threatened, or the ponies, or our home? How much more so when the thing in danger is our half-life, our other self?"

"Is there no way to experience love without this fearsome thing?"

"None. Think on it. You fear for Yellow Puma and your family, even for Bear Paw and Little Eagle and Otter. Why would you not fear for me?"

He considered this and answered, "But it is deeper and more awesome than other fears."

I thought quietly for a moment. "Isn't that because the rewards of our love are deeper and more awesome? Nature balances things, Cut. The rewards we accord one another are weightier, so the penalties are heavier."

"You are a better Yanube than I, Billy. You travel the straight Red Road. You have found your Special Direction, what our Lakota friends call the Seventh Direction, while I still search for mine."

"Nonsense! If ever someone had a proper sense of direction, it is you. You undercut your value to me … and to your people."

"My people can wait," he said through a tight throat. "Right now, I want to love you right here in the open, so prying eyes can understand what I feel for you."

"Then do it. Some, should they see us, will understand; others will believe we are merely dogs copulating in the dust."

"Then their opinion will not matter."

He came to me and gently touched the scabbed flesh at my temple. The finger moved to my cheek. He tipped my chin upward and covered my lips with his. When he stepped back, I slipped his buckskin shirt over his head, revealing his sculpted chest and deep armpits. His dark, almost black aureoles roused me mightily. He released his chaps and loincloth to stand gloriously naked, his flesh puckering in the early spring air. Dark Warrior thickened and grew until it stood throbbing with the beat of his heart.

I rushed to throw off my clothing, but Cut stayed my hand, preferring to accomplish that himself. Then he laid me on the cold planking of the porch and covered me with his warm, muscled body. Before I knew what he intended, he slipped down my torso and took Pale Hunter between his lips, almost costing me too much. I managed to relax and enjoy the sensation of my manhood being lovingly washed before exploding in a mighty orgasm. Then he planted Dark Warrior in the private place that belonged to him alone. He thrummed me lustily, rending my flesh with mighty strokes. When he burst and shuddered through his ejaculation, he grasped my hand and raised it into the air with a great shout.

"This is my beloved Win-tay to whom I have just been a husband! This is my beloved Win-tay, who I have pleasured like the man he is!"

The words echoed against the three hills of our homestead. One of the dogs, West, I think, howled in response.

CHAPTER 8

Cut Hand was more a mother hen than a husband after our scrape with the man-stealers. He hovered close every minute of the day, but I was patient, allowing time to dim the memory of his fright. Eventually, he resumed hunting and fishing and racing Arrow against other ponies when the *tiospaye* moved but a mile east of us in the spring. Many of the young men were inveterate gamblers, and while Cut was not immune to the affliction, neither did he indulge it to our bankruptcy.

Yellow Puma seemed to repair slightly, yet he was not well. Badger played the flute, sending his love medicine to Butterfly, but things were not to the point where anyone was making predictions. I sincerely hoped she would see he was a good man.

Spring and summer were ideal. *Skan*, the sky, remained mostly a clear blue, and *Tate*, his companion-brother, the wind, laid a gentle kiss upon *Maka*, the earth. *Wakinyan* came to cleanse and nourish sparingly.

One day, two squads of dragoons led by three officers galloped into the Mead. The dogs put up such a fuss one of the men pulled a pistol.

"I would not do that, were I you!" I called from the porch.

"Then call the beast off," the senior officer yelled.

I gave the signal, and South slunk back to the porch. Two of the officers dismounted; a third saw to the men. With some unease, I wondered how long it would take Cut to get here.

"Am I addressing Mr. William Strobaw?" the captain asked as he removed a military hat to wipe sweat from his forehead with a blue sleeve.

"You are," I replied shortly, still miffed over the threat to my dog.

"Captain Charles Jamieson, at your service, sir. And this is Second Lieutenant James Morrow."

The captain was a mutton-chopped man in his thirties; the lieutenant, a baby-faced blond not more than a few months out of the Point. When he finished dismounting the troop, a more seasoned lieutenant with a silver shoulder bar was introduced as Smith. This latter officer left me discomfited in some undefined way.

"What can I do for you gentlemen?" I decided to be civil. "I can offer tea or coffee, but I do not traffic in spirits."

"No, thank you," the captain shook his head. "I believe you are the trader for a band that calls itself the Yanube." At my nod, he continued. "This is a courtesy call to let you know we are building a fort on the upper reaches of the river some fifty miles to the northwest. You are now under the majestry of the Yanube River Military District. We will patrol this area on an irregular basis to accustom the savages to our presence. You may call on us at any time in case of trouble."

"Thank you, sir, but I will have no trouble. The Yanube are peaceful and disposed to mind their own business."

"Are they praying Indians or heathens?"

"They are not Christians, but are devoted to their own system of belief. You won't find better people, Captain. They offer no trouble, only friendship."

"Trouble does not always come from the direction you expect, Mr. Strobaw," the officer warned. "Renegade white men are beginning to appear in the territory, and the Sioux are showing signs of restlessness. I take it this band is Sioux."

"Siouan, is more like it. They are undoubtedly kin, but are not a part of the Seven Council Fires."

The officer's expressive eyes showed interest in my description of the Sioux, but he moved on to his next question. "If I understand correctly, there are other Indians in the area."

"The Pipe Stem Draw People claim lands to the west. These two bands tend to rub up against one another, and there is trouble now and then, but usually nothing too serious."

"How are the tribesmen armed, Mr. Strobaw?" Smith put in.

"Lightly. They are no threat, as I have said."

"I would like to visit this Yanube village if you will direct me toward it."

"You have not asked my advice; however, should it be sought, I would send one man under flag to the village to request permission," I replied.

"I thought you said they were friendly," Smith snapped.

"Not hostility, sir, but courtesy. But I see some of them are here now."

Surprised, the military officers turned in the direction I indicated. Not one of the men had been aware of the Indians' approach. Cut, accompanied only by Bear Paw and Little Eagle, topped the eastern hummock and trotted toward us. All were armed, but the weapons were not displayed threateningly. Otter would be close by to summon help if it was needed.

"Captain Jamieson," I said when my mate slid from Arrow's back. "This is Cut Hand, Scion of the People of the Yanube. His father, Yellow Puma, is chief of the band."

The captain saluted. "Would you please tell him –"

"I speak your language, Captain," Cut interrupted.

"Excellent!" Jamieson introduced his officers and repeated the essentials he had related to me. I expected Cut to show off his command of English, but he was sparing with his words about halfway to the point of rudeness.

The troops left soon thereafter. In all that time, the blond-headed officer, Lt. Morrow, had said nothing. He was the junior of the bunch, and likely stood a little below the meanest sergeant in his comrades' estimation. The shavetail rode his gelding with an excellent seat – one most likely learned as a child at his father's manor. Aristocracy playing soldier, I judged.

"I don't like it!" Cut raged as the dragoons disappeared to the west. "Nobody asked them to come here. How can they just move in like that?"

"Ask the Mohawks," I said, "and the Shawnee and the Six Nations. These Americans do what you and the Sioux did when you came to this country. Nobody invited you. You had the strongest warriors, so you moved in. Now the Americans do the same."

Little Eagle fumed. "Are you claiming they are stronger than we are?"

"I know a little about the American military. If there's a fort then there are at least two hundred soldiers. Can you raise two hundred warriors?"

"One of the People is worth –"

"As many of the enemy as he can kill. Unfortunately, that is true of the soldiers, also. Besides, you don't have artillery pieces capable of throwing a shell over that hillock and shattering this whole building."

"Nobody has that!" Bear Paw snorted.

"Teacher does not lie," Cut said quietly. "He told us this day would come. He told us how it would happen. When he speaks, we must listen and learn."

#

Resplendent in red sash and suspenders, that night I sat on the blanket with the headmen at council to discuss the visit by the Long Knives and the new fort to the west. The entire *tiospaye* congregated in the clearing before Yellow Puma's dwelling to hear the debate. Fortunately, most of the hot heads had not earned a man's name or counted coup and had no right to speak at council, else the attitude might have been worse than it was. At last Yellow Puma asked my opinion.

"The decision how to treat these soldiers belongs to the People, but if I can shed light on the situation, I will be pleased to do so. This is the army that defeated the great British redcoats in the east almost sixty winters ago. They beat the tribes east of the Big Muddy and shoved them to the far shore. Some have resisted, but none have stood against them. But this is a big country, so they will be slow to swallow this land."

"They have a stronghold west of us!" Lodge Pole growled.

"And they have already been to the western ocean, as I told you. But it will take time for the Americans to come in such numbers as to seriously threaten you. Were I in authority, I would send messengers to the Seven Council Fires and even the Pipe Stem to see what they intend to do. Then I would decide what is best for the women and children who will inherit what you sow. I would not be guided by pride and arrogance, but by what is best for the People." Then I told of the great numbers of soldiers back east and enumerated the forts along the Missouri and to the west. I explained about the big guns, the artillery pieces.

After trying to frighten them to death, I explained the great debate over black slavery and the rifts in the white man's world, expressing the opinion that one day these men would fight among themselves. I told of the rumors of trouble in Tejas. In short, I tried to give these proud, peaceful people some hope in the face of the apocalypse rolling headlong onto their Great Plains. I sat down to mutters of discontent.

Yellow Puma made it to his feet alone, but it was not easy for him. His recent decline was troubling. "It is my belief what has happened calls for no heavy decisions on our part," he intoned. "We can suffer visits by these people if they are simply scouts to test the temper of the tribes. Our reaction to these incursions is meaningless beside that of our larger brothers of the Seven Council Fires. They will determine the fate of this country. Teacher's advice is good. Cut Hand and Badger will visit their fires and determine their mood. Bear Paw and Lodge Pole will go to the Pipe Stem and speak with Great Bull. Teacher will remain and talk more on this matter to me. Is it agreed?"

I died one of my "little deaths" as my spouse rode away the next morning. While waiting for Yellow Puma to send for me, I wandered the camp. Butterfly, washing clothes at the river, paused long enough to visit and cast long looks to the northwest, although I knew not whether they were for her brother or for Badger. I teased her a little about the young warrior, but she did not respond as I expected.

Spotted Hawk was in his lodge and picked my brains more thoroughly about the army situation. It was flattering to have this old man give my opinions such import. Wisdom comes with age, and my twenty and three years were far too few to merit much.

The summons came when the sun was at its zenith. Yellow Puma and I ate alone on the north side of the lodge, although Bright Dove and Butterfly took a meal in their own space, occasionally rising to serve some new morsel, always moving sunwise, or as I termed it, clockwise, the direction of all traffic in the tipis.

"Your words at council last night were hard to hear. They do not bode well for the People. But I believe them to be true."

"The tribes have a difficult time ahead of them. Some will not survive what comes."

"The People must survive," he grunted. "My young men would like to take to the hatchet and chase the soldiers away when they come back."

"That would not be wise, but young men often are not. That is why the gray hairs lead the *tiospaye*. I am no smarter than the next man, but neither am I less knowing than a child. I tell you the history of what happened where I was born. And from this history I can see the repetitions as they occur. I know what is going to happen, but not when nor the exact manner."

"If you held my responsibilities, what would you do?"

"Urge my young men to keep their tomahawks dry. There will come a time when there is killing enough to sate any blood lust. Keep that time as far in the future as possible. If the weight you bear were mine, the Americans would know me as a peace chief. One day their military will fight among themselves over black slaves, but that might be many, many snows from now. If you can hold the peace until that time, who knows what will happen after that?"

"It will not be easy. Each man is free to do as he wishes. I can control my young men only so long as they believe what I am doing is right. If I do the wrong thing, this *tiospaye* will melt like snow before the sun, each man taking his family to another fire."

"Is that not better than leading each man to his death? But these soldiers have not yet challenged the People in any meaningful way. You should be able to hold your hotheads for the present."

"Yes," he agreed. "We have time."

I was shocked to realize our conversation had tired Yellow Puma. Was he more ill than he appeared? Although I longed to ask, that would be impertinent. I posed another question in its stead. "When do you expect Cut Hand back?"

"Perhaps not for a phase of the moon," he replied.

With a sudden emptiness in my gut, I made as though to rise. "If you have no further need of me, I will return to our home."

"Take Little Eagle and Otter with you in case you need to send a message."

Before I could rise, he stayed me with a hand on my shoulder and inquired as to my contentment with life among the Yanube and with his son. It was unlike this man to pry into personal matters, so I replied carefully.

"He has been good to me, and I believe I have been good for him."

"He seems satisfied," Yellow Puma said. "I set my heart against your union until Cut Hand had other wives and children, but you have been good for him. My son is more serious and grows in wisdom each season. He is a contented man."

Uncertain how to reply, I resorted to their term of universal meaning. "Hah!" Then I retreated outside, my cheeks burning with pride.

# # # # #

At sixteen, Little Eagle was so full of himself he was a burr in the bum. With his dangerous, demanding Crying-for-a-Vision quest behind him, he had claimed his man's name; he was now Lone Eagle. Making matters worse in my eyes, the budding warrior fed his growing confidence by counting coup on a recent horse raid. Even so, when the immature side of him surfaced, he reverted to the fetching youngster of two years past. Yet, thanks to Lodge Pole's sly squib last autumn, I was vaguely uncomfortable alone with Lone Eagle in my own home. The same, of course, could be said of Otter's presence although he was merely a child. Still, to my white man's mind a claim of debauching a child would be an even riper scandal to propound were I set upon the ruination of another man.

It was Lone Eagle's arrogance that eventually led my mind away from such nonsense. In Cut's absence, he cast himself as my guardian and expected me to defer to him. When I did not, he grew sullen. We reached a tacit truce after three days. I went no farther than the barn or the horse enclosure without informing him, and he stopped trying to control my every movement.

After reporting to the council on his and Lodge Pole's contentious talks with the Pipe Stem, Bear Paw came to the Mead to fill me in. Their efforts had yielded little. The other band had been loathe to discuss matters with a Yanube.

Hard on the heels of his departure, the dogs commenced to raise a ruckus. I stepped onto the porch to find Carcajou on the path at the south edge of the meadow. He lifted a hand in the universal sign of peace – palm outward to show he held no weapons. Afraid Lone Eagle might level a rifle at the man from the cover of the house, I called the boys outside. Giving the signal to the dog, I signed Carcajou to approach. When he was near enough to hear, I turned to the house.

"Lone Eagle, go to the village and tell Yellow Puma the son of Great Bull has come to confer with me following his talk with our emissaries." I delivered these instructions in argot, so Carcajou could understand.

"I am needed here," the youth said airily. "Send Otter."

"You are needed as a messenger. Do not be impertinent! Do your duty. Tell Yellow Puma the Pipe Stem wish to hear my words for themselves."

Carcajou nodded, apparently realizing I was getting rid of a hothead. Grudgingly, the hothead took his departure.

"Otter," I said to the youngster who stood with a wry, knowing smile on his face, "I will call you if I need a message sent." Unlike his companion, this rum boy minded. He turned and went inside the house.

"We will talk where the sun can warm us," I said, pointing to a place some distance from the porch. "But first can I offer food or drink?"

"Nothing," he said, retreating to a spot of his choosing, not mine. Always the courteous host, I followed and took my seat in the grass opposite him.

"You have frightened the Yanube children out of their wits. Is this why you came? To scare them off their land."

"If you believed that, you would not be here, Carcajou. You have seen the soldiers who came uninvited. You have observed more American wagons this past season than ever before. The Pipe Stem are as good at reading signs as anyone. Go to the Sioux for their opinion. Go to the Mandan. Go to the Sauk; they are the last to feel the white soldier's boot on their neck."

"I am here, so I will listen."

I repeated everything I had seen and heard. During the telling, Lone Eagle and Bear Paw appeared on the hill to the east; two of Carcajou's warriors materialized out of the line of trees behind him. Both parties waited warily.

When I finished, he speared me with his immense eyes. "Win-tay, your words are sincere, but I will reserve what I believe. Even so, I will relay them to my father. Perhaps we will go to the Seven Council Fires for their counsel in the matter." He gazed at me a long time. "You are different, Teacher. I don't know how, but you are."

"I am a friend to any man who shows me friendship. I prefer efficient peace to wasteful war. In this country, that makes me different."

"Do you find yourself drawn to me, as I do to you?" he asked bluntly as we rose and shook hands, Indian style. Then he turned and proudly strode away.

CHAPTER 9

Cut arrived at the Mead ten days later, well ahead of my expectations. Once he bathed and ate, he told me what he had learned. By virtue of numbers and ferocity and military prowess, the Sioux dominated these plains. They were a large nation of seven divisions speaking three dialects, Dakota, Lakota, and Nakota. The Teton, a Lakota-speaking tribe, claimed its own sub-branches, among them, the Ogallala, Hunkpapa, and Siconjou. While the whites used Sioux as overarching name for these proud people, they referred to themselves as the Seven Council Fires. As was true of most tribes, they did not speak with one voice.

Cut and Badger visited several different fires and found the Sioux no better prepared to deal with the situation than the Yanube. The round bellies, while cautious, were agitated by the white man's incursion and the westward push of the Nakota-speakers who had been displaced by European settlers. The young bloods howled to take up the hatchet, and Cut's greatest fear was these hotheads would go out taking the Yanube high bloods with them. He understood perfectly that unless all the nations rose at once in a unified front, to take up the tomahawk was worse than futile – it was suicidal.

"And," he concluded, "there isn't a leader to bring them together." Cut leveled a look at me. "You are a white man, Billy. Why do you give us counsel?"

"Not because I wish harm to befall my own kind. There is no danger the Yanube or Sioux will defeat my people. In a battle maybe. In a hundred perhaps. But in the end those who resist will be overrun. I merely want the Yanube to have the life they love for as long as possible."

He fingered the rose knops I gathered to brighten the rude table where we sat. "Your words are little comfort, but true, I think. Even about the buffalo?"

"Even about the buffalo," I agreed sadly. "But that time is not yet come."

"I am tired," he sighed. "Come to bed, so we can make love to one another's bodies and minds and spirits."

103

He covered me with a yearning that tore my heart from my breast. Then he made love to my mind and spirit by tolling the things that drew him to me. When he finished, I moved my lips to his well-formed lobe and recited my litany to him. His lids drew heavy, and I allowed him to slumber while I wept unmanly tears into his hair.

Both of us were in a better mood on the morrow. As was his custom, he walked every inch of our merestead, seeing for himself the condition of the animals and the fields that provided us with foods not native to these plains. It was near onto noon before he spoke the words I had been thinking since last eve.

"Teacher, would it be of value for you to visit a white settlement and listen to those you meet?"

"Yes, I believe that would be profitable," I admitted.

"Good. Then we will leave tomorrow."

"I must do this thing alone if people are to speak plainly to me, Cut."

"I cannot allow it. I will be dead until you return." He frowned.

"No. You will go on living and care for this place. You might even do some unmanly chores since we have no true woman to carry that load."

"We could get one," he said quickly. He was merely tickling – I think.

"From what I hear, the Yanube believe Dark Warrior is worn out on the backside of the Red Win-tay, so no woman will have you … unless you have in mind one of those old crones who have lost both husband and children."

"Hah!" he cried. "I could show you!"

"You better not!" I snapped. "Dark Warrior is mine. I only lend him to you, so you can pass water."

He laughed. "Once again, I believe you."

It was my turn to frown. I could not undertake a venture like this with a secret between us. "Cut, I want to tell you something, but first give me your solemn oath not to act on it." He tried to squirm out of such a vum, but in the end gave it. "While you were gone Carcajou came to the Mead." Feeling a modicum of shame, I told him the whole of it from our first meeting to our last.

Anger flushed my spouse's features; frustration followed closely since I had bound him with an oath. The gold in his strange eyes glowed as if lit by an internal furnace. "Perhaps Lodge Pole is a better judge of people than I am!" The profane words struck my ears like a physical blow. He looked as if he wished to reclaim them, yet was unable to contain the next ones, albeit they came out in a less accusing tone. "Does he have reason to want you?"

"I have admitted the attraction, husband. But I swear by all that is holy to me, I gave him no reason to understand I was interested."

His ire lasted the remainder of the afternoon, but when we rode to the village to inform Yellow Puma of our intent, he allowed our legs to touch occasionally. Once home again, he thrummed me so thoroughly his clemency was obvious.

I drove the wagon into the village the next morning with a bum that complained of every jolt and a pipe sore to the touch. Nonetheless, I hummed "Yankee Doodle Dandy," a tune not ordinarily on the lips of a good Tory lad. With the Yanube's furs and what I took from our stores, the Conestoga carried a respectable load. Lone Eagle and Otter agreed to tend our stock while Cut accompanied me part of the way. Fifty miles in a loaded wagon translated into three good days of travel when most of the journey had to be made over game trails.

Cut tied Arrow to the tailgate and shared the wagon's bench with me. We spoke very little, but his presence was welcome. He left me the third morning with firm instructions not to drink too much or trust too much. To my surprise, I was reluctant to enter a town peopled by my own kind, a measure of the comfort I took from my adopted aboriginals.

A sizeable settlement with the unfortunate name of Yawktown had grown up around Fort Yanube. Despite my earlier reservations, my excitement began to mount. There was a sawmill, a general store, a livery, several saloons, a doctor's office, a barbery, a frippery for used garments, and even a bank! Thinking of the sheaf of currency in my boodle, I stopped there after making arrangements to board the team at the livery stable.

The banker was flustered over the variety of medium I presented: red, green, blue, yellow, foreign, domestic, continental currency, even a few bank bills. The man shook his head and said it would take some time to calculate values. I agreed to leave the paper and return the next morning.

The banker informed me the general store did some trading, so I gave the place a try. I was suspicious of the merchant's squint, but in time discovered it to be an eye condition, not a statement of character.

Caleb Brown was a southerner who grew distressed with conditions in Southampton County, Virginia, and moved his family west on the heels of Nat Turner's Insurrection in August 1831. Brown shared my conviction that warfare over the slave question lay ahead. Cautious about stating his own position, he merely ventured that the economics of slave labor were becoming questionable.

The mercantiler accompanied me to the livery to look over my goods. The sheer size of the load unsettled him a bit, but in the end, he made a bid, which was neither overcast nor so low as to be scandalous. Relieved of the responsibility of the People's furs, I trusted him to make payment the following morning.

All of my gold and most of my silver remained hidden at the Mead since such coins are specie in any man's book and were an invitation to be knocked in the head and abandoned in some alley for their gain. But I had brought a little of the silver and all of the copper to finance this venture. Reckoning there was sufficient for a room and a meal, I proceeded to the Rainbow House, an inn and eatery, as well as a drinking establishment. No ordinary, the Rainbow was quite a respectable place. After a decent meal, I drifted into the common room, which resounded with the noise of revelers, many in uniform, as was expected at an army post.

"Good evening, Mr. Strobaw."

I turned to face the blond-headed officer who had accompanied Captain Jamieson down the Yanube a month back. "Good evening, Lieutenant Morrow."

"May I stand you a drink?"

"If I may return the compliment." I trailed him to a table in the far corner of the room where the commotion of other men's conversations was less diverting.

"Your trading post is quite interesting." He raised his glass after a florid Irishman filled our order with the house ale, which turned out to be a dark and strong potion. "It seemed almost a blockhouse."

"When I first arrived in the country, the idea of defense was appealing. There has been only one assault; however, it was rather half-hearted." Realizing I was giving information rather than gathering it, I added, "Tell me, sir, what is the news from back home?"

"Not much," he said wryly. "You knew, of course, that President Jackson has been reelected?" I nodded. "Remains to be seen what this new Democratic Party will do for us, but Old Hickory's intentions are well known. My friends tell me Congress will establish a Department of Indian Affairs this year to be responsible for overseeing the resettlement and welfare of the tribes."

That was sour news, indeed. "Providing it is funded," I probed.

"I am informed it will be. Jackson is determined on removing the remaining Indians west of the Mississippi. There is already a territory set up for them where they will doubtless be better off."

"Better off being evicted from their homes? Deprived of their way of life? Separated from their means of existence? I seriously doubt that, Lieutenant."

"They will be provided subsistence … at least in the beginning."

Declining to state my opinion of such subsistence, I changed direction. "And what of our Indians out here? How will the Bureau interface with them?"

"That is not clear. There will be some displacement, I'm sure. There are too many settlers moving west to leave things completely undisturbed."

"What is your unit's mission?"

"To keep the peace and provide security for routes to the west. Frankly, our biggest worry in this immediate area are the Sioux. They seem powerful and obstreperous Indians."

"I have been living on their fringe for the past two years without molestation. A few come by the Mead now and again, but since I do not stock strong drink, they are mostly interested in ammunition for their weapons. How often do you intend to patrol my particular sector? Should I alter my goods to accommodate your troops?"

"They want for little except the strong drink you mentioned."

"And that I will not handle. In my mind, it is too dangerous. Raids have been made on arsenals and whiskey barrels. I want none of it."

"You are a wise man, sir. May I ask if you are tarrying long in town? Captain Jamieson or Major Wallston might wish to host you a dinner."

"I take it this Major Wallston is the commandant at the fort?" At his nod, I continued. "Unfortunately, I am leaving tomorrow after my business is done. Perhaps another time. Tell me, do I detect the soft tones of Virginia in your speech?"

"Yes. I was raised on a plantation a few miles downriver from General Washington's Mount Vernon. I should say President Washington, but to my family he was General for so long that we still err in assigning him that station."

"May I ask what called you to the military, or is it a family tradition?" He appeared to flush somewhat at the question.

"No, a personal decision," he replied as Caleb Brown joined us. Since they were acquainted, Lt. Morrow remained with us for a brief while longer. When he departed, Mr. Brown and I discussed prices and politics until it was time to retire.

The following morning, I was at the bank when it opened, and was frankly surprised at the weight of the count the banker gave me. Some of the bills I had thought paltry were pennyworth, while some I prized were severely deducted. I took a portion of the funds in coin and deposited the remainder, carefully explaining that upon withdrawal I would accept no Bills of Currency issued by the bank itself. Some banks had over-extended their credit, resulting in losses. Banker Crozier, a hunched, spare man who looked to be cast from the standard mold of his profession, assured me my requirement was not a problem.

After filling most of my needs from Caleb Brown's wares, I set about shopping elsewhere. A three-footed, long-handled griddle for pancakes and a sheet-iron roasting kitchen completed my equipment for fireplace cooking. A small wheel with a foot treadle for spinning went into the load. I eyed a simple loom fit only for weaving a plain over-and-under weave called tabby, but decided I could construct one myself. Four lanterns and a flaxseed press proved irresistible as I pictured Cut and me reading and writing well into the night.

The gunsmith was well stocked, and I was delighted to purchase six percussion weapons and a supply of cartridges. Two handguns and a heavy gauged shotgun rounded out my purchases there.

To my surprise, the tailor was a Jew. I had encountered a number of them while hesitating in New York City to debate the course of my future, but none since. Abraham Kranzmeier was a bearded, pleasant man with a heavy European accent that fell soothingly on the ear. His son, however, possessed the sharp tongue of a harpy. Several bolts of middling cloth and a hunting frock were his contribution.

At each establishment, I introduced myself and spent a few moments discussing the weather and the Indian situation. As a final order of business, I made a courtesy call on the fort to take the measure of this Major Wallston.

He received me cordially in his office, a place no bigger than my fronting room and probably a bit ruder in construction. In fact, I did not find the fort to be a first rate effort, although the men marching or performing calisthenics appeared a cut above their environment, and the post's horseflesh looked well-tended.

Elijah Wallston, Major, United States Dragoons, was a man beyond his prime but still capable of field life. Once past the pleasantries, he reverted to type and put hard questions to me regarding the situation in my part of the country in a manner that demanded cooperation. I gave it to him, declaring the Yanube peaceable, but like all the tribes possessed of a few hotheads. I admitted they were as perplexed over the army as was the army over them.

I considered confessing the fate of the two man-stealers, but withheld that information as one – together with their ponies and wares – had been hidden beneath the ground at my insistence. The other felon had been swept away in the Yanube's spring runoff and never seen again. Fearful some of the young bucks who thought my caution foolish would excavate the two buffalo guns, Cut and I rendered them useless by dropping stones weighing at least a quintal squarely atop them.

When asked about the Sioux, I allowed him to conclude they were waiting and watching like everyone else. I learned a split about the strength of the fort and its armaments. I also gleaned there was a new redoubt on the lower Yanube a hundred miles southeast of Yellow Puma's encampment. When the Major escorted me outside his headquarters, I glimpsed a brace of wheel-mounted field pieces. I also spied Lt. Morrow bawling out a platoon and managing not to sound like an underclassman announcing commencement.

Tardy in my departure, I resisted the urge to remain another day and sent my team down the rough road to the east, following my earlier ruts across the flat country. Night overcame me almost before the wagon was out of Yawktown's lantern glow. I drifted off to sleep beneath the Conestoga missing my beloved mightily. An hour later, something woke me.

"Cut? Cut Hand, is that you?" I demanded. "Where are you?"

"Here, wife," came the soft reply. He lay behind me. How he managed to come up on me in the dark, put Arrow to pasture, and slip into my blanket without alerting me was one of the things that made Cut Hand who he was.

"Only one sleep in the white man's town, and already your senses are dulled. What if I had been Carcajou?"

"Then one of us would have died." I turned and reached for him.

"Unfortunately, it would have been you. How did you know it was me?"

"I knew you'd skulk off in the distance like some mangy dog."

"A dog is a noble animal. He does much work for us."

"All right, I surrender. You'd find something noble about anything I name you. But you know what I meant. Kiss me," I said, changing the subject.

"It will take more than a kiss to forgive your insults."

"Here I am. Take what you want."

He did – with unusual gusto, which told me he had feared for my safety.

# # # # #

The council convened upon our return to hear my report. Cut and I presented Yellow Puma and Spotted Hawk new percussion rifles. I carefully explained that the two hundred or so troopers at Ft. Yanube were armed with weapons like these. They were good horseback rifles, short, yet with sufficient caliber to knock a man from the saddle or a buffalo from the herd. One so armed could fire two times while warriors with inferior arms shot once, as it needed no spark to set off the priming. The simple drop of a hammer accomplished that trick.

The men around the fire examined the rifles and talked animatedly among themselves. I followed with the news of the four field pieces and once again explained how they could heave shells that destroyed everything within the span of two tipis. News of a second fort down river brought exclamations of alarm, none more vocal than Lodge Pole's.

When I finished, Yellow Puma rose unsteadily to his feet. "My people, I have led you for these many years. For the most part, we have lived in peace, excepting our skirmishes with the Pipe Stem, and neither is set upon destroying the other. Each has his place.

"We know Teacher as one who speaks the truth, even when it is painful. Now, I will put questions and beg he hold to his usual custom. You have told us of your people's prowess as warriors. We understand their greed for land and gold and furs. Now tell us something of your way of life."

I held my tongue for some time, trying to glean what he was seeking. "If there were Americans in the same number as my fingers and thumbs standing before us, all of one hand and the thumb and forefinger of the other would be farmers living on their land and plowing fields and raising foodstuffs to feed their own families with a surplus to trade for things they need. The remaining fingers of the second hand would be merchants and gunsmiths and fabricators and bankers to handle the coins others use to pay for their goods. And they would be military men such as you have seen with your own eyes.

"Americans possess a will of such stubborn strength no one has yet been able to stand against them. Seen as individuals, they are not always notable. The preacher who yelled at you last summer was a subject of derision. Put him with ten others, and he becomes a different person. The traders, Hatcher and Rickles, were impressive men, but with ten others they will stop a buffalo stampede.

"The white man lives under a written code of law that all may read and understand." I stretched the truth to make a point. "Every child grows up knowing if he steals or kills, the force of those laws will crush him. But above all else, the white man is human. He is able to do great things, but he is also capable of great errors. His code promises justice to every man, but because men administer this code, there are injustices at times. To some, the red man's word is not as good as the white man's. Nor is the black man's, nor the Jew's, nor the yellow man's. This is where the human fails the code.

"Let me tell it to you this way. If a white family traveling through the land of the Sioux was slain, the American dragoons would punish the Sioux. They would not punish the Sioux who did the killing, but all the Sioux because of what some did. Hear me! Should your leaders decide on peace, but some of the young bloods take up the hatchet, the punishment will be administered to the entire *tiospaye*. This is the truth … the plumb truth!" With this, I sat down.

There was absolute silence until Lodge Pole shouted from the other side of the fire, "This is not just!"

"No," Cut's low voice growled, "nor has Teacher declared it so, merely the truth. Now I tell you this. After the winter snows come and go, I will travel to this fort up the Yanube to see the army leader. Teacher has told me he seems a hard man, but one who lives by his rules. I will hear his words and see if I draw the same measure. While I trust Teacher with my life, one of us who must live under this justice-that-is-not-justice must judge the matter for himself."

Yellow Puma struggled to his feet. "My son has spoken his aim, and I approve. But all should know my heart. Yellow Puma will be a peace chief until he is given reason to turn to war. My paint will not be red until the white man smears it upon me himself. I ask my young men to leave their knives in the tipi. When the Blue Coats come again; they will be welcome until they make themselves outcast by their own actions. We need not like them, but we must respect them as human beings and men of power. That is all I have to say."

On the way home, I reviewed all that had happened. Was I stirring up these people for nothing? The dragoons had molested not a single Yanube. No white men had come to the village and made trouble or sought advantage over these folk. Still, I knew what would come. The People must be prepared. I glanced at Cut riding at my side.

"I am afraid, my love. Afraid I'm frightening people needlessly."

"No." He shook his head. "Already I understand what is to come better than before you spoke. If you had not given your counsel, I would be waving my rifle and screaming no one rides through these lands without our permission. I would be one of those firebrands you fear so much."

"You should understand this, as well," I sighed. "When you look at a Welshman or a German or a Jew, you see a white man. When a white man looks at a Sioux or a Yanube or a Mandan, he sees an Indian. If the Sioux anger him, he will make little distinction when seeking his revenge. That is why your thinking is right; you should talk to the Major and let him see you as an individual rather than a race. He must understand the Yanube are not the Sioux."

We dismounted and scratched South's ears before putting away the ponies. I paused on the stoop before blurting, "I'm going with you, Cut."

"I hope so!" he exclaimed.

CHAPTER 10

Tatanka was late coming in '34. The Yanube elders were fretting over their winter supplies when Lone Eagle and two other youngsters raced into camp with news the great bison had finally been spotted. The herd seemed thinner, and the slaughter was not so great this hunt. Although Cut said that happened from time to time, I could not help but wonder if my prediction was already coming true. Likely, this was not the case as the white men were not yet so numerous on the plains. Whatever the reason, the kill was sufficient for the coming winter. Once the carcasses were harvested, Cut and I participated in a Buffalo Dance and a feast of fresh meat at the *tiospaye* that night. The drums threatened to undo all my work as the hotheads fired up on home brew.

Too sated to make the trip back to the Mead, we slept in the bachelor's tipi. Nonetheless, Cut managed to vent the pent-up need generated by the kill. He lowered my britches and molded himself to me beneath the covers, moving so gently I did not believe he could achieve a climax. He proved me wrong. He suppressed a groan by biting my shoulder; I felt the familiar spurt of his hot seed.

We took our share of the buffalo to the Mead, and I was salting and smoking meat when West let me know someone was coming. Up to my armpits in gore, I looked up to find Splitlip Rumquiller waddling to meet me. I was never happier to see a rough, bearded face. He ignored the blood and gave me a bear hug.

Cut let out a cry of welcome and stepped off the stoop to join us.

"Thet there arse a yers still looks mighty good ta these old eyes," the frontiersman said, stepping back to look at me.

"Better watch out, Cut Hand understands every word you say now."

"Hah!" Cut exclaimed. After receiving his own greeting, he added, "If I was going to share, it would be with my friend, Splitrum. But I'm not going to share."

"Don't blame ya none. Damnation! Cain't decide which one a ya's the purtiest!"

Split accepted our invitation to spend a few days and settled in easily. He was horseback, but said he had a few stores back in Ft. Ramson, the new military post a hundred miles to the southeast. He was Indian trading, but got a hankering to see Cut Hand and his country wife, so he came to chew the dog. He brought the tidings that Wild Red Greavy was dead, killed in a fight in a particularly nasty ordinary better than a year back. They'd partnered, but Red was too fond of drink and women to be trustworthy, so Split pulled it and went off on his own. He latched onto a button down in Spanish Territory, and when the mists cleared from his mind, Split learned he'd married a Crow woman stolen by the Apache. Too much trouble for the pleasure she gave, he agitated her until she got mad enough to divorce him.

The old mountain man gave us other news, most of it somber. Trouble with the Santee frightened the Minnesota Territory to the point where the army was called out. So many of the Indian nations were on the move west it was possible trouble might come from that source rather than the Americans or the local Indians. A scheme to pry Tejas – they called it Texas nowadays – away from the Mexicans and admit it to the union spurred fresh talk of a war south of the border. Riots over whether new territories would be admitted to the union slave or free splintered the national psyche. Somebody named Joseph Smith claimed to have found and translated some golden tablets into something called the *Book of Mormon*, upon which he founded a church. Smith declared the Lord Jesus had visited the New World and ministered to the natives. Some suspicion as to their morals attached to these Mormons since they were said to marry multiple wives. Cut demanded to know the sin in that.

Split was genuinely impressed by the relationship Cut and I enjoyed. He satisfied himself Cut wore the britches, but also concluded I didn't act the usual Win-tay. Before unrolling his blankets on one of the two beds for guests in the east fronting room, he looked Cut squarely in the eye.

"Er the two a ya likely ta be having at it in there?"

"Likely," Cut answered before I could say otherwise.

"Shore hope all the excitement ain't too much fer my ole heart!"

That night, Cut rogered me with all the enthusiasm of a raw youth demonstrating his prowess to his first doxy.

The Yanube gave Splitrum a reception deserving of his reputation. The old man demonstrated a rough frontier courtesy born of long experience. When he seemed disposed to give straight answers to sensitive questions, I went down to the river in search of Butterfly, so Yellow Puma could compare our information without the embarrassment of doing it in front of me.

Later in the evening while Cut was in the bathing room Split looked at me with concern. "Thet Yella Puma's a sick man, Billy."

Before he left the next morning, Split let us know a detachment of troops was scheduled to leave Ft. Ramson next spring on transfer to Ft. Yanube. They'd likely follow the river and come through us or at least close by.

# # # # #

Exactly a *senight* after Split left, there was a ruckus at the south end of the meadow. I looked out the door at the same time Cut walked stiff-legged up beside the stoop. Carcajou and two others stood waiting patiently.

"Get in the house," Cut snarled at me.

"Cut, don't –"

"Go in the house, wife," he said, deliberately putting me in my place. Normally, he used the term fondly; this time it wounded. Nonetheless, I obeyed because I wanted to arm myself. Cut had nothing except a skinning knife.

As there were three of the Pipe Stem, I grabbed three rifles and stood in the shadow of the doorway, cradling one of the weapons for easy use.

The Pipe Stem moved not a muscle as Cut approached. Pride and love and fear battled for ascendancy in my heart as I watched my mate calmly face his enemy. I could hear nothing from where I stood, but observed much agitated head shaking. Finally, Cut turned his back on them and returned to the porch.

"Teacher," he called. I stepped out onto the stoop. "Carcajou wants to talk to you. He has heard Splitrum was here."

"You can tell him what Split said as well as I can."

"My word is no good with him. Will you speak to him, or do I send him away?" Cut's face was clear. If he harbored jealousies, they did not show.

115

"I will talk to him, but don't interfere."

"Hah!" he said, neither agreeing nor disagreeing. Nonetheless, he gave the sign to call off the guard dog and beckoned Carcajou forward.

"I would hear Splitrum's words," the Pipe Stem said without preamble.

"You could have asked Cut Hand."

"Why would he tell me the truth?"

"Because Cut Hand never lies. Even when it is to his profit, he does not lie. When you know that, you will have learned something valuable for the future."

Carcajou eyed Cut Hand blandly. "Nor do I lie, Yanube."

"Hear me, Carcajou," I said sharply. "It is the same with me. I will never lie to you, and I will never lie with you. I belong to this man. If he dies by a stroke of lightning, I will still belong to him. If he dies by the hand of a Pipe Stem, I will still belong to him."

"Does he need his Win-tay wife to protect him?"

Cut reacted with a growl and reached for his knife, but I spoke loudly and stayed his hand. "He needs no protection from anyone. But there is no advantage in either of you killing the other, Carcajou. One day, he will lead the Yanube; and one day you will lead the Pipe Stem. The time will come when both fires need vigorous leaders who deal straight and fear no man. You are both courageous; I hope you can also be wise."

"Teacher, I will say this thing, and then never speak of it again. You are different from others. That difference has pulled me toward you, but I now understand what you hold in your heart is not in the manner of some silly girl who plays with men. I am sorry for this misunderstanding, as I truly felt you had a list for me. This is finished.

"And to Cut Hand I apologize. I took your interest in this Win-tay as a dalliance. Now see you I have truly taken him to wife. All who know of Cut Hand know he is a man. We will never be friends, but I now put aside our personal differences and vow to make no effort to harm you for private reasons. Should conflict arise from duty to my people, that is another matter."

"I hear you, Carcajou. And while I would like to carve your belly, I will also give my pledge. There will be no personal vengeance."

The situation defused, I filled in the Pipe Stem scion on Split's news and speculations. Carcajou asked a few questions and then rose.

He did it like Cut. I envied both men their ability and grace. I always got up by degrees; they did it in one effortless movement.

I did not realize the depth of Cut Hand's rage until the Pipe Stem left. He looked as if he wanted to crawl my hump. If he tried, he'd have a fight on his hands. We'd fight like men, not a man and his distaff.

"What did you do, make moon eyes at him?" he demanded.

"I swear, Cut. I did nothing." I assumed we were having a reasonable discussion. "Do not let Lodge Pole's poison come between us."

"It is not Lodge Pole standing between us, wife," he said in a quiet voice. "Let me understand. Carcajou goes to the trouble of courting you and insulting me because you did nothing to show your interest in him?"

It was colder than the weather dictated at the Mead for three days. Cut remained on the peck, busying himself in the village to avoid confronting me. The second night he did not come home, doubtless to make me believe he was resting in some girl's arms. At nightfall, my heart and mind concluded this was nonsense, but dawn found them in agreement on the obverse. He came riding up mid-morning as I slung a pan of wash water over the end of the porch, very nearly hitting him in the face. Had I wanted, that's where it would have landed for I timed it to perfection. Putting on an innocent face, I expressed false contrition.

Lone Eagle showed up after a week's absence, and I was overjoyed when he spent the night because Cut would have to move back with me. Alas, I reckoned without a complete understanding of the situation. He threw Lone Eagle on the floor on the west side and claimed the bed opposite Otter. By right of age and standing, Lone Eagle dispossessed Otter who rolled up in his blanket before the fireplace. I slept alone in a cold bed.

The thaw came the next day when Cut sent the two boys on some fool's errand. He sat at the table while I prepared a meal.

"Come here, wife," he said. I ignored him. "Billy, please come here."

I claimed the chair opposite and leveled a look designed to inform him I would brook no nonsense. It was probably only calf's eyes.

"I am sorry, Billy," he said at great cost. "You have a way of taking the sting out of things, for making it easy to come over to your way. But sometimes when you do it, it hurts. You begged that Pipe Stem dog for my life."

"Nay! I did no such thing. I put to rest once and for all the idea he could ever have me, and he apologized. From a man like that, an apology is something."

"A man like that! You think he is a special man?"

"He is the Pipe Stem's Cut Hand. That makes him very special."

"Damnation! You always wiggle out of it. You speak in circles like all white men so nobody understands you."

"Then let me make it clear. I love Cut Hand, Scion of the Yanube. I love nobody else. I want Cut Hand. I want nobody else. I love him so much I won't even ask where he was the night he did not come home. I love him so much I want him to fuck me in every orifice he can fit!"

He laughed then, and Pale Hunter danced a jig. "Lone Eagle and Otter will be back soon. Do you want to shock them?"

"That's their problem. Mine is that I am excited beyond all reason by your presence. Only Dark Warrior knows how to settle that excitement."

I was watching the sweat form on his broad, clear brow as he worked over me when the boys returned. Cut ignored their noises in the other side of the house while he finished what he had started.

# # # # #

We accompanied the band on the trek to the winter quarters again. The Conestoga made heavy hauling so much easier that I began thinking on acquiring a wagon for their use. The winter camp was on the far side of the Yanube this year, about fifty miles south-southeast of the Mead. Since Yellow Puma entered the cold season an ill man, Cut wanted to remain in the encampment, but when his father insisted, we returned to the Mead. Joy at finally being alone was tempered by worry over Yellow Puma. My mate felt he should have remained with the *tiospaye*, and the cold northers, when they came, blew right through his heart.

Although I seldom accounted for the days, it must have been sometime near onto Christmas when the dogs alerted us to intruders. We found them barking at a wagon at the edge of the meadow. Curious,

I called off the dogs and bade the man at the reins approach. From the way he stumbled through the knee-deep snow, he was in a bad way. Cut and I dragged him into the house.

"Family!" he mumbled, shivering violently. "Wagon!"

Shrugging into my heavy coat, I plowed through the snow and crawled up into the seat. A frightened young face stared down at me. The boy pointed a rifle that looked as frozen as he was.

"Easy, son. We're just going to the house where it's warm. Your pa's already inside. Wouldn't you like to put your feet to the fire, too?"

There was no real comprehension on his face, but the lad allowed the barrel to waver away. A woman's voice called from somewhere in the back of the wagon. A young female whimpered.

We set the whole family to thaw before the fireplace in the west porthern of the house while Cut and I moved their wagon into the lee of the building. Their horses joined our own in the barn. The animals were in poor shape, and I despaired of one of their number surviving. The towheaded boy of about ten clung to his father's leg and moaned when Cut came into the house. The little girl, a year or so younger shrieked and buried her head in her mother's skirts. The wife visibly reacted, as well. That was not a good sign. It was evening before Benjamin Bowers recovered sufficiently to tell his story.

Under the authority of a trainmaster called Boggs, ten wagons started out from St. Joseph, Missouri, much later in the year than was customary and delayed at Ft. Ramson to await the arrival of spring. Courting an additional fee, the trainmaster induced three families bound for Yawktown to proceed the remaining hundred and fifty miles to Ft. Yanube

The party ran into a blue whistler of a storm and hunkered down to wait it out. When the weather cleared, the travelers found their food exhausted and the way blocked both fore and aft by mounds of fresh snow. The men formed a hunting party, fighting their way to a small stand of trees lining a frozen creek bank where they came upon the carcass of a deer. As they fell upon it, three Indians stepped out of the forest and made clear by sign they claimed the slain animal. Since the kill was fresh, it is likely the red men spoke the truth, but at the moment, truth did not enter into play. When the warriors became insistent, the trail boss shot one of the natives. A small battle ensued over the deer. Surprise and superior firepower won the moment for the immigrants.

The meat provided by that deer proved costly, indeed. The next morning, a group of Indians showed up to articulate their anger by shouts and forceful gestures. The trainmaster shot one of the warriors mortally. The others returned fire. Boggs, the cause of it all, recovered his mount and was last seen fighting snowdrifts to the southeast, drawing a goodly number of the attackers with him. The remainder pursued the assault on the wagons. All seemed lost until something called the Indians off. As the warriors beat a trail in the direction Boggs had fled, Bowers assumed the coward had been caught.

Following the attack, Bowers discovered the rest of the party dead. Five adults – assuming Boggs had received his just desserts – and one child, plus who knows how many of the Indians died for a scoundrel's greed and stupidity.

Fearing the Indians' return, Bowers packed only the essentials for his new life abandoning most of his personal goods to the elements. As they had covered more than half the journey to Ft. Yanube, he hitched six of the strongest animals to a wagon designed for a team of four, killing two of the beasts fighting his way through drifts that should have stopped him cold. It was a testament to the courage and determination of that broad, stocky man that he made it as far as Teacher's Mead. We now understood the children's reaction to Cut Hand.

These four survivors were important testators. If Bowers told the true story of the battle to the army in the manner he related it to us, the thing might not have much of an afterclap; otherwise, retribution could come to anyone in the area. Welcome or not, we had guests until the thaw. Fortunately, our personal stores were adequate, but the strain of more large horses dependent on our fodder might prove a problem.

Cut immediately undertook a campaign to desensitize the children to his presence. He spoke only English and read stories aloud to Timothy and Beth. Further, he did something totally out of character by making himself useful to a flighty, finical Mrs. Bowers. Slowly he managed to blur the image of red men slaying women and children.

Bowers was a cooper by trade and spared as a locksmith. He was also a decent farrier. We used the long winter months to construct barrels and kegs, something always needed, and to replace our locks with more substantial devices from his depleted stock. All of my heavy team animals received new shoes as Bowers sought to earn his keep and express his gratitude.

Cut made the children rackets, which they quickly learned to use. There was nothing of the climate-struck about the small fry; both Timothy – whom Cut dubbed Timo – and Little Beth, the appellation he attached to her, pitched in with chores and clamored to go trapping with us. Quite comfortable with me, the two grew slavishly devoted to Cut. The family was pleasant, although Mrs. Bowers, a thin, nervous woman, tended to be a croaker, always looking for disaster in every event.

In a sense, their misfortune was a boon. While I selfishly wanted Cut to myself, interacting with four additional souls diverted his attention from concern over his father and the matter that Yellow Puma's illness foreshadowed. He reserved the dark hours of the night for these cares, which was why I overcame my reluctance to have congress while strangers were in the house and reached for him in the privacy of our bed

# # # # #

The first signs of spring occasioned a debate among us. The drifts blocking the trail on our bank of the river were awesome, yet Ben Bowers was anxious to get to Yawktown. No doubt a cooperage would find adequate country custom, and, of course, he also had his other two trades to fall back on if need be.

Reluctant to allow the family to proceed without going in aid of them, we concluded now would be the ideal time for Cut to visit the fort. Thereafter, we could cross the Yanube on a bridge just outside of town and make our way to the winter camp farther down the river. This would occasion trespass deep into Pipe Stem territory, but it was a risk Cut was eager to take.

Hence, we set out for the fort fully a moon ahead of our intention. It is fortunate we went with the family. There were times when double teaming was the only way to gain passage through a drift or hub-deep muck. I, of course, had the Conestoga to carry our furs and to assist the *tiospaye*'s move back north.

We were granted immediate admission to the commandant's office. The news of the battle on the Yanube had not reached the military; indeed it had no idea wagons had departed Ft. Ramson so late in the season. Ben Bowers told his tale faithfully. Immediately, the officers in the room turned to me.

"Who were the tribesmen?"

"It was not the Yanube. They were on the far side of the river some fifty miles to the south. So far as I know the Pipe Stem were also south of the water."

The Major faced Cut. "You, sir, can you identify the raiders?"

Despite Cut's understanding of the need to be courteous, he flushed a full shade darker. "Major, I can only tell you who they were not. As Mr. Strobaw said, my people were far to the south."

The fort's commander recovered himself. "Forgive me. It was not my intention to make accusations. As I understand it, you are the son of Yellow Puma, the leader of the Yanube band, is that correct?"

"Yes. My name is Cut Hand in your language."

"Which you speak beautifully," the Major interjected, rising to extend a hand. Cut gave him a firm American shake. "Do you also agree it is unlikely the Pipe Stem were involved?"

"Yes," my husband replied.

The Major turned to the officers of his command. "That leaves the Sioux, gentlemen. The first of many encounters, I fear."

Surprisingly, Bowers spoke up forcefully. "Sir, I would like to point out once again it was the natives who were set upon by Mr. Boggs. He proved to be a thoroughly disreputable character all around. He engaged in gross misconduct with us and did even worse to the inhabitants of the land. On my oath as a Christian, sir, Mr. Boggs killed that Indian with no warning at all. When they came in greater force to protest, he slew another."

"Did you fire your weapon, sir?"

"I did, but only when the wagons were engaged. By that time, the devil had been unleashed, and there was no stopping the slaughter."

The rest of us were dismissed while the Major spent additional time with Cut Hand. Captain Jamieson took the opportunity to ask that the bodies of the settlers be delivered to the post when the thaw permitted. I declined, explaining Indians avoided the dead except to quickly dispose of their own, a prudent policy that helped avoid contagious diseases such as often swept the Europeans.

I returned to the commandant's quarters in time to understand Major Wallston nursed a healthy respect for my mate. They had progressed to the point of discussing how certain flora and fauna were best prepared for eating.

Caleb Brown purchased our furs, giving us a near-decent price. He was pleased to meet Cut Hand since he had very little contact with the original inhabitants of this country. Banker Crozier, somewhat flustered to find an Indian in his establishment, nonetheless overcame his trepidation and gave us the benefit of a few minutes of his time. Jones, the gunsmith, would be of some import in Yawktown; consequently we spent time in his place of business, as well. Cut, impressed with the armory's range of goods, bought another scattergun since he had seen me bag pigeons and waterfowl with mine. Before the day was done, we turned our wagon out of town and crossed the Yanube on the white man's bridge.

Cut inundated me with countless questions about the fort and town. At first I perceived it as a thirst for knowledge about a foreign world, but by nightfall, I understood that in part it had been a delay of a more painful subject never far from our minds. I broached it directly after we set up camp.

"It is time, Cut Hand," I said simply.

"Billy, I cannot do this thing. I love you beyond all reason."

Dark Warrior sought me so desperately when we turned to our blankets that I took charge of our love-making. Cut rogered me with a quiet desperation and settled into my arms afterward. Normally, he sheltered me with the afterglow of his embrace; tonight, his broad back lay against my chest revealing the depth of his inner turmoil.

At length he spoke again. "I have been thinking on this. Our life is good together. If this is so, why must we change it?"

Hope flared and died. "Because you are not with the People. You are of them, but apart. Your nights are spent at the Mead with me. You have no family to aid in understanding their needs. You have no wife to interact with the women of the band and draw them to you."

He lifted his head slightly and smiled. "The women respect you."

"Maybe so, but they do not discuss pregnancies or the prowess of their husbands or the flow of their menses with me." I sighed so deeply, his torso shifted with my breath. "You must live among them."

"And you won't leave the Mead." He stated a truth.

We were silent, each taking solace and strength from the other until we fell asleep in a hollow twenty yards from the wagon.

The following day we crossed into Pipe Stem territory. Though they probably had not moved from winter quarters, a few out-parties might be scouting. Nonetheless, Cut spent most of his time on the seat beside me except for occasional forays on Arrow to check for danger.

"I have thought on the matter," he said as he stepped from Arrow's back onto the wagon. "I will take a woman to wife. She will bear me sons. You will live at the Mead until the winter move, and then you will come with your husband to live like a proper wife in his lodge until we return north. You are my first wife and always will be, Billy, but my loins are potent. I can satisfy both of you."

An ache arched through my chest. "No, I will not share you. I can't."

"Then we will return to the Mead and live there forever."

"And I will have made you an outcast. That would be painful to us both."

"Pain seems destined. Now we must determine the lesser torment."

"Cut Hand," I fought to keep bitterness from of my voice. "This thing is plain and allows no evasions. We must resolve it in some manner. You need a proper wife and children. Else when Yellow Puma dies, they will turn to Lodge Pole who will dig up the tomahawk and lead them against the army. Failing that, they will drift away to other bands. Without Cut Hand to lead them, the Yanube will cease to exist. Are you willing to be the cause of that?"

"No," he answered deep in his throat.

"Do you know who you would marry?" I asked the fearful question.

"Yes, Morning Mist. Do you know her?"

"Slightly." I was stung because he had not confided this to me. "Have you spoken to her?"

"No, but there are ways to tell she will be receptive."

"Will you need all of our horses for the bride price?"

"You speak as if this is a thing already determined! Yet you tell me you cannot abide it. What am I to do?" He leapt onto Arrow's back from the moving wagon and was gone for a long time. Once I heard the sound of a bugling elk in the distance, but it was Cut Hand recklessly venting his frustration.

When we arrived at the winter camp, Cut's decision was forced upon him by his father's condition. The once husky man could hardly rise. He walked only with the assistance of Bright Dove and Butterfly. His mind was still sharp although his voice sounded like the piping of a whooping crane. He greeted us with great joy and assured us he was healthier than was true. I sincerely wished I knew more of medicines. I was only able to provide him with a modest dose of saffron to ease his wracking rattle.

Bear Paw cornered us immediately, and Buffalo Shoulder, clearly showing the strain of his shunning, joined us more cautiously. Expressing delight and relief at their kinsman's early appearance, they warned that Lodge Pole was taking advantage of Yellow Puma's illness to usurp some of his functions. People were beginning to go to the big Indian for advice and help.

While Cut made the rounds of the camp, I tarried with Yellow Puma, as he desired company. When all else were gone from the tipi, he spoke softly.

"I fear I am causing you distress." He paused. "You know Cut Hand must take a second wife."

I noted his careful choice of words and was appreciative of it. "Yes."

With considerable effort, he shifted on his blankets to look me fully in the eye, something these people do not often do, considering it rude. "You are a strange man, Teacher. It must be true that you are a Win-tay for my son is young and full of juices, yet he spreads none among the women. I always thought it would take two wives to handle his virility. You do this adequately alone.

"Yet, you are not a Win-tay in other matters. You cook the meals and tend the household chores, but someone must do this even among the bachelors. You are a man, Teacher, in all that counts. This is a sick old man's way of saying he is proud you care for his son as you do. But I am fearful of what will happen when a woman is introduced between you."

"As am I."

His hearing was still with him, and the words reached his ears. "Teacher, in the seasons you have been with us, I have never asked anything personal of you. All of my demands were for the *tiospaye*. And ultimately, what I seek now is for them, too. But it is also personal because it arises from concern for my son." The dark eyes found my own and held them. "I know what is in your mind, Billy," he used my given name to personalize his request. "You will tear apart the relationship rather than share him. Do not do that, my son. I beg of you. Share him, at least for a while. He will need you for what is coming."

Yellow Puma held up a hand to forestall my reply and to signal he needed to rest a moment. "He has grown apart from his people, and Lodge Pole takes every opportunity to point it out to others. Cut Hand still has their trust and respect and will find his way back, but until that is accomplished, he will need you at his side."

Finished now, he awaited my reply. "We have talked of this, Father-in-Law," I acknowledged his station. "Would the young woman of his choice be willing to share him with me?"

"You make more of this than there is, Teacher. You will cope."

As he was tired, I left his lodge and wandered the camp. Cut was out with the horse herders, so I looked up Butterfly to see how she fared. She had gained some maturity, but underneath she was still the delightful young woman I knew. She denied interest in any of the young swains and swore that she would die a dried up old maid, causing me to laugh. She rounded on me.

"A lot you know! You and Cut Hand live up there in your stone lodge and keep everyone else out!" She stalked away with a womanly sway I had never noticed before.

That night Cut Hand joined me in the bachelor's tipi. He had moved at a dogtrot all day, helping with chores throughout the village. Repairing weapons and spreading damp black powder to dry had occupied my time.

"They wintered well," Cut noted as he sat opposite me. "But I will lead a hunting party to find fresh meat for another moon. We leave tomorrow. I will follow the river south and east. I'm taking most of the warriors because I want it done quickly, and I'd feel better if you stayed to protect the village."

He paused. "If the soldiers come, take the People and move back from the river. There is a stand of trees to the south lining a small creek. Abandon everything and simply take the people. If you are not here when I return, I'll look for you there. I'm going to leave Otter to help. Lone Eagle is putting up a fuss, but he's staying behind, too."

"Cut," I said slowly, "I have been considering our problem. Marry Morning Mist. I will be your second wife. I won't be very good at it, but I will try."

"Billy," he said, obviously relieved. "You will do this for me?"

"If I want you, Cut Hand, then I must do it. Who knows, perhaps Morning Mist and I will get on like sisters."

He cupped my neck in his strong hand. "Bear Paw will keep everyone out. I want to mate with my wife."

Briefly, I wondered at the silhouette we cast against the skin siding as he raised my legs to his shoulders, but I didn't care. Cut entered my channel masterfully. I grew rampant. He came in a flurry of mighty thrusts that reached virgin territory in my fundament. Then he pulled me atop him to flank his belly. Pale Hunter nuzzled Dark Warrior lovingly with each lunge. When I washed him with my seed, my handsome warrior husband took me again, just to prove he could!

CHAPTER 11

It is my opinion that Lone Eagle, mortified at being left behind with the women and children, would have defied Cut Hand had not Yellow Puma requested his protection in the absence of other able-bodied warriors. Trapped by his sense of loyalty, he took out his frustration on me. My refusal to defer to him soon drove the young man to stabbing the frozen ground with his knife as if it were my belly. Snapping off the tip on a hidden stone did little to improve his disposition. The youth threw himself aboard his pony and raced away to spend most of his time in isolation, riding in wide circles around the campground.

It was he who reported a group of warriors approaching the camp. Packing one rifle and my scattergun, I recovered Long and rode out to meet the strangers with Lone Eagle and Otter at my side. A few half-grown youngsters and men past their prime chased down horses from the herd to follow us.

We broke the ridge and halted to watch the five mounted warriors as they pulled up to observe us in similar fashion. Doubtless, they waited to see if others crested the hill behind us. At length, a solid-looking man of middle years urged his mount forward. When he raised his hand to show it was empty, I bade my companions hold still while I rode out alone to meet him. I was less worried about the stranger in front of me than Lone Eagle at my back. Doing something rash was not beyond him, especially as he was on the nettle from a perceived slight. As we halted at ten paces, I discerned the warrior must be Sioux. Although he played Indian, keeping his broad face immobile, I could imagine his confusion at facing a white man on the edge of the Yanube winter encampment.

He immediately proved me wrong. "Hau! Greetings to Teacher, the Red Win-tay, wife of Yellow Puma's son. I am Stone Knife. My companions and I are riding south to see the new fort on the Yanube for ourselves. They say that it will send many white men here when winter breaks its grip." The dialect was Lakota.

I nodded. "They will come. After the snows melt, a detachment of dragoons is to move out on its way to Ft. Yanube. There will be other white men who follow, but I believe they will come slowly."

"Hah!" This proud lord of the plains neither accepted nor denied my judgment. He glanced over my shoulder, and I knew my army of children and ancients had arrived at the crest of the hill.

"On your way south you will come across Cut Hand and the men of the camp hunting for game. Please tell him all is well. Will you take nourishment with us? We have meat should you need it. And Yellow Puma would make you welcome."

"Yes, he would extend his hand. Thank you, but we will continue our journey. Tell me, is my old friend well?"

"As well as most men carrying his years," I hedged. From the man's look, I suspected he read the real meaning between my words – else the news of Yellow Puma's plight had already traveled down the moccasin path.

"Once we get a look at this American fort, perhaps we will return this way. But when I arrive at my own fire, I will speak of meeting the Teacher," he said by way of farewell.

"And I will tell Yellow Puma I have met the famed warrior, Stone Knife," I responded, unknowing whether or not he was a personage of merit.

"Lakota!" Lone Eagle said when I returned to the others. There was a measure of respect mingled with derision in the word. "I must warn Cut Hand!" he cried, turning his pony.

I grabbed his rein. "They are not wearing paint, Lone Eagle. The Sioux party knows Cut Hand and his warriors are in front of them and will approach in peace. There is nothing to fear, but Yellow Puma must be told of Stone Hand's passing."

Frustrated in his attempt to join the men, he angrily jerked his leather free and pushed his pony into a gallop back to the village. If he could not have the one; he would have the other – he would deliver the news to his chieftain. Otter merely gave me a bemused look. Sometimes he was more mature than his senior.

Lone Eagle, Otter, and I alternated with those from other bands scouting the camp's perimeter. There was no more excitement until Otter reported the men were coming home. Cut rode up, tired from the hunt, but on a high rope. They had been moderately successful. The People would have green meat to mix with the jerky and pemmican. He reported that Stone Knife had teased him about where a man put his pipe in a wife like his famous Win-tay.

It was not until we were alone in the bachelor's tipi a few minutes later that the thing eating at him came spilling out. "There was trouble." He slung his long gun on the blanket and folded his legs to follow it down.

"Let me guess … Lodge Pole."

My lover grimaced and told the tale. The men dispersed in small groups to make their hunt, a usual custom. Scouts had warned that two soldiers rode the trail on the north side of the river, and Cut went to the water's edge to watch their passage, standing in full view, his hand lifted in greeting. The dragoons took note, but made no pause in their journey.

"Messengers, most likely," I interrupted the flow of his dialogue.

"They were not yet out of sight when someone fired at them. The blue coats leaned over their saddles and got out of there without looking back."

"Neither was hit?"

"No, but I saw leaves cut from the tree above one rider's head."

"Who was downriver of you?"

"Several. One was Lodge Pole."

"But why would he do something chuckle-headed like that?" I demanded.

"To make trouble for me. I was the only one in plain sight."

"He cannot be stupid enough to believe the soldiers can identify a lone Indian from across the river."

"Perhaps not, but our trail will lead right back to this camp."

"Could it have been Stone Knife's people?"

"They were well ahead of us. I sent Bear Paw to warn them what had happened."

"So the soldiers could be on the move already."

"Perhaps we should pack up and start north."

"A fleeing man is assumed to be guilty."

He thought for a moment. "You are right, Billy. If we do not face this now, it will follow us and grow as it travels."

"You have to find out who fired that shot and clip his horns."

"First, we must let everyone know the danger."

# # # # #

Yellow Puma sent messengers to summon representatives of all the bands in the winter village. As this was not the Yanube council, I did not sit on the buffalo robe, but stood at the side of the crowd. From the gabble of voices around me, it was clear the entire camp already knew what had happened. Why not? Their own returning men would have told them.

After the pipe ceremony, Cut helped his father to his feet. The man's voice reminded me of a reed flute because of the windiness behind the weak words.

"Our men have returned from the hunt to report a serious incident that can cause trouble for all of us. You should hear of it for yourselves." With that brief announcement, he sat back on his blanket with Cut Hand's help.

Then my mate, strong and unbelievably handsome, stood tall before the gathered throng. My eyes sought out Lodge Pole in the forefront of the important men seated on blankets and buffalo robes. Huge lips pursed, he studied his hands as if he had never seen them before.

"My people, cousins," Cut's strong voice rang out over the multitude. "As we hunted along the river to the southwest, two American dragoons rode the opposite bank in the direction of the fort. As they passed, one of our party shot at them."

The crowd stirred uneasily. On half a dozen faces, I read six different reactions. Shock, dismay, delight, fear, unconcern, outrage. My heart sank when I understood some among the group countenanced the reckless act.

"The soldiers were not injured and they continued on their way without firing back at us. But the commandant at the fort may decide to investigate the matter and punish those responsible."

"Who fired at them?" a voice asked from the crowd.

"I know not," Cut answered honestly. "I stood on the bank watching the soldiers as they passed. While it pleases most of us that the soldiers may have been frightened, it should also concern us. I had given the peace sign. What if the Americans decide the peace sign leads to betrayal? If they believe that, then we can no longer trust their white flag of truce.

"What if they take this attack as an uprising?" Cut Hand continued. "I have been to one of their forts. I have seen their fighting men. I have seen their big guns mounted on wheels that fling shells over hills and fall from the heavens on camps, rendering them helpless."

He strode off the carpet of buffalo robes into the midst of the crowd, past the men to the edge of the women at the back. "What if they decide that to ignore this thing would embolden our young men and invite more trouble? Your sons and daughters," he nodded to the women, "will feel their fury the most. This is a serious thing and must be discussed seriously."

He strode back to his place beside Yellow Puma and sat down.

"We must determine who is responsible," Round Head, the misco of another band, agreed. "And he must be punished."

Lodge Pole undertook the laborious process of removing his long frame from the ground. He reminded me of myself in the act of rising, except there was considerably more of him to lift.

"Who led the hunt?" he growled in a voice that reached the far ends of the camp like the roar of a feral animal.

With only a short pause, Cut scrambled to his feet. "I organized the hunt, as you well know. Because of that, I am responsible. And I will face that responsibility when the soldiers come."

"So you admit you put the People in jeopardy! You led the hunt. Your people fired on the soldiers. You put us all in danger –"

"No!" a voice shouted from the back. "Cut Hand is not responsible!"

Buffalo Shoulder elbowed his way into the far end of the crowd. Gasps went up from the Yanube in the council.

Lodge Pole sputtered. I had never seen a grown man actually sputter until that moment. "You have no right!" he shouted. "This man is shunned! He is responsible for the deaths of three Yanube! He speaks, but has no voice!"

"He is not shunned by my *tiospaye*," Round Head said firmly. "I will hear what he has to say."

But Lodge Pole was not finished. "I see it now. Cut Hand permitted this sot to participate in the hunt even though his own *tiospaye* punished him for getting drunk and failing to warn of an attack on their village that killed three of the People. What happened, Buffalo Shoulder, did you get so bottle-fevered that blue coats looked like moose? What kind of leader allows a shunned drunk to go on a hunt with decent men? This man is worthless!" the giant scoffed. He turned his back on Buffalo Shoulder.

"Still, I will hear his words," Round Head insisted.

"Yes, I had been drinking," Buffalo Shoulder admitted. "But I can tell the difference between blue coats and moose. And I can tell the difference between Cut Hand and a giant. Lodge Pole fired that shot. I saw it with my own eyes."

"Liar!" The huge man's bellow frightened children at the back of the throng.

"There was another with him," Buffalo Shoulder stood his ground. "There is another who knows the truth."

Had it not been such a serious matter, it would have been comedic. Each man looked to his neighbor and then searched across the heads of others. At long last, a young man stood. He was a member of Lodge Pole's wife's family who went by the name of Bois d'Arc.

"Buffalo Shoulder speaks the truth. Lodge Pole shot at the soldiers and claimed he could lay it on the back of Cut Hand."

"Liars!" the big Indian screamed. Children whimpered. Camp dogs barked and slunk away. The very light seemed to fade from the sky. "They lie to protect their own." Then abruptly changing tactics, he appealed to the hotheads in the group. "What are we, men with our stones removed? We have always hunted where we pleased, roamed where we wanted without asking permission. Now we shuffle along behind the white man like pet dogs. Not me! I am a man! Who is with me?"

A few accepted the challenge, but Cut stepped forward to put an end to it.

"I hunt where I please," he shouted over the war hoops of a few young men. "I walk where I wish. But like honorable warriors in the day of my father and the time of my grandfather, I do not shoot from ambush to provoke the anger of a mighty enemy from personal ambition!"

Yellow Puma struggled to his feet without assistance and moved to the center of the group. "Lodge Pole, you have coveted the leadership of this band from the very day you arrived among us after you were made unwelcome by your own kinsmen. You have done this thing to discredit my son in the eyes of his people. The act, itself, was despicable. The fact it endangers not only my *tiospaye* but all others in this winter camp is unforgivable. You will no longer throw a long shadow over my people; you are banished from the Yanube forever. You will leave our camp and never return. If you disobey, then any man is free to kill you. I will take my leave now and permit the other headmen to make their own decision in the matter. And know this, Sioux! If the soldiers come, none of us will pay for your perfidy."

I cannot imagine the cost to that sick, proud man to march in firm steps out of the crowd back to his own lodge. Cut Hand and most of the Yanube left with him. I trailed along with the women.

# # # # #

We did not have to wait long for the arrival of the soldiers. Sentries alerted the village the following morning that a troop was drawn up in a skirmish line about three English miles to the southeast. The camp's warriors formed their own battle line behind their leaders. Bear Paw and one of the other band's young men took mounted groups to flank the dragoons. Then we helped Yellow Puma aboard his white stone horse and rode out unarmed in advance of them all. Cut ordered me back to camp, but I ignored his entreaties – as he expected I would. I bound a white rag made from one of my under-shifts to a pole, so our intentions could not be misconstrued.

We knew no one at Fort Ramson, and indeed, the officers who came to meet us were strangers. Yellow Puma put all of his remaining strength behind his voice as he hailed the military men ten paces ahead of him. Cut Hand translated his words.

"Welcome to our American brothers. I am Yellow Puma, misco of the People of the Yanube. We know why you are here and are anxious to end this matter as it should be, without violence and in the spirit of friendship. I am known to your brother officers at Fort Yanube as a peace chief."

The leader of the troop, a mature man wearing captain's bars, gaffed his horse two steps closer. "We have heard of you, Yellow Puma. We know you as a good man who desires peace. But perhaps you do not control your young men."

"It is true young men of both our peoples do not always behave as they should, but we iron-hairs do the best we can."

"We come because two of our messengers were fired upon along the Yanube River. The army cannot ignore such dangerous acts."

"Nor can we," the misco agreed. "When our hunters reported the incident upon their return yesterday, we held our own council and identified the culprit."

"Then you can turn him over to us and the matter will be finished."

"The matter is finished," the chief said in a firm voice. "The Sioux with snake blood who took refuge with us after his own turned their back on him has been sent away. None in this village will shelter him. The Teton will not allow him back. He has nowhere to go. He will be a problem no longer."

"Give me his name, Yellow Puma," the captain insisted.

"His name will never again be spoken by any of our people. He is dead to us. You have my word he alone turned his medicine gun upon your soldiers."

The officer edged his horse over to me. "Would you be the Mr. Strobaw who trades for these people?"

"I am," I acknowledged.

"Perhaps you are not bound by their custom."

"I participated in the council. All I can do for you is confirm what Yellow Puma has said. But I see you have your own Indian scouts with you –" I allowed my voice to trail off. The captain understood.

The officer turned back to Yellow Puma. "One troop will pass south of your village. The other will cross the river. Please assure the women and children we intend no harm."

"Thank you, Captain," the chief replied.

We returned to our warriors, and Yellow Puma collected them in plain sight of the dragoons to demonstrate he had had strength at his back when he chose to parley. I hoped the Americans appreciated the significance of this as they passed through our lines and set about the task of finding Lodge Pole's trail.

I do not believe they succeeded as some months later I heard of a gigantic Indian killed in a drunken brawl down in Indian Territory.

CHAPTER 12

The next day Cut Hand began his courtship of Morning Mist, which had all the earmarks of a short affair. Only the close scrutiny of the entire village kept her from crawling into his blankets that very day. The next fortnight was as painful for me as any I remember. I slept on a cold bed in the bachelor's tipi while Cut rotated between his father's lodge and a bedroll beside mine. A bargain was struck, horses were exchanged, and the marriage was accomplished quickly. A week before the move northward was expected, Cut Hand took Morning Mist to bride. Their wedding night, spent in a new tipi near to his father's, was pure agony for me. Images of Cut mounting his new bride left wounds like a flint blade. Pale Hunter shriveled, and my testes crawled upwards, seeking cowardly shelter. I was wracked with a physical pain as if my very soul struggled to escape its corporeal body.

To my surprise, after the wedding ceremony, Yellow Puma, supported by Bear Paw and Lone Eagle scratched at the doorway where I sheltered. The ailing man sat across from me; the other two settled comfortably on either side.

"Tonight is not a night for Teacher to be alone," Yellow Puma said. He gestured toward Bear Paw, and the latter passed an earthen jug to me.

Strong drink and I do not mix well, but tonight it was welcome. I recall neither my companions' departure nor the remainder of the night, but when I woke to a headache and harsh stomach the next day, I was wrapped snugly in my blankets. Lunging to my feet, I staggered outside, seeking some secluded area, nearly soiling my clothing from every orifice before finding a measure of privacy.

I had not realized I wandered so far from camp until each step back drew more leaden than the one before. I needed Cut to –

Oh, my God! Cut! He would be with her! He was a new groom; I was sick, alone, and abandoned. I dropped to my knees and flopped onto my belly in the cold, half-frozen grass. My chest ached until I passed out in the mud and snow.

"Wife? What are you doing out here?"

Cut's voice startled me back to my senses. I raised a frozen cheek. "Too much to drink."

He roared with laughter. "Do I carry you back like some weak, swooning woman?"

"No, but you can help me up." I grasped a strong, brown arm, and he hauled me upright. "Can … make it … now."

For three more days, I endured the torture, clinging to the forlorn belief that each sunrise brought us closer to the time of departure for the Mead. Morning Mist was everywhere. Most women do not touch their men in public – not so this new bride. She clung to him possessively. To my tortured mind it was a silent proclamation he no longer needed the support of his old Win-tay wife.

Then disaster struck! At least it was a disaster to me. A heavy bank of dark, lowering clouds slowed the snowmelt and delayed the People's departure. Otter and Butterfly stayed nearby to lend quiet, unassuming support. Even the self-important Lone Eagle found opportunities to do things with me. It was an uncommonly unselfish offer from this handsome teen, and I was grateful. In fairness, except in events he perceived a challenge to his manhood, Lone Eagle was a pleasant youth.

When the departure for the north was delayed yet another week in deference to the weather, I could stand it no longer. I informed Cut I was returning to the Mead.

"You can't!" he exclaimed. "You can't get across the river."

"I will load the wagon and go by way of Yawktown to trade furs for supplies. The People have some plews that should bring a prime price. Afterward, I will head home."

"I won't let you go!" He grew angry.

"Why?" I snapped. "You don't need me! You're otherwise occupied."

He dropped his gaze. "I know it's hard for you, but this is … what was it I read in those books? A honeymoon? Yes, this is our honeymoon. But it will soon be over. And you are wrong; I need you more than ever."

In my pitiful desperation, I half-believed him. "We shall see, Cut. But you don't need me right now. Let me go home to tend our animals and do some trading on the way."

"I will send warriors with you, at least through the Pipe Stem country."

"That will only provoke trouble. I am going alone."

His eyes softened. "Will you be there when I return?"

"Yes." I met his gaze steadily. "When I leave you, Cut, I'll tell you first."

His pride nicked, he withdrew slightly. "So be it. I will gather the furs and whatever else we have for trading. Lone Eagle and Otter will accompany you."

"No," I said firmly. "I leave tomorrow … alone."

"Very well." He turned away.

I busied myself loading the wagon before taking a solitary meal, politely declining an invitation from Yellow Puma's household. Otter came to the bachelor's tipi to sit with me until my husband appeared.

"Wife," Cut said, walking up to me and clutching my shoulders. "I did not want you to leave with bad feelings between us."

"I'm glad," I whispered as he drew my shirt over my head. He took a few moments to finger my bare torso before removing the rest of my clothing. He must have had a friend guarding the entrance, as he showed no nervousness over being interrupted. Cut lay with me then, confirming his love, drawing out my own responses, retying the bonds that held us until I was afire within and without. So far as I could tell, Dark Warrior had not suffered contamination from his coupling with Morning Mist. I slept in the afterglow of his flanking, trying to ignore a persistent niggling at the remote edges of my aura.

Cut and a half a dozen friends traveled a league with me along the bank of the swollen river. Finally, the others withdrew and gave us a moment alone.

"I love you, William Joseph Strobaw," he pronounced solemnly. "Why must things change between us?"

"Damnation! Things have changed!"

"Not so deeply as you seem to believe."

Mindful that he opened and closed each day by speaking to his Great Mystery, I gave words to the thing that had worried my mind last night. "Cut, do you remember when I first took you? I imagined my God frowning down on me and preparing to strike us for being sinners of the flesh." He frowned, seeking to understand. "That went away when I realized what I held for you in my heart was true love. And then we made vows to one another that reaffirmed my belief. God no longer tortured my mind." I had all of his attention now.

"But when you came to me last night, and I enjoyed your body, the physical demonstration of your love, I experienced it again – the disapproval of my Master. According to my laws, you legally belong to someone else now, a woman; and that is the natural order of things."

Cut shook his head slowly. "According to our laws, I still belong to you. He clasped me to his breast, oblivious to the warriors who watched from a distance. "Oh, Billy, what have I done? I did not understand your struggle! Why didn't you tell me?"

"Because I had settled it. Because I had no idea it would intrude again. Because I love you, and because I love the Yanube, I will do what I can for as long as I can endure it. But I have to fight another battle and come to an understanding with my Lord anew."

He held me at arms length. "How can I help you with this battle?"

"You can't. This is one I must fight alone."

He drew me to him again, kissing me hard on the mouth, exciting my passion before releasing me and vaulting from the wagon onto Arrow. Without looking back, I urged the double span of blacks forward. The wagon moved with a clink and a creak across the rough bench of hard prairie stretching alongside the Yanube River.

# # # # #

This time I was aware of the Pipe Stem brave as soon as he materialized on the horizon, although I kept doggedly to the faint trail. Whatever happened was beyond my ability to change it. He paced me for half a day and then disappeared. It was no surprise therefore, when I topped a rise and found three warriors barring my way. One was Carcajou.

The Pipe Stem climbed from his pony to the wagon seat without my slowing. "Hau, Teacher," he said. "I will ride with you a part of the way."

"Welcome, Carcajou. How has the winter been with you and your people?"

"We have endured … most of us. My father, Great Bull, died when the snows came the hardest."

"I am sorry," I said. "I have heard he was a good man."

"A hard one, but a good one. I would have you ask me what you asked him when you saw him last."

"If I would be welcome at the fire of the Pipe Stem?"

"You would be welcome. You did not know of this, Teacher, but from the moment you spoke plain and true to me in front of your stone house, you have been under the protection of Great Bull. No Pipe Stem would harm you. He respected your words and reputation that much. Now you travel under mine."

"That is good to know."

"Our winter grounds are not far. Will you make that visit now?"

I would have preferred to keep on the road to Yawktown, but he seemed intent on my accepting his invitation. The wagon and its white drover occasioned a great deal of excitement in the Pipe Stem town. Small Horse, recovered from his burns, emerged from a lodge marked by poles holding medicine bundles. He solemnly greeted his chief and his guest. The old man was quite loquacious, especially around the council fire that night. About all I could contribute was the fact that a detachment of soldiers would soon be coming up the south bank of the Yanube and that the army was on the nettle because of Lodge Pole's actions. That, of course, required the telling in full.

Carcajou came to talk in the bachelor's tipi set aside for me that night. In the warmth of the interior, he threw off his coverings, exposing his broad, dark chest and strong thighs. I felt a familiar stir of interest. He was handsome in a totally different way from Cut Hand. Darker, shorter, straight-nosed, cant-eyed, he could have been a Chinese warlord lounging before me.

"What is this medicine you have? Does Double-Woman to give you sexual power over men?" he asked abruptly.

"I hold no power over men."

"You examined me with such interest that I quickened," he said as if to refute my denial. "Two strong men lust for you. Cut Hand took you to wife; Carcajou has admitted his desire. This is not power?"

"It is only a power you give to me, Carcajou. I loved Cut Hand from the first moment I saw him. I pursued him and forced myself on him. It is you two who hold the medicine. His power is such that I deserted my own people to come with him. Your power makes me want to forget my pledge to him."

"Hah!" he said. "So I did not imagine it."

"No," I recognized this was dangerous ground. "I look on Carcajou and find myself wondering what it would be like to lie with him. But I will never know as I have made a vow."

"I could take you now and do what I want with you."

"Yes, but it will be to my shame. If you would disgrace me then so be it."

"Why would it be shame?"

"Because my religion promises punishment for one who breaks a vow. But more importantly, because of the love Cut Hand and I hold in our hearts for one another." I continued before he could interrupt. "Between Carcajou and me there is respect and the bond of friendship. But neither of us can claim love. You would bed me for the novelty of it, nothing more; I from curiosity, which would then turn to shame, and our friendship would be gone."

"Perhaps I would be better than Cut Hand. Maybe I can claim your love."

"And what would you do with it if you succeeded? Are you willing to make me your wife before the whole band?"

"I could put the lie on my lips and claim so, but you are right. I think we would both get great pleasure from our coupling, but we shall never know. I will confess something to you. After our last meeting, I looked up a youth in our village who is considering the Win-tay life. It was pleasant, nothing more. To be certain, I went to him again. The same. But just as it is different with some women, so it would be different with you."

"It is different with some women because of feelings you harbor for them."

"I will allow you to rest now. You will be on your way to the fort tomorrow." It was not a question but as a statement. When he rose, he permitted me to see that he was aroused. I almost reached for him, but resisted.

"You are well-named," I growled. "A wolverine is a wily beast."

The next day, two Pipe Stem warriors escorted me until I was almost within sight of the bridge. Thereafter, a buckboard and I were the only travelers on the road in the early April chill. The livery agreed to look after my Conestoga, so I reserved a room at the Rainbow and headed for the public bath. As I waited my turn, Second Lt. James

Morrow entered, and we refreshed our acquaintance. I expressed surprise the public facilities drew military custom.

"Too rushed and hurried an affair at the barracks," the blond-headed, baby-faced officer explained. "It's all right for getting clean, but once in a while I like to sit and soak."

I had no more than settled into the long galvanized tub used for these affairs than the lieutenant claimed the one adjacent. This was a social gathering place, so the tubs were grouped with the head of one at the foot of the next to accommodate gentlemen wishing to hold conversations. The life of the dragoon had sculpted the young officer well. Bronzed forearms paled into white flesh, and the dark "vee" of the tan at his neck drew the eye.

"Oh, Lord," he sighed blissfully as he lowered himself into the hot water. "That feels sinfully good."

"Don't say that," I cautioned, "else some preacher declare it so."

"True. Ahhh," he exclaimed, his lids slipping halfway over blue eyes. I thought he slept until he spoke again. "And how was your winter, Mr. Strobaw?"

"Uneventful, except for nursing a family of four in my midst."

"Oh, yes, the Bowers family. I understand he's set up his own establishment … a cooperage, I believe. He will probably do well. There is always a need for barrels and kegs."

"Then they are well?" The officer nodded. "Maybe I'll look them up," I mused.

The Lieutenant had scant additional news. The detachment from Ft. Ramson was not expected until later this month. Captain Jamieson had already left for the Boggs Ambush Site to recover the settlers' bodies. The Major was inclined to fault the trainmaster, so retribution would not be sought, although an effort would be made to impress upon the tribesmen the seriousness of attacking settlers. I sensed the lieutenant's eyes examining me as I stepped from the bath after adequately steeping the poisons from my system.

The Bowers were happy to see me, and insisted I share a meal in their home that evening. Timo and Little Beth peppered me with questions about Cut Hand. Their interest in him was inexhaustible. Doubtless in their dotage, they would regale others with tales of their own personal wild Indian.

The following morning, I visited Caleb Brown who informed me he had made a connection with Mr. J. J. Astor's American Fur Company and was seeking responsible investors to purchase pelts on its behalf. Since the merchant seemed an honest and honorable man, at least in our dealings, I risked five hundred American dollars with him. Even though this venture did not promise huge immediate returns, it would continue to earn something in excess of the interest the bank paid for so long as I saw fit to leave the principal or until the collapse of the agreement with Astor's group. Hence, in a sense, I was a party to buying my own furs.

My business transacted early, I visited the gambling room at the Rainbow, which claimed a hard-earned dollar in small bits and pieces before I gave it up as an ill-conceived idea. Intent on one dram of whiskey to be tossed back and forgotten, I found myself standing beside Major Wallston and the dark-headed Lieutenant Smith.

After pleasantries, the senior officer asked about the state of the Yanube. I advised of the confrontation with the Fort Ramson troop and the reasons why. I also told of Yellow Puma's health and Great Bull's death, naming Carcajou as the band's new leader. Both officers expressed interest in the character of this new chieftain. I gave my frank opinion – he was a good man, but a little removed when it came to dealing with Americans.

The Major asked after Cut Hand by name, and I told of his wedding. A slight flicker in Smith's eyes led me to believe he knew something of my station. Following that, I retired, slept, rose, and departed for home.

Captain Jamieson's prior passage was clearly written on the land. The troop had marooned to the south of my clearing between the creek and the river, raising concerns over the dogs.

The hounds were unharmed and so delighted to see me they deserted their posts to leap around Long's feet at their own peril. The pony and the dogs were amicable antagonists. The canines couldn't resist a friendly nip, to which Long responded with a not so friendly kick. A good feeding settled the animals down. The horses in the barn had exhausted their stock of piled fodder, so I tossed fresh hay from the loft before tackling the mass of half-frozen urine and fecal matter. Before night fall, smoke poured from all of the Mead's chimneys.

Memories of Cut Hand almost spoiled my return. The comforts of home receded into the dark corners of the room as lamplight replaced the sun's glow. By the time I took to my bed, a sharp physical pain rose in my chest as jealous images of him rogering his new wife claimed me anew. My sleep was poor that first night at home.

Early the next morning, barking dogs drew me to the door. A delegation of six Sioux warriors strange to me stood waiting for an invitation. I called off South and beckoned them forward, growing a bit nervous as they crowded into the west fronting room. Their first request, made in the Lakota dialect, was for liquor. Finally convinced I had none, they sat on my floor to talk.

"Soldiers passed by," the leader announced.

"Yes, it was a detachment from Ft. Yanube on its way to recover the bodies of the settlers killed last winter on the north bank of the Yanube."

Hooded eyes and firm lips told me nothing. "What did these soldiers say?" their spokesman asked

"I was not here," I said, knowing they had seen my wagon tracks on top of the shod hoof prints. "I went to the Yanube winter camp and took their pelts to the trader in Yawktown. When I was in the white man's town, I spoke to an officer who told me the army considers the attack to be the fault of the Americans."

They reacted to the information with visible surprise. "Why is this?"

"The family who survived the fighting wintered here at the Mead. This Bowers is an honorable man. He told the commander of the fort the trainmaster killed one of the People over a stag. Then when the People came to protest, he slew another. The attack on the wagons came after that."

"So the army is not mad?"

"Oh, yes, the army is mad. The army is angry whenever an American is killed, just as the Lakota are angry when one of theirs dies at the hands of others. But this anger is constrained by the knowledge the tribesmen, whoever they were, were wronged first." I added this to let them know the Indians involved had not been identified. "But if the dragoons meet even the slightest resistance, there will be blood spilled."

An angry mutter went around the group.

"There can be an end to this thing if the tribesmen do not confront the troops until the memory of it has faded," I continued.

"Unless, of course, the blue coats find something at the massacre site that identifies the attackers."

Their talker, a weather beaten man with a droopy right eye, studied the floor intently. "I am told there is nothing."

I gifted the leader with an old pistol and the others with knives and hatchets before they left. They gave me a handsome silver fox pelt some New York matron would envy as a neckpiece for her coat.

Once again, bedtime brought pain and jealousy. Determined that I was a bigger man than this, I worked hard the next day to get my place in order and to take stock of stores in the cavern. The People would need supplies when they arrived.

I went to sleep the following night behind an hour's worth of sincere prayers. Wrestling with my problem, I decided if I was right with my God a month ago, I was right with Him now. After all, I had not committed adultery, I concluded with warped logic. If the Good Lord judged us all by the same measure, only Cut had done that.

# # # # #

The Yanube arrived a week later. I rode Long to the river crossing and watched the camp pass over. They were tired from the journey, but happy to be back. My heart dropped into my boots when Cut splashed across to greet me.

"Hello, wife," he said to remind me of my oath.

"Husband," I replied to let him know I remembered.

"It is good to see you. Tonight I will remain in camp, but tomorrow I want to hold you and put Dark Warrior every place he can be made to fit!" His laughing face turned serious. "Have you made peace with your God?"

"Yes. If there is sin, it is yours."

He frowned. "How can that be?"

"I hold myself for my mate. You spread yourself between two."

He turned away in genuine confusion. Now my task was to survive until tomorrow night without succumbing to green-eyed beasts.

I loaded the wagon for the village, practically clearing out our food stores. I did so with no reservation; the People needed the strength only red meat provided. The remainder of the day was spent helping where I could. The merchandise received for the band's pelts constituted another wagonload, which I delivered the next morning.

Yellow Puma surprised me by appearing stronger than a month ago. "My son," he greeted me warmly. "The provisions you supplied are welcome."

"Thank you, Yellow Puma. You are looking better."

"I am feeling fit. I will be with you for a long time to come."

"That is good. On my journey back through the land of the Pipe Stem, I learned Great Bull has traveled on. Carcajou leads his people now. Also, an officer at Ft. Yanube informed me the detachment from Ft. Ramson will pass this way any time now. Probably on the other side of the river." The rest should be said, as well.

"I received a visit from the Sioux after I got back. They know of the soldiers' coming. They also asked about dragoons who passed on this side of the river heading east. I told them the troop was on its way to recover the bodies of the settlers massacred last winter. Cut Hand told you of that?"

"Yes. What is the mood of the soldiers?"

"At this point, they are blaming their own. The Sioux said the dragoons would find nothing to dispute this."

"Hah," he grunted.

"What they will find are the bodies, including women and a child. That will inflame them. You must be careful when they pass this way."

Yellow Puma sent for Cut Hand and several others to hear this news from my own lips.

"I understand being angry because of your dead women and children," Bear Paw said. "But what has this to do with us? We did not kill them."

Cut spoke before I could. "Because to them a red man is a red man, and there is no difference. If you cannot find the Indian who killed this child, slay another so he can't do it to some other child."

"That is the thinking of some, and that makes them dangerous." I was chagrined some still did not comprehend what I had preached for years. "It is like our own hotheads, I suppose."

Otter and Lone Eagle accompanied me to the Mead when I left camp that afternoon. I did not wish their company, especially if Cut was coming later, but each seemed eager to see the place again. As I feared, both claimed beds in the west side and turned in soon after dark. Their day had been full.

Cut Hand came quietly not long after. I heard his low voice speaking to the youths in the other room before he came to our side of the house.

"Billy!" he said, giving me a hug. "Will you come bathe me? I need to wash in our shower. Your strange contraptions are becoming precious to me."

I did as he bade and washed his naked body from the top of his head to the heel of his foot. He tarried beyond the capacity of the hot water container and had to rinse in the cold. Poor Dark Warrior shriveled at its touch.

Cut took a great deal of care as he covered me that night. At the first spurt of his seed, he thrust so deeply I felt we were one!

"Beloved," he whispered hoarsely. "I have missed you so much. I have been afraid for you every minute."

"Except when you're fucking her," I said waspishly, ruining the moment. "Forgive me, Cut. I've never had to share you with anyone before."

He allowed me to rest for a glass, that time it takes for sand to pass through the middle of an hourglass, and then entered me so easily, so naturally, so erotically I was lost in him until he finished with me. Then we slept.

Lone Eagle, fairly dancing with excitement, woke us the next morning with news the soldiers were coming.

Captain Jamieson and two sergeants were seated on a blanket before Yellow Puma's tipi when we arrived. Two derelict wagons rested in the midst of a full company of dragoons. The young troopers looked nervous.

The Captain allowed the medicine pipe ceremony to be completed before he rose to greet us, clasping Cut's forearm in the Indian way. "Ah, Cut Hand. It is good to see you again."

"Captain Jamieson. Welcome to our village. Are you in need of anything?"

"Thank you, no." Jamieson turned to me. "A sad business, Mr. Strobaw. As you can see, we located the spot where the killings took place. Women, a child. It's ungodly!"

"Some of your men don't look too happy."

"Would you be, sir? They carry the bodies of murdered folk."

"No, but I wouldn't be looking to take it out on innocent people, either."

"Nor are we," the Captain answered, the harshness leaving his voice. "But it's hard for them to understand. They're just boys, some of them."

Judging from the looks of the two sergeants, the boys were not the problem.

"Has there been any word on the perpetrators?" he pursued the issue.

"I thought that was agreed. Boggs was the perpetrator."

Jamieson's muttonchops twitched. "I mean to ask if word has filtered down as to who he may have attacked."

I shrugged and stated the obvious. "Likely some of the Sioux, but there is no way of telling which ones."

The troop moved out before the young bloods of either race became too agitated. Yellow Puma's warrior's muttered depredations against the blue-coated soldiers just as Captain Jamieson's did against the buckskins, I expect.

Cut surprised me and remained at the Mead that night. This time he chased Lone Eagle and Otter out of the house and barred the door. I understood his actions when he engaged in one of his more energetic and audible thrummings. I almost laughed in the midst of his climax when I caught sight of a deeper darkness at one of the paper lights at the window. Those rascals were outside listening to his performance. We'd have been better off if they were in the house; the door was thicker! Mischievously, I let out a bellow: "My God, Cut! You're magnificent. A stallion! A bull!"

# # # # #

Each day seemed to deliver an unexpected event. Mine came on the morrow after Cut left for the village. I found the demure form of Morning Mist standing with two friends just at the end of South's patrol. I should have obeyed my instincts and spun on my heels leaving them where they were. Instead, in the hope of promoting amity, I recalled the dog and motioned them forward.

As Morning Mist neared, her submissive posture evaporated. She came up the steps and stared up at me rudely. "I would see my husband's other dwelling," she announced and marched past me into the house.

Two giggling girl-women trailed after her. They picked up things randomly and threw them aside with only a casual glance. My neat house was turning into a shambles. I stilled an instinctive protest as Morning Mist ambled into the private side of the house. She went first to the bed, and the three of them stood tittering. Then Morning Mist sat on the thing and bounced, squealing delightedly. Before I could protest, she lay back, moving her broad hips. It wouldn't have surprised me if she had raised her legs, but there was a point beyond which even she would not go. She turned over and sniffed the covers.

"Yes," she announced. "It is Cut Hand's bed. I would recognize his aroma anywhere." Pure showmanship. He had no aroma.

When they flooded the bathing room by mishandling the spigots, I lost my temper and shooed them out of the place. The other two fled, but Morning Mist strode haughtily to the door. I had not seen the last of that one.

Two nights later Cut showed up, obviously flustered. He flopped on a chair opposite me at the table. A deep frown puckered his brow.

"What?" I demanded grumpily.

"Don't be like that. I haven't said anything."

"Not yet. But when you do, I won't like it." In a flash I understood. "You know your other wife was here, don't you?"

"Yes, I heard. She … she wants to try the bed."

"So build her one."

"She wants to try that one."

"She wants to flaunt it in my face," I hissed.

"Damnation, Billy! I'm not asking you to stay and watch."

"You want me to leave my own house so you can flank her in my bed."

"I could just do it," he flared.

"Then do it," I said in a deadly tone of voice as I rose slowly to my feet.

"All right, I'll tell her no," he backed away. Cut left shortly thereafter, as angry as I had seen him in awhile.

He made me pay for my refusal for a fortnight. According to my imperfect calendar, the month of July had commenced before he walked through the door as if nothing had happened. Finding me at the table washing some root vegetables, Cut grasped my shoulders and drew me to him in a passionate kiss. What Otter thought, I do not know. He fled the house.

When Cut left the next day, I was sore all over, and he was walking funny.

CHAPTER 13

The following morning, Otter and I returned from fishing to find my door ajar and the dogs agitated. Blood at the end of the meadow led to where South lay with deep wounds in his flank and head. He valiantly tied to crawl to us, whining in shame that he had not dealt with the intruders. I ran to the porch, shotgun at the ready.

The fronting room on the east side was a shambles. The two bunks lay in splinters. The long table I used as a trading counter leaned drunkenly on three legs. Bursting through the door to my living quarters, I found Morning Mist hewing at my bed while the two girl-women who had accompanied her the other day worried over the kitchen table. Seizing the closest women by the hair and slinging them forcefully through the doorway, I spun as Morning Mist rushed me with her hatchet. It fell harmlessly from her nerveless grasp as I twisted her arm savagely. Shrieking as only an enraged Indian woman can, she spewed threats and imprecations as I tossed her bodily from the porch. The others made the mistake of fleeing across East's guard area; one lost half her skirt before escaping.

I took the wounded dog from Otter and examined the animal's injuries. "Find Cut Hand," I snapped.

The irony of it! The beast had survived wolves, soldiers, and marauding warriors, only to fall to the spite of a jealous woman!

Cut arrived to comfort the injured beast before going to the barn for our supply of sawn wood. I joined him after tending our faithful friend, and we set to work. Before *Han,* darkness, led in *Hanhepi*, nighttime, much of the damage was mended, although my dressing mirror was smashed beyond repair.

"She is the spawn of *Unk*!" I snarled, playing lose with one of the creation myths. "She should be cast into the water like her mother!" Recalling my incredibly naïve remark before their marriage, I snorted sourly. "Sisters!"

Cut giggled then, actually giggled. "The sisters from hell!"

"I'm glad you find it funny!" I roared. "How did she get in, anyway?"

"She stole my key to the stock lock. It won't happen again, Billy."

"How do you know? How do you know she won't shoot the other dogs and poor South, if he survives."

"Because I beat her. I beat her in public and declared in front of everyone I would divorce her if she did not stop behaving like a fool."

"Beat her? Damnation, Cut, that would just make me more determined."

"She is not you, my love. I meant my words, and she knows it."

But Morning Mist was not so easily tamed. She made life so miserable that Cut, figurative hat-in-hand, asked to spend one night in the house – meaning in my bed, of course. Stubbornly, I refused until I realized he was rent between two people who should love and support him. My lack of cooperation was not helping. As distasteful as it was, I finally agreed.

When evening came, Otter and Lone Eagle hung around the west end of the house pitching the iron with me, a game where a heavy object is tossed at a hole in the ground. Imagining what was happening in my bed at that very moment distracted me, allowing the boys to beat me handily. When Cut and Morning Mist came out of the house, I hid in the barn to avoid her smug face. Out of sight of the others, I retched sour bile. As Cut once pointed out, love carries heavy penalties.

# # # # #

Morning Mist and I were taking a horrible toll on Cut Hand; he grew haggard, not from sexual exertion, but from constant tension. I made certain none was present in my home. It worked for awhile; he began spending more time at the Mead. But when others came for him at awkward hours, we recognized he was the leader of the *tiospaye* in all but name, and to take his rightful place among them, he needed to live in their midst.

Finding some excuse to banish Otter and Lone Eagle from the house, I wept for three days, a very unmanly thing to do, but then I wasn't a man. I was a creature, half-man, half-woman, and thoroughly rotten! Never insensitive to my moods, Cut returned and remained with me for five days, undermining my determination. But my decision was firmly resolved, although I did not act upon it for some time, being human enough to hope the situation would change.

Then Cut's father took a turn for the worse. When I went to his side; Yellow Puma's pain-filled eyes read the hurt in mine and released me from my promise.

As preparations began for the fall move, I informed Cut that Otter was driving the wagon to the new encampment. He lifted an arched eyebrow.

"I'm staying here," I announced.

He came to me before the move for a night of tender love, something I will remember for the rest of my days. We turned at opposite ends and embraced Dark Warrior and Pale Hunter simultaneously, climaxing almost as one. Then Cut took me from behind so that his long, lean body pressed full length against mine as he fucked the seed out me. We slept a few minutes, but I woke as he withdrew his shriveled pipe. He lay beside me on his belly.

"Lie atop me, wife," he ordered.

I obeyed, and for the first time in my life, I experienced the joy of my groin resting against hard male buttocks. As my cock sprang to life, he allowed Pale Hunter to ride the crease between his buns until I came in the most exciting, tumultuous, gripping, erotic orgasm I had ever experienced.

As he left the next morning, Cut paused at the door. His look was penetrating, sad. "Goodbye, wife. I'm sorry. I tried to make it work."

After he was out of sight, I drove our stock into the band's herd and went to help the People where I could. When the last horse crossed the broad, shallow Yanube, my eyes teared again.

I waited at the Mead for a week to be certain Otter had delivered my letter to Cut Hand. I had entrusted the missive to the youngster with instructions to hand it over upon arrival at the new winter camp. I remember every painful word of that hateful page:

"My Love. I promised not to leave without telling you first. Otter will have handed you this letter ere I depart the Mead, so that pledge is honored, no matter how cowardly; I had not the mettle otherwise. But you understood before ever you read this.

"I considered a standaway, a separation, but concluded it would resolve nothing. I do not leave because I no longer love you, rather out of deep feelings for the man who has been my one, my only, my greatest love! It is my wanch, my misfortune, Morning Mist and I cannot abide one another. Consequently, we are killing you and squandering the goodwill of a fine people. That is not only foolish, it is unforgivable. Morning Mist cannot leave, so I must.

"Therefore, I have placed a pair of your moccasins outside the door, divorcing you in accordance with custom. You are released from your vows and responsibilities, as I consider myself released from mine. The Mead, of course, is yours.

"I hold no bitterness, Cut Hand. I will always remember you as the most magnificent and honorable man I have ever known. Take care of your people for they are mine, as well. Love. Billy"

I departed my home at Teacher's Mead despondent and in pain in the fall of 1835. Time and history were passing me by. As I later learned, a crazed man named Richard Lawrence made an attempt on the life of Andrew Jackson the prior January, but both shots misfired. Doubtless there would be attacks on other presidents, but none would ever succeed. This warning would serve to strengthen the security around our chief executive until it was impenetrable.

I took only three rifles, my shotgun, pistols, and personal possessions with me – and the hoard of gold and silver coins, of course. The northers held off, so the trip took only two days, but it seemed I traveled a hundred years. I rented a stall at the Yawktown Livery for Long, a box at the bank for my gold, and a room at the Rainbow for my carcass.

One night in that room was sufficient to goose-pucker my flesh. The noise on the street below my second-floor window disturbed me more than was called for. Living in the wilderness taught me to listen with a constant ear since rustling grass or breaking twigs might herald the Angel of Death. Men laughing and talking and spitting right below the window constituted a cacophony, and the clop of a hoof brought me bolt upright in my unaccustomed bed. Strange, I had not experienced this during my previous short visits.

Missing my own bathing room more than anything else, I visited the establishment's privy reserved for gents and then sought out the local bathhouse. A shave and hot bath revived me, and breakfast in the Rainbow's dining room gave me courage to face the day and worry over what to do with myself. One phase of my life was ended; another had yet to reveal itself. What was I qualified to do? Hire out as a scout for the government? Become a professional hunter?

The former was out of the question. I would never put myself in the position of running down my friends, as a scout could conceivably be required to do. Professional hunter resonated better and would have the advantage of keeping me out of town for a good part of my time. Of course, I could settle a piece of ground and farm. That is what I was raised to do, but the task of building another homestead seemed oppressive at the moment.

Reviewing my station, I found it acceptable. None of the gold in my possession had been touched, and doubtless far exceeded the value of the remaining silver and my account at the bank. When I checked on the latter, I was pleasantly surprised to find it considerably buffered by the proceeds of financing Caleb Brown's fur purchases as a factor for the Astor organization.

To reconnect with American civilization, I visited the Jewish tailor and had clothing made a cut above my usual habit. Abandoning my signature red garments for the drab of small town society was surprisingly difficult; I felt absolutely common. The sturdy boots from the local cobbler chafed feet long accustomed to the soft comfort of moccasins. Further, they made a resounding clump against the boardwalk, robbing me of any ability to move about quietly. Apparently, that was in accordance with the usual custom, for the local citizenry seemed inordinately taken aback at another's silent approach. Silence equated with stealth, and stealth with chicanery.

A visit to Caleb Brown brought an invitation to dine with the merchant. I accepted gratefully. Filling my day was already presenting a problem. Discerning circumstances were different from previous visits, Mr. Brown probed as to my intent. I shared my plans to the extent they existed.

Later that evening, I dropped by the inn's saloon for a dram of spirits prior to retiring. Halfway through my libation, Captain Jamieson and the Lieutenants Morrow and Smith appeared at my elbow and offered a drink.

It would have been a more pleasant evening without the presence of Smith. Within the hour, he proved a dour earwig of the worst sort, concurring with anything the Captain said and withholding judgment until learning the bend of Jamieson's twig in the wind – except on the subject of the "tribesmen," as he termed them, depersonalizing an entire people and reducing them from a society to a mere meaningless term. He was harshly outspoken on that subject as he got deeper into his cups, raising the suspicion he was a pot valiant, a poltroon of the worst sort who drew his courage from John Barley-

Corn, or more ominously, from behind ranks of armed troopers. Frankly, he was bigoted about the red man, and as such was a dangerous man. Even the Captain felt moved to caution him over some of his comments, although I gleaned Jamieson, himself, feared the Indians more than was reasonable.

Smith reluctantly ended the roundhouse by complaining that his duty as adjutant compelled his return to the post. Jamieson decided to accompany him, but Morrow remained for another drink.

The atmosphere altered with the departure of the other officers. James Morrow visibly relaxed and initiated a timid conversation, inquiring about Cut Hand and things of more personal interest. As we talked, I observed this attractive military officer. In the company of others, he was stiff and stolid; when alone with me, he was affable and pleasant. In this, he was not unlike my friends among the Yanube. He had a finely drawn face, somewhat narrower than my – than Cut Hand's. The blonde hair went well with his tanned features. He had lost the "mother's milk" look, leaving him a handsome, virile young man.

As I finished my drink and declared it time to retire, he seemed reluctant to end the evening. Perhaps it was more comfortable here than on the post. In the lobby, he offered his hand, which I took in the American manner. On impulse, I stated I would not be averse to a final drink in my quarters. Lt. Morrow accepted readily.

Once in the room, he grew unaccountably flustered, and I knew my instinct had been correct. Even so, I had no idea how to advantage the situation, although I was attracted in that vague way Carcajou affected me. This young lieutenant was no Plains warrior, but his build was trim and firm and demanding of my interest. He had leaned out since last spring; his uniform no longer hugged him so tightly. I was suddenly desirous of seeing him naked again. Unbidden, my pipe stirred.

As we sipped generous drinks, I decided upon a course of action. Walking to the door, I paused before deliberately turning the key in the lock. He swallowed hard as he stood in anticipation, his staff clearly outlined against the blue of his trousers. Cut's image flashed before me, almost costing me the will to continue, but Morrow's eager, frightened features motivated me.

His hungry eyes followed every move as I undressed. With a soft moan, he tore off his uniform and fell to his knees in front of me. His hands found my flanks and caressed my flesh. I fell on the bed, taking him with me. His kisses did not stir the blood, and this disturbed me for I had never sought assignations merely for sexual release, except with that long-ago doxy.

When he eagerly took me into his mouth, I forgot such nonsense. Lt. James Morrow had done this before; he was good at it. I cautioned him to go slowly else I come too soon. He worked at me as if this were a thing he enjoyed, as I took pleasure in doing it for Cut in my past life. With that thought came a pang of regret interrupted by an explosion of ecstasy. Once the moment was over, I was perplexed. Did he expect reciprocity? Morrow came up off of me, leaving my flesh as clean as if washed by a clear rill, and moved into the crook of my arm, his head buried in my neck.

"Was that all right? It … it has been a long time. I was afraid I had forgotten how to do it properly."

"That was good," I proclaimed, floundering in unfamiliar waters. I knew nothing better than to speak my mind. "I'm not certain what happens next."

"Can we stay this way for a while? And later maybe you can –"

"Maybe I can what?"

He made no reply.

"Lieutenant … James, speak plainly. That's the only way I know how to deal." Then I understood. "What is it? Do you want me to flank you?" A tremor shook him, and I was sorry for my vulgarity. "Damnation, man! Why didn't you say so?"

I had never fucked a man before, and I soon understood why Cut placed such great store by it. James accepted me with an open-mouthed sigh of pleasure. I labored above him, dripping the sweat of my exertions onto his chest. He made no exclamations of rapture, but gratification was plain to see in his face, and it drove me to greater efforts. When my release came, it was strong and satisfying, yet not tremendously powerful. I kept at it until he flogged himself to a long, forceful orgasm. Exhausted, I fell forward upon his chest and lay panting. It was hard to see him as a leader of men at that moment. As I rolled off of him, he whispered his thanks.

"No need to thank me, I enjoyed it as much as you did."

"Did you? I never knew if it was about pleasure or power."

We lay with the lamp on low wick while he spoke of how he first came to lie with a man, his father's Ganymede, a sixteen-year-old serving boy, when James was but twelve.

"He was Portuguese … Eduardo. He came into my bath once with hot water and stayed to watch me. His eyes … they were huge and brown. When he looked at me, I got excited. I could see he was, too. He took it out. I'd never seen one like that … hard, I mean. I took him, but when he came, I almost choked to death. He got scared and ran out of the bath." James shifted his weight and continued living in the past.

"He had this patch of black hair around his penis that fascinated me. I wondered if I would ever have hair like that. The next day I went up in the hayloft where he kissed me on the lips. I didn't even know you did that. Damnation, I didn't know any of it. But I did by the time I came down from that loft. He stripped me bare and put his thing inside me. It hurt at first, but then I could feel him rubbing my channel. When he came I felt warm inside. It was another year before he made me ejaculate. He did it with his hand while he was inside me."

"How long did this go on?"

"For two years, until we were caught. My father beat Eduardo and sent him away. He put me in a boarding school."

James had been tossed from the boiling pot into the fire pit. His roommate shared the boy with two friends, and on occasion, all three fucked him at one sitting. Then he had been accepted at the military academy where they promised to make a man of him. Since that time, the constantly terrified James had abstained from carnal encounters, not only with his own kind but also with women, indeed, with himself.

With James's departure from my room in the wee hours, came recriminations. I had sullied the manhood of a southern gentleman! Nonsense! James had been ready and eager for the leap. Had I not serviced his needs, he likely would have erred with someone who would take advantage of his station. I snorted aloud. In some quarters that was called – what was that new-fangled word? Rationalization.

Suddenly, I achieved an erection that had nothing to do with James Morrow as I recalled the feel of Cut against me, the warmth of his living body, the generosity of his soul, the beauty of his mind. Unmanly tears flooded my eyes; loneliness overwhelmed me. I prayed to my formidable God that Cut Hand and the *tiospaye* were well. My heart hardened into pig iron as I imagined him lying in Morning Mist's arms. Despondent to the point where the derringer on the table beside my bed appeared seductive, I turned away and came to the odd conclusion I had betrayed him tonight. Maybe I was a closet Catholic who, once taking the vows, can never lay them aside.

In the cold light of day, I shrugged off those feelings, of course, and continued to see James. Despite the newly discovered confirmation I was a common sodomite, I grew truly fond of him and looked forward to inspecting his naked body, sunburned at head and arms, blue-veined white everywhere else. He gradually progressed from shy to proud of my inspection, and each time expressed his thanks following our copulation. I finally came to understand his gratitude was for not treating him with derision post coitus as others had.

#####

As James Morrow became a regular fixture in my life, I was reintroduced to the fear Americans engender in sodomites, something of a shock when laid against the more accepting attitude of the People. Nonetheless, I cottoned to the danger before disgracing myself in the eyes of the Yawktown community.

When the weather finally began to turn with the coming of the Goose Moon, I gathered articles needed for my new life as a hunter, but when I purchased a buckboard, I acknowledged the past four months had been nothing but flam. The items that went into my boodle were things I would require at Teacher's Mead. James knew I planned to leave with the thaw on a hunt, but I have no idea when he recognized I was returning home, possibly when he saw the wagon.

The night before my departure, a few friends hosted me a frolic at the Rainbow House. Brown, Crozier, Kranzmeier – they were all there. Major Wallston and Captain Jamieson came by for a brief while. Then James and I discretely retired to my room. He appeared reluctant to do much except hold onto me tightly. At length he raised his head, the blue of his eyes faintly visible.

"Why didn't you tell me you were going back?"

"I do not know when I made the decision; I drifted into it. I would have told you tonight."

"You're going back to him?" I had long since confessed Cut Hand to James.

"No." I laid a finger across his full lower lip. "That part of my life is over. He belongs to his wife now. There's no place for me except as friend and counselor."

"How can you stand to be around him?"

"I cannot answer that. But Teacher's Mead is my home; the Yanube are my family. And Cut Hand is my friend. If they will allow me, I need to go to them."

"Billy," he reverted to his original shy self. "I will resign my commission and come with you if you will accept me."

"That would not be a good idea. You have a profession. There's steel in you, James. It's well covered by the velvet, but it's there. Enough, I think, for you to be good army material. But don't go getting into trouble with some enlisted man. That would ruin your career and put you in prison. It would be like being back in school except worse." I felt the shudder run through him.

"I'm going to miss you. This has been the best four months of my life," he cried. "Fuck me! Be rough with me, Billy. It will have to last a long time."

I did my best. My rigid staff invaded his handsome body harshly. I flanked him long and hard, and after a short rest, I gave him my seed again, desperately seeking to deliver an experience to remember. I must have been at least partially successful as he was unsteady on his feet when he left for his quarters on the post.

CHAPTER 14

I invested the gains from my venture with Caleb Brown in the Yawktown gunsmith's entire stock of percussion rifles and cartridges. I also bought a new dressing mirror and had the glazier throw enough blown glass lights for all of the windows at Teacher's Mead and several to spare.

Although I delayed my start for the Mead late into the thaw, the going was rough. My wagon was a buckboard, and Long Wind did not take kindly to being hitched beside the sturdy black I had purchased. He cast sullen looks over his shoulder designed to convey his humiliation at this change from proud Indian pony to draft horse. Patience, I urged. It would only be for a few days.

The homestead had weathered well. Deep snow drifts choked the north side of the building all the way to the hillock. A rangy dog approached, growling threateningly. It took a minute to recognize South. He had not only recovered from Morning Mist's hatcheting, he had survived the winter. Slowly, the beast lowered his hackles and allowed me to approach. West snarled his disapproval from some distance, but he, too, eventually recognized me. East, a tough bitch trailing three scrawny pups, allowed herself to be cajoled. North did not show his muzzle, nor did I ever find sign of the carcass. Removing a few haunches of smoked meat from the cavern, I fed the half-starved canines. Then with some trepidation, I entered the house.

A ghostly coat of gray dust shrouded the interior. A sheet of paper covered by Cut's fine hand pinned to the inside of the door remained undisturbed until flames blazed in all the fireplaces and the horses were tended. Then I sat at the table with his epistle.

"Beloved. When I discovered your desertion, I was angry beyond all reason, and Morning Mist despaired of my sanity. Then I remembered my pledge that you were free to return to your people although you would rip my heart from my breast and take it with you. That you have done.

"If you are reading this, then welcome home! You have returned, and perhaps my heart can be restored to its proper place, and a friendship bound by love and respect can be revived and strengthened.

Know this – Cut Hand loves you always, William Joseph Strobaw. Even so, I recognize the strength of your reasoning and accept that we are divorced. Knowing I can never cover you again is hurtful, but if that is the case, I will endure. We will endure. Love. Cut"

I dropped my head to my arms on the planking of the table. How did I ever believe I could leave him? Whether or not there was a physical relationship, the object of my devotion was here, and here I belonged.

I reread the letter, noting with pride the beauty of his composition. While most of the people in Yawktown could neither read nor write, this wild son of the plains penned a hand the envy of Moorehouse College. I further recognized the People must be back from their winter quarters.

This was affirmed when Otter sauntered through the door as though I had never left. He delivered the sad news of Yellow Puma's passing during the winter followed quickly by the death of the misco's old friend, Spotted Hawk. Badger now served as shaman. The fate of the band was in the hands of a new generation of leaders.

My young friend also brought the welcome news that Buffalo Shoulder's shunning had been lifted even though he still indulged alcohol more than was seemly. Otter laced the sour among the sweet; Cut Hand was now a proud father. Morning Mist had laid a great belly and delivered a boy-child named Dog Fox. Damnation! Cut's seed was powerful! He must have lined her on his first covering.

Otter was coming fifteen now and looked the part. Gone was the baby fat from his lean frame. Fully as tall as I, his shoulders flared over ribs muscled with sinew and gristle. The light, genderless voice had broken, taking on an adolescent timbre. There would be a bush around his pipe now, and that organ would have lengthened and broadened. In actions, however, he was the old Otter, well named because of his playful ways and sudden bursts of energy. He spent the night with me, bedding down in the east side of the house while I crawled into what had once been my marriage bed and the scene of countless beautiful couplings.

Lone Eagle showed up the next day, and the change in him was startling. Just shy of eighteen, he looked to be two years older. His deep, vibrato voice and self-conscious swagger announced to the world "here walks a man." Arrogance rode his shoulders more comfortably now, mellowed by confidence, smoothed of the brash, uncertain edges.

He, too, acted as if there had been no interlude since our last meeting. They both spent the night.

Cut Hand, Bear Paw, and Buffalo Shoulder appeared the next morning. All of my jealousies fell away at the sight of Cut Hand's magnificent bearing and physical beauty. Our handshake was long and endearing. Finally, he stepped away and allowed the others to greet me with much pounding of backs and sly ribbings.

Cut and I sat alone at the kitchen table before the fire while the others inspected my new rifles. He told me of Yellow Puma's last days, and how his father spoke of me with affection. Toward the end, the ailing man complimented his son on his wisdom in selecting Teacher as his first mate. We both sat without words, working through fresh sorrow for the loss of a father and a friend.

His mother and Butterfly lived in a tipi beside Cut's own as a part of his household. Bright Dove still mourned the loss of Yellow Puma, but was managing to cope. Butterfly had spurned Badger's advances so long that the young man took another wife. He would still have her, but Cut feared she would never be a second wife to any man. So she languished, a juicy fruit working its way toward shriveling age. I almost laughed aloud. Butterfly was younger than my twenty and five years.

Cut questioned me about life in the American settlement, but would not ask what he wanted answered most. I volunteered the response.

"My friend, I formed a liaison while I was away. I did not rest easy over it because I was breaking a trust. But it happened."

"You broke no trust," he answered solemnly. "We laid aside our vows. Was it the yellow-haired officer?" Surprised, I glanced up at him. "He had eyes only for you while he was here. Was he good for you?"

"He allowed me to survive. I'm not certain I would have otherwise."

"You were a man for him," he said with certainty. "That is good. Now you know the great joy I experienced when coupling with you." Once again I looked at him for an explanation. "He was only strong enough to be your woman. But I am grateful he helped you survive."

"Not just survive. He gave me back my life." Cut had no response to that. "Are you not disgusted that two Win-tays lay together?"

"Some men defy convention. You are one of them," he answered simply.

Choked by my emotions, I escaped the subject. "I understand you have a son. Are you sure you didn't poke your pipe in Morning Mist when we had that fight? She puffed up awfully fast."

He smiled. "No, my friend. I held true until I took her in marriage. But Cut Hand's seed is strong. Did you not feel its power often enough?"

"I sometimes thought I would conceive even without woman's parts."

"I have a vow to request of you. Give it or not; the choice is yours. But if you accepted Carcajou, either to husband or to lie with, I would feel betrayed."

"You have my word," I replied with a pang of regret.

# # # # #

The entire *tiospaye* extended a hearty welcome when I visited the next day. I paid my respects to Bright Dove and noticed how empty the lodge seemed without the commanding presence of Yellow Puma. Butterfly was lovely and wrapped in a new mantle of maturity the loss of a loved one sometimes bestows.

Morning Mist's look of venomous triumph changed into false welcome when Cut came to the lodge opening. He gave me a bear hug and ordered food and drink to be brought. That did not sit well with the wife ascendant, but she served with all the grace of a Boston hostess. Her composure slipped when Cut initiated the conversation in English. A party of Nakota Sioux had marooned at this very place and moved on only reluctantly when Cut Hand informed them this was the site for their summer camp. One day, he sighed, there would be trouble with the Sioux.

Cut had decided he would be a chief who chose the peaceful way for as long as he was permitted to do so. I understood what he meant. When the Americans started coming as they were said to be streaming to the Oregon country, then conflict would be inevitable. It irked to be able to see so plainly that a simple, healthy, peaceful life like this would one day no longer be possible. What I could not see was how the tribesmen would survive. I shivered, something that did not escape Cut's notice. He must have understood, for he did not ask its cause.

His most immediate worry was Butterfly. "She does not favor any of the young men," he complained. "She is content to go with the other women as they do their daily chores."

"Some buck will come along to spark her interest. She grew up with these boys. It may require new blood like with her first husband. Has anyone new joined the band?"

"They come and go. More than in the old days. That, too, is worrisome. How will I manage everything that is coming?"

"Sunrise by sunrise," I replied.

I tarried with him, mostly to spite Morning Mist, but I could not in good conscience keep him longer. Otter was hoeing the garden plot in preparation for planting when I returned to the Mead. Lone Eagle lounged on one of the porch chairs eating a jubal, a sort of sugar cake I sometimes baked.

"Hah!" the latter said. "Look what I found," he tossed a hand casually in Otter's direction. "Is he your Win-tay now?"

Even now, I reacted like the white man I was. "Don't start those rumors, Lone Eagle, or you will never be welcome in my house again! I remember you doing woman's work in this very place when you were not much younger than he is. Did that make you my Win-tay.?"

"Of course, not!" he objected, puzzled by my vehemence. "It was but a joke, Teacher. I meant nothing by it."

"And by such jokes are lives ruined. Don't joke about it again."

He drew himself to full height. "A man says what he wants!"

"Wipe the crumbs from your chin and stop acting like the back end of a horse," I snapped and went to join Otter in the garden. Surprisingly, Lone Eagle did not stomp off in righteous indignation, but sat back down and finished the sweetbread.

A few days later, a lanky youngster visited the Mead, announcing himself gravely as Long Toes. As he handed over a small parfleche as a gift, I noticed he carried a flute, the sure sign of a smitten tribesman. My first swain had come to vie for what had belonged to his leader. I almost laughed aloud. He could not have been more than seventeen. Before I could react, Lone Eagle strode through the doorway.

"What are you doing here?" he demanded.

"I ... I came to see Teacher."

"Get out of here!" Lone Eagle thundered. Embarrassed, the young man forgot to protest the challenge to his pride and fled. "I didn't think he had the stones," my self-appointed protector muttered. "He's been bragging he was going to lie with you."

"Lie with me? What was his name again? Long Toes? Does that apply to his pipe, as well?"

Rather than join in the teasing, Lone Eagle was scandalized. He seemed to get that way around me quite a bit. "Don't talk like that! He's just a child."

"About your age, isn't he?"

I did not see Lone Eagle again for several days.

Life settled as near to normal as possible absent Cut's physical love. On occasion, I caught a look of longing on his face and was tempted toward carnal relations, but I recalled the near destruction of this fine man as he was whipsawed back and forth between Morning Mist and me. I loved him too much to subject him to that again.

Late in the spring, I was pulled to the door by the din my dogs were raising. Two of East's pups had survived. One I named North and trained him to his namesake's duties. The other was dubbed House and made a guardian of the immediate premises of the homestead. In truth, he spent a lot of his time inside the house slobbering on anyone who would give him a friendly scratch behind the ears.

I called off my guardians as two platoons of dragoons rode into my meadow. Otter joined me on the stoop. Captain Jamieson strode up to shake hands by way of greeting. Lt. Morrow dismounted the troop before joining us.

"Mr. Strobaw, a pleasure seeing you again, sir," the Captain enthused. "If you will allow the use of your creek to water the men, I believe they are seasoned enough to drink upstream of the horses."

Smiling at his joke, I nodded permission. Lt. Morrow bawled an order, impressing me with his command voice.

"Out feeling the pulse," the Captain replied in answer to a question. "I'm taking one platoon north to call on the Sioux; Lt. Morrow is visiting the Pipe Stem after we parley with the Yanube. I understand Cut Hand leads that band now."

"Yes, sir, he does. A word of caution, Captain. You're going to find some strange faces among the Sioux. There have been groups moving through this country from the east, putting pressure on the tribes here."

"I see. And the Pipe Stem?"

"They are led by Carcajou. He will be wary and suspicious, but he will listen to what you say if you can find an interpreter."

"Splendid. Now, if you would be so kind as to send your Ganymede to summon the chief of the Yanube, we can parley under the cover of your stoop."

"Otter is not my Ganymede," I said more sharply than intended. "He is a free warrior of the Yanube and understands every word you say."

"My apologies," the Captain said, nodding to the tall youngster.

"As for sending for Cut Hand, no, I will not. I would not presume to summon the chief of this band. My advice is the same as the last time, send a trooper under flag and request an invitation to the camp. Otter will accompany him, if you wish."

An hour later, we passed the pipe around the council blanket before Cut Hand's lodge. Even after all these years, my system was no more accepting of tobacco. I always experienced a moment of giddiness after drawing on the calumet.

Jamieson nodded toward the red stone pipe when it came to rest in Cut's lap. "Impressive piece of work."

"Yes," I agreed. "Like most things, it is symbolic to these people. The stem is male; the bowl, female. There is a healthy trade in this red stone, which comes from the east. This medicine pipe represents one of the *tiospaye*'s treasures."

The Captain addressed his mission, reinforcing the army's wish for friendship and warning we would see more patrols. Cut Hand translated the English words into his own language and then turned back to the officers, his glance lingering on the Lieutenant for a moment. He accepted the Captain's words as true and said that like his father, he was a peace chief.

The flowery fluff out of the way, Cut bore down with hard questions. Why were the Nakota-speakers being driven west? Why were there fewer buffalo? Was it true an American settlement was going up on the Yanube halfway between Ft. Ramson and Ft. Yanube?

Would the American army's friendship translate into better weapons for their friends? I believe Jamieson was truthful insofar as his authority extended, but he gave the Yanube scant comfort.

It was late before the confab broke up, and the officers gratefully accepted my invitation to house at the Mead for the night. The troops pitched tents and bedrolls in the meadow before the cabin while the officers appropriated the bunks in the west fronting room. Both expressed gratitude at the offer of my bath. Lt. Morrow went about his libations while his captain and I sat at my table to discuss news from the east.

Old Hickory's term was ending, and Jamieson believed the vice president, Martin Van Buren, would succeed him. The next item explained his mission better than anything else. On March 2 of this year, the Texicans declared themselves independent. On March 6, the Mexican army overran a fortified mission called the Alamo at San Antonio de Bexar. Some famous names died there, Crockett and Bowie, among them. If the United States was dragged into a war with Mexico, the military would be hard-pressed to field large armies in the North Country. This and the continuing squabbles over black slavery were telling on the Americans.

James emerged from the bath clothed in his trousers and little else. When Captain Jamieson disappeared to take his own shower, James was standing before my new mirror combing his hair. He smiled as I moved up behind him to lean my groin into his buttocks. He shuddered in excitement at my touch. When the sound of water trickling from the shower stopped, I moved away.

# # # # #

As the army left my meadow the next morning, Otter materialized in a state of mild agitation. "Don't you like them?" I teased.

"Some are all right, but I don't like the ones with stripes. They tried to get me to go find them women. When I wouldn't, they wanted me to service them. They got angry when I refused. So I went back to the village last night. I am sorry I left you alone with them."

"I was fine, Otter. I'd rather you protected your manly little backside than hang around for me." He blushed, but he smiled as well.

"They'll be back in a few days. They're meeting back here to return to the fort."

"Yes, I know. I heard Three Stripes tell Two Stripes."

"The Sergeant told the Corporal," I corrected.

That evening, Cut and a few others came to hear my views on this latest incursion into their territory.

"So the American army will now fight the Mexican army?" Cut asked as I finished relating my news.

"That is a possibility. The reason for this patrol was to determine the temper of the tribes in case the army becomes tied down. If trouble breaks out there will be no reserves to support them, and there will also be fewer new troops to guard roads, so the flow of settlers may slow. Of course, I have no idea how long the war will last – if it comes."

The next afternoon, James led his platoon back to the Mead anticipating a rendezvous with Jamieson. Lone Eagle and Otter both stood on the porch as the troops arrived. Before long, teenage curiosity overcame natural reserve, and they circulated freely among the Americans. I kept a wary eye on both. If Lone Eagle was propositioned as Otter had been, I would not have bet on the outcome. The youth didn't have his rifle with him, thank God, but he wasn't above using his skinning knife if he perceived his manhood challenged.

I watched from the stoop as James got his men settled. The soldiers' small rag houses quickly popped up in two long, orderly rows. The horses were watered, fed, hobbled to the west of the house, and placed under guard. Understandable, I suppose. Cut and his warriors were skilled horse thieves and considered it an honorable act if their foes were the victims. The troopers were likely justified in considering that they and their mounts fit into this category.

When the enlisted men were eating from their provisions, James turned to his own needs. He came from the bathing room that night naked and rampant. He laid his trim form atop me and looked into my eyes.

"I have not stopped thinking about you since you left," he said hoarsely. "Those months you were in town were the happiest of my life. I recognize your love lies elsewhere, but you are entitled to know that James Carlton Morrow loves you deeply." He moved to my roger, taking an unbearable amount of time. Whenever he sensed I was on the edge, he would shift to my stones or my belly or some other part of me

171

until I cooled. My long delayed orgasm was almost painful at the point he finally allowed it to occur.

He kissed me with my juices still upon his lips. "That's what love tastes like," he whispered. "I made it last because it has to hold me for a long time." He lay beside me, and I feared he had dropped off to sleep. Then he moved down my body again, exciting me anew. I crawled between his legs. "Now!" he begged. "Give me something else to remember!"

James fair wore me out with his demands. There came a point where pleasure and satisfaction fell away, and it became a matter of endurance. He was insatiable. Toward dawn, I told him "no more." When he stepped out onto the porch to greet his men that morning he was refreshed, revived, rejuvenated; I crawled around the house like an overused jackass.

Otter and Lone Eagle showed up giving one another such looks and giggles that I checked the cavern door. The lock was dust-free. The rascals had crawled through the secret passage and watched from the trapdoor in the bathing room. The lamp had been on low wick, so they had a good view of my bare bum as I flanked the good lieutenant. Seeing me at the cellar door, the two made themselves scarce, but not before they put the spare key back where I stored it. They merely put in the wrong side of the bag.

James began to worry when Jamieson had not put in an appearance by the evening. That might have been why he only had me mount him twice. He was preparing to put his troop to horse and start a search the next day when one of Cut's scouts brought word the Captain was a league away.

Jamieson was an uneasy man when he rode up. Over a cup of fresh coffee he filled in his lieutenant and me. An unusual number of Sioux swelled the camps, as I had warned. He counted Santee from Minnesota and Wisconsin in greater numbers than expected. There was definitely an exodus occurring.

Cut Hand appeared at the Mead within the hour. Jamieson greeted him with a firm handshake, but not before Cut's eyes slid from James Morrow to me. Captain Jamieson got down to business as we took our places around the kitchen table. The three men Cut had brought with him sat on the floor with Lone Eagle and Otter.

"Cut Hand, I am worried about what I saw up north. There are a bodacious number of Sioux up there," Jamieson said.

172

"Yes," Cut answered calmly. "I told you of the migration."

"Migration isn't the word. It's an inundation. They're straining the land. Some of them are going to have to go somewhere, and it seems the likely place is south. This country isn't so filled up as their own."

As the two men spoke, the boys kept up a running translation for the other Indians who did not speak English.

"One band has already set up camp twenty of your English miles to the northeast," Cut acknowledged.

"What will you do if they come closer?"

"Nothing. They are our kinsmen. They will come no closer than necessary. When it gets too crowded, we will move."

"Like everyone else," the Captain muttered, glancing at me. Was he was seeing the same future I did?

# # # # #

The army did not show the flag for the rest of the summer, making me wonder how many men, Mexican and American, were dying down on the Rio Grande? Had the United States entered the war?

Some of Cut's young bloods succumbed to rising sap and raided for horses, touching off retaliation. One morning, I found South nuzzling a fallen warrior curiously. I managed to get the unconscious youth into the house and onto my trading table in the west fronting room. A bullet had passed through the flesh of his side. Working quickly while he was out of it, I bathed the wound in antiseptic and closed it, sacrificing one more cloth shirt to a wounded Indian.

Alerted by the dogs, I went to the porch as Lone Eagle strode to the front of the house, a scowl on his handsome face. The rest of a chase party sat their ponies at the end of the meadow and jabbered excitedly.

"Where is he?" the young Yanube demanded.

"Inside. He is injured." Anticipating what was to come, I planted my feet in front of the door. "You cannot have him. He is unconscious."

Taken aback, he actually recoiled. Lone Eagle became enraged. "I shot him! He is mine! Get out of my way!"

"Lone Eagle, you will have to fight me to get to that youngster. Damnation, man!" I used the term deliberately. "He's but a boy."

"Do not do this to me!" he pled. "The others are watching."

"Then go back and tell them you will take the enemy's mount and weapons and send him home afoot to relate the folly of raiding Yanube horses."

"Where are his weapons?" Lone Eagle grabbed onto this idea as a way out of his dilemma.

"In the grass where he fell, I guess. He had a knife I laid there on the steps. The pony is munching grass near the west hummock."

Lone Eagle swept up the skinning knife and stalked back to the edge of the meadow. In a few minutes, he held up an old flintlock and let out a whoop. His companions joined in. Triumphantly, he recovered the boy's pony and led his small band toward the village.

An hour later, the dogs told me strangers were coming. The day was dying, but the light was good enough to see Carcajou with several of his warriors at my meadow. I stepped to the porch and called him forward.

"He is here, Carcajou. He's been injured, but he will recover."

The subject of the discussion staggered out the door and sagged against a pillar, looking wan and hurt and young.

"I cleaned and cauterized the bullet wound, but he hit his head when he fell off his horse, so he's apt to be dizzier than normal for one of that age. His weapons and pony are forfeit."

"Thank you, Teacher," Carcajou replied, beckoning two of his warriors forward to take the wounded youth. "I would talk," he added, turning back to me.

"Then come inside my house. Do you drink the white man's coffee?"

"Only to be polite."

"Then come in and be polite."

Carcajou was unaccustomed to chairs, so he sat at my table gingerly. "You are looking well, Teacher."

"My name is Billy, Carcajou. I would hear you speak it once before my time expires."

Ignoring my sarcasm, the Pipe Stem misco made an effort. The name came out like Cut used to pronounce it. "Bil-lee."

"Close enough. Now, what can I do for you?"

He asked about news of the army, and I related all I knew, including the fact the United States might go to war with Mexico. Carcajou then turned personal.

"And how are you, my friend? The People say you divorced Cut Hand and left to live among the Americans at the fort-town up the river."

"All of which is true. But I came back."

"To him?"

"No. To my home."

"So now you are free of your oath. I did not know Cut Hand was a fool."

"He is no fool, Carcajou," I flared. "He had a duty to his people, and being with me got in the way of it. I am free, my friend, but I am not available."

"The time for that is past, Bil-lee. I took the Win-tay boy as my wife."

That got my attention. "Did not your first wife object?"

"Why would she object? He is strong and helps with her work. And he can hunt and fight if that is required. It is a good arrangement for her. Ah, I see. Yes, he made it work with her, but this boy is no Teacher. He is pliable and molds himself into a proper role."

"That is my trouble. I don't fit anyone's role."

"Yes, Cut Hand is a fool," he mused. "I would not battle for you now because you would upset my peaceful household." He leaned forward slightly, his impressive shoulders hunched. "But if I had you, I would never let you go!"

Carcajou left a vacuum when he took his leave, but Otter soon came to keep me company. I have no idea where he watched and waited, but he always knew when I was alone. I was grateful for his presence. Correctly perceiving my mood, he insisted on a writing lesson and soon had me charmed out of my depression. He wrote almost as well as Cut, though his vocabulary was not as sound. We finished the evening reading aloud from Poe.

When Otter came from the bathing room not yet in his loincloth, I came near to calling him to me. I knew he would have come, but there was something wrong with pressing a man's desire on a youngster only fifteen. Of course, his body was not that of a child. His shoulders were even wider than last year; his hips lean but muscled. The crown of dark hair at his groin had grown in thick and luxurious.

The Good Lord's countenance haunted my dreams that night, thunderously denouncing my lascivious thoughts of Otter. In a bargain for peace, I promised never to touch another except in an act of love, not lust – a promise that would be sorely stretched in the future.

CHAPTER 15

I drew breath easier once the summer solstice and the Sun Dance Ceremony passed. Dances were dangerous as the blood tended to run high, and the greatest ritual of all was this annual ceremony where the White Buffalo Pipe excited a grand passion among the tribesmen.

One day, Otter broke into my musing by drawing me to the porch to point out a black, lowering cloud to the south across the river. The roiling monster dragged a thick, dirty tail that sucked up dirt and brush and grasses. Evil in its purest physical form!

"Tornado!" I hissed.

"*Iya* left the water," Otter said quietly. "And *Wakinyan* went after him. They fight awful battles, and it is humans and animals who pay."

Iya, I knew, was a giant, the son of *Inyan*, the First Being, and *Unk*, the Mother of Contention. The Thunder-being, *Wakinyan*, who brought rains and cleansed the earth, was the mate of *Inyan* and jealous of this illicit offspring. Unable to touch the giant so long as he remained in water, she sought to destroy him whenever he came ashore. But inevitably, *Iya* escaped the vengeful supernatural and fled back into the depths. That is why tornadoes follow rivers.

The dogs yipped and howled and buried their snouts between nervous paws as the twister harried the plains beyond the Yanube with an earth-shaking roar. We watched warily, poised to seek a fraidy-hole in the cavern if the thing turned our way. But it slowly meandered to the southeast, away from both the Mead and the *tiospaye*. Even from this distance, Otter and I felt the pull of the hydra. From time to time, the devil-wind lifted its foul funnel like a monstrous black buffalo wolf raising its leg to piss upon the plains. Occasionally, snaky tendrils dipped to the left or the right. Eventually, the beast disappeared into the distance. Then the rains came, and Otter turned inside the house to burn cedar as he had been taught to do during thunderstorms.

One morning, the dogs barked with the kind of excitement that told me a friend was coming, probably in some haste. Otter muttered that it was Bear Claw.

"Butterfly! Stolen!" the big man shouted before turning his mount back toward the encampment. Otter and I were only minutes behind him.

A group of women had gone to pick wild flowers, but when they were ready to return, Butterfly was nowhere to be found. At first, they called out, believing she might have fallen asleep. When that brought no results, they searched frantically, fearful she may have been struck by one of the serpents that sometimes sheltered in the shade of the bushes.

They found the basket with her blossoms scattered and crushed. Signs told of a fierce struggle and two men making off with her on horseback toward the north.

Cut and I, trailed by a dozen warriors, followed the sign northward. Belatedly, the fugitives devoted some effort to covering their tracks, but Cut did not hesitate. He made straight for one of those strange islands found on the plains, an isolated pine-shrouded knoll. Within minutes we broke the trail of Butterfly's abductors and found her abandoned and unconscious in a sheltered glade. I examined her quickly.

"No broken bones. She's been beaten and probably ... assaulted," I added in a low voice. "She will live, Cut."

He turned to his men. "Take her to her mother. Teacher, come with me."

Others in the party clamored to accompany us, but these rapists were obviously Sioux, and to approach a camp with a large armed party might provoke something the Yanube could not handle. So with no warriors in attendance, Cut and I tracked the culprits straight into one of the encampments. Cut seemed to know some of the *tiospaye*, but I recognized only one – Stone Knife, who apparently led this band.

"Welcome, Cut Hand. Teacher. Will you take food and drink with us?"

"Thank you, "Cut replied, "but we are on a mission and lack the time to be courteous. Forgive us for that. Two men stole and raped my sister. We trailed them to this encampment. This is not an act of friendship between kinsmen, Stone Knife. This is a crime, and the criminals must be punished."

Stone Knife pursed his lips thoughtfully. "Are you certain this was not a romance, a thing between hot-blooded youth?"

"She was forcibly removed. We found where she escaped her captors once and was retaken. They left her on Elk Mound, unconscious and bleeding. The cowards ran straight to this fire."

"Rest a moment, Cut Hand. Wait before my lodge. My wife will give you water to cool your thirst. I must talk with some of my people."

Outwardly calm, Cut agreed, but the force of his grip on the water cup revealed the depth of his rage. My own condition was not much different except I was not so stolid as to conceal it. We sat for at least two glasses, and most hourglasses in these parts measured by the half-hour. At last Stone Knife and several others came to sit opposite us.

"Cut Hand, it pains me your fireside has been wronged by our own. Things are not good with us. Too many strangers claiming kinship are among us. It was two of these Santee who committed this crime. They have been banished from this *tiospaye* and no longer enjoy our protection. Again, I am sorry for your troubles."

With that, the men stood and walked away. The *tiospaye*'s council had rendered the harshest possible penalty, freeing us to pursue individual justice.

"Come on!" Cut said, performing that miraculous maneuver that took him from a seat to a standing position. We recovered our ponies, waved our thanks to the important men of the band, and headed out to locate the trail of the two fugitives. Out of the corner of my eye, I saw Stone Knife wave to the east.

"This way!" I cried, bringing Long Wind sharply right. Cut followed without question. Before long we crossed the trail of two ponies stretched out in headlong flight.

Too smart to rush after them, Cut let the men wear out their mounts. We adopted a trot both Arrow and Long could maintain all day. Only when tracks indicated the ponies ahead of us had slowed, did he urge Arrow into a gallop. *Wi,* the sun, burned the blue from the sky and left it liverish, but we pushed ahead. We crossed a freshet and paused for a drink and to allow the animals to blow, reasoning the men ahead of us had done the same. During this respite, Cut eyed the trail in the grass on the other side of the rill with suspicion. He rose and walked a short distance.

"They doubled back," he said upon his return. "They went up or down this creek. It is not so large as to hide the tracks of two ponies. You walk upstream, I'll go down."

The two had split up. I trailed the one who fled north. My quarry kept to the water for a league before breaking east again. I tracked him into the darkness of night as long as I dared and then made a cold camp.

At mid-morning the next day, the apples in front of me were growing fresher. By high sun, I raised a horseman in the distance. Of course, he could see me, as well. He urged his pony into a fast run which gained him little. Long kept a steady lope, and by the time the man's pony was winded, my mount still had a great deal left. Abruptly, the brave wheeled and took a stand. The broken, discordant tones of his death chant came across the distance. He would run no more.

I was near enough to see the shock on his face as he realized it was a white man who came for him. He threw up his rifle and wasted a ball; it did not even pass close enough to hear. He began the cumbersome effort of reloading until he realized I was too close. Dropping the weapon, he seized his tomahawk. I paid him the honor of shooting him from the saddle; an honor because I was not about to engage in hand-to-hand combat with a fully-grown Sioux warrior. I respected their abilities too much for that.

When I reached him, I was dismayed to discover how young he was, likely only a few years older than Lone Eagle. Angered and saddened by the thoughtless cruelty of this youth and his companion, which resulted in the brutal rape of a young woman and the death of one or both of them, I sat beside his body and fought my emotions. What a waste of a life – of lives, probably. If only these people understood how little they could afford such losses. If only they could see what rolled across the vast prairie toward them.

At length, I stirred and considered the idea of taking his scalp to prove Butterfly had been avenged. Instead, putting that ghoulish idea aside, I gathered his pony, his weapons, and something he would never part with while he lived, the small medicine bag concealed in his breechcloth. There were not enough rocks to cover him, so I rolled his lifeless body into a depression and hacked clumps of dirt with his hatchet to make a thin grave covering. It would not protect him from animals, but it was the best I could do.

Then I retraced my steps, allowing Long to pick his own gait. Near sundown the next evening, I approached the small creek I had crossed earlier and spotted Cut heading north trailing a strange pony behind him. He lifted a medicine bag, and I responded in kind. Butterfly's rapists had paid for their crime.

We snared a hare and roasted it over an open fire while our ponies grazed and rested. The freshet pooled shallowly amidst a scraggly grove of locusts, so we stripped, each checking the other's nakedness to see if it was as remembered, and then we sat in the water to soak away the day's poisons.

"I fear you are too far-sighted," Cut observed with a sigh as he leaned against the bank and settled himself more comfortably in the pool.

"How so?"

"Many of the things you have foretold have taken place." That cried out for no answer, so we sat in silence until he spoke again. "And the buffalo, too?" he asked his perennial question in a low, half-believing voice.

"Even the buffalo," I rendered my stock response. "If I could change it by denying it, I would do so."

"I know, my friend. I know."

We talked about our lives and the events beginning to shake this beautiful land, one of which had just seen its culmination. We spoke of everything except our personal desires. When I lay beside him in my blankets that night, my erection was painful; I wager his was no less urgent.

We made the village the following day. After bestowing the criminals' weapons as gifts, Cut stood in view of all who were assembled and scornfully dropped the two medicine bags into a fire.

Butterfly lay inside Bright Dove's lodge wrapped in a thin blanket even though the evening was not yet cool. Her bruised and battered face dispelled some of the regret I harbored over the death of the Santee; her broken spirit erased the balance.

"She has been asking for both of you," Bright Dove said quietly. "She will be all right physically, Cut Hand. It is her spirit that needs mending." The woman laid a hand on her son's arm. "Is it finished? Truly?" He nodded. She was, of course, asking if there would be recriminations from the Sioux.

Strangely, Butterfly drew as much comfort from me as from her brother, and since Cut had demands upon his time, it fell to me to console her. She slowly came out of whatever dark place her mind had gone to hide from the horror. A *senight* passed before I heard her laugh for the first time since the rape. It was a feeble effort, but it was something. That marked a watershed. The young women who visited her now returned to their true selves, laughing and giggling and gossiping shamelessly.

Morning Mist often left the infant, Dog Fox, with us, presumably to lift her sister-in-law's spirit, but I sometimes could not escape the thought it was to free Morning Mist of caring for the babe. That judgment was likely pure spite on my part because it was clear Cut's wife loved her child.

Butterfly's face was still marked by dark bruises when she ventured outside on my arm. We walked to the river where she sat watching the fast-moving stream. Some of the young men stopped to engage her in conversation, but she responded poorly, and we spent most of our time strolling alone. Her body had recovered its strength, but her mind was still fragile.

Otter's face expressed relief when I finally returned to Teacher's Mead, and the youth promptly took off on business of his own. He had earned the respite. Otter had remained at the house while I slept in the bachelor's tipi during the girl's recovery.

The morning after my return, my second swain appeared. This one was my own age or greater, someone I knew vaguely. He was pleasing to the eye and vigorous in his approach, but I did nothing to encourage him. He was patient, showing up at my door every day for a week, ignoring Otter who was there all the time and Lone Eagle, an occasional visitor. Both of the boys got a laugh out of my discomfort. The last time he came, he left in evident confusion because Butterfly had stopped by the Mead for a visit, and he walked in as I was holding her in my arms to nurse her through a weak moment.

His disillusionment must have been great. When I escorted Butterfly back to the village, word had spread we were suitors. Cut emerged from his lodge with an eager look on his face. When the sly questions began, I looked at Butterfly, who returned my gaze, and I did not bother to correct false impressions. I would whisper in Cut's ear later, but in the meantime any protection against unwanted romantics was welcome.

Mark Wildyr

I never held that private conversation with her brother. She seemed favorable to the idea of a relationship, and it did not discomfit me unduly. A naturally happy woman, she began to bloom, leaving behind all visible signs of her assault. We even exchanged shy kisses and warm embraces.

Word came that the buffalo had been sighted, and the village moved to replenish its larder. Though reduced, the great beasts' numbers were sufficient to meet the Yanube's needs – this year. To further confound matters, a party of Pipe Stem conducted its hunt within sight of our own. I was reminded of my unsettling conversation with Cut as we returned from hunting the two Santee.

As soon as the meat was put away, the hides prepared, and all other usable parts distributed, I cleaned myself carefully, had a long talk with Otter, and went to look up Cut Hand. He was taking his rest in front of his lodge.

"Cut Hand, I would marry your sister, if she will have me."

"She will have you, old friend."

"I can offer ten ponies and three new percussion rifles."

"Is she worth all that?" he laughed, abandoning the hard bargaining usual in such an event.

"More, dammit! I'll give twelve ponies, but that's my limit!"

He roared with laughter. "If I say eight, will you increase it to fourteen? Agreed, William Joseph Strobaw. If she will have you, it is done."

I frowned. "I … I thought you said she would."

"She will. She will. Go ask her now."

I proposed to Butterfly, sister of Cut Hand, Headman of the Yanube, on the riverbank in the full view and hearing of a dozen giggling, gesturing women. I was not so skilled as to attempt the love flute, but she did not seem to mind. She blushed prettily and said yes.

# # # # #

Cut got as drunk following my wedding as I did at his, but for different reasons. Before Butterfly and I escaped to Teacher's Mead, I was scandalized to find Otter as inebriated as the rest of them … and him only fifteen!

They were not too intoxicated to cause mischief. The guard dogs drove us to distraction because of drunken Indians skulking

183

around the premises. We endured endless whoops and hollers and falsetto shrieks of ecstasy. Recollecting the not-so-secret entrance, I placed heavy items on top of the trap and closed the door to the bathing room to bar Otter and Lone Eagle from spying on us. Since they had watched me bugger an army lieutenant, the two rascals would not be averse to seeing how I did with a woman!

But when I lay shyly at her side, Butterfly began shivering uncontrollably. I caught her to my breast, uttering soothing sounds. She froze against me until I assured her I could wait until she was ready.

"What if I am never ready?" she cried in anguish. "I love you Billy, I really do. I have since Cut Hand brought you to us. I was jealous of him for a long time. I've thought about doing it with you lots of times. But now –"

"What those men did to you is too fresh. When we make love, Butterfly, it will be right for both of us. I can wait."

"But you want to, I can feel it. Your penis is big and hard!"

"I can wait," I said again. And it was true. My pipe had reacted, but the will behind the act was weak. I could have performed but was frankly relieved I need not, at least this night. "Butterfly, this will be between us and no one else."

"Yes, my husband," she said in a small voice.

She kissed me the next morning, but scrambled out of bed when I came awake. We settled immediately into a pleasant routine. It was nice having a woman to cook. Butterfly revealed me as a coxcomb, a mere superficial pretender to the culinary arts. She mortified meat vigorously so even the toughest parts became tender morsels. She demanded I construct a hastener, a metal reflector, which cooked the dishes more evenly than I ever imagined. Both of these simple things, and a host of others she revealed, had been beyond my ken.

After a week, she invited Otter back to his bunk on the other side of the double house. He took two more days to show up out of politeness.

It was another phase of the moon before we made love. I had regularly kissed and touched her gently in private places seeking to ease her fears. One night, when I moved away, she caught me back to her. I slowly undressed her, and even more slowly tasted her silken breasts and belly. Her mons rose subtly, covered by thick, velvety hair.

She made no protest when I bared my flesh; indeed, her small fingers closed around me curiously, mentally measuring me against her dead husband, I'm sure. She trembled as I entered her, though I knew not if it was fear or excitement. I thrust gently until she rose up to meet me. I grew more frantic; she was a match for me. Before I erupted, she had her own series of small explosions. Finished, I hovered above her and gently wiped the sweat from her forehead.

"It was as I thought it would be, husband," she murmured.

"It wasn't too frightening for you?"

"No. I understand you are not like those other men. You only want to love, not to hurt. I am healed of that fear now."

"Good. I love you, Butterfly."

"Was I –" she fumbled. I suspected she wanted to know if she was as good for me as her brother, but had not the way of asking.

"I took much pleasure in it." In that statement, I did not lie, nor did I answer her implied question. No one would ever be as good as Cut Hand.

By the middle of the morning, I knew something was terribly wrong. She was sharp to Otter once, but apologized immediately. Well able to read storm warnings, the youth nodded his acceptance and disappeared. It was past the middle of the day before she turned to face me, tears in her eyes. "I deceived you."

"How so?" I asked, startled. At least whatever was bothering her would now come out in the open.

"I am with child!" she blurted. "I knew it when I took you to bed last night."

"That is no surprising estate, Butterfly. You are a lively young woman, and those were vigorous men who took you against your will. Nor is it of consequence so long as you took me because you care for me. It is natural to seek comfort in times of stress. But let me tell you one thing, Butterfly Strobaw, and you had best hear me on this. When that child arrives, I will love him and treat him as if we conceived him together last night." She clutched at me and cried tears of relief. Then I acted the typical husband. "And don't you ever suffer something like that alone again! I am your husband! You tell me your cares before they become worries."

"Can we speak of another thing?" I grew wary, but consented. I am certain she could sense the reluctance through the tensing of my shoulders. "All agree this thing between you and Cut Hand was extraordinary. Do you love him yet?"

"As deeply as ever, Butterfly. But Morning Mist and I were wearing on him. In the end, we would have destroyed him. She could not leave because she ensured he would lead the band. And with his leadership, they have the best chance of survival."

"He still loves you, too," she murmured against my chest. "Sometimes I still get jealous. So does Morning Mist," she added in a tone somewhere between a swipe and a stricture.

"No need. We have vowed never to lie with one another again. On the return from hunting the Sioux, we bathed together and slept without touching."

Otter came back the next evening. I missed the little dickens when he was not around. Little! Hah! He was a lithe fifteen edging toward six English feet, and not yet finished growing. The arrogance that shrouded Lone Eagle at this age was missing. Otter was a strange youngster. He showed none of the aggression of the born warrior, but he had been on horse raids and displayed unquestioned bravery in difficult situations. Lone Eagle tended to treat him as a younger brother, but when Otter had his fill, Lone Eagle knew better than to push. He might be bigger and stronger than Otter, but the older youth understood the dogged determination hiding beneath the boy's placid exterior. And frankly, Otter was brighter than any of them. He read, wrote, and spoke English better than most fifteen-year-old American schoolboys, and had shown considerable skill at arithmetic and the basic sciences. He liked to learn.

#####

I was probably not the enthusiastic lover Butterfly had a right to expect. I flanked her on a regular basis, but without the joyful spontaneity of the lovemaking Cut and I had shared. Yet she seemed satisfied, and I came to love her in a true sense. I treasured her presence and her company, and even her occasional fits of anger. While this was comfortable for both of us, that is all it was, the placid love of older folk, not the passion of people our true ages.

Nonetheless, I recall those as happy days. The homestead prospered. With Butterfly taking efficient care of the inside of the house, Otter and I tended the animals and the garden. In fact, we extended our planting area to the size of a true merestead.

Butterfly was quick with child the day she went down river with some of the women to dig sassafras roots shortly before the *tiospaye*'s winter move. Otter and I were picking some vine vegetables when he stood and motioned to the east with his chin. With growing alarm, we watched a rider thunder recklessly toward us.

Otter, quicker than I, ran for our horses while I stood frozen by an unnamed fear. Buffalo Shoulder was the herald this time. Butterfly was hurt. I ran for my bag of medicines and leapt to Long's back from the porch. The three of us rode through the village at breakneck speed. My heart plummeted at the snarl of people gathered south of the campground. There was a stillness about them I did not like.

Throwing myself from my pony, I stumbled, regained my feet, and rushed forward. The crowd opened before me. Cut sat splayed on the ground with a limp Butterfly cradled in his arms. A large, headless rattlesnake lay a few feet away. With a moan, I fell before them and took her from her brother. She was dead. The creature that killed her was immense, a grandfather snake missing his rattlers and filled with venom to spare for a small woman like Butterfly.

Cut looked at me with pain-filled eyes. "It struck her in the neck. There was nothing anyone could do, Billy. Not even you. You couldn't have saved her even if you had been here. She went too quickly."

"We'll never know, will we?" I cried hoarsely.

The child was gone as well, of course. Too small for life on its own, it died when Butterfly's heart froze from the poison. I carried my wife in my arms all the way to the campground, staggering drunkenly the last hundred paces. I laid her before her mother's tipi on soft, silk grass blankets. The frozen mask of her agony had softened, but one would never mistake her stillness for slumber. With a great shudder, I wondered if this was the retribution of Almighty God for my sins. But why take two innocent lives to punish me? And she was innocent. She never had an impure thought in her life. Earthy, yes. Given to moments of genuine anger, at times. Yet, spite and hate and deceit were not her way. There was no venom in her except that injected by the fangs of the serpent.

I insisted on a white man's burial at the Mead and chose a spot with good drainage to the west of the house. The entire village came to watch the ritual of laying away a loved one. I prowled the plains for days afterward until I found a fitting free stone. Lone Eagle and Otter helped me lift it into the buckboard. I spent two days engraving her epitaph.

Butterfly Strobaw, Daughter of the Yanube
and Beloved Wife of William Joseph Strobaw,
Lies Here Together With Her Unborn Child.
1815-1836
May God Shine His Face Upon Her.

CHAPTER 16

Otter wanted to remain with me when the *tiospaye* moved to winter quarters, but he was needed to drive the Conestoga. The boy had been so proud of making the four big blacks do his bidding he neglected to consider the consequences of being the only Yanube capable of doing so – to say nothing of seeing to the care of the beasts and the repair of the prairie schooner, itself.

I spent the first few days after the band crossed the river constructing a sturdy fence around Butterfly's grave from my store of precious planking. I made the plot middling big since someday I would lie there. Perhaps Otter as well.

That done, I became a glazier, installing the glass quarrels brought from Yawktown last spring. I had guessed well so the panes fit snugly, although some of the frames required a bit of chiseling. Almost immediately, the house grew warmer while the fireplace's greed for wood abated.

The day after I finished, West made a moderate fuss over a heavily bundled figure standing at the fence surrounding Butterfly's grave. Angered by the morbid interest of a stranger, I burst out of the house absent either coat or weapon and stomped across the rapidly freezing ground to discover the stranger was Carcajou. I should have taken my cue from the dog who failed to put up a significant objection.

"Teacher," he greeted me solemnly. "I see you have found new grief."

"Butterfly, my wife," I said. I assumed he knew of my wedding, as he seemed to know much of the happenings at Teacher's Mead.

"So I heard. I came to offer my sorrow to bolster your own."

"Thank you. Can you stand some coffee?" I asked, shivering.

"Ugh," he made a face. "But you need some. This is not a day for shirtsleeves. Here," he threw out an arm and enfolded me in his buffalo robe. "Hah! There was a time when such an embrace would have inflamed me. Well, perhaps there is something of it left. When I get back to my fire, I will give my Win-tay a tumble and think about you."

He glanced around the interior of the cabin curiously. "We are moving tomorrow. We waited longer than usual because one of our women was ailing, so now we must hurry." He grimaced over his cup of coffee and added an ungodly amount of sugar. "Uhm. Better," he announced. "I came because I heard of your trouble. That one," he inclined his head toward the graveyard, "had great misfortune in her life. The whole countryside admires how you and Cut Hand faced the Sioux in their own camp and tracked down her rapists. Then to find happiness with you only to have her life snatched away."

"Thank you for your thoughts. Cut Hand will appreciate them, as well."

"I do not speak them for him. I speak them for my friend, Bil-lee." He paused a moment for a taste of his coffeed sugar. "Have you talked to any of the army men since they were here at snow melt?"

"No, I've spoken to no one."

"I traveled to the eastern fort this summer, the one they call Ramson. This war with the Mex-i-cans, did not take place. The white men in that place they call Tex-as fought them off without help from the American army."

"I would never have guessed it."

He sipped again. There was more to come. "They say this big officer at Ft. Yanube, this Ma-jor, is being sent away. The new chief at Ft. Yanube will be the one with two bars."

"Captain Jamieson? But he's too inexperienced for a command like that!"

"It is true, Bil-lee. He will get the yellow leaf on his shoulder."

"Who will take his place?"

"Someone with a strange name like Sniff."

"Smith?" I was dismayed. "But he's an incompetent!" My God! James would be under his command.

"This is not good news?" Carcajou frowned.

"No, it is not. Major Wallston is a seasoned officer. Captain Jamieson is a decent man, but doesn't have the depth … the experience. Smith is a bigot of the worst stripe, if I am any judge. He will now be in charge of the patrols, and I don't trust his judgment."

"Then we must be careful."

"Yes. May I ask a favor?" His expression told me he did not like what I was going to ask. "Cut Hand should know of this. If I write him a letter, can you see it is delivered before the snowfall comes?"

He made no reply for a minute. "I will do this because you have shared information gathered for the Yanube with the Pipe Stem. Do not ask it often."

When I placed the note to Cut in Carcajou's hand, he turned it over thoughtfully. "Cut Hand can understand what you wish to tell him from this scratching?"

"He learned to read and write a long time ago. I can teach you, as well. It would be good to know such things when dealing with the white man."

"Prolonged exposure to you, Bil-lee, might wear out the bum of my Win-tay." At the door, he turned serious again. "I always remember what you tell me, Teacher, and many of your predictions are beginning to reveal themselves. For the first time in my life, the Pipe Stem took their buffalo within sight of the Yanube. And the Sioux were not far removed. The pressure on the land is growing. My cousins, the Lakota, tell of many kinsmen coming from back east confirming things you explained to us. I am sorry you are such a prophet because what you see in the future is not to our advantage."

"Carcajou, if I could prevent it, I would."

"This I believe. Goodbye, my friend. Your message will be delivered."

# # # # #

The first norther, a blue blizzard to match my mood, breached my protective hillocks to seize the Mead in its grip, and I wintered alone for the first time. Never had a season seemed so long. I rapidly exhausted the diversion of reading. The storms came fast and furious, and I wore a fresh trail through the snow every day to talk to the livestock and check on their condition. I took to mucking out the barn daily although the snow was too deep to carry the waste far, so I spread it over the garden area, hoping the thing would not be overdone and burn up the crops next year.

Threshing was cold weather work, so I dragged out my grains and took up a wooden flail until sweat poured from me despite the cold. I brought all of the dogs inside for comfort, but they were not broken to the indoors and created such a mess that I booted them all out except for House. He had a modicum of manners, and I needed company.

The full weight of the season had not yet descended before I was driven outside by sheer boredom. Bearing a rifle and with the shotgun strapped to my back, I donned rackets to escape four walls and beavered down, setting traps liberally and harvesting an abundance of prime blue pelts.

Chess and checkers played with oneself leave something lacking. I held solitary conversations, which I found quite witty and enlightening. In truth, some of my personal philosophy found voice during that long winter. I began a journal, writing down with the utmost honesty what happened to me on this sojourn through life, my actions, my thoughts, my fears, my emotions – my *tun* as Cut would say. Perhaps someday some soul may be more enlightened about men with different tastes because of it.

The wolves became almost a pleasant diversion. I spent many a day and night tracking them, daring their ambush and almost falling prey to it more than once. West, my faithful guardian of the barn and the graveyard grew bolder than was wise and paid with his life. The leader of the wolf pack fell to my anger in recompense. The feral beasts were not so aggressive after his loss.

Nights were worse than days as my thoughts were free to roam. I missed Butterfly bitterly. Cut weighed heavily on my mind, his masterful body and wonderful intellect and joyful spirit so real I could almost reach out and touch him. Once or twice I pictured him lying with me while I stroked my hungry shaft until it spewed loads of sperm into the air. At other times James leapt to mind, so different from Cut, yet so giving of his love.

The remainder of the winter was spent training House to assume the responsibility for the west side of the clearing. He was too old by this time to rename, so we now had South on the south, East on the east, North on the north, and House on the west, which offended my sense of logic.

The thaw came without my realizing it. One day, I observed a sun dog, one of those pale, rainbow-like spots between clouds that often herald impending changes in the weather, and the next morning woke to the sound of dripping water. After assuring that my spigots had not failed in the bathing room, I opened the door stark naked and observed icicles slowly disappearing from the eaves. That dripping sound was snow dissolving from my roof. Of course, the warmth of the house sped the process, but even the snow load on the trees was not so great, and the crick had shed its skim of ice, running free and clear.

Suddenly realizing I had become water-shy, I scrubbed a winter's worth of dirt and dried sweat from my body and set to work scraping off a lengthy beard, seriously considering adopting a moustache. Yet I admired the clean, clear features of the Yanube men so much that I ruthlessly cut the hairs from my face. Would that I could accomplish this task as they did, with an Indian razor, two shells used for plucking or, more recently, the metal tweezers I brought from Yawktown. These tools were now highly prized trade items. Then I opened the house to the cold and aired out the close, musty odor of winter.

My joy was unwarranted; it would be weeks before the People returned. But I could at least see an end to my stark isolation. The snows had been abundant that winter, so the river flowed deep and angry, well beyond its normal run. I took to roving the northern bank anxious for some sign the abatement was underway, but I had my field turned and ready for planting ere a single Yanube scout appeared on the opposite bank to let me know by signing that all was well with the band.

A few days later, I traveled a distance to the southeast to check a good walking place where the stream was wide and shallow and lined with a shelf of hard rock. Even there the water was too swift for safe passage. As I tested the current with a few steps into the river, Long swung his head, ears rotating wildly. Immediately, I brought him around. Some fifty yards away stood a party of six mounted Indians. Stone Knife lifted his hand to show it was empty and urged his pony forward.

"Hau, Teacher," he greeted me. "I see you have survived the winter."

"And you, too, my friend. How goes the hunting?"

"Too many two-leggeds; too few four-leggeds," he grumbled. "But we do not hunt. We were on our way to see you."

"Me? How can I help?"

"There is trouble. Your words as they have been repeated to me have always counseled peace. Because of the respect you have earned, I heeded those words. Now, my heart is stirred to anger. As once you and Cut Hand came to me, I now come to you."

"Tell me what has happened."

193

"Soldiers followed three hunters to my fire saying they tracked men who killed a settler family close to the fort. They brought a white man who was there when the attack took place. I allowed them into my village, believing they came honorably. This white man claimed the three returning hunters were the killers. But none had been absent from camp long enough to travel that far, Teacher. Mine was a squaw camp since most of the men were away hunting, and I watched like a helpless woman while the soldiers took those three men away to Ft. Ramson. One was my son."

"I have no influence at that fort, Stone Knife, but I will go there and argue for them. Have your scouts found any trace of the men the army tracked?"

"No. If there was a trail, the soldiers' passing covered it."

"Can you find where they might have eluded the troops?"

He looked at me squarely, a rare thing among these people. "There is no such sign."

I nodded toward the party. "Are these five men of standing in your band?"

"Yes, they are of my council."

"Ask each to come to me in turn to tell me what he saw with his own eyes. That way I will have testimony to present to the soldiers."

# # # # #

I departed the Mead armed, provisioned, and carrying a portion of my gold coins. The buckboard held all of the furs taken that winter. Two of Stone Knife's Lakota helped me ford the river using rawhide ropes to secure the wagon from the current. They then shadowed me on my hundred-mile trip.

A town similar to Yawktown had grown up around the military post. First, I found the fur trader and spent far too long dickering over the price of my peltry to establish my bona fides. The wagon, loaded with provisions for my return, was housed in the livery stable. I opened an account at the bank, depositing a few gold coins after reaching the firm understanding any withdrawal would be in like specie.

I ate at a restaurant, took a room at an inn, and paid a likely-looking youngster to carry a written message to the fort commandant asking to see him the next morning. He returned with a note that Major

Wallston would receive me at ten on the morrow. That was a pleasant surprise and a stroke of luck. Major Wallston knew me from Fort Yanube; therefore, I need not waste precious time proving I was no feather merchant.

The Major was downright pleased to greet me. His office in this post seemed a little larger, but his staff was made up of tin soldiers, green Point officers eager to prove their mettle. Wallston appeared embarrassed by their enthusiasm.

While I am no pettifogger trained in the law, I presented Stone Knife's case calmly and logically. The Major questioned the lieutenant who led the platoon in pursuit of the miscreants, and I was dismayed at the youth and inexperience of the man. As questioning continued, it became apparent the platoon was as unseasoned as he. Its sergeant had recently been transferred from a post in New York State.

The Major sent for the civilian who identified the three Sioux, but he was nowhere to be found. It required two days to locate the man pilfering the homestead that had been attacked. When the troops came upon him, he and another man were digging holes around the burned barn. By the end of my fourth day at Ramson, Major Wallston knew the truth.

These two pimps had heard rumors of gold hidden on the homestead of this unfortunate family. They murdered the farmer, his wife and fry, torched the buildings, and raised an alarm at the fort, claiming an Indian attack. One of the whoresons, acting as a volunteer scout, led a troop of dragoons up a well used trace until he chanced upon the trail of a hunting party that took him right into Stone Knife's camp. The young officer who fell for the hoax did not know how lucky he was to still be wearing his hair. The Major explained it to him in great detail.

Three relieved young men strode out of the fort's gaol still cloaked in the impressive dignity of this tribe of mighty warriors. Two of them rode in the back of the buckboard; the third took his place beside me on the driver's bench. I came to understand before the trip was out this stern-faced man was Stone Knife's son. The trio was solemn and reserved until we camped the first night beside an old buffalo lick. Then youth and enthusiasm at being free surfaced, and they became happy youngsters, joking with one another, tickling about things that happened during their confinement.

Stone Knife met us a day's journey from his camp; his relief at recovering his young men almost cracked his stolid demeanor. He thanked me profusely and advised that the Yanube would arrive at the river on the morrow.

With this news, I hurried home to prepare for my people's return. My people! They were that in every sense of the word. These were my family, my friends, and my foundation upon this earth.

Anticipating the crossing Cut would choose, I awaited the appearance of the first scouts. A lone warrior splashed across the still swollen walk and greeted me with a great shout. It took a second to realize it was Lone Eagle. The youth had sprouted another inch and filled out to the proportions of a fully-grown man. I wondered if he had taken a wife and asked about the matter.

"No," he replied uneasily. There was a tale to be told there, I surmised. "But it is time I start thinking about it," he went on. "A man needs a good wife."

My joy was unbounded when I raised Cut Hand's tall form astride Arrow. Because the water was still high, Cut stationed warriors along the walk to help the young and the old across. As the Conestoga hove into view, he caused ropes to be affixed to the wagon against the eventuality it might slide downstream. I took inordinate pleasure and pride in Otter's skill in handling the contraption. All made the crossing without event.

The site of the summer camp was about two leagues from Teacher's Mead. There was no time for visiting with friends until the village was set up. Hunting parties went out immediately. The horse herd was driven to a broad bench above the river where herdsmen gentled them until the beasts knew they were home. The mares were inspected to see if any were ready to drop colts prematurely. Small injuries were looked to. The People's horses were well tended.

The Conestoga needed some tightening of bolts and minor repairs, but Otter was already working on those. He was taller, maybe even a spit broader through the shoulders, but the face was still that of the man-child I held dear. He greeted me solemnly, breaking into an uncontrollable smile when I complemented him on the condition of the horses and the care he was giving the wagon. He indicated he would be home tomorrow night.

Home! Teacher's Mead was unquestionably his home. No child in this band was without family, but Otter came as close as any. His mother and father had crossed the divide long before I came to live among them. Likely, Otter looked upon me as this closest kin. He had spent most of his time with me since I met him on the south side of the Yanube with Bear Paw and Lone Eagle and the others five years back in the spring of '32.

By nightfall, things had settled down, so conversation was possible. Cut sent for me to take my customary place on the blanket at his right and asked about the news I sent in my letter. He was relieved to learn of Major Wallston's posting to Ft. Ramson, and intrigued by my successful representation of Stone Knife. As did I, he considered this full payment of the debt we had incurred to the Lakota.

Later, in private, Cut resolved the mystery of Lone Eagle's disquiet over the question of a wife. The young man had been caught dallying with a girl and had to ease her father's sense of outrage with three ponies. Now the youth was virtually impoverished.

The young warrior was sitting on my porch, impatient for my arrival, when I finally reached the Mead. I bit back a teasing remark about his recent encounter. Still, he took offense.

"So you think it's funny?" he demanded as I lit a lamp in the fronting room.

"Am I laughing?"

"On the inside you are, and some of it leaked out onto your mouth. She's the one who wanted it. Felt me up until I couldn't stand it any more! I didn't even get it in her. They found us before I even got it in!" He was offended he had to pay for something he hadn't enjoyed.

"You're not the first young man in that condition."

"I had to give up all my ponies! What am I going to do? Cut Hand says not to raid for horses any more. I'll never get enough animals to pay for a bride. I'm ruined! All I've got left is my war horse." He meant his riding pony.

Recalling something I'd heard while at Yawktown a year back, I told him of a herd of feral horses south of the Little Island Mountains.

"I'll go tomorrow! I'll come back rich!"

"You'll come back with a lot of work ahead of you. Those horses are wild. They won't be worth much until you break them."

Ever the conniver, he came up with an answer. "I'll trade two for one. Two wild horses for a riding pony."

"Sounds good, if you can catch enough horses and find enough dunces."

"I will," he announced confidently. "Tried to get the old man to take my furs, but he wanted horses."

Upon learning he had a store of furs, I proposed we travel to Yawktown for supplies and then find the herd ourselves, adding, "You can have all we capture. I will leave Otter to tend the Mead"

"You would do that for me?" Lone Eagle eyed me a minute. "Yawktown. Hah! You just want to see that yellow-haired officer again. We watched you fuck him, you know. Otter and me. We watched from the bathing room."

"It's 'Otter and I.' I hope you got an eyeful."

"I know your pipe's bigger than his. He didn't act like a Wintay." He grinned and added. "Except when his head bobbed up and down on your staff, and when you put it up him. Course, you don't act like one either, but you are. Cut Hand really used to throw it to you. We listened at the door."

"Don't be crude, Lone Eagle. What I am is my business."

# # # # #

Halfway to Yawktown, we came across a patrol led by my friend. James had no news of import except his unhappiness over the new command at Ft. Yanube. He respected Major Jamieson but loathed and distrusted his new superior, Captain Smith, all of which he confided as we stood well apart from his troop. In this we agreed, although Jamieson did not stand quite so high in my estimation as in his.

Lone Eagle asked a hundred frivolous questions after the troop passed. Did it hurt putting your thing up that? Didn't it squeeze too much? Did it get dirty? Did my thing have tooth marks? What did I like best? When I had my fill, I kicked Long into a trot to shut him up, but Lone Eagle was having too much fun. His rich baritone rang over the countryside as he continued the tickling banter.

Caleb Brown probably added a dollar's value to the total of Lone Eagle's packet because I brought him there. The youth went around the store gaping like a country yokel, which in a way he was, but rediscovered his arrogant disdain before long. He insisted on wandering the town and chanced upon the gun shop. Lone Eagle must have handled every weapon in the place before bargaining for a better rifle and a scattergun such as both Cut and I owned. He ended up settling for a new repeater. After that, we bought ropes for the making of a corral and departed civilization to take up our hunt.

Once we crossed the Yanube on the bridge and headed south, the western edge of the Little Island range appeared in the distance. The recent snowmelt had succored the grass so that it brushed our ponies' bellies as we abandoned the rough road and cut cross-country. The horizon stretched to eternity. Only the hungry raptors – hawks and eagles – soaring the blue sky above in search of prey reminded us that despite the deceptive serenity, the desperate, deadly game of life went on unabated.

We located the herd two days later. They were magnificent beasts likely descended from the first horses brought to this world by the Spaniard, Juan de Oñate, in the late 1500s. Led by a big, black, white-blazed stallion well experienced at avoiding hunters, they haunted the buffalo ground along the river south of the Little Islands. The animals had good pasturage, available water, and the wooded foothills for shelter.

Despite his youth, Lone Eagle had the patience of a good hunter. We watched the herd for three suns to establish the rhythm of their days. The stallion spotted us, of course, but after a time, grew accustomed to our presence. Once, a great lion came down from the hills and spooked the herd, but that was to our advantage. We watched where the big black led his harem. The next day, Lone Eagle approached the herd, and the stallion took a second escape route.

After two more days of quiet approaches, the horses finally repeated a pattern. We now knew the stud had three established escape routes. While the herd was down on the plains grazing, we constructed blind corrals to block each of the three paths along which the black led his mares when spooked.

Yelling and waving our arms, we came at them from two different directions. The black's head came up; he neighed a warning and was off. The wily stallion nearly out-coyoted us, heading in a new direction, but Lone Eagle managed to turn him toward one of the usual escape pathways. The black surprised us again, tearing right through our ropes and limping up the hill to freedom. A few of the mares managed to follow him before Lone Eagle blocked the gap with his pony, and I closed the rope gate at the rear.

Our flimsy corral held more horses than we could handle, so the rest of the day was spent picking out the best. Mares that were too aggressive, we turned loose. Finally, Lone Eagle had fourteen mares and immature stallions haltered and tied apart from the others. We then cut the ropes and hazed the balance of the horses up the hill where the stud stamped the ground impatiently.

We left for home each trailing seven horses. Three small colts followed their mothers. Figuring to put as much distance as possible between the herd and ourselves, we traveled until it was too dark to proceed safely. Still the stallion tried to raid us that night, but we had rigged a stout picket line to hold the mares, and one of us stood guard. I came close to shooting him before he finally gave up and raced away; I will forever be grateful he still ran free.

After the initial euphoria, during which I had to listen ten times to the story of a capture I had participated in myself, Lone Eagle grew uncharacteristically quiet. That night after I rolled into my blanket while he took the first guard, he tarried at my side for a moment.

"It's like us and the white man. Those wild horses were living free until we came along and changed everything for them."

"Yes, that's a good way to understand what's happening." As I realized Lone Eagle had matured into a discerning young man, my pipe hardened beneath my blankets and I smothered a sudden, intense lust for this handsome youth. I might have succumbed to my overwhelming desires had he not spoken.

"They're going to make us live like them, like white people, aren't they? What happens if we won't?"

"Then they will kill you."

"They can't! We're warriors. There are too many of us!"

"The dragoons will come like grasshoppers. They will cover the land."

"Don't talk like that! Why do you do it? You know it makes us sad."

"Because I want you to understand and survive."

"We will survive," he said with all the confidence of inexperience as he glanced around the immense, moonlit plains, unable to imagine the truth of my words. As I examined the greatness of this land, I sheltered a small doubt myself.

I lay in my blankets for a long time listening to Lone Eagle walk the perimeter of our small camp, talking softly to the horses as he passed them. It was all I could do to refrain from giving myself release, but eventually I fell asleep despite my condition.

The next morning, we set off again, hugging the foothills and passing near the spot where I had first laid eyes on Cut Hand. Three mounted warriors picked up our trail as we neared the Yanube. Despite his objections, I insisted Lone Eagle go ahead of me, arguing that any ambush lay ahead, not behind. I wanted the men to see it was Teacher accompanying one of the Yanube. If Carcajou's warrant of protection still held, perhaps they would leave us alone; although seventeen horses – nineteen counting our own mounts – were a tempting prize.

The colts refused to enter the river when we reached a good walk across the Yanube. Lone Eagle roped two of the little beasts, dragging them protesting through the fast, shallow tide. The third evaded him, and since the Pipe Stem were drawing close, he abandoned it.

Lone Eagle was no longer a pauper when we rode into the village. Cries of congratulations greeted us from all quarters. Even Cut Hand came to the horse pasture and pronounced the animals superb. Never one to waste such an endorsement, Lone Eagle promptly traded six of the animals for three riding ponies.

Otter was glad to see me when I got back to Teacher's Mead, peppering me with questions about the hunt while I bathed. As I dried off, it occurred to me that no back-east husband had seen his wife naked as often as these folks had seen my bare bum, especially Otter. The People's attitude toward the flesh seemed far healthier than that of my own countrymen.

Lone Eagle came later that night, jubilant over his skill as a horse trader. Long after I retired to my bed, I heard the boys in the other room as Lone Eagle made a legend of our hunt and the daring and skill required to execute it.

CHAPTER 17

Immigrant traffic increased considerably during the summer, driven by widespread unemployment back east. New York banks stopped making payments in specie because Old Hickory had created too much credit, which resulted in inflation and speculation in western lands. Multitudes headed west in a desperate search for a better life. Martin Van Buren replaced Jackson, becoming our eighth president and the first to be born after the signing of the Declaration. At long last, the black slave situation intruded on our part of the world.

Hastily summoned to the encampment, I found a huge Negro defiantly facing a crowd of curious Indians. Shirtless and gleaming like melted tar, the man's back was lash-scarred, the mark of an obstreperous slave. The whites of his eyes showed when he spotted me. Be this help or horror, they mutely asked.

Claiming his name was Hiram Moses, the near-giant resisted admitting he was an escaped slave until Cut, in his literate English, assured the man we had no intention of turning him over to the authorities. Hope flared briefly until I explained how often the dragoons scouted this particular country.

Hiram Moses overnighted at the Mead where he was an object of fascination to Otter. My young friend watched closely to see if black soot washed from the man's skin in the bath. Otter knew better; he had read all the books in my poor library, but the reading and the seeing are two different things.

Hiram objected to taking his meal at the table with Otter and Lone Eagle and me, claiming he would be more comfortable in the barn or on the porch. I decried his decision even though I fathomed he was reacting to a lifelong habit of subservience to the white man. No doubt had I not been present, he would have willingly sat at the table with my two Yanube friends. Eventually, I relented and allowed him to carry his plate to the barn. Otter, still fascinated by this black stranger, joined him. The limits of Lone Eagle's curiosity had been reached, and he ate at his usual place at the kitchen table. He left immediately after devouring the last crumb on his tin.

In like fashion, Hiram would not sleep in the house that night, which might prove fortuitous should any dragoons show up at the Mead. I attended him as he settled his great bulk in the hay of our loft. Otter's curiosity deserted him at that point, and he announced he would rest in his bunk in the western porthern. He had a few questions, however, which he put to me when we returned to the house.

"Have you seen anyone like him before?" my young friend asked.

"What do mean 'like him'?"

"You know. Black like that."

"Many. I saw many when I was back east."

"Where do they come from?"

So we spent the remainder of the evening seated at the eating table while I provided Otter facts he already knew from his reading of books, but was struggling to place into context in the reality of the thing. He finished the long discussion with a final question.

"Are … are they human?"

"What is your guess as to the answer?" I gave his question back to him.

"I guess so. I mean, he looks like us … but he doesn't either."

"Am I human?" I asked.

Otter snickered. "Of course, you're human."

I spread my hands. "Why? I'm not the same color as you? I'm different, am I not?"

That brought an outright laugh. "You're different all right. But … but –"

I waited him out as he struggled to express himself."

"But you don't look like an … an animal," he finished.

"I am an animal. So are you. So are all human beings."

"I know that, but you know what I mean."

"Not unless you express it, I don't," I forced the issue.

"He sorta looks like pictures in some of those books. Of animals, not humans."

"Otter, there are people who deny that Indians are human. And by Indians they mean Yanube and Sioux and Comanche – all of the People. I believe they are wrong. So, too, are they wrong when they claim black Negroes are not human. They think, act, walk, talk, feel love and pain and everything you feel."

"Dogs feel pain and love and eat and sleep like we do, too."

"Yes, but they do not talk – not in the manner of men – nor think. Humans reason in ways far beyond other animals. We are able to plan things, use our hands and minds to create tools and other useful items. And this, in my opinion, gives us a soul. And, a soul is both a blessing and a curse."

"How so?" Otter leaned forward over the table, intent on my answer, his young face frowning in concentration.

"It is the soul that makes man – reasoning, rational man – act fairly toward his fellow humans and other animals, as well. And it is the soul that is forfeit should he ignore the lessons of his God. So let me ask you your own question. Is he human?"

Without hesitation, Otter replied. "Yes."

"Good. I agree. Now let's go to bed."

The following morning, I was generous with my provisions in outfitting the escaped Mississippi slave, gifting him with a sturdy pony and one of the older percussion rifles in my stock. As he prepared to take his leave, I offered a few copper and silver coins. The man accepted them eagerly and then raised his weapon against me, demanding the remainder of my currency.

"I sorry, Mista Billy. Ya been good ta this old field hand, but I runnin' fer ma life. I kilt ma overseer when he hurt ma woman. I needs all I kin git."

"Mr. Moses, the first thing you must learn is to prime your weapon," I lied, praying he was unfamiliar with long guns. "The second is to be grateful for what help you are offered."

The powerful man gave his rifle a confused look. "I kin still take ya," he warned, raising the barrel like a club.

"Yes. And you will find a hundred Indians on your back ready to tear you apart. It's not the men you need fear as much as the women. They'll flail you alive inch by inch." I built upon the fiction read in some of my books; I had never seen these Yanube women perform any such acts, although Morning Mist leapt to mind with the words. "Take what you are offered and go. You'll find no more welcome here."

Defeated, the big Negro reclaimed his impressive dignity. "I hopes ya never finds yaself no slave, Mista Billy. It eat out the decent in a man. Lord Jehovah, forgive me!"

"Doubtless he will," I replied. "Your best direction is north to Canada."

I never learned what happened to the unfortunate man.

#####

Numerous mounted patrols from both Ft. Ramson and Ft. Yanube agitated the Indians, drawing delegations from the Sioux and the Pipe Stem seeking counsel. Cut Hand and Carcajou finally sat on the same blanket to make medicine, smoking a ritual pipe before chewing the matter of the Long Knives thoroughly and digesting nothing. Cut Hand harangued his people to refrain from joining other bands in raiding or harassing white settlers. The Pipe Stem sachem listened to the exchange without comment, but later confided he would take the same position with his own young bloods.

The Americans did not make the Indians' decision easy. Rumors of gold on the upper Yanube drew hundreds of opportunists before being quickly proved false. Even then, scores of ox-drawn freight trains bearing homesteaders continued to roll into the tribes' territories.

Then the inevitable occurred. Lone Eagle came for me mid-morning. Two wagons of settlers passing some miles south of the river had been attacked. Out-parties, drawn by the smoke, spotted the burning wagons from afar and reported that the military had arrived with Indian scouts from foreign tribes.

The affair was no concern of the Yanube – except Buffalo Shoulder had not returned from visiting a passing party of eastern Sioux. Cut Hand, with me at his side, observed from a distance as the troops rode up into the Little Island Mountains. Worried, he sent messengers to the village for more warriors. Distant gunfire reached our ears in the afternoon. We waited all day on a rise as our numbers slowly grew. There was no attempt to hide our field camp that night; fires fed by buffalo chips signaled our presence for anyone to see. There was much sour talk around the *tiospaye*. Hot-heads agitated to ride down and lay in ambush at the edge of the foothills. It was an ugly scene; one I feared would get out of hand. I accompanied Cut in numerous rounds of the camp as he tried to talk the anger and fear out into the open and dispose of them. Few got much sleep in the dark hours.

The next day, the troops filed down from the mountains. Upon confronting such a large party of Indians, the commander of the outnumbered dragoons formed his men boot-to-boot in a skirmish line.

Even from this distance, we could see the troops held four mounted prisoners.

"I pray he is dead," Cut muttered in a voice meant for my ears only. He glanced at the warriors who had made their own skirmish line. "I don't know if I can control them if he isn't."

"Do you want me to go meet them?"

"No. I want you to go with me." He beckoned Bear Paw and Lone Eagle forward. I followed the three warriors down the slope. The line of troops halted and sat waiting. To my horror, the officer in charge was Captain Smith.

"Mr. Strobaw," the man said with a casual salute. "What is your business here?"

"I am here with the misco of the Yanube. He has come to see the situation for himself since these are his grounds."

Smith turned in the saddle and gestured to his prisoners. "Are these his, as well? These fellas some of your redskins, Mr. Strobaw. Or his?"

I refused to take umbrage at his tone. "No, they are Sioux, probably Santee pushed from the east." I pointed with my chin, Indian fashion. "Except for that one. He is a Yanube visiting the Sioux. Buffalo Shoulder is a good man."

"A good man, eh? Do good men murder innocent white men and women? Two men, two women, and three children. All dead, all crowned."

"The Yanube do not scalp," I said quickly.

"No, and they don't raid settlers, neither," Smith answered with a sour swipe.

"May I speak to him?"

Smith paused before giving his permission. But it was not I who nosed his pony to Buffalo Shoulder's; it was his leader, Cut Hand. The Captain and I halted a pace or two behind. I stood ready to translate for Smith.

"Buffalo Shoulder," Cut greeted his clansman. "I see you have gotten yourself in trouble again."

Buffalo Shoulder shrugged as well as possible with his hands bound behind him. "Nothing I can't handle."

"Hah," Cut rejoined. "This officer tells me some wagons were burned and whites killed. If you tell me you have not done this thing, then I will fight for you."

"You know how it is. You get drunk, and somebody says let's go have some fun. I never intended to harm those people."

"That was your intent, but what did you do? Did you kill?"

Buffalo Shoulder's chin shot up. "I was with them. What they did, I did."

"So for the pleasure of a drink, you put your village in jeopardy. Because of a drunken rout, I have the pride of your people lined up against these soldiers. Was it worth it, Buffalo Shoulder?"

"You should have been with us, then you would know, old friend."

"I was with my people taking care of my responsibilities. I was doing as a man should do, not throwing my life away."

"Go home, Cut Hand. Take my kinsmen with you. This is not your fight."

"That I will sadly do, my friend. I have a duty to them, and that duty does not drive me to throw away their lives for your foolishness."

"Then go and take care of our people. I will face what comes like a man. I don't want to live if I can't live like a man! When was the last time we raided for horses? When did we last count coup? When did we race through a camp and spread fear of the Yanube? This is no life for a man; I am finished with it."

Cut flinched. "Do you understand what they will do to you, brother? They will put a cord around your neck and hang you until the breath leaves your body. That does not sound like the way a man should end."

Buffalo Shoulder's eyes narrowed as he replied, and I altered the faithfulness of my translation at that point. I spoke his words as "However they kill me, I will die like a man." What he actually said was, "I will die like a man."

As Cut Hand turned Arrow and rejoined Bear Paw and Lone Eagle, I paused, hoping this military popinjay could understand plain English.

"Report that the chief of the Yanube came to see for himself what happened here. He spoke with his clansman, Buffalo Shoulder, who admitted his part in the attack on the wagons. Cut Hand judged for himself the justice of what is going to happen, and has honored your majesty. With a superior force at his back, he has shown himself a fair-minded man of peace. Someday, when someone needs to remember this, I pray you will be as honorable a man as he, Captain."

Disturbed by the arrogant, gloating sneer on the man's coarse features, I took no comfort my words were heeded. Angrily, I touched a hand to my hat brim and wheeled Long about. The four of us regained the rise and turned the line of Indians back toward the Yanube. It was a narrow thing. When the distant sing-song death chants reached our ears, some of the younger warriors faltered until their chief continued on his path. Lone Eagle's battle with himself over what was right in the matter was painfully obvious. He desperately wanted to go to the aid of Buffalo Shoulder, as did we all, especially Cut Hand, who had played with his friend in the dirt as a child.

The shots, when they came, were fired like a volley. Cut looked at me pleadingly. With Lone Eagle at my side, I rode back to the crest. The four prisoners had broken away; deliberately courting death. All were cut down. Soldiers rolled the bodies into blankets as one of the army scouts watched us carefully.

The council that night was a noisy and contentious affair. Buffalo Shoulder's cousin decried the betrayal of his kinsman, declaring that honorable men were bound to ride to his aid. Were the Yanube so infected by fear of the whites they could not stand up for their own? The furious young man's words found favor with some in the assemblage. Cut Hand heard every last voice before he rose.

"It was not I who betrayed my oldest friend, but he who was unfaithful to us. For five summers, we have spoken of this time in open council. Those who had ears have heard. Those who had a thirst for liquor or raiding or killing have heeded those callings rather than the logic of the changing world. Buffalo Shoulder put us all in danger. He got drunk and helped kill seven people who were no less human than we. He created a widow among us and a son with no father."

Cut Hand paused and took a shaky breath, his pain obvious. "We could have fought the soldiers, and perhaps Buffalo Shoulder would have fallen anyway. But Bear Paw and Lone Eagle and Badger and all the men with me would have faced the bullets of those dragoons, and many would have died. There would be more widows and more orphans. And when other Long Knives came for their revenge, this band would cease to exist." Abruptly he sat down.

"What does Teacher have to say?" someone asked from the back.

"He is a white man! You know what he will say!" another voice spat.

Surprisingly it was Lone Eagle who reacted to this slur. He sprang to his feet and threw back his shoulders self-consciously.

"Teacher is a white man who is not a white man. His flesh is white; his blood is red, like ours. In his mind, he is one of us. He stood with us against our enemies. He warned us of what is to come. He is our teacher, our prophet. He tells things as they are. He lies for no one. He has warned us against his own, told us of their way of fighting and thinking. He has taken a wife from among us. He is my friend, and I will hear no unjust words against him!" He flopped down and grew silent. I was impressed by the eloquence of this nineteen-year-old warrior.

Bear Paw rose. While not yet one of the round bellies, he was known as a serious man and had standing among the council.

"I will say this, and then I am done with the matter. I know few things beyond doubt, but this one thing I do know. Cut Hand led us down the peaceful Red Road today. I would have taken the contentious Black Road and battled the Blue Coats, but I am thankful he was wiser than I. If he had not been, before the moon turned her back on us again this village would be finished. Your bodies and the bodies of your children and your horses and your dogs would lie as fodder for the vultures and the rats and the skunks. The Yanube would exist no more. While I do not hold my own life too dear, I do those of my wife and my children and my family and my neighbors. Let no one doubt that Teacher is one of us. He has proved it many times. He killed for us. He provided weapons and ammunition for us. He hunted for us. But most of all, he is a counselor and a friend."

There did not seem to be much left to say after that, so the affair slowly broke up. Cut wanted to talk, causing us to invade Morning Mist's lodge where we drank more than we should have. Cut Hand relived his childhood with Buffalo Shoulder, and I listened as a friend should do while the pain washed out of him like corruption from the pox.

Lone Eagle and Otter were both at Teacher's mead when I fell off my horse in front of the steps. They lugged me inside and dumped me in bed, clothes and all. Sometime during the night I was sick in the chamber pot.

There were a few desertions from the *tiospaye* after Buffalo Shoulder's death, although it was likely a positive development as most were hotheads. How futile and foolish that young man's death had been. I prayed to Almighty God it would provide an object lesson for those who remained.

CHAPTER 18

One day, as Lone Eagle stood on the front of the steps of the Mead talking to two of his friends I caught myself examining his strong, wiry frame with the same lust I experienced on the wild horse hunt. When he glanced up unexpectedly, I quickly turned aside to go take stock of the arms and ammunition in my small armory. Lone Eagle soon followed, giving me a long, insolent gaze but saying nothing. That evening, Otter and I ate alone; Lone Eagle went elsewhere.

I was almost ready to retire when the young warrior arrived back at the Mead and asked to wash up. I lay flat of my back so as not to snatch glances of his fine body since he left the door to the bathing room open. When he strode out to comb his hair before my dressing mirror, my pipe and my eyes betrayed me. Lone Eagle was proud of many things, but none more so than his long black mane. Normally held in two braids, it hung below his shoulders when loose. I watched the play of muscles in his back and buttocks as he combed his glorious black crown into a shining mass.

He paused to watch me through the mirror. Abruptly, he threw down the comb and walked naked to the bed. Slowly he drew back the covers, revealing my pulsing pipe. He moved closer and spread his legs. I sat up to push him away, but he resisted my insincere efforts. He pulled my head to his belly

"No," I said, my tongue teasing the black pelt at his loins. But it was useless. I accepted him and was lost. His long pipe rose, randy and ready. His big, curved cock filled my mouth, blocking my airways. His lush pubic hair tickled my nose; his heavy stones beat a tattoo against my chin. He was relentless, fucking my mouth as if it were a vagina, ultimately achieving orgasm with a great shout. His taste was different from Cut Hand's, more musky, but not at all unpleasant. His muscled body shuddered from the force of his release.

I was pleased when he spread me beneath him. Lone Eagle was experienced, but only with women. When I reached my own climax, he was so astonished by my spasming channel that he flanked me anew with all the vigor of a nineteen-year-old in the prime of life. I was almost glad when it was over – almost.

Afterward, he studied me by the lamplight. "You are mine now, Billy," he declared, using my name for the first time. "I have taken you to wife! I will tell the council tomorrow. You will do this with no one else. Not even when your army officer comes sniffing around next time. Do you hear me?"

I would have laughed except it would hurt his pride. He was the young man giving instructions to his bride, and he expected they be followed to the letter. He might have a surprise or two coming, but not over the matter of fidelity. I had only the capacity to love one man at a time.

The next day, I rooted around in a trunk trundled back with me when I returned to the Mead until I located what I was looking for. My scarlet garters and red shirt and brilliant scrivener's ribbon looked good to my eyes. They felt better to my skin and refreshed my sense of who I was nearly as much as my new husband. On my next visit to the village, no one commented on my return to the habit of yesteryear, but sly eyes scanned the colorful apparel and smiles touched many lips. The People now knew the Red Win-tay had come among them again.

He flanked me at least once daily from that night until it was time for the village to move. We were a week into the affair before he declared his love, although he was sincere in what he said. We fought often, but it mattered not. He always came to my bed expecting to exercise his husbandly rights. He never flagged in his efforts or in his enthusiasm.

The big battle came over the winter move. He announced that I would join him on the trek and live in the village during the exodus. I adamantly refused. He threatened to beat me; I invited him to try. He seriously considered it before slinking out of the house and absenting himself until the middle of the night when he returned to beat me in his own way – one that was acceptable.

On the day of the move, he packed and mounted his pony, ready to splash across the Yanube with the rest of the band. I said goodbye to him in good cheer. He surprised me by leaning down and planting a kiss on my lips. Public displays of affection were not his way. Maybe he did love me.

He was back two days later in the midst of a sudden snow squall. It was a mistake, but it was too late to send him south again. He had cabin fever within a *senight*. I occupied his mind by drilling him in reading, writing, and arithmetic until he balked. Like Cut, he regarded chess as a game of war and worked until he mastered the rudiments. He read more than ever and even helped, albeit sparingly, with the womanly chores of cleaning, preparing food, and threshing grain.

He made sexual demands at all hours of the day and night. No one had ever inspected me as he did, not even Cut, peering into every crevice and crack, poking as if he were examining an old nag. For orneriness, I returned the favor and discovered I enjoyed the byplay. No portion of him was unattractive, even the baser parts. He was clean and healthy and comely all over.

I was surprisingly happy with him that winter, even when he grew testy at the confinement. He took to the rackets, fair weather or foul, accumulating more furs than usual. The People were not fur traders in a serious way, relying on the buffalo for their requirements, but they took pelts when the occasion presented. Trapping required long hours and jaunts a considerable distance from the Mead, often in deep snow. I joined him from time to time, but discerned he required some time to himself. Besides, I needed to tend the household chores. Lone Eagle was a good trapper. Next spring, his cache would require a trip into town to exchange them for supplies.

My new husband had a run-in with the wolf pack over a beaver and required the repair of his arm. He disdained my laudanum as I sewed his flesh in neat stitches with a boiled needle and thread. He neither flinched nor made a noise. He was all man, this warrior of mine. Afterward he showed his gratitude by fucking me enthusiastically. He was willing to flog the sperm from my pipe with his hand, but that was as far as he would go. Anything more would have been unmanly to his way of thinking.

Shortly before the first thaw, the dogs warned of someone approaching. A party of four Indians appeared on the footpath at the far edge of the lea. Although they carried an ominous air – dressed in ragged buckskins and muttering among themselves rather than hailing the house – I ignored my better judgment and went outside to call off the dogs. They must have been unknowing there were two of us, because when I beckoned one man to approach, he shuffled forward and lunged at me once he drew near. His bear hug constricted me to the point I was unable to reach my skinning knife, and I would be in for it when the others joined the ruffian.

I sensed rather than saw South attack one of the number, but another circled behind and threw a sour-smelling arm around my neck.

Lone Eagle shot out one of my precious hand blown quarrels, knocking the assailant from my back. The man pinning my arms to my sides fell backwards, taking me with him. The force of our fall broke his hold, and I snatched my knife from its scabbard and flailed at the thuggish fellow repeatedly. He was so thoroughly bundled with deerskin and blankets, my blade was having trouble doing much more than inflicting minor cuts.

He twisted out from under me and grappled for a hatchet he'd dropped when he seized me, and I got serious about the matter. My knife found the soft spot to the left of his spinal cord at the neck, and copious amounts of blood ran out of him, taking his life with it.

Another raider fell to South and House. When I called the dogs off, the man was not dead, but probably would be if left to the elements. He refused treatment of his wounds and ran after the fourth man who had deserted him. We lugged the two we had killed a considerable distance from the Mead and left them for the wolves. The callousness of this act disturbed my conscience not at all. It was impossible to break the frost and bury them in this climate.

After the killings, Lone Eagle exhibited the same arousal Cut experienced following acts of violence, and thrummed me near unto exhaustion. Later, I made the mistake of fingering his magnificent chest. He looked at me closely and mumbled he required a moment of rest before trying again. To my dismay, he not only tried, he succeeded.

# # # # #

Lone Eagle was even happier than I when the first of the People splashed across the Yanube in the spring. Cut had waited longer than usual to return, allowing the water level to drop considerably. When I saw women carrying new babies, I understood. A number of the bucks had not waited until the cold winter months to line their women. I watched closely until Morning Mist crossed and observed she was not wearing a cradleboard. It occurred to me at that moment she was ill-named. Morning Mist was too beautiful an appellation for this sour sow.

Cut paused to greet Lone Eagle and me. "I see you two did not kill one another over the winter."

"Thought about it," Lone Eagle retorted.

"He was not alone in that," I said. "If he did not wield such a good hand with the broom and the mop, I might have considered it myself."

"Hah!" Lone Eagle regarded his chieftain closely to judge if he discerned I was teasing. He must have been satisfied on the matter as he dropped it.

I looked at the people streaming across the Yanube. "You've a surplus crop of babies. What's the matter with Cut Hand? Have you lost your potency?" I immediately understood it was the wrong thing to say.

Cut frowned angrily; then his brow cleared. "We lost a child. It got all twisted up in her belly, and the midwife was unable to save it. It … it was a boy. The birthing hurt Morning Mist badly. Dog Fox may be our last."

"I'm sorry," I said. "It was a stupid joke."

He reached across the distance and laid a hand on my arm. "Don't worry, old friend. I know you would not hurt me on purpose." He turned to my husband. "Did Teacher set you to your letters and numbers?"

"Without end," my spouse complained. "I put up with it as long as I could. He chased me out of doors in a snowstorm with his reading and writing and figuring. Landed me right in the middle of a wolf pack."

"There's something you ought to know," I turned serious. "Four Sioux attacked us before the winter broke its hold. We killed two and wounded one, but he and his accomplice got away. We didn't recognize them, but if you get questions from any of the camps, you know what happened.

"Uh," he acknowledged. "I missed you," he added in a low voice. Lone Eagle bristled beside me. "Don't get all stiff-legged," Cut snapped. "I am telling a friend how I missed his friendship and wise council."

That night when Lone Eagle asked if I still loved Cut Hand, I replied honestly. "I will always love him. But I have grown and changed. I do not love him in the same way. You need not fear him or any other man," I added, laying a hand on his smooth chest. "I am yours and yours alone for as long as you want me. I ask only one thing. When you are finished with me, tell me. Do not go slinking off to other beds and crawl back to mine."

"I have not done that to you," he responded indignantly. "I told you, Billy. I love you. And my words are true. You said them back to me, and I believe them true, as well. I have shown you my love the only way I know. Is that not enough?"

"It is for me." I stroked his silken skin. "But you are sometimes a mystery to me, as I am to you. Often, neither acts the way the other expects."

"That is true, wife," he answered. "You are not as dutiful and obedient as you should be, but I have always forgiven you."

The next day Otter returned to claim his bed in the other side of the house. Lone Eagle was unusually vocal in his flanking that night to let the youngster know he was taking care of business.

I puzzled over this casual attitude toward Otter. Normally, the tribesmen did not permit others of mating age near their wives unchaperoned, and Otter was now a man according to their lights. He had his Vision Quest this past year and earned his man's name, River Otter, although he remained Otter to most. I concluded finally that the boy was yet a little brother to Lone Eagle, but the day was coming when he would pose a threat to my jealous, virile spouse.

# # # # #

The summer and early fall were uneventful except for the burning of the countryside to refresh the land and encourage new growth next spring. If *Wakinyan*'s lightning bolts failed to accomplish this, the tribesmen set "cold fires" to burn out the brush and fallen wood that caused hot ones.

When James and his troop rode into the meadow shortly after the burn, Lone Eagle materialized almost before the officer dismounted. My husband sat close by my side at the eating table while we conferred. Once his point was made, Lone Eagle moved away slightly, but watched us through hawkish eyes, especially when James gifted me with a copy of Hawthorne's latest work called *Twice Told Tales*.

The news my military friend brought was not encouraging. There had been clashes between settlers and Indians north of Ft. Ramson, one so severe it involved a field piece. Settlers were clamoring for the removal of the tribes to reservations like the colonial "praying towns" of old so that missionaries could convert them.

Information from back east was by necessity somewhat dated. The country was still in the grip of the Depression of 1837 with no end in sight. The slave issue virtually paralyzed the country. Pro-slavery rioters at Alston, Illinois, killed Elijah Lovejoy, a prominent abolitionist publisher, and smashed his printing press. The number of Supreme Court Justices had been raised from seven to nine. As one of his last acts, Andy Jackson recognized the Republic of Texas. Somebody named John Deere produced a steel-bladed plow in Illinois. Michigan was admitted as the twenty-sixth state just this last year.

James remained over, sleeping on the east side in Lone Eagle's old bed. My young husband was noisy in the exercise of his marital duties that night. Doubtless the countryside knew when he achieved orgasm. James was duly warned to keep his distance, to say nothing of the platoon of dragoons sleeping in our meadow.

Tatanka appeared on the trace in season that year, but he was considerably more skittish. The bison had been hunted relentlessly all during the annual migration. The camp compiled ample stores, but the men had to work harder to accomplish the harvest. The kill was spread over a great distance, so the women's task was no easier. Long Wind performed well, as usual, and I brought down two cows. This year, I tried the raw liver the Indians considered a great delicacy and decided to do without such tasties in the future. I wondered if Cut Hand would cover Morning Mist with the same fervor he had me after such hunts. I spoke into Lone Eagle's ear until he was inflamed into a little thrumming of his own!

So far, this was the best year since my divorce from Cut Hand, but clear skies to the west sometimes usher in storm clouds from the east. Tibo Jaquez de Velasquez arrived hard on the heels of the buffalo hunt. Yanube scouts had warned me of the wagon passing on the south side of the river within sight of the village. Therefore, it was no surprise when it turned north and splashed across the thin-running Yanube at the Mead. As the team pulled into the lea, I observed a man of middle years at the reins and a straight-backed youth with a proud seat aboard a fine-looking, long-necked mount. They were obviously father and son – or perhaps grandson – bearing a striking resemblance, one to the other. Hawk-eyed and eagle-nosed, they brought with them an aura of

Old World dignity. The two resembled the People more than they did me, but there was a difference. Of Latin blood and temperament, I decided ere the first of them dismounted.

"*Señor*," the older man called from his wagon. "May we rest our bones in your meadow and partake of water from your *ria* – your creek?"

"Certainly," I called as Lone Eagle and Otter walked up to the porch from wherever they had been.

"*Gracias*." The man climbed down from his wagon, a contraption considerably greater than a buckboard but less than a Conestoga. As his feet hit the ground, he shrugged as if throwing off the weariness of lengthy travel. The man left the watering of his team to his younger image and strode with firm step toward the stoop.

"May I introduce myself," he said in strongly accented English. "I am Don Tibo Jaquez de Velasquez, late of Chihuahua, Mexico. And that," he tossed a glance over his shoulder at the young man, "is my grandson, Carlos."

Carlos went about his business with a grace that was unusual for a man of seventeen or eighteen winters. The grandfather, who appeared older at close inspection than at first glance, mounted the steps and offered a strong, leathery hand. He removed a broad, flat-brimmed hat embellished with a heavy band of what appeared to be silver set with a blue-green stone holding brilliant golden flecks. Turquoise, I judged.

"Do I have the honor of addressing Mr. William Joseph Strobaw?" Jaquez continued.

"That you do, sir. And this is Lone Eagle and River Otter, two warriors of the Yanube tribe. They are conversant in English."

The courtly man took the time and effort to move to each and deliver his greetings.

"Will you take refreshment," I asked. "A meal, perhaps?"

"Thank you. Victuals would be welcome. We have been at a strong move since leaving Ft. Ransom. If it would not be too much trouble," he added.

"Not at all," I responded. With my eye for masculine beauty, I found my attention on young Carlos. Slender as a willow whip – but with good shoulders – he stood, legs spread, holding his gelding in loose rein, allowing the animal to drink. His gaze was centered on Otter with an intensity that could only be described as smoldering. His dark, expressive eyes moved slowly up and down my young friend's body. That one, I was certain, would have picked a doll in the stead of an arrow had some grandfather tested him as a child. Curious, I glanced at Otter. The boy had obviously noticed the attention paid him; his color was high. He dropped his glance before that piercing gaze.

"Otter," I said, occasioning a start from the youngster, "would you see what we have to feed our guests?"

The boy almost bolted for the door of the house.

"Carlos," Jaquez called. "Fill a canteen with fresh water and bring me some, *por favor*."

"*Si, mi abuelo*," the youth responded.

My guest and I appropriated the two chairs on the porch of the cabin and settled in for some talk. Lone Eagle, took a seat on the steps, well within earshot. He stared at Carlos with some hostility.

"And where are you bound, sir?" I asked. I had to engage the man in talk, else I would have laughed at my mate's jealousy, even though it seemed misplaced. Otter should have been his concern.

"To Ft. Yanube. We will winter there and then proceed on to the Oregon Territory."

"You are somewhat north of the usual route, are you not?"

"That is true; however, I had a delivery to make at Ramson. Some uniforms I contracted with the army to transport." He paused before adding. "And then I had a message to deliver – to you and an individual called Cut Hand, I believe it is."

"Cut Hand is the misco of the Yanube. You passed his village on the way here to the Mead. And what is this message, sir?"

"I had the privilege of making the acquaintance of a mountain man by the name of Rumquiller back in St. Jo. Splitlip Rumquiller, he was called. You know of him?"

"I traveled to this territory with him back in '32. How is the old coot?"

"Alas, my message is not good news. Mr. Rumquiller succumbed to injuries he suffered when a wheel collapsed on his wagon. It was loaded with heavy equipment, and he ended up beneath some of it. He tarried for several days. As we were acquaintances – friends even – I remained nearby until the end. When he knew he was going to meet his Maker, he asked that I inform you of his circumstances should I travel to this part of the country." Here, Jaquez paused to inscribe a cross on his forehead and torso "Indeed, it was to

221

discharge this request that I accepted the contract for delivery of the uniforms to Ft. Ramson."

"That was uncommonly kind of you, Mr. Jaquez."

"Not at all. Split and I had done some business from time to time, and he handed over his purse to ensure I would not forget to convey his respects and inform you of his demise. I am pleased that obligation in now fulfilled."

We spoke awhile longer, exchanging tales of our mutual friend. I was grateful for the reminiscing as the news hit me hard, leaving my bowels queasy and my nerves inflamed. I settled down some as talk turned to news from the Southwest. Don Tibo confirmed what Carcajou had told me – the Americans did not enter the war when Texas declared its independence. After the rebels suffered the rout at the Alamo, they redeemed themselves at the battle of San Jacinto, capturing the Mexican President, Antonio Santa Anna, and winning their freedom without the direct aid of the Yankees.

As soon as we finished our meal of antelope jerky, beans, and tubers, I asked Otter to go inform Cut of Splitlip's fate. Carlos contrived to accompany the boy to the village, but his senior held him close.

The two Jaquez – man and boy – remained overnight, sleeping in our western fronting room. I rejected Lone Eagle for the first time that night, fearing noise of our lovemaking would inflame young Carlos and send him rushing into the darkness in search of Otter. Our friend had opted to desert us and sleep in the bachelor's tipi in the village that night.

Cut Hand made his appearance before the wagon departed the Mead to hear of Split's death for himself. We both stood in the grip of sadness as the Jaquez men clattered off to the west on the way to Ft. Yanube. Otter did not show up until the wagon was well out of sight.

# # # # #

When talk turned to the move to winter quarters, Lone Eagle made it clear he expected us to accompany the band. Even though I refused, he traded for buffalo skins and brought them home for me to construct a proper tipi. When he found them stored in the barn, he lost his temper and came close to trying to thrash me, but settled for an earnest round of cursing, first in argot and then in English.

Even though it was a busy time for him, I looked up Cut Hand for a conversation. "Am I so impossible to live with?" I opened. "I couldn't make it work with you, and now I'm wrecking it with Lone Eagle. Am I so impossible?"

"Yes," he answered calmly. "You are totally impossible and outrageous. Impossible because you are a man in your own right and exercise your will as a man. Outrageous because you are the greatest fuck a man can have but refuse to act the part of a proper wife. You are also the wisest and best of friends."

"So I am destined to end up someone's boon companion."

"There is something you should know, Billy. Lone Eagle has told everyone he will be with us on the move this year. To keep him here would cost him much, perhaps more than he is willing to pay. And," he added, "he's been showing interest in a girl." My shoulders sagged. "I am sorry, but this is information you should have before making your decision."

So I acquiesced to my husband's demands and wintered with the Yanube, but once committed to the idea, I made the best of it. Huddling beneath thick buffalo blankets on frigid nights was conducive to good carnal relations. I came to understand why so many Yanube babies were born in August and September. If the men spread their women as often as Lone Eagle did me, then it was inevitable. I wondered what the People thought of his roaring orgasms, but no one ever gave a clue by word or glance.

The one part of village life I could not countenance was working side by side with the women to boil our clothing or prepare our meals. Morning Mist walked the camp to gossip on the days I washed clothes. She never spoke to me, but talked around me, making waggish remarks that were difficult to ignore. To give them heed, would be even worse. Another woman could pull her hair and punch her belly, but I was not free to indulge such satisfaction, nor did I wish to. All I wanted was to have this long, dreary, cold, blustery season behind me. Thank God I had brought South with us. While the dog was bothersome, he was also protection against the unwelcome presence of Morning Mist.

If I suffered, Lone Eagle prospered. He was as proud as that feral stallion we had stalked because he prevailed upon Teacher to accompany him to winter camp. Not even Cut Hand had been able to accomplish that feat. He only began to wilt as the thaw came upon us.

But to me it seemed as if an entire twelve-month had passed before we started the trek back to the Yanube.

CHAPTER 19

I am certain Lone Eagle came near to demanding we live in the village for the remainder of the year, but he made no determined fuss when I returned to Teacher's Mead. I saw to the livestock we'd brought back, put the dogs on guard, and built two good fires, so the place was warm and a meal simmered in the fireplace by the time Lone Eagle arrived home.

"Where's Otter," I asked, aware that sometimes he did not appear until the second night.

"I told him to stay away," my lord and master answered breezily.

"You did what?" I rounded on him with a ladle in my grip. A cold hand grasped my heart as I realized my earlier fears had come to pass.

Surprised, Lone Eagle stuttered. "He … he's too old to hang around like he does! Have you looked at him lately? He's a man!"

"This is his home!" I snarled. "Go get him."

"I will not. People will talk. His pipe's too big."

"Go tell him to come home," I said in a deadly voice.

"You act like he's putting it to you!" my husband complained.

"You know better. He doesn't think of me that way, and I don't do it with anyone but you."

"You better not," he said lamely. "But I will think about it and give you my decision tomorrow."

"Decision my bum! This is the boy's home. You can't deny it to him!"

"He can sleep in the bachelor's tent … tonight."

Lone Eagle's sulky tone promised no vow to go for Otter on the morrow, but half a pledge is better than none. Our row did not dampen his enthusiasm that night; he thrummed me deliciously, rogering me from behind with his lean body atop mine. As irksome as he was at times, Lone Eagle was a magnificent stud.

When Otter returned home the next night, I took another look at the boy. The youth was eighteen now with all the attributes of a young man. His britches were filled out, and the soft buckskin of his winter shirt stretched across broad shoulders. The sight gave me pause. I remembered young Carlos Jaquez and his obvious lust for Otter.

All of the men in my life were uncommon in looks. Cut Hand, the most striking, possessed a classical handsomeness that caused people to tarry for the simple pleasure of observing him. James had a man's body with an adolescent's fetching features. Lone Eagle was handsome in a darker, leaner way, what my sainted ma had called devilishly handsome, Lucifer at his most seductive. Carcajou, although never a lover, was a heavier kind of masculine beauty. Otter's comeliness was classical like Cut's, dangerous like Lone Eagle's, and stolid like Carcajou's. I hoped he would find a young woman worthy of his seemliness.

# # # # #

Spring brought the first serious trouble since the Pipe Stem raid five years earlier. When we heard shots from the village, Lone Eagle and Otter grabbed their weapons and headed out the door. Their horses were at hand, still tethered to the front porch from a short hunting foray, so they were well away while I delayed to close up the place. My key was in the lock when a lead ball smashed into the stone at my side, splintering me with rock fragments. I scrambled back through the door and slammed it shut. A bullet smacked into it where I had stood but a moment earlier. Opening my front drawing window, I peered through the gun slot.

Three men stepped out of the trees at the end of the meadow and stood conferring for a moment, their eyes fixed on the guard dog at their front. As they moved to advance on the house, South brought one of them to his knees. Without hesitation, another of the villains shot my protector. Furious, I fired, dropping one attacker. Before I could pick up another rifle, House and East hit the other two. I grabbed a pistol and ran out the door, shooting one man in the chest as he was about to knife a dog. The other lay flat on his face, begging for mercy. East gave him a chewing before I bothered to call her off.

Rifle shots echoed over the east hillock as I checked the fallen dog. Our faithful friend was gone, shot in the head. Leaving East and House snarling atop the one man still alive, I turned to the fallen men and received a surprise. One was Indian; the other, white. The prisoner also turned out to be white. Fretting over the continuing sound of gunfire from the direction of the village, I calmly knocked the man in the head, removed all weapons from the area, and left the dogs to guard him while I threw a halter on Long and took off bareback.

I abandoned the trail, which skirted the thin forest off to the east and took to the trees. Slowing as I detected movement ahead, I grew cautious until I came upon Lone Eagle and Otter abandoning their mounts. I slid off Long's back and joined my two friends. Afoot, we cautiously approached the sound of battle. As we topped the rise, the cause became clear.

A force of whites, Indians, and mustees had attacked the village, trying for furs and horses. The fools did not realize these people were not prolific trappers. I raised my rifle, vaguely aware that Lone Eagle and Otter had done the same. We fired simultaneously, as if in a volley.

With us behind them and Cut's larger force in front, the raiders took real losses before fleeing to the north. Declining to chase the scum, we rushed down into the village despairing of the loss of friends. Fortunately, however, the *tiospaye*'s scouts had discovered the gang before the attack, so the Yanube's losses were held to two, virtually a miracle given an attack by a score of gunmen. Even so, that was a tremendous loss for a small band. I hoped Stone Knife was in the vicinity to finish off the filthy pimps!

A breed and two whites, including the one lying unconscious at the Mead, were among the living when we checked the fallen men. A general clamor went up from the Yanube, demanding their own justice since a senior member of the council had died in the assault.

"Cut," I said beneath my breath. "This could get ugly. You have to do something."

"What would you have me do?" His face was flushed with emotion.

"Take them to Ft. Yanube. Turn them over to the army."

"To what end?"

"To protect your people from recriminations. There must be seven or more dead men and these three live ones. Half of them look to be white."

"So we are unable to protect ourselves from attack?" Bear Paw asked.

"No. And we have done just that. Now we must see there is no afterclap. That no one can falsely claim we unjustly killed."

My words raised a storm of consternation among Cut's tribesmen, but I continued to argue for turning them over to the army. In the manner of these people, there was much loud decrying of my position, but eventually, I prevailed when Cut recognized the value of showing the commandant we were peaceable even when provoked.

The next morning, Lone Eagle, Bear Paw, and I undertook the fifty-mile trip to Ft. Yanube. With each of the three prisoners tightly bound and trussed securely to my buckboard, we traveled straight through without stopping.

Major Jamieson accepted the prisoners and heard our story. Afterward, he pressed me for details.

"Did you recognize any of the men who escaped?"

"No. Although I can tell you some were bloods, some native, and some white. Just like the seven who were killed."

"Describe them."

I raised my eyebrows in surprise. "Generally rough hewn, scruffy men. The whites had raised beards. None of them smelled like lilac water."

"How were they dressed?"

Belatedly, I came to understand he was seeking a particular face among the raiders, and eventually he confessed the leader of this particular gang, which was becoming an increasing problem in the area, was an army deserter – one of his own sergeants.

Jamieson expressed the belief the attack on Cut's people was to tie them down while three of their number hit the Mead. Apparently, word had seeped around town that I held hefty accounts in the local bank, some of which had been deposited in gold.

Infuriated that my business had become the subject of rumors, I stormed out of the fort and marched into the town, my companions at my back.

Banker Crozier squealed like a stuck porker when I demanded the funds from my accounts. Upon learning the reason, he acknowledged he had discharged a clerk who was said to be among the outlaws. This explanation, appearing reasonable, caused me to reconsider, but not before he conceded another one-quarter of a percentage point in interest on my accounts.

Bear Paw had never been in an American town before and expressed a curiosity about everything he saw. Since I was unwilling to waste a trip, those craven killers had ridden atop what trade goods we had. Before my business was finished with Caleb Brown, my two companions wandered off. Fearing the worst, I followed a trail of vaporous women scandalized by two half-naked men wandering the streets. Damned if I didn't discern a gleam or two in some of those vacuous eyes. I caught up with the two men trying to buy a parasol from a matron who couldn't decide whether to be outraged or amazed by savages speaking better English than most of her neighbors. Her umbrella had caught the eye of my two friends because it was collapsible.

I soothed ruffled feathers and escorted the two of them to the livery where we recovered our horses and wagon. They disdained helping load the buckboard at Brown's store, as this was clearly woman's work. I left Caleb to puzzle over why my two servants didn't lift a finger, relieved they had not heard his comment, else they'd still be explaining they were no one's servants but warriors of the Yanube.

Within a month, I was summoned back to the fort to testify at the trial of the three desperadoes. None of the Indians were required to appear, but my testimony was sufficient for a sentence of hanging.

Upon my return to the Mead, Otter would not look at me when I greeted him. Abandoning the buckboard, I rode Long to the village. When I sat down with Cut Hand, he displayed an uncustomary dis-ease.

"All right, what is it?" I demanded after reporting the results of the trial.

"That girl I told you about? Lone Eagle has taken to courting her."

"What!" I brayed.

Lone Eagle was waiting on the porch when I got back to the Mead. "Wife," he said sharply, seeking to establish his authority. "I need some of our horses. I would take another wife."

I said nothing, merely seized his arm and flung him off the porch into the dirt. He scrambled to his feet and started for me, but apparently decided better of it. I was seven years older, but had him by some ten pounds. He halted, legs apart, arms planted on hips, looking so handsome in his outrage I could have dropped down and taken his pipe right there in the open.

"What's the matter with a second wife!" he demanded.

"If you take a wife, she will be your only wife."

"Be reasonable," he pled. "Those are my horses anyway. When I married you, they became mine."

"That might be your way, but it's not mine. Keep your hands off my horses. You want to get married, do it with your own property."

"See! You aren't a proper wife! You don't act like a real wife. You just let me come to bed with you because you like my pipe! You don't love me!"

"You've a funny way of showing your love," I came back at him. "You want to bring a woman into my house and flank her right in front of me."

"What's the matter –"

I stomped into the house, leaving him sputtering in the meadow. Moments later I heard his pony thunder toward the village. Otter slipped in from the barn or someplace.

"Am I so bad to him?" I demanded.

The lad looked as if he wanted to flee again, but manfully answered. "No. You're good to him."

"Why does he want another wife?"

"Some prefer doing it to girls. That's what they're made for."

I came down off my mad and laughed. "Yes, that's what they're made for. But if that's what he wanted why didn't he get one in the first place?"

"Probably because he was too anxious to get you," Otter answered and eased out the door.

Lone Eagle came home after I went to bed that night and made a mess trying to take a shower. From all the stumbling around, I gathered he was drunk. When he fell on me, still wet from his bath, he proved his condition, but he also demonstrated it did not inhibit his ability to fuck. His pipe was just as hard and hungry, his thrusts as strong and manly. I submitted, not because of his insistence, but because I wanted him very badly at that moment. I sensed his love slipping away. The flanking was rough, but tremendously satisfying.

He gathered some provisions early on the morrow, informing me he would be gone for a few days but refusing to tell me where. Rather than follow him, as was my inclination, I sat on the porch to reason things out. He needed horses. So he was either going on a raid by himself or back to the feral horse herd we had hunted two years earlier.

My heart fell into my stomach when I realized he was determined on taking this girl for a wife. He had accepted the denial of my wealth and was remedying his problem the best way he knew how.

He was away so long I determined to search for him. Any kind of evil could have befallen him – Indian, American, or natural. Before I worked up to it, Cut came by the Mead. Seeing my agitation, he let me know he had sent a scout over the Little Islands who found my mate patiently stalking the black stallion and his harem of mares. Lone Eagle was all right.

Although he was too polite to ask, I knew Cut longed to know what I would do if my husband brought home another wife. Would I suffer for Lone Eagle what I had not for him?

"I don't know, Cut," I answered his unasked question. "It will not work if he brings a woman into the house. Will it work if he lives here and in the village as well? My heart tells me to try. My mind tells me it is hopeless."

"I was sad beyond all reason when you left me," he said unexpectedly. "I loved you more than anyone on Turtle Island. I would never have permitted anything to come between us except what did. I always hoped it would be far enough in the future for you to become accustomed to sharing a home.

"But as unhappy as I was for myself, I despaired for you. How could you find happiness? At least I had someone to share my lodge, and I had my duties. When you went to the white man's town, I wept. There, I have told you something no one else in the world knows. I cried like some child who has dirtied himself. But in the bottom of my heart, I knew you would be back. I only wondered when and if you would be alone. I half-hoped you would bring someone back with you.

"When you and Butterfly married, I was overjoyed. I saw you loved her in your own way, and if the passion was not great, at least it was sufficient. But fate took her away, and I feared for you again. I was pleased when Lone Eagle took you. He is arrogant and impetuous, but he is a good man. The sad thing is that he is content. Oh, he fights with you, but what man does not fight with his mate? And I suspect he comes back to apologize the only way he knows."

"Then why?" I asked through a collapsed throat.

"He has it in his head he wants to marry this girl and father a child. His real need is to prevail over you. In his mind, the man of the family's word is law, that whatever he decides is the way it should be. He has not learned what many of us know, the wife gets her own way, she just never says no. You say no to him, Billy. It drives him crazy."

"Then the mistake is mine."

231

"The mistake is two different cultures. In his, you do not say no to him. In yours, you are free to agree or disagree. He will stay out there until he gets his horses. Then he will come back and marry the girl. He is bound on it. You have lost him unless you will share him."

"I cannot, Cut Hand," I said sadly. "No more than I could share the one I loved above all others."

I wept some of those unmanly tears Cut mentioned after he left until I heard Otter's step on the porch.

# # # # #

Events unfolded as Cut Hand had foreseen. Some days later, Lone Eagle returned, thinner but immensely proud that he led ten ponies. With what he already owned, he had more than enough horses for his prospective bride.

After he cleaned up, he took me to bed with such gentleness and sensitivity I almost lost my reason. But when he informed me afterward he was going to offer the ponies to the girl's father on the morrow, I told him goodbye. He sulked and spent the rest of the night disturbing Otter's sleep by angrily tossing and turning on a bed in the other room.

The eve before the day of his marriage to a pretty little girl named Swallow, I put Lone Eagle's possessions on the porch and went to inform the council I had divorced him. When I got home, Lone Eagle had removed his things from the house and taken a small parfleche he knew I favored. In its place, he left a beautiful, beaded hairbine he wore on special occasions and a letter. While the missive was not as finely crafted as the one Cut had left penned to the door of the Mead, it still spoke the mind of a young man whom I had learned to love, as well.

"Billy. There is sorrow in my heart as I write like you taught me to do. For two winters we have been together. My friends said I could not remain faithful, but I did so. I want you to know this.

"It is my fault that you are throwing me aside. It is not yours. In my heart, I know this thing I want to do is not what you want, but it is what I am determined. So I will never have the right to spend my seed in you again. I will miss that very much. Like I will miss your company. When I see you again, do not turn your face away. I would not blame you, but I hope you do not. I want to be your friend. I took your parfleche to remember our love by, and left you my headband.

Cast it in the fire if you wish, but my heart will burn if you do. Love. Lone Eagle"

I taught these people too well. They expressed themselves better than I can with all my years at Moorehouse College.

Otter stuck close by after Lone Eagle's departure, and that helped make the days endurable, but the nights were dark islands of sleepless agony. I was not yet finished wallowing in self-pity before the events of the world caught up with me again. Cut summoned me to council one afternoon, and upon arriving I found Stone Knife seated on the blanket.

The Sergeant's Gang had struck his camp the day before. Enraged, the Sioux fought off the raiders and pursued them, slaying a large number of the renegades at the cost of three warriors. Stone Knife now had two prisoners and a score of corpses strewn about his territory, many of them white men. One of the captives was a ruffian who wore the blue coat with faint marks where there had once been three stripes. Stone Knife's young men wanted to kill the prisoners and throw their carcasses to the dogs, but their misco sought Teacher's counsel on the matter.

After I related what happened at the trial of the three men we turned over to the army, Stone Knife agreed to bring the two captives to the Mead, so I could accompany him and two of his warriors to the fort with the prisoners. To my surprise, Lone Eagle insisted on going with us.

My former husband showed up before Stone Knife and his people arrived, walking into the house as if he had never left it. He helped himself to a pone spread with maple mel and asked after my health. Grateful for his nonchalant approach, I could have hugged him. The grace and beauty of his masculinity excited me to an erection despite myself. Fortunately, the dogs announced Stone Knife's arrival at that point. Alas, there was no guardian to our front door since South was gone, but the other animals kept us well warned.

#####

Major Jamieson was delighted with the capture of his former sergeant. Stone Knife told his story with great dignity and modesty, and Lone Eagle proudly translated it into English.

The Major entered the attack on Stone Knife's camp into the record, so no guilt attached to the Sioux. He paid over a reward for the renegade and sent a wagon full of supplies back with us. I noticed Lone Eagle and Lt. Morrow exchanging hostile glances a couple of times.

As we were leaving town, Lone Eagle pulled up beside Long. "Aren't you going to him?" he asked bitterly.

I halted, forcing him to come back to me. "Why would you deny me the pleasure of his company? You have your wife. Why shouldn't I have someone?"

He studied the empty horizon for a full minute. "Go back if you wish. He will take your cock up his ass, but that is all you will get from him. You require more."

"And where do I find that?" I demanded, recognizing the truth of it.

"Back where you belong," he answered cryptically and turned away.

CHAPTER 20

When the buffalo came later than usual that next year, Cut suffered a long gash in his hip during the hunt. As Badger was elsewhere treating injuries, I had the task of repairing his manly thigh, a bittersweet chore. Tonight he would flank his wife with more caution than abandon.

As talk turned to the coming winter move, Otter announced he was not going with the band this year. Secretly, I was relieved. I had considered wintering at Yawktown, but it was not something I desired.

We accompanied the caravan a few leagues south, so Otter could check on the Conestoga's green new driver. Lone Eagle rode beside me for a distance chatting about his hope of becoming a father, giving me another clue to our failure. Swallow had missed her menses, which he took as a sure sign of his prowess.

Cut Hand also sought my company, although he had much to do during the march. His people had prospered, so few actually walked on these journeys any longer. I was proud of the way he had managed the affairs of his people and took this opportunity to tell him so.

"Would that I had handled my own equally well," he responded sourly. "I crave love at my fireside. Oh, she loves me in her own way," he added quickly, as though ashamed of his outburst. "But it is not the best way. Once I had a wife who loved unselfishly."

"Cut Hand, your wife keeps a good lodge and sees to your son, who is a healthy and happy three-year-old. She is denied more children, but I wager she takes care of your needs. Many men do not have so much."

"As usual, you are right. Tell me something, friend, when will you begin teaching Dog Fox?"

"As soon as Morning Mist consents to it."

"She will consent," he said grimly. "I want all of your knowledge poured into his head. I think he will have great need of it."

"Then let Otter and me have him next summer for a time each day. If there are others who would have their children learn, send them as well. Maybe I'll become a real teacher."

"You are a real teacher," he said, kicking his horse forward in aid of a woman having trouble with her load.

Otter and I did not reach the Mead until dark. After supping and bathing, he seemed in a spleen over the prospect of a long separation from his people. Seeking diversion, we took out the chess set, and his mood eased. Sensing he was loath to go to his own bed, I suggested he move his blankets before the fireplace in my room; an offer he readily accepted.

Before the northers wailed snowflake tears, we had seen to our winter needs. Food was plentiful, wood and chips were stored, our brook ran cold and clear, the animals were put away safely, and I would not be alone again this year. For the first time since Lone Eagle left, my spirits rose.

A prolonged snow storm took care of that. We studied and read and worked at chores, yet the urge to get outside the four walls bore down upon us. Our rackets got us a distance from the house, but the white snowscape and leaden skies made the out-of-doors a prison, as well. Otter worked on mending furniture on the west side of the house or took to the barn for an hour at a time. I walked in one day as he stood in the west fronting room smoothing down a pelt and realized with a shock that his garments outlined an erection. Normally, I would have teased him, but for some reason I withdrew quietly.

Later, I challenged him to a game of Euchre, which he accepted with false cheer. What a mistake I made in not insisting he remain with his people for the winter! After the first game, he announced he wanted his bath. We lifted the hot water to the shower, and I heated another pot. Otter's back was to me; and I briefly admired muscles I had never noticed before rippling down its length.

His bath complete, Otter helped prepare my shower. I took a long time with it, in no hurry to reach my solitary bed. The bathing room was snug and comfortable. I likely kept things too warm, wasting fuel I would rue later, but we had moved to the same side of the house and would save firewood in that manner.

One lamp burned low as I stepped into the common room. Otter was not at the table or in his own blankets, so he must have gone to the other side of the house for some reason. I padded naked to my dressing table and drew a comb through hair in need of cutting, something I despised doing. Movement caught my eye in the mirror. I turned. Through the gloom of this unlighted corner of the room, I discerned his form. He lay belly down on my bed, brown flesh glowing golden in the faint lamplight. My throat seized up. I moved bedside to protest that he did not have to do this for me, but no sound escaped my larynx.

My struggle for words died as he reached to stroke my belly. He played with the light brown hair trailing from my navel to my bush. He nuzzled me with his lips. Glorying in his touch, I fell across him. He rolled us over and placed his head on my belly with my pipe trapped between us. I pulled him up to me; he put a hand against my lips.

"I want to, Teacher. I've wanted to for a long time. But you never looked at me like you did the others."

"You were a child, Otter! How could I look at you that way?"

"I love you, Bil .,. Billy," he said, faltering over my given name, which was unfamiliar to his lips. "I understood Cut Hand. He found you and brought you here. You belonged to him. But when that was over, I wanted you to see me. Lone Eagle thought it was fun to watch you and that army officer do it, but I didn't like it. It hurt. And then Lone Eagle coveted you. I could see it happening, but I kept hoping you'd look over him and see me."

"You weren't yet sixteen when Lone Eagle took me."

"I got hard for you all the time. I used to go out in the barn and take care of it, so you wouldn't see me that way. And at the same time, I wanted you to see."

"You are a beautiful young man, and so help me, I want you."

"Then lie back and let me do it for you."

He lay between my legs and tasted my sensitive places. Inexperienced, he suffered some difficulty in taking me. Once, he raised his head and smiled ruefully. "How can that yellow-headed officer do it so easy?"

"Practice," I gasped, anxious for him to resume.

He lowered his lips back to me, and the sight of his dark head working over my pipe brought me to climax. I pulled him to my lips and kissed him, my own juices fresh on his tongue.

"I want to be your wife, Billy."

My heart jittered. This tall, virile young man was offering himself to me in any manner I wanted. His own pipe pressed against my groin, proving his desire. This was not a favor to me – it was his own true lust, his own need.

Cautiously, I made my entry of his virgin body. Each time I halted to give him rest, he urged me on, meeting every thrust with one of his own. He came before I did, crying in joy at ejaculating with a hard pipe flanking his channel. His inner muscles gripped me, milking my cock like a dairyman pulling cream from a teat.

We slept then, and I woke fearful of his reaction to our intimacy. He lay studying my features intently. I moved to take his pipe, but he stopped me.

"A husband doesn't do that for his wife!" He sounded shocked.

"You have a lot to learn," I smiled, acquiescing for the moment. I mounted him to watch his handsome, beardless face. Sore from the previous night, he could not completely hide the pain, but when I faltered, Otter locked his heels behind me and pulled me firmly into him. The excitement of his male beauty drew me to climax in record time. I stroked him until he was writhing beneath me. The strength of his ejaculation was astonishing. He squittered far, this young colt of mine. Moments later, I was consumed by another orgasm.

I gasped for a breath above him. We were still joined together by my shriveling pipe. "That was magnificent, Otter. Truly wonderful."

"For me, as well." His black eyes wandered my features as if burning them into his memory. "Just like I imagined it would be. It … it was my first time, you know."

"I thought maybe that Carlos fellow managed to corner you before he left," I tickled. "He disappeared once while you were in the barn."

My young companion – nay, my young mate – took umbrage. "I didn't do it with him! How could you say that?" His outraged features softened into a smile. "But he tried. He walked up behind me when I was forking hay in the loft and rubbed up against me. Grabbed my thing!"

I chuckled at his sour expression. "And what did you do?"

"I turned the fork on him. He almost fell from the loft."

"He was handsome," I continued my teasing. My cock was firming again with all this bawdy talk.

"Not like you," Otter reached up a hand to touch my cheek. "Nobody is handsome like you."

"Nay. Many are more seemly than I. You, for instance."

His eyes widened. "Me? I'm ordinary."

"If you are ordinary, my love," I replied, using those words for the first time with him, "then I am coarse beyond description."

He moved his hips, and I responded. I thought I was sexually exhausted before, but that was nothing to the shell of a man I was when Otter finished with me.

After that, the long winter months seemed ridiculously short. I took him bending over the counter in the fronting room on the west. I fucked him lying flat on the kitchen table. I laid him out on the trading counter and stroked his cock so slowly he was a long time reaching orgasm and was sore for the rest of the day. At length, we came to our senses and went about pursuing goals other than draining one another of seed.

Otter went out alone to run traps on the upper creek, and I ran shivering after him at the cry of a hungry wolf. He looked up in alarm as I came running over the hill frightened out of my wits. His mood turned to indignation when he learned I was afraid for him. He had been taking care of himself for ten years now, he reminded me. Then he grew delighted over my fear for him. He laughed aloud and asked if we were married yet. I told him yes. As soon as the band came back, I would declare it before the council.

# # # # #

When the People returned, Cut Hand was first across the river for a change. He looked at the two of us sitting our ponies and knew immediately.

"Teacher, River Otter, I am happy for you," he said simply.

"Thank you, Cut Hand. I will declare it to the council this evening."

"Good. But make it tomorrow night, and we will drink to it."

"Agreed. It is proper that Cut Hand gets drunk with my husband." With those words, Otter dispelled any doubts about our situation.

"My friend," Cut Hand said, "this time you have found a passion that will last. This young man has loved you since his voice changed. By the way," he added. "Lone Eagle is a father. Little Yellow Flower greeted the world just before we started our move."

I was happy for my former husband. Maybe a daughter would settle him down. I told him as much when he splashed across later,

239

cradling a small bundle in his arms. His wife rode behind looking tired and weak.

"She is a beautiful child." I made my pronouncement over the small, wrinkled face squinting up from a cocoon of blankets.

"No, but she will be when she becomes human," he answered with uncharacteristic modesty. "What is it I hear? I am happy for you. Otter will be good for you, and you have always been good for Otter. It is a natural thing."

The following night, I stood beside Otter and declared to the council I had taken him to wife. He acknowledged this as his true wish, and it was done. No one seemed surprised since he had been a part of my household for a good part of his life. If the roles we played were unexpected, no one let it show.

On the way home, barely conscious from Cut Hand's promised drunk, I mused that in March of this year, 1840, I had turned twenty-and-nine-years, and my handsome, Win-tay wife was a full decade younger.

My Win-tay wife poured me into bed where I soundly slept away our wedding night.

CHAPTER 21

I had three marvelous years with Cut Hand and six additional moons marred by the presence of Morning Mist. Even so, he was the one who set me on my life-path, bringing me face to face with my true nature and introducing me to those who became "my people."

Poor Butterfly was but a brief sonata. I have often wondered at our future had fate not intervened to deprive me of her sweet presence and that of the child that would have been mine – though not of my blood.

Lone Eagle and I enjoyed one another for two tumultuous years. Our couplings – both of the body and the mind were aggressive and explosive. In the end, I failed him as I had failed Cut Hand. Alas, a woman's womb was stronger than what I had to offer.

The next ten snows with Otter were magnificent. That beautiful young man was attentive but unassuming, eager but not demanding, loving but not possessive. His feelings were easily damaged, yet he was difficult to raise to anger. I finally understood what Cut Hand and Lone Eagle meant about a proper Indian wife. He ran my household efficiently, worked beside me on our farm, hunted with me, and when desperadoes appeared, fought for me.

Mindful of his vulnerability should something befall me, I revealed my hoard of gold and silver coins and spent hours drilling him on the worth of ducats, pieces of eight, sovereigns, half-joes, and all the coins in my treasury. I pounded the value Americans gave these scraps of metal into his skull. He shook his head, amazed they were coveted above horseflesh. In fact, I feared he did not truly comprehend the lengths to which some white men would go to possess such a bonanza as they represented.

We had long since taken in Dog Fox and a dozen of the band's children to implant foreign information into their bright little minds. Morning Mist gave Cut grief at turning over her child, but he put his foot down firmly on her small toes, and the boy became an eager learner. When her time came, Yellow Flower attended our impromptu school, and was later joined by a brother and sister. It was a matter of vast pride that I remained friends with both my former husbands.

As smoothly as my personal life was proceeding, it was not the same for the Great Plains. Westward pressure continued at a steady pace. Strange Indians appeared each year, not always peacefully. The Sioux were finally goaded into reprisals against white encroachment. Murders of individual Indians occurred without punishment, but armed resistance brought harsh reprisals. Many times over those ten years, the Blue Coats came through our territory on their way to punish some band prodded into revolt. Cut's young men became increasingly restive, and a few joined other chiefs who were not so doggedly committed to peace. The buffalo came in dwindling numbers.

In that distant world east of the Missouri, the United States suffered growing pains. The Iowa Territory, established by Congress in 1838, encompassed much of the lands the Yanube occupied. General Winfield Scott and seven thousand soldiers forcibly removed fourteen thousand Cherokee from Georgia and Tennessee to Indian Territory in Arkansas and Oklahoma. Joshua R. Geddings of Ohio, a Whig, became the first abolitionist congressman. The following year, some fool proposed cutting a canal from the Atlantic to the Pacific across the Isthmus of Panama.

The census of 1840 counted some seventeen million souls in the United States, and I tried in vain to make the Yanube understand what a host that represented. The war hero, William Henry Harrison, got elected to the White House, but old Tippecanoe's lungs killed him with pneumonia, and his vice president, John Tyler, became president. In '44, the country annexed the Republic of Texas as a territory, occasioning the long threatened war with Mexico the following year during the administration of yet another president, James K. Polk, a Democrat. The fighting went on for a couple of years, seemingly so Old Rough and Ready, General Zachary Taylor, could vie with Old Fuss and Feathers, General Winfield Scott, to determine who could best whip the Mexicans. Somewhere in the middle of it, Texas was admitted as the twenty-eighth state.

In 1848, the Treaty of Guadalupe Hidalgo ended the war, costing the Mexicans Texas and some five-hundred thousand square miles from New Mexico across to California and up into parts of the Colorado and Wyoming territories. Soon afterward, somebody discovered gold near Sacramento, California. Hopes the rush would drain off some of our own settlers failed to materialize. Zachary Taylor must have killed more Mexicans than Winfield Scott because he got himself elected the twelfth President, but he didn't last long either. They say cholera put Millard Fillmore in his chair.

Closer to home, by the year 1850 we began hearing talk of proposed solutions to the Indian problem in the west. Treaties protecting the Miami, Shawnee, Delaware, and others were scrapped by settler aggression. After another defeat of the tribesmen at Fallen Timbers, the resulting Greenville Treaty ceded most of Ohio and parts of Indiana to the Americans, although it also recognized the principle of Indian sovereignty. The talk and the trend were unmistakable; the nations would be herded into reservations. To what mean piece of fallow earth would my beloved Yanube be shipped?

I tried to prepare them for what was to come, but my concepts were no longer the vague notions of eighteen years ago. Now I was talking about the reality of the army rooting them out and carrying them off to some foreign land. Cut was cautious in his embrace of my warnings because he would face a revolt if the *tiospaye* truly believed what I was saying. We had a long private discussion the evening before the band left for winter grounds in the late fall of 1850. He listened patiently to my alarms and reminded me he was widely known to favor peace.

Cut considered leaving Dog Fox with Otter and me that winter, so he could complete his studies. Nearing fifteen, the boy was as handsome and well formed as his father. His presence was sweet pain to me, since he looked out of his father's deep black eyes studied with golden points of light. He was acquiring the arrogance of his warrior class without the awkwardness Lone Eagle suffered at that age. Unfortunately, he adored both Otter and me too much for Morning Mist to turn him over to us for the winter.

Acknowledging my happiness with Otter these last ten years, Cut ventured onto the thin ice of recollecting our own love. He laughingly recalled my bumbling attempt at fellatio as he lay bound to a tree. He described the startled look on my face that quickly turned blissful when he fucked me the first time. As he spoke, I felt a powerful, unrequited lust for this handsome man.

After we saw the *tiospaye* across the Yanube River, Otter and I went about preparing for the coming winter. Over the years, we had perfected our routine, and were seldom afflicted with cabin fever. We saved sufficient chores and projects to keep us busy during the long winter months. This season promised to be a squaw winter, for although the People had already moved, the weather still held the warmth of the sun during the day, while the nights were merely chilly, not cold.

We no longer had the dogs to warn of the approach of strangers. House, the last one, had died this past summer. It was Otter's sharp hearing that alerted us this time. James Morrow, sporting new captain's bars, and a troop of hard-riding, dusty dragoons bore down upon us from the east. That surprised me. Normally he approached from the west. Both of us went to greet him with broad smiles. Otter held none of the jealousy that had infected Lone Eagle. My friend's failure to return our cordial greetings alarmed me.

"I fear I'll not be welcome this time, Billy." He dismounted wearily. "I have bad news. Tragic news!"

A band of raiders had destroyed a farm located south of the Yanube on one of its small tributaries, murdering the farmer, his wife, and three growing children. The homestead lay just east of the route Cut Hand and his people likely took. Alarms went out to both Ft. Ransom and Ft. Yanube, some twenty miles closer. Captain Smith led a strong troop on a forced march and found signs of movement to the east and to the southwest.

Smith took the bulk of the dragoons and followed a solitary set of tracks to the southwest, figuring they would unite with the broad lodgepole trail of a moving camp they had cut earlier. The Captain sent James to the east where he intercepted a troop from Ramson in hot pursuit of the murderers, a gang of mixed bloods, renegade whites, and Indians. They overtook the raiders, recovering horses and other goods from the looted household. When James raced to report the success to his superior, he discovered a horror.

As best he and others could piece together later, Smith approached Cut Hand's moving band of Indians from the rear. Cut's scouts warned him of the dragoons' approach. He had also been told of the farmer's murder by the scout whose tracks the soldiers followed. Knowing the local military commanders recognized him as a peace chief, Cut halted his column, wheeled about with some of his warriors, and rode to meet Smith.

Captain Smith drew his troops into a skirmish line and cut down the Indians at point blank range. Cut Hand fell in the first salvo. The others tried to flee, but were shot from their horses. The remaining warriors rallied around their women and children, but the charge slew most of them.

James, with tears in his eyes, looked down at where I had collapsed to my knees and told me it was a massacre, very few escaped. Smith returned with his own troop to Ft. Yanube after instructing James to deal with stragglers. Instead, my friend came straight to me.

"Why?" I wailed, not really expecting an answer.

"I don't know, Billy. He feared the Indians irrationally. The recent uprisings petrified him beyond reason. Maybe he panicked when Cut Hand approached with his warriors. Or maybe he's just a rotten whoreson who took advantage of a situation simply because he could!"

Fighting my way to my feet, I told Otter to bring the wagon. Understanding what I was about, James insisted on accompanying us. At that point I cared not what he did. The sight of that blue uniform was repugnant to me. Yet James had disobeyed orders to deliver the terrible news in person.

Before I could gather the supplies we needed, shooting broke out in my meadow. I rushed to the porch to find the troopers running toward a fallen figure. With a moan, I leapt from the porch and elbowed them away. Lone Eagle's bleeding body lay sprawled in the grass.

"He jumped us, Cap'n!" one of the privates cried, pleading for understanding.

I ignored them and gathered my dead husband in my arms, carrying him to the burial plot where Butterfly rested. James set some of his men to hacking out a grave. Before setting a foot toward the south, I saw that beautiful man wrapped in a blanket and covered with earth. The hairbine he left for me years ago went around his brow; his medicine pouch was secreted on his person.

We found Lone Eagle's dead pony less than half a league from the Mead. Injured in the ambush, the brave was making his way to me when he saw the troopers in the meadow. Wounded, probably dying, he made one last desperate attempt to take some of the enemy with him. A death song on his bleeding lips, Lone Eagle charged into the troops firing his rifle and raising his hatchet.

We almost tore the wagon to splinters reaching the massacre site. My poor people had not got even half their journey done. The vast horde of vultures brought home the reality of James's story more than the sight of the bodies themselves. The troopers spread over the countryside firing weapons to scare off the carrion birds. I found Cut Hand first, and a cry escaped me at the sight of his flesh torn by army bullets and rapacious birds. He was handsome even in death. I wrapped him in a blanket and left him where he lay. Then we went about the grisly task of collecting the bodies of my fallen people and burying them in a huge common grave in a natural hollow.

At first neither Otter nor I would allow the soldiers to touch them. James let us discover for ourselves the enormity of the task and then quietly ordered his men to help. We examined each still form, seeking to identify everyone. The little tots were the worst because of the damage done by the birds and the bullets. I found Bear Paw near his friend and chief. Lone Eagle's wife and children were there. Badger lay near his family, but nowhere could I find Morning Mist and Dog Fox. I hoped by some miracle they had survived.

We returned to the Mead in the dark of night. Otter had said nothing to me all afternoon. He was discombobulated, as was I. James and his troopers paced us, refusing to allow us to proceed without them. At the Mead, he ordered a new grave dug, and we laid Cut Hand to the right of his sister. Now this little yard held two husbands and a wife.

James stayed the remainder of the night, although he remained outside with his men. Otter held me to his breast while I wrestled with the certain knowledge I slew my beloved and his people as assuredly as if I unleashed the volleys that felled them. Cut Hand trusted his person to the military; he delivered his *tiospaye* into their hands because I had preached peace, peace, peace! For eighteen years, I told him to make his intentions known and trust to the honor of the military. Now he was dead. They were dead.

When I recovered consciousness the next morning, James was preparing to move out. He entered the house and located me at the kitchen table. Otter was nowhere to be seen.

"Are you all right, Billy?" James laid a hand on my shoulder.

"No, but there's nothing either of us can do about it. Where's Otter?"

"He is down at the river. We talked a little this morning. He's a good man."

"One of the best. They all were, my Yanube."

"I'm going to file a report," James said. "That whoreson won't get away with this!"

I rose and faced him. "You will ruin your career. Nobody wants to hear about an army officer killing Indians."

"Career be damned! This is a matter of what's right. I'm going to send a report to Major Wallston; he's about to get his silver leaf. He knew Cut Hand, respected him. He'll listen. And the captain who led the Ft. Ramson troop went back with me. He saw the scope of the slaughter with his own eyes. Not all the troopers will lie for Smith. We'll raise a stink about this, Billy. Might not do us any good, but they'll hear from us."

"I'll write letters," I said immediately. "The President and Congress and the War Department. What about Jamieson? Can we count on him?"

"I doubt it," James answered slowly. "I'm afraid you were right about him. He's not a bad man, just not very strong. Smith was acting under his command, so he might feel his neck is on the line, too."

"Then I'll put it there. Copies of all my letters will go to him; maybe he'll give us Smith to save his own career."

"Perhaps, Billy, but don't count on it. Don't count on anything."

"Thank you, James. Congratulations on your promotion. It was good of you to come tell me in person and then help to … do what had to be done."

I surrendered to a deep despair after the troop left, grieving alone for a time before going to the door. I spotted smoke half a mile away at the edge of the river and knew Otter was purifying himself after handling all those corpses.

I gave him privacy until well after high sun and then succumbed to my need for him. I walked to the small brush-covered hut he had constructed for his *inipi*, his sweat lodge. Shucking my clothing, I crawled through the opening. He was at prayer; I waited until he opened his eyes before speaking.

"Are you all right?"

He peered through thick banks of steam. "How can a man be all right when his whole world has been destroyed?" Then he moved to my side and put an arm around me. "I am sorry. So long as I have you, an important part of my world still exists. I am yours, and you are mine. Nothing else matters."

"Except to see that the pimp who destroyed our family pays. And he will pay, Otter. I swear this. From this moment on, I exist for two things, your love and our revenge."

"He will not pay. All he killed were some red dogs."

"Red dogs with voices! Red dogs with friends who have voices. You will see. You will see!"

He, the young man who had endured the medicine lodge's enervating steam for hours, pulled me out of the mists and led me to the river where we washed the last of the poisons from our bodies and came alive again in the pure, frigid waters. Collecting our clothing, we walked home naked in the cold autumn air. He sat me before the fireplace and brushed the circulation back to normal in my limp body.

I returned the favor and discerned this was not the Otter I slept with the night before. To that moment I viewed him as a mere youth. But a strong, fit man of twenty and nine snows submitted to my touch now. I knew just as certainly that our relationship had altered. He proved me right when his hard pipe, fully as big and strong as Cut Hand's, pierced me that night. Our roles had changed. He was the proud Yanube warrior, and I, his Win-tay wife. It was a welcome change. I accepted his seed gratefully, gaining momentary respite from our tragedy and discovering anew how deeply I loved him.

Otter crawled over me in the dead of night. A small fire flickered in the fireplace grate, so I was able to see him dimly.

"What is it?" I asked. I was not so much sleepy as dim-witted from lack of sleep.

"Somebody's outside," he whispered.

We drew on clothing, claimed our weapons, and slipped the bars on the front door. My hinges are always oiled, so we made no noise as we gained the porch.

"Over here!" Otter hissed and disappeared around the west end of the porch. Fearful for his safety, I laid a rifle barrel across the corner, keeping it high so as not to harm him. In moments, he was back, leading a woman trailed by shadowy figure. From their tattered dress, they must have been survivors of the massacre.

Spiriting them inside before stirring the fire, I was shocked to behold the drawn countenance of Morning Mist in the dim light. The slender youth behind her was Dog Fox. Happy to see any survivors of that dreadful slaughter, I clasped her arm. "Are you all right?"

"Y … yes," she gasped and about collapsed. I led her to a chair and forced both of them to sit. Otter was already warming food. "Oh, Teacher," she wailed. "It was awful! They cut him down while he rode out with open hand. They killed them all!"

"How did you escape?"

"After they killed the men, they came for us, shooting the women and children. Dog Fox was with me because I had asked for his help. He grabbed a rifle, but I saw it was hopeless. I –"

"She struck me with a rock so I fell down and lay senseless while my friends and relatives were shot down," the youngster said bitterly.

"She saved your life," I told him. At the moment that meant less than nothing to him, but in time he would come to appreciate her action.

Morning Mist continued. "And then Bear Paw's wife fell against me. I lay beneath her until the Blue Bellies passed. As soon as I could, I got Dog Fox to his feet, and we escaped. We … we went to Stone Knife's camp, but he had already moved. I did not have any other place to go."

"I'm glad you came," I assured the woman who had wrecked my life. The time for all that was past. Now it was survival.

"The army has already come and gone, so you are safe here for the moment, but I am doing something that will make it more dangerous. I am going to the fort and seek justice for Cut Hand and our People. There are those who will listen." I studied the two sad figures. "There is one thing. Your husband … your father is out there lying beside Butterfly. As is Lone Eagle."

The old enmity lighted her narrowed eyes. "So you have all of your husbands and your wife with you!"

"Yes, because I would not leave them in a common grave where the rest of the People lie. You may visit him tomorrow."

After they were settled in beds on the west side, sleep was impossible. Otter and I sat at the table drinking coffee. His deep voice interrupted my thoughts.

"She hates you. You hate her. So now we will live in a house of hate."

"You are wrong. I do not hate her because she saved the most precious thing in the world to me, except for you. She saved –"

"The boy," he finished. "Cut Hand's son. He who would be yours if you had woman's parts." Otter looked at me. "He is a good boy. He has more of his father than his mother, I think. He would have rather died, you know."

"Yes, and like Lone Eagle, he may yet find a way to do so. But that will pass as his juices flow, and he learns life is good to have even in difficult circumstances."

"This makes your life harder, I think." Otter nodded his handsome head.

"Yes. I have always sought to be a truthful man. Now I must learn to scheme, cozen, flam. If he is to survive … if you are to survive, I must do so. And the first lie I tell will hurt you, I'm afraid. If anyone comes to the Mead, I will refer to you as my servant, as one who is invisible."

He smiled wryly. "Just like I used to be."

"You were never my servant!" I cried.

"No, but I was invisible."

I sighed acknowledgement of that fact. "Otter, I need some time at Ft. Yanube. I hope the weather holds off as I must go before winter. If I can't get back will you see to them?" I nodded my head in the direction of our sleeping guests.

"They will be safe with me."

CHAPTER 22

I left at dawn without disturbing the two exhausted sleepers. I had not gone far before an armed warrior blocked my way. Given that word of the murders would have spread far and wide, I did not know what reception to expect even though I recognized the man as a Pipe Stem. He gave the empty-hand salute, and we nudged our ponies forward.

"Carcajou would speak to you," he said quietly. "We are preparing to move to winter quarters, so he was unable to come himself. It is not far."

My friend sat on the ground before the skeleton of his tipi and invited me to join him while his wives completed the task of taking down the lodge. He waved his warriors away after our medicine smoke.

"Teacher," he asked when we were alone, "are you well?"

"No, not well, but I am alive."

"We heard what happened."

"Then you know I killed him."

Despite his usually stoic demeanor, he started. "What do you mean?"

"All these years, I preached peace in his ears … yours, too. And what did peace gain him? Three bullets in the chest! If he hadn't listened to me, he would be alive today."

"Are you so maddened by misery you cannot know what drivel you speak? Cut Hand walked his way through soldiers and white settlers because of the knowledge you gave him. I have done the same. Because one criminal with the double bars on his shoulders murders him on the plains does not make you responsible. Cut Hand and I were not friends, but I respected him. I respected him because he had the intelligence to listen with open ears and decide what was best for his people. He knew what came from your mouth was best, so that is the way he took."

"That may be so, Carcajou, but the words I speak now are to trust no one. Assume no one comes in peace."

"Listen to your own tongue, Billy." He had mastered my name by now. "They are words that have always been there, words I have always heeded."

"I must be on my way. I am going to the fort to see if I can stir up trouble for the captain who murdered my people. I am going to stir it all the way to the Big Father in Washington if I have to."

"You do so at your own risk. Teacher's Mead may no longer be safe."

"Then so be it. This thing must be done. Carcajou, once again I ask a boon. If any inquire about me, tell them I live at Teacher's Mead with my Indian wife and son and my servant, Otter."

His eyebrows climbed. "Your wife?"

"Morning Mist ... Cut Hand's wife ... escaped. His son is with her. And if Otter is seen as my servant, perhaps be will become invisible."

"How long will she stay?"

"Until I find some place safe for her."

"She will likely go to the Sioux. Or perhaps remain with you."

His words haunted me the rest of the way to the fort. Surely, she would not want to remain, but if she did, I must suffer it because of the boy.

Yawktown had grown to the point where the city fathers had seen fit to change the name to Yanube City. My friends from the old days had become men of substance, and I was about to use their influence to the full extent of my ability. Since it was late when I arrived, I took a room at the Rainbow Hotel, as the establishment was now called, and bathed in one of their new baths. Each floor had a fully equipped bath with a zinc-lined tub.

Early the next morning, I called on the land office and made certain the title to Teacher's Mead and the one hundred sixty acres around it was correctly entered. The government had surveyed some years back, permitting me to exercise my right of purchase under the 1841 Pre-Assumption Act. Now I made a bid for contiguous land. If no one contested my offer, I would own forty thousand acres of land lying astride the Yanube River. I bid an outrageous nine cents per acre, seriously denting my account at the bank. It seemed politic to pacify

Banker Crozier, whose influence I would need, by agreeing he could draft most of the cost from my account with the bank at Ft. Ramson.

The most crucial part of my scheme rested with the next call. Abraham Kranzmeier, the Jewish tailor, now had four young seamstresses and two sons working for him. Despite his age, he arrived at the shop each day to inspect every stitch that went into garments made in his name. I had given him custom over the years, and we held one another in esteem. He flicked a bushy, gray eyebrow when I asked to speak in private, but wordlessly led me back to a room furnished like a comfortable parlor in a home. He offered a cup of expensive imperial tea with lemon and settled back to stroke his long beard and listen.

"Abraham, I come to you because if anyone in this town understands the yoke of oppression, it is you. I intend to do something not exactly proper, not for my own personal gain, but for the protection of people who will need it in the years to come."

I paused for him to volunteer some comment. "I heard what happened to your Indian family. You come on behalf of the survivors."

"I have a beautiful piece of ground at Teacher's Mead. When my time comes, I want to make certain it goes to my intended heirs."

The old man took out a crooked, elaborately carved pipe, and for one minute I thought he was going to offer it in ceremonial observation. "So you see the same future I do," he said, settling the pipe comfortably in the corner of his mouth.

"Indians are going to become the Jews of America," I answered. "They will be denied ownership of their own land, citizenship in their own country, and forfeit their very lives if no protection is offered. I seek to provide a few of them this protection."

"You want to will them your property."

"Yes, and my testament will not be honored unless I fix things a little. So I come to a respected member of a community with a long history of surviving hostile systems."

"In other words, you come to an old Jew. An old Jew whose nephew, although he bears a gentile name, is the clerk for this territory. Tell me what you need."

I wanted a record of a marriage between me and Butterfly, a woman of the Yanube band, in the spring of 1834, some two years before the actual event, and a marriage license to go with it. I wanted a record of birth and a birth certificate for William Cuthan Strobaw as issue from this marriage for any day in December 1835 plus a baptismal certificate in the Methodist Church, one of the more active in the area. The old man listened and then named a sum, explaining it was not payment to him but the cost of having the items created. I handed over some of my hoarded gold coins and asked him to expedite the process. I wanted as much time between this and my own demise as possible. Time often perfected titles.

This business completed, I retired to my room and began writing letters. They were difficult to compose, not only because of the emotion behind their content, but also by reason of needing them to be documents of a logical, educated mind that would not be put off by delay and frumpery.

James knocked on my door after the evening dinner hour and told me of the rumors flying about the fort. Captain Smith's account of the Battle at Hampton's Homestead, as it was being billed, was already forwarded to the War Office. I showed James my efforts to date, and he handed over a working copy of his own report lodged with Major Jamieson only this morning. There were minor discrepancies between the two, but that lent credence that each had made his own independent observations.

The next fortnight was not pleasant. My letter of accusation, together with copies of missives posted to the White House, the Indian Bureau, the Territory's Congressional Delegate, and the War Department, were delivered to Jamieson. I remained in town and held myself available to answer questions.

Once, Captain Smith, himself, faced me in the commandant's office before a gathering of his peers and promptly lost his composure, referring to me as an Indian lover guilty of aiding in the murder of white men. He, of course, referred to the Sergeant's Gang, although in the recesses of my mind, I held the secret knowledge of the slaying of the two man-stealers. I remained true to my bearing – solid and dignified, I hoped – and in my opinion, his loss of control did not fall to his favor.

Nonetheless, to make an officer of the United States Army pay for the killing of heathen Indians, no matter that many were women and children, was no easy task. I had seen newspapers and penny dreadfuls decrying savage, murderous red Indians of the western frontier and comprehended the mood of the public. After the facedown with Smith, I hastily posted another set of documents to the authorities with additional details, including the names of some of the enlisted personnel required to take part in the action. Caleb Brown, Banker Crozier, Abraham Kranzmeier, Benjamin Bowers, and others of my acquaintance also posed questions to the authorities over the misnamed Battle at Hampton's Homestead.

The weather turned fierce on my return to Teacher's Mead, but I pressed on, anxious to reach home. Otter and Dog Fox were both happy to see me safely back. Morning Mist, now recovered, acted as if the place were her own. I would have none of it, and sat her down at the kitchen table to tell her so.

"Morning Mist," I shook my finger in her face, uncaring the rudeness of the act, "you are here by my sufferance. I have been willing to forgive past wrongs and a hateful countenance, but I will no longer suffer such actions. Behave as a guest – no! Behave as a servant and carry your own load, or I swear I will throw you off the place and have you live or die in the cold."

Her puckered features creased into a hateful smile. "You will not do that, Win-tay. You will not do that because of the boy – my son. You covet him too much."

"If this is true, woman, then beware. There is nothing to prevent me from throwing you out into the snow and keeping Dog Fox for myself."

The look on her face revealed she had not considered that possibility. Had she the means to do so, Morning Mist would have set up a lodge of her own. Recalling the time she came at me with a hatchet after her marriage to Cut Hand, I closely watched my back for a *senight*.

The winter was as miserable as any I recall. Only Otter and Dog Fox allowed me to survive. It was not Morning Mist's hateful presence that oppressed; it was the knowledge that all those beautiful souls were gone, a thought that started me on the path of healing. Those souls were gone, but where? If God were just, as I believed, He had taken them unto Himself and treasured them as dearly as I. In a further effort to repair, I resumed lessons to Dog Fox, attempting to include Morning Mist as a peace offering. She would have nothing to do with it and discouraged her son at every opportunity.

That was when I saw the boy for the man he would become. He handled his mother deftly, never outright rebuffing her, but manipulating the woman to his will. He pursued his lessons diligently

255

and gave me as near proximity to Cut Hand with those haunting, gold-black eyes as was humanly possible.

#

Given the uncertain state of my household, I decided it was time to review my plans with Otter. In the dead of night after he had inflamed and then satisfied every fiber of my physical being, I explained I was arranging to leave the Mead and its environs to the boy rather than to him because Dog Fox, or William Cuthan Strobaw, as he was to be renamed, should outlive him by years. If examination of title survived my death, I did not want another test of ownership until many years later.

The remaining gold coins secreted in the cavern, however, were Otter's alone. Over the years, I had cautiously exchanged the more valuable pieces at the banks in Yanube City and Ft. Ramson for a greater number of gold and silver coins of reduced value. My goal had been to excite less interest when exchanging such coins for goods or services. Now this had an added but unintended benefit; an Indian spending an occasional coin should not draw undue attention.

Otter heard me out and strongly urged that I not to take Morning Mist into my confidence, perceiving her as one who would grasp any opportunity to further her own fortunes, even at the expense of her son. Once I was gone, Otter would find himself evicted if she had her way, whereas Dog Fox would understand the place was really Otter's so long as he saw fit to live there.

By spring thaw, Morning Mist and I were at one another's throats daily. One or the other was constantly on the peck. She was a hateful woman who brought out the worst in me. I know not where the thing would have ended had not Stone Knife, now an old man, stopped by the Mead after the thaw. Morning Mist, at the rag-end of a thrown fit, quickly accepted an offer to join his camp since there were already a few Yanube with him. I despaired of the boy's departure, but it was necessary at this juncture.

It was well into spring before Otter agreed to the next step in my plan. We journeyed to Ft. Ramson where we were not so well known as at Yanube City and set about legally changing his name to Joseph Strobaw Otter. He insisted on keeping his own name, but proudly accepted part of mine. He stood before the court dressed in civilized clothing with his long hair shorn into a white man's haircut, and spoke to the magistrate in perfect, unaccented English. The clerk was impressed in spite of himself. I carefully explained that Otter was a nephew who had recently come to live with me and accept my civilizing ways. Thus, I managed to get the totally false claim of one-half white blood entered into the record.

I rested at the Mead for a day before undertaking another trip to Ft. Yanube alone. Abraham handed over the precious documents I required, and I promptly had them copied and certified at a local lawyer's office where a will was drawn leaving my entire estate to my son, William Cuthan Strobaw.

Major Jamieson's reception was not as cordial as usual. He treated me distantly. Apparently, Jamieson had received queries from higher authority over the Hampton's Homestead Affair. This rendered him uncertain over my influence in Washington City – a circumstance that afforded me some measure of protection, I finally concluded.

James was in splendid isolation, totally shunned by the other officers of the post. Such treatment was not unexpected, and he bore it with the best possible face. Nonetheless, I knew our dinner together that evening was a rare treat for him. Caleb and other influential men took note of his plight, and made a point of extolling the virtues of the junior officer. It was to our fortune Jamieson was a weak man. James advised by messenger a few weeks later his exile was easing.

Otter undertook regular visits to Stone Knife's camp; I, less frequently. On my last one, the old man asked if I wished to have Morning Mist back among my household. I hastily declined.

CHAPTER 23

For two long years, I posted letters and inquiries concerning the Yanube Wipe-Out, as the incident came to be retitled, even though my prosecution was unpopular in some quarters. Although Smith never confronted me again directly, I received oblique messages. Miscreants shot up the front of the house in the middle of the night, shattering two of my precious window lights. The Pipe Stem told me later there had been soldiers in the area.

A party of Nakota-speakers unfamiliar to me marooned on my doorstep demanding liquor. When I denied having any, they informed me I lied; the Blue Coats said I stocked it by the kegs. I took two of their ringleaders through my house and barn to convince them otherwise. Eventually they went away after chopping up the edge of my porch with hatchets out of ennui.

In early October 1852, a message reached me from James advising that while Captain Smith would not be brought to trial for his crimes, he had resigned his commission under threat of a Blue Ticket, a bad conduct discharge. In no small part, the man was caught in his own loop because the tribes were rendered hostile by his cowardly, murderous actions. He professed to be returning back east, but James recommended caution, as Smith was an angry, vengeful man who had taken refuge in strong drink as the pressure on him grew.

Otter grimaced sourly and said at least the whoreson would not be in a position to assassinate anyone else. It was a short measure, not what we wanted but better than we expected.

A few days later, a Sioux arrived to warn that a white man with a packhorse was on the trail from Ft. Yanube. He was an army man, yet not an army man, wearing the shirt but not the decorations of a real Blue Coat. It could, of course, be any veteran on the drift, but there was no doubt in my mind the man was Smith.

Otter was at Stone Knife's camp on one of his visits to Dog Fox, so I set out to meet the murderous thug on my own. The man lacked the stones to face me honestly, and I was not about to submit to a bullet in the back when I least expected it, so I determined to put an end to the thing once and for all.

Long Wind had been put to pasture, and I now rode a quick, maneuverable pony named Arrow after Cut's old mount. When Smith and I settled our score, the pony would help me survive.

Three hours later, I grew worried. I should have encountered Smith unless he left the path for some reason. Paying closer attention, I bent to the trail and found prints of his horse and pack animal. Turning about, I followed his tracks, at times covered by my own slipshod passage. A hundred yards on my backtrack, I broke sign carelessly unobserved in my earlier passing. Two individuals intercepted the man, and four horses left the trace, heading north. The sign went cold in a small brook. I searched up and down the rill, but located nothing further except a splash of blood on a bush at the edge of the bank. I plucked and shredded the stained leaves.

At first, I suspected the Pipe Stem of extracting revenge for me, but discarded that notion. Carcajou would have found some way to let me know. And it was a Sioux, not a Pipe Stem, who warned me the man was on his way. Finally, I settled on the unthinkable. Among the Yanube, a seventeen-year-old is already a man with a man's obligations. In a few months, Dog Fox would be seventeen. If it had been my mate with him, Otter would bury the horses and personal goods to avoid exciting the interest of some law dog.

When my husband came home the next night, I failed to raise the question, and he volunteered nothing. So far as I know, ex-Captain Smith was neither seen nor heard from again.

# # # # #

Dog Fox spent a few days with us the following summer. Although he was practically grown physically, I judged his mind too young to contemplate deeper matters. Besides, the question of how to handle his mother was not yet resolved. The bright, handsome, young man showed demonstrable progress in his studies; he had read each and every book he took with him when Morning Mist left the Mead. His favorites, he could quote virtually without fault. The boy looked so much like his father that I wept silent tears the first night he was with us. Otter understood and held me quietly in his arms.

My hand was almost forced when Stone Knife came to talk me out of a twist of tobacco. The pressure on the band was too extreme; they were moving west. I argued the white man was there, as well, but the old chief felt he had no option. When it developed he was moving only fifty miles to the northwest, I rested easier.

Carcajou came next to say he was taking his *tiospaye* in tandem with his cousins, the Lakota. I sighed with sadness; that meant our country would be opened to strange bands from the east and more settlers than I wanted to face. It also meant I had to do something to outline my boundaries. An American squatter on the Mead's patented land could cause serious legal problems in the future.

Otter and I labored long and hard to raise obvious markers. They worked reasonably well, although a few were maliciously torn down. Two families had to be removed from my land at gunpoint, but they moved only across my boundary line to become unwelcome neighbors. Some, as I came to know them, were decent folk, but they were where they ought not be. This land belonged to the Indians.

# # # # #

In the summer of '54, Otter came home from a visit to Stone Knife's encampment with another rider in tow. I stepped to the porch and was pleasantly surprised when a taller, more mature Dog Fox smiled at me and clasped my arm affectionately.

"Uncle Billy," he greeted me.

"Dog Fox, it's so good to see you." I looked at Otter, who nodded. With a catch in my throat, I joined them at the table, a cup of coffee clasped in my mitt.

"She has married," Otter spoke into a comfortable silence, "and Stone Knife moves farther west before the winter. He will likely join the Ogallala at Ft. Laramie."

"Then it is time," I murmured.

The youth shot a curious glance at the two of us. "What is it, Uncle Billy?"

"Son," I experienced a strong emotion at the word, "the red man's time is almost run. In a short day, the army will herd your kinsmen onto reservations and turn them into white men without the attendant rights and privileges. There will be hardship, starvation, killings, wars, terrible suffering on both sides, but the red man will lose. I can think of only one way to give you some measure of protection from this. Even this might not work, but it is the best I can do.

"You must learn to call me by another name," I continued, laying a hand over a strong brown arm shaped exactly like his father's as I told him he must become William Cuthan Strobaw, the issue of William Joseph Strobaw and his wife, Butterfly. I told him he must cut off his shining glory, his long hair, and learn to wear trousers and call me father. And I told him why.

"When I die, William, this property will be willed to you. The official records show my marriage to your Aunt Butterfly, and the birth of a son to that union. Her death certificate has been filed showing she died giving birth to a child … you. According to the white man's official records, something by which he lives and dies, you are my son, and in this bag," my hand touched a parfleche on the table, "is a birth certificate making this an official fact.

"If I passed over and my will was probated today, I do not believe the law would permit you to inherit the more than forty thousand acres of this Yanube homeland I have purchased. But I am planning on hanging around a few years in the hope times and attitudes and laws will change, so the Mead will be yours. It comes with only one condition. Otter has earned a warm corner and must always have a home here. He is never to be denied anything. He knows this place will be yours, and he understands why. He is reconciled to it. But no matter who comes to live with you here, no matter who you marry, you must give me your sacred word Otter not only has a home, but is also made to feel welcome. In truth, you will be holding the farm in his stead until he comes to join me."

"You have my oath, father." The young man entered into the spirit of the thing. "But what of my mother?"

"She rests beneath the earth outside that window," I replied.

"What of Cut Hand's widow?" he restated the question.

"That is up to you. She hates me, son. I do not know what she has told you, but surely you are aware I was Cut Hand's Win-tay wife for three and a half years. I loved your father and only gave him up, so he could build a family and assume the leadership of his people. Morning Mist would not accept me as his mate. She had her own reasons, I suppose, but never in my life have I tried to harm her. Just understand that she will never be my friend. And if she discovers what we are doing, she will wreck it. She will cost you your inheritance."

The boy's eyes flicked toward Otter who answered his unasked question. "Yes, we are together now. He has been my mate for fourteen years. He has been good to me, as I have been good to him."

"So I must be my father's sister's son, and that of his male wife," he said, but there was no sting behind the words. "I knew of this thing with Cut Hand," he admitted, "and I have always loved you, Uncle Billy. I knew he loved you, too. I will be proud to call you father. I will not like losing my hair, but I'd rather be scalped that way than the other." He made feeble joke of it.

"And I have loved you, son, like you were my own since Cut Hand brought you to me to start learning."

"My new name ... you gave me the middle name for my father, didn't you?"

"In his honor, yes. But I couldn't make it exact because –"

"Because it sounds too Indian," he finished. "So must I become a white man at heart as well as in name?"

"You must be who you are, William. It matters not what we call you."

\# \# \# \# \#

So that fine young man joined our household and lived a solitary life, learning to be a farmer and rancher in the white man's way. William eagerly sought contact with young people of his own kind, but that was difficult with the camps as far removed as they now were. He saw fit to visit his mother only three times in the years he has been with us. I do not believe this was his choice. Rather, it was Morning Mist making him pay for his desertion to the hated Win-tay. I am quite certain she believed he flanked me daily. Nothing of that sort ever happened, of course; I truly considered him the son of Cut Hand and myself.

Fate intervened to lend a hand in his future salvation. One of the families homesteading across the boundary of our land had three sons and a honey-haired daughter. Dog Fox ... pardon William ... fought the boys at least a half a dozen times before they learned to respect him. It was not easy for William. Indians do not fight in the same manner as white boys, and he was impatient of the boxing lessons I gave him. He preferred rushing in and ending the affair in any manner possible.

263

We asked our neighbors over for picnics and dinners, and one of them responded – the neighbor named Jacobsen with the honey-haired daughter and three feisty sons. The other neighbor, whose name I do not recall as he did not last long in this country, had obvious prejudices and never set foot through our door.

The shock of finding Otter and William well educated prompted a request from the Jacobsens to teach their children. Otter and I readily agreed, and friendships budded.

In time, a romance did as well. Using William's forged baptismal certificate, I saw him married to Mary Jacobsen at the Methodist Church in Ft. Ransom, which was the name of the town as well as the army post.

CHAPTER 24

I am not certain when I first felt the thing within me, but I saw looks of consternation on Otter's face long before we spoke of it.

"What is it, Joseph Otter?" I demanded one day.

"Why are you not eating? You are losing weight."

"I don't know. I have no appetite ... except for you."

"Hush, the children will hear you."

"You are becoming a prude, Otter."

"There were not whites in the house before. Now we have a white woman tending our William's manly needs, and we have three muddied little things that can't decide whether to grow up looking like their handsome father or their pretty mother. And it is not proper to speak of such things to your servant."

"Oh, Otter, I wish I could stand on the walls of the fort and proclaim how dear you are to me."

"You cannot, so don't talk foolishness. Act like a proper wife for once."

"I never have. Why should I start now I'm near fifty years old?"

# # # # #

The pain did not come until the following spring. By then I knew I had a canker feasting on my heart and liver and kidneys – my pluck. Otter plied me with tonics to ease my discomfort. When they gave only limited relief, he grew melancholy until we stood at the little graveyard one day. He looked at me with understanding in his eyes.

"You will see them again, Billy."

"If there's a God in heaven, I will."

"Will you give them my love?"

"Yes. I will tell them what a fine man you came to be. How you rogered me with the best of them and kept me content for twenty years."

"Twenty years. So long, but not so long." He looked around the homestead and watched the children playing happily. "I will miss you."

265

"And I you."

"I will come to you soon."

"Not before your time." I nodded in the direction of William and his wife working the sourdough keg on the porch. "They may need you yet."

"When you are gone, I'll be more of a danger than a help."

"Otter, you've got to promise me you won't –"

"I will wait for my time," he assured me, a hand on my arm. "Besides, you're not gone yet."

"I soon will be, husband. Who will you turn to?"

"No one. There is no one after you."

"You are a man in his prime. You need someone."

"Past that, I think." He patted his flat, muscled stomach.

"I wish … Never mind."

"I would fuck you, wife," he said in a steady voice. "Now."

"You'll have to lock the door. The children –"

"The children will be fine. It is I who needs looking after at this moment."

"Then let's go look after you," I said, trying to hide a sudden pain. He was not fooled, but he was a magician, caressing me, teasing my flesh, expunging the discomfort with his hard manhood. He flanked the seed plumb out of me, proving how much of a man he really was.

# # # # #

I was tired – physically tired and weary of pain – but there was still something to be accomplished. The Jacobsens had brought word of trouble in the east. This war I had prattled about foolishly for thirty years seemed about to become a reality. A few days later, as Otter lay panting at my side, I reached over to stroke his beautiful flesh.

"I must go to Yanube City. And it has to be tomorrow, I think."

He sat up immediately. "You're not up to the trip, Billy. Is it something I can do for you?" Characteristically, he put up no fuss when I shook my head.

Otter would not permit me to sit Arrow, but took me in the buckboard. His decision proved wise when I spent a good deal of time lying in the bed of the rough contraption. He hazed all night, never stopping until we reached the town with my insides well scrambled. Before retiring to a room at the Rainbow and resting to husband the strength I would need, I sent a message to the fort asking James to visit me that evening.

He came, and the shock of my appearance was plainly stamped on his face. "Billy!" he exclaimed.

"It's all right, James. I'm all geed up, but at the moment I'm resting comfortably. Otter brought me. Drove straight through from the Mead. Sleeping in the livery with the wagon right now, I imagine."

"Damnation! I'll get him a room."

"No need to stir up that kind of fuss. He's fine where he is. It's you I'm worried about. Tell me what's happening out there in the big world."

"It's as you've been predicting. President Pierce wasn't able to settle the slavery question any better than anyone else, and it got worse under Buchanan. The Supreme Court struck down the Missouri Compromise in 1857 with the Dred Scott Decision. In fifty-nine a crazy zealot named John Brown attacked the U.S. Arsenal at Harper's Ferry, West Virginia. He got hanged for his trouble, but it stirred up both sides. Last year, Abraham Lincoln was elected president on the Republican ticket. South Carolina seceded from the Union claiming the Doctrine of States Rights. In April, their troops captured the U.S. Arsenal at Charleston. It looks as if most of the slave states will join them. Might have already happened."

"So it's full-scale war, isn't it? What will you do, James?"

"Resign my commission and accept one in the Army of Virginia."

"Are you so anxious to ruin your career and give your life for those same bastards who raped you all through school? Tell me, James, if you'll permit a personal question, what happened to your father's plantation when he died?"

"It's mine now. My brother's running it. I haven't seen it for years."

"The North will win, you know that, don't you? They have the men and industrial capacity. And they have right on their side."

My friend bristled. "Are you so certain?"

"Aren't you? You're a smart man, James. You understand the military. A lot of boys are going to die and be maimed for life because one power structure wants to preserve a corrupt way of commerce that deals in human beings."

"It makes no difference if they lose; it is a matter of honor."

"Listen to yourself. You sound like that shock-pated youth I first saw almost twenty-eight years ago. Idealism! What's that ever got anybody except dead? James, sit out the war right here. You're needed to counteract the Smiths of the army. The War Office will realize you come from Virginia. They will not want you back there, so they'll leave you here where you can do some good. Think man, your brother will be a Virginian for you. If the South wins, he can protect the plantation. If it's the North, salvage something for them."

We argued far into the night. Exhausted and in a great deal of pain, I kept doggedly to my pretenses, wearing him down. James agreed to consider the thing carefully before doing anything rash. Upon taking his leave, he helped me to bed and planted a kiss on my numb lips. I whispered weakly for him to stop at the livery and have Otter come for me in the morning.

I drank up my supply of laudanum like some poor sot guzzling strong drink, but it did not keep the beast feeding on my bosom at bay. The next morning, Otter insisted I rest a bit longer while he found me something to eat. To my consternation, he dawdled away a good portion of the day, but I must have slept because he woke me to load my carcass aboard the wagon.

My mate drove to the bank where Banker Crozier – and I now realize I do not recall his Christian name – came to the wagon to serve me himself. I closed my account to restore my hoard of gold and silver coins for Otter's use. I then said goodbye to Caleb Brown, selling him my interest in the fur trade. Ben Bowers had to do with a short, sad goodbye. Abraham Kranzmeier had passed on years ago.

At nightfall, I asked Otter to halt the wagon. I wanted to star-pitch beneath the big Comanche moon one last time.

"Isn't it beautiful, my love?" I whispered as we lay side-by-side gazing at an incredible display of stars and lustrous gasses dominated by an immense Big Dipper, which he called the Seven Persons. "I have slumbered beside Cut Hand and Lone Eagle under the welkin, but we have never slept beneath the stars. I wonder why that is?"

"It does not matter because we are doing it now. Are you strong enough to accept me?"

"If you're strong enough to give it."

"Hah! You will see. I will show you."

In truth, my conscious self visited elsewhere during a part of the thrumming, although I stayed with him as much as possible. I would not have much more of this handsome man, and I strained to take what enjoyment of him I could.

"The best ever!" he lied gallantly when he finished. He laid his head on my chest, and I stroked his white man's haircut, longing for the long locks of his youth. What had I done to earn the love of such a man?

That was yesterday. Today, Otter brought me home to Teacher's Mead and wanted me to go to bed, but I had other things to do. First, I set out the final words in my journal, completing it with the notation as follows:

William Joseph Strobaw, also known as Teacher and the Red Win-tay to the People of the Yanube,
this final day of October,
Year of our Lord 1861, at Teacher's Mead on the Upper Yanube

Thereafter, I said goodbye to my tall, handsome, well-formed son and his wife and children. I gave them the hard chink from the sale of my fur venture, specie sufficient to see them through a few years, although the farm would provide all they needed. This fine Indian man and his white wife and blood children would be affluent beyond most people in the territory. I prayed to God they would be able to conceal that fact, and told them so.

I asked Otter to help me to my bed where he lay beside me while I uttered my farewell to him. That took some time and all of my strength. Above all, I wished him to understand what he meant to me, how dearly I held him. When that was done, I thought over the words I had set down in the tome clutched to my aching chest, and decided there were too many secrets for it to survive. I told Otter I would toss it into the fire – tomorrow.

EPILOGUE

October 1862, Teacher's Mead on the Upper Yanube

Major James Carleton Morrow closed the journal and stared at the cover. Yes, the tome should likely be fired to preserve the secrets it revealed. But, it also told the personal histories of remarkable men and women. It portrayed a time never again to be seen on the Great Plains. It encapsulated the wisdom of this man called Teacher. Sighing, he withdrew the journal from the fireplace.

Billy Strobaw's prophesy was proving itself at his very moment; the nation was rending itself to pieces in a terrible war. The Confederates had whipped the Union at Manassas and seemed to be winning everywhere. Yet there was no doubt Billy would also be right about the final outcome he predicted from his sick bed a year ago.

James Morrow rose from the kitchen table and strode to the porch of the sturdy building. He studied the handsome Indian father as he and his two young sons vamped a plow, making one serviceable by salvaging parts from another. The wife, well along with her fourth, shelled peas and instructed her daughter in the art of food preservation. James knew Billy had talked him into staying at his post to help protect the inheritance of these people. It was a good and honorable purpose, and he would do what he could.

Finally, he stepped from the porch and joined Otter standing at the fence of the little graveyard. It was difficult to tell from the erect carriage the man carried forty and one years. James read the rough stones used to mark the graves.

Lone Eagle, a Warrior.
Butterfly Strobaw, Wife of William Joseph Strobaw.
Cut Hand, Peace Chief of the Yanube.
William Joseph Strobaw, Teacher.

James moved to the Indian's side. "Otter, I am tired. Before long, I am resigning my commission, war be damned, and retiring to some acreage north of the fort. I don't suppose you would come with me?"

271

The dark, handsome warrior surveyed the length and breadth of Teacher's Mead through large, liquid eyes before turning to the army officer. Joseph Otter now understood what his beloved Billy had meant when he said, "I wish –"

"Yes, James. I will come."

The End

ABOUT THE AUTHOR

Born and raised in a small Oklahoma town, Mark Wildyr has had a lifelong interest in history and Native American peoples and their cultures. After taking an undergraduate degree in history, Mr. Wildyr served in the United States Army and then pursued a career as a businessman. He presently resides in New Mexico, the setting of many of his stories, which explore developing sexual awareness and intercultural relationships. Approximately forty-seven of his short stories and novellas have been acquired by Alyson Publications, Arsenal Pulp, Cleis Press, Companion Press, Green Candy Press, Haworth Press, STARbooks Press, and *Freshmen* and *Men Magazines*.

In *Cut Hand*, his first published novel, the author indulges his passion for both history and First Nations.